D1632152

PASQUALE'S ANGEL

By the same author

FOUR HUNDRED BILLION STARS

SECRET HARMONIES

THE KING OF THE HILL

ETERNAL LIGHT

RED DUST

IN DREAMS
(Edited with Kim Newman)

PASQUALE'S ANGEL

Paul J. McAuley

VICTOR GOLLANCZ

LONDON

First published in Great Britain 1994
by Victor Gollancz
A Cassell imprint
Villiers House, 41/47 Strand, London WC2N 5JE

© Paul J. McAuley 1994

All rights reserved. No part of this publication may be
reproduced or transmitted in any form or by any means,
electronic or mechanical including photocopying,
recording or any information storage or retrieval system,
without prior permission in writing from the publishers.

The right of Paul J. McAuley to be identified as author
of this work has been asserted by him in accordance with the
Copyright, Designs and Patents Act, 1988.

A catalogue record for this book is available
from the British Library.

ISBN 0 575 05489 1

Photoset in Great Britain by
Rowland Phototypesetting Ltd, Bury St Edmunds, Suffolk
and printed in Great Britain by
Mackays of Chatham plc, Chatham, Kent

To Valerie

17th April 1994.

Salai, I want to make peace with you, not war.
No more war, I give in.

LEONARDO DA VINCI,
from his notebooks

PART ONE

The Feast of Saint Luke

1

Morning, just after dawn. The sky, for once clear of the murk spewed by foundries and manufactories, the rich blue of the very best four-florins-to-the-ounce ultramarine. Men ambling to work along the Street of Dyers, leather-aproned, long gloves slung around their necks, hair brushed back and tucked under leather caps. Clogs clattering on flagstones, cheerful shouts, the rattle of shutters raised as the little workshops opened up and down the street. Apprentices hanging skeins of coloured wool on hooks over workshop doors: reds, blues, yellows, vibrant in the crisp slanting light against flaking sienna walls. Then a hollow rapid panting as someone started up the Hero's engine which by an intricate system of pulleys and belts turned the paddles of the dyers' vats and drove the Archimedes' screw that raised water from the river. A puff, a breath, a little cloud of vapour rising above the buckled terracotta roofs, the panting settling to a slow steady throb.

Pasquale, who had drunk too much the night before, groaned awake as the engine's steady pounding shuddered through the floor, the truckle bed, his own spine. Last year, when things had been going badly – the scandal over the commission for the hospital of Santa Maria Nuova, and business, never more than a trickle, suddenly drying up – Pasquale's master, the painter Giovanni Battista Rosso, had rented rooms on the second floor of a tall narrow house at the eastern end of the Street of Dyers. Although one room was only a closet, and the second, where Pasquale slept, was not much more than a passage with a bed in it, the main room was airy and light, and had a pleasant aspect over the gardens of the Franciscan friars of Santa Croce. On winter mornings, Pasquale had lain late in bed and watched the swarming shadows made on the ceiling of the narrow room by the lanterns of the dyers' workmen as they passed by in the cold dark street below, and in spring he had turned his bed to face the opposite window so that he could watch the trembling dance of light and shadow cast through the leaves of the trees in the garden.

But all that summer he had been woken at first light by the Hero's engine, and now its vibration mingled with the queasy throb of his hangover as he groped for and failed to find his cigarettes.

Too much wine last night, wine and beer, a great swilling indeed, and then he'd taken a turn at watch over the body of Bernardo, he and three others all armed with pistols in case corpsemasters discovered its hiding-place, all of them drinking thick black wine sweet as honey, waving the weapons about and as likely to shoot each other in drunken jest as any corpsemaster. Poor Bernardo white and still, his face seeming rapt in the light of the forest of candles burning at the head of his coffin, the two silver florins that shut his eyes glinting, more money than he'd ever had in his short life. Twelve years old, the youngest pupil of Jacopo Pontormo, Bernardo had been knocked down by a *vaporetto* that morning, his chest crushed by its iron-rimmed wheel, and his life with it. Altogether a bad omen, for he was killed on the seventeenth of October, the eve of the feast of Saint Luke, the patron saint of the confraternity of the artists of the city.

Other noises rising, floating through the open window. Automatic cannon signalling the opening of the city gates, their sounds arriving one after the other according to the law of propagation of waves through air, first near and loud, then farther and fainter. The clatter of a velocipede's wooden wheels over cobbles, its rider cheerfully whistling. Women, calling across the narrow street to each other, the small change at the start of the day. Then the bells of the churches, far and near, ringing out for the first mass. The slow heavy tolling of Santa Croce itself mixed with the beat of the dyers' Hero's engine and seemed to rise and fall as the two rhythms pulsed in and out of phase.

Pasquale made a last futile swipe for his cigarettes, groaned and sat up, and discovered himself fully clothed. He had a distinct impression that a surgeon had bled him dry in the night. Rosso's Barbary ape sat on the wide window-sill at the foot of the bed, looking down at him with liquid brown eyes as it idly picked at calcined plaster with its long flexible toes. When it saw that Pasquale was awake it snatched the blanket from his bed and fled through the window, screeching at the fine joke it had played.

A moment later a human cry floated up. Pasquale thrust his head out of the window to see what was going on. The window overlooked the green gardens of Santa Croce, and the young friar who had charge of the gardens was running up and down the wide white gravel path below, shaking an empty sack like a flag. 'You keep that creature of yours inside!' the friar shouted.

Pasquale looked either side of the window: the ape had disappeared. He called down, 'He *is* inside. You should be inside too, brother. You should be at your devotions, not waking up innocent people.'

The friar said, 'I tell you, he was after my grapes!' He was red in the face, a fat young man with greasy black hair that stuck out all around his tonsure. He added, 'As for innocence, no man is innocent, except in the eyes of God. Especially you: your profane and drunken songs woke me last night.'

'Well, pray for me then,' Pasquale said, and withdrew his head. He couldn't even remember getting home, let alone singing.

The friar was still shouting, his voice breaking in anger the way that fat men's voices often do. I'll see to your grapes, Pasquale resolved, as he lit a cigarette with trembling fingers. The first puff was the test: the trick was not to inhale too deeply. Pasquale sipped cool green smoke cautiously, then more deeply when it seemed that he would not lose the contents of his stomach. He sat on his rumpled bed and as he finished the cigarette thought about angels, and Bernardo's sweet dead face. Bernardo's family would try and smuggle their son's body out of the city today, taking it back to Pratolino, beyond the jurisdiction of the corpsemasters.

Pasquale poured water into a basin and splashed his face. Combing his wet springy hair back from his forehead with his fingers, he went into the main room of the studio and found his master already at work.

Rosso and Pasquale had whitewashed the walls and floor of the big airy room just two weeks ago, and even at this early hour it glowed with pure light. The ape was curled up in the brocade chair, the blanket wrapped around itself, snoring contentedly, hardly stirring when Pasquale wandered in and Rosso laughed long and hard at his pupil's bedraggled state.

Rosso was working by the big window that overlooked the street. Its shutters were flung wide. He was using a feather to brush away charcoal from the lines of the underdrawing on the canvas that, sized,

13

primed with oil, lead white and glue, had been standing against one wall for more than three weeks and was now propped on the worktable. He was barefoot and wore only his green work-apron, girdled loosely at his waist and falling to just above his knees. A tall pale-skinned man, with a shock of red hair stiff as porcupine quills, a sharp-bladed nose, and a pale-lipped mobile mouth. There was a smudge of charcoal on his forehead.

Pasquale picked a big goose-quill from the bundle on the work-table and lent a hand. Rosso said, 'How are we this morning? Did Ferdinand wake you up as I asked him? And what was the good friar shouting about?'

Ferdinand was the Barbary ape, named for the late unlamented King of Spain.

'He waited until I was awake before he took the blanket. And he did it because he likes my smell, not because of anything you told him. You couldn't get him to drink a glass of water by asking if you chained him for a hundred days in the Araby Desert. As for the friar, he has a jealous soul. Do you like grapes, by the way? I've an idea to make our friend shout so loud he'll burst.'

'You'd have Ferdinand steal those grapes? You persuade him to do it, and I'll believe you can talk to him with your fingers.'

Pasquale switched away the charcoal dust that had accumulated at the bottom of the canvas. The lines of the underdrawing had to be all but erased, or else they would show through, or even worse, tint, the oils.

'Master, why are you doing this now? Shouldn't you be dressed?'

'Why, I only just this minute got undressed.'

'Out with your bumboy, I suppose.'

'That,' Rosso said, 'is none of your business. Besides, just because you couldn't sweet-talk Pelashil into giving you more of that poison, there's no need to take it out on *me*.'

'Pelashil? Did I try?' Pasquale did remember talking to her, never quite an argument, he more and more insistent about wanting to try the híkuri again, and she telling him that a drunken man would only be bewildered by the visions it gave, but she had come up and given him a kiss later, in front of everyone, and told him to come and see her when he was in his senses. Pasquale groaned, half in pleasure, half with guilt. Pelashil was the servant of Piero di Cosimo, a Savage brought back from the friendly shores of the New World and widely held to be his common-law wife. She was twice Pasquale's age, dark and heavy-haunched, but Pasquale was attracted by the challenge of keeping her attention long enough to make her smile. She had no time for small talk, and if conversation bored her she would turn away. Her silences were long, not so much sulky as self-absorbed; her sudden, flashing smile was all too rare. Strangely, what Pasquale took seriously, the euphoric híkuri dream, the sense of diving deep into the weave of the world, Pelashil maintained was nothing more than entertainment. She wouldn't even listen when he tried to tell her what he'd seen after he'd chewed the shrivelled, nauseatingly bitter grey-green button she had fed him in her hot, brightly decorated little room.

Rosso, who understood his pupil, laughed and made the sign of a cuckold's horns on his forehead. 'For shame, Pasqualino! You take advantage of a poor crazy old man.'

'Perhaps I want to follow in his footsteps, and see for myself the New World. We could go, master, you and I. We could make a fresh start over.'

Rosso said, 'I'll not hold you to your contract if you want to leave. God knows you've learned all you will from me. Go if you want, but don't break an old man's heart and steal his servant. Old men need the warmth of women.'

'Think of the light, master, and think that a man can live like a king for the rent you pay for this place.'

'A king of Savages? What kind of honour is that?'

'I know you will tell me you have your reputation here,' Pasquale said. 'I'm sorry to have mentioned it. You should get dressed for the procession.'

'We have plenty of time before the procession.' Rosso stepped back and looked critically at the underdrawing. It was the deposition of Christ, looking down the length of His dramatically foreshortened body as He was tenderly cradled by His disciples.

'Surely this can wait.'

'I have to finish it in two weeks, or I'll be fined. That's what the contract stipulates.'

'You've been fined before. And we have to finish the wall for that light-show.'

Rosso had agreed to paint patterns on a newly plastered wall as part of an artificer's scheme to amaze and entertain the Pope. Years ago, the spectacles celebrating the visit of a foreign prince would have been entirely provided by artists; now, they were reduced to assisting in the devices and designs of the artificers.

'We will paint the wall tomorrow. I can't afford to break that contract, and neither can I afford to break this one. We're close to asking Saint Mark for half his cloak. Listen, if Signor di Piombino likes the picture, he may offer his private chapel to us. How would you like that, Pasqualino? Perhaps I would be able to engage new pupils.'

'You'll have to find a new bed, then. Mine is too narrow for two, and has a groove in it so deep I dream I'm buried alive.'

'It has to be narrow to fit in the room. Ah,' Rosso said with sudden exasperation, 'what's the point of new pupils anyway!' His mood had swung around as it so often did these days. Pasquale knew his master was not recovered from the business with the director of the hospital, who had seen devils in the sketch of a commissioned painting where saints should have been, and loudly proclaimed how he had been tricked to any who would listen. Rosso said, 'Maybe I'll let you do the whole chapel, Pasqualino. But I feel like painting this, at least. It's time it was finished. And there's that panel you've been working on. When are you going to make a start on it? As for this, don't worry, it'll be a piece of piss to do. We'll start by shading it across, right side brighter than the left. I sold one of your prints, by the way.'

Pasquale had found some of yesterday's bread. Chewing hard, he said, 'Which one?'

'You know, the kind the women buy, the kind for which they never quite dare ask outright. She was a pretty woman, Pasquale, and blushed all over, I swear, as she tried to make me understand what she wanted. Put some oil on that bread, although how you can eat after all you've drunk . . . you won't spew, I hope.'

Pasquale had made a number of studies for that kind of print – they were called stiffeners, in the trade. He had found a model in one of Mother Lucia's girls, a compliant whore who would pose for pennies, and hold the same pose for an hour or more without complaint. He said, 'Which one exactly? How much did you get?'

'An early one,' Rosso said carelessly. 'Very virile, with cocks running rampant through it.'

'That? It was pirated this spring.'

'Yes, and the copy has improved on your original – the passage with the arms of the man holding the bladder and cock on a pole is much freer. Still, our blushing customer wanted a print of the original, which is a compliment of kinds, I suppose.'

'Well, I'll do another.' Pasquale wiped oil from his hands on a bit of cloth and picked up the blackened goose-quill. 'Are you really going to use this underdrawing, or are you going to start over again?'

'Oh, I think this has promise. Although I don't like the positioning of the two figures lifting the legs. Maybe I'll move them back a little.'

'It will spoil the lines of their arms, surely. Besides, if you lift a heavy weight, your arms are close to your sides, so they must be close to the body.'

'Here's my pupil, telling his master what he's about.'

'What about my fee for the print?'

'As for that, it is already spent. Don't look at me like that Pasqualino. One must pay rent.'

'Yesterday you said the rent could wait.'

'I didn't mean for the studio,' Rosso said and winked.

'Which bumboy was it last night? The Prussian with the scar?'

Rosso shrugged.

'He's a thief.'

'You don't understand a thing, Pasqualino. Let an old man find love where he can. Is it your hangover making you mean?'

Rosso was twenty-four, only six years older than Pasquale.

Pasquale scratched the ape around the ears. The animal stirred, and sighed happily. Pasquale said, 'We should get ready for the procession.'

'We have hours yet.'

'We have promised to collect the banners from Master Andrea. Master . . . do you think he'll be there?'

'It would be very rude of him not to be.'

Raphael. They didn't need to name him. His name was on everyone's lips in the three days since he had arrived from Rome in advance of his master Pope Leo X.

17

Rosso added, 'In any case, I must dress appropriately, and I haven't quite decided . . .'

'In that case I think I'll have plenty of time to try and teach the ape something.'

They arrived late, of course. Rosso was famous for being late. Instead of dressing he lounged about in his work-apron, moodily staring at the cartoon, then started sketching Pasquale in red chalk while Pasquale tried to teach the ape to climb down a rope – not as easy as it seemed, for Barbary apes are not great climbers, and certainly not of ropes. Rosso was still in his odd changeable mood too, reluctant to leave and yet restless. By the time he had thrown on some clothes, he and Pasquale had to run through the streets to reach Andrea del Sarto's studio, and still they were late.

Master Andrea was in a bate because of some business with his new wife. His pupils hung around the front of the studio, where rolled processional banners leaned against the wall. Their master's angry voice rose and fell from an open window above. Cheerful with holiday spirit, in their best clothes, the pupils passed a fat marijuana cigarette back and forth and munched on the plump juicy Colombano grapes Pasquale and Rosso had brought with them, and laughed at the story Pasquale had to tell. He had a rope burn to prove it; at one point on its way down the ape had panicked and had nearly jerked the rope from his hands. By and by more painters and pupils drifted along – this street housed a dozen studios, mixed amongst the workshops of goldsmiths and stonemasons. Someone had brought a flask of wine, and it too was passed around.

Master Andrea came out at last, a portly man dressed in black velvet, with a belt of braided gold thread. His face was mottled, and his hands trembling as he smoothed back his long hair: he looked like an angry bee, shot out of its hole to see off intruders. He was in fact a kindly man, and a good teacher – Rosso had been his pupil, so that in a way Pasquale was his pupil, too – but he was prone to rages, and his new wife, young and pretty, provoked him to fantastic jealousies.

Rosso put his arm around his former master, talking with him as the group made their way to the Piazza della Signoria while Pasquale, a banner-pole on his shoulder, followed amongst the other pupils.

18

He felt frumpy, still in the clothes he had worn the day before – he really didn't have anything better to wear, things being what they were, but if he had not been so drunk, he would have taken off his doublet and hose and tunic and laid them under the mattress before going to bed. At least he had thought to scrub his face and hands, and anoint his palms with a rose-water receipt of Rosso's. He had brushed his curly hair until it shone, and Rosso had put a circlet in it, and called Pasquale his little prince of Savages, just to annoy.

The party gathered other painters and their assistants and pupils as it went through the streets, and by the time it reached to the Piazza della Signoria there were half a hundred. The same number was already waiting in front of the Loggia, chief amongst them Michelangelo Buonarroti, towering over all by sheer force of personality, clad in a white tunic so long it was almost a robe – to hide his knock-knees, Rosso said, adding that, even so, had he possessed a thunderbolt, he would have made a passable Zeus.

Raphael and his entourage were not there.

The hired band struck up with shawm, sackbut and *viole da braccio*. Banners were unfurled, bright with gold and ultramarine, like flowers suddenly blooming in one corner of the stony fastness of the piazza. Following the example of the other pupils, Pasquale socketed the pole of his banner in the cusp of the leather harness he had put on; even so, his shoulders soon started to ache as wind tugged the heavy banner to and fro.

Not many of the passers-by took notice. The importance of the confraternity had dwindled, and they seemed a small, insignificant group, dwarfed by the big stage that workmen were hammering together in front of the Palazzo, in preparation for the Pope's imminent arrival.

The hammering didn't even stop as the blessing was read from the steps of the Loggia. What with that, and barked orders as companies of city militia drilled across the square's vast chessboard, and the noise of the signal-tower atop the Palazzo della Signoria as its arms clattered and weaved in a kinetic ballet, the frail voice of the old Secretary to the Ten could scarcely be heard as he pronounced the annual blessing. The priest shook holy water towards the assembled painters even as the Secretary was led off by his attendants at what seemed an undignified speed. The priest muttered a prayer, sketched a cross in the air, and that was that.

The procession set off, gathering itself into a ragged line as people jostled for position. Gradually, they wound out of the piazza, through the shadow of the Great Tower. Square, studded with narrow windows and balconies, and machicolations and platforms clinging to its smooth stone as swallow-nests cling to a barn, the tower reared so high into the sky that it forever seemed to be toppling as clouds moved behind it. It nailed down the north-western corner of the colleges and laboratories and apothecaria and surgeries and dissecting-rooms and workshops of the new university which had replaced an entire neighbourhood of crooked streets where once goldsmiths had worked, an interlocking complex of red roofs and white colonnades and terraces all overlooked by its architect, the Great Engineer himself, who in his Great Tower brooded hundreds of *braccia* above the common herd, perhaps even now watching the procession of the Confraternity of Artists creeping like a line of ants at the base of his eyrie as they turned towards the Ponte Vecchio. They had to march in single file, a heavy traffic of carts and carriages and *vaporetti* thundering past, before they turned to strike out along the wide promenade beside the river.

Pasquale, holding up the pole of a banner painted with the likeness of Saint Luke, benign and white-bearded, and painting one of his portraits of the Blessed Virgin (there were three, now at Rome, Loreto and Bologna), kept an eye on the river as he marched. He loved to watch the ships go by: the small barges which were the work-horses of the river-transport system; the paddle-wheel ferries; the big ocean-going *maonas*; and, on occasion, a warship on some mission that had taken it far from the naval yards of Livorno, prowling with its screw drive like a sleek leopard amongst domestic cats.

Sunlight fell through a rift in the clouds. The banners glowed; the musicians beat louder and everyone picked up his step. Pasquale's heart was lifted at last, and he forgot his headache and his uneasy stomach, where bread and oil made an unwelcome weight, forgot the ache in his arms from holding up the heavy banner. Gulls, which followed the Grand Canal inland, were flakes of white skirling above the river-channels. Cries, far cries. He could dream of taking sloe-eyed brown-skinned Pelashil back to her native land: the New World, where white, stepped pyramids gleamed bright as salt amongst palm-trees, and every kind of fruit was there ready to fall into your hand if only you reached out for it, and flocks of parrots flew like arrows from the bows of an army.

The river was divided into channels, and the channel nearest the shore ran with strange colours that mixed and mingled in feathery curls – dye-works and chemical manufactories poured out mingling streams which unlike pigments did not mix to muddy brown but formed strange new combinations, chemical reactions fluttering across surface in exquisite patterns as if the water had been stirred to life. Along the full flood of the raceway channel, water-mills sat in chained lines strung out from the piers of bridges, their water-wheels thumping and churning, their machineries sending up a chattering roar. Most drove looms, trying to compete with the modern auto-matic machineries of the manufactories on the far bank. At night some went freemartin, cutting the mooring of their rivals, trying to jockey upstream to get advantage of a stronger current. Sometimes you could hear pistol-shots carrying across the water. The journalist and playwright Niccolò Machiavegli had once made a famous remark that war was simply commercial competition carried to extremes: and so here.

At the Ponte alla Grazie the procession turned away from the river, plunging into a warren of narrow streets between tenement buildings faced with soft grey *pietra serena*, stained with black streaks by pol-luted rain and crumbling away through the action of the tainted air and smokes poured forth by the manufactories. At street level, workshops and *bottegas* had opened their shutters for the day's busi-ness, and their workers came out to cheer the procession as it went past. They especially cheered Michelangelo, who marched with stead-fast dignity at the head of the procession, his white garments shining amongst the blacks and browns of the other masters. Florentines loved their successful sons, most especially if they were prodigals. Even better, Michelangelo had returned because of a furious argu-ment with the Pope over the tomb of the Pope's predecessor. He was seen as having upheld the honour of Florence over the wishes of her old enemy: not for nothing was his most famous work the statue of the giant-killer, David.

21

So at last the procession reached the homely church of Sant'Ambrogio, in the neighbourhood where most painters worked. In the years before the Confraternity had broken with the Company of Saint Luke and its physicians and apothecaries, who in truth had long bankrolled their impoverished artist brothers, the service had been held amongst the marble and bronze of the church of Sant'Egidio, in the hospital of Santa Maria Nuova. No more.

A fine rain had started. The drums beat on as the procession filed through the narrow door into the homely little church, with its plaster walls and shadows up amongst the rafters, and the noise of the reciprocal engines in the manufactory across the street.

Raphael was not there, either.

2

The mass was almost over when Raphael finally arrived. He swept in at the head of a gaggle of assistants and pupils, and the bustle at the door of the little church turned everyone's heads. The idlers at the back, who had talked all through the service in the casual way of Florentines, the church being simply another public place that, except for its altars and chapels, was as secular as any other, stopped talking and gaped and nudged each other. The masters and pupils in the congregation glanced back, every one of them – with the exception of Michelangelo, who sat stiffly at the far end of the front row of seats in exactly the same pose he had held throughout the mass (and in which pose Pasquale had surreptitiously sketched him), not deigning to look back at his rival and yield him the satisfaction of recognition. Even the priest paused for a moment, before continuing with his blessing of the host amidst the ringing of many small bells. As Raphael and his followers doffed their raincapes to reveal fashionably black machine-cut tunics, doublets and leggings, the six-piece orchestra wheezed into the *Agnus Dei*, the ageing castrato coming in half a beat late, and almost everyone in the congregation began to whisper to everyone else.

Rosso nudged Pasquale and said in a stage whisper, 'God's second favourite son blesses us.'

Pasquale couldn't help looking around to stare at the great painter. Raphael sat at ease amongst his assistants, some of whom would be masters in their own right if they had not chosen to serve Raphael. As who would not? Raphael earned more than any artist in either Rome or the Florentine Republic, and so more than any in all of Europe and the New World. Like Michelangelo, Raphael had taken the New Age to heart. In the age of the individual, he had become his own man. He took commissions as he chose, and his own fame made the rich, both the old money and the new, fiercely contest in bidding for his work, while the poor decorated their houses with shadow-engraved reproductions of his work. No other artist had that kind of cachet. Michelangelo did as he pleased, and usually fell out with his clients as a result, but only Raphael made sure that his clients got what they wanted while painting as he chose.

'He's come back to his roots to make sure they're as bad as he remembers,' Rosso said.

'He has paid his florin,' Pasquale said, meaning that Raphael had the right to celebrate mass with the Florentine Confraternity of Artists on the day of their patron saint because he had signed his name in the Red Book and paid his fee. Because Pasquale had been eager to catch a glimpse of Raphael, now he felt that he must defend him.

'About the only one here,' Rosso said, which was almost true. The Red Book of the Confraternity recorded more debtors to Saint Luke than creditors, for few bothered to pay a whole florin to become a recognized master in a guild whose best days were gone, while those like Raphael Sanzio of Urbino or Michelangelo Buonarroti didn't need a confraternity to promote their interests. Pasquale had heard Master Andrea grumble, as the procession had filed through the church door, that they were less than the rat-catchers' guild now, that once upon a time the whole street on which this little church of Sant'Ambrogio stood had been crowded with a joyful procession, all come out to see a single painting leave the studio of Cimabue, and where now was that ardour?

But the processional banners were still bright, for all that their finery was patched and faded, older than the century. And even in this little church there was evidence aplenty of the Golden Age, when image had sung straight to God. There was a flaking fresco of the Annunciation over the first altar, and, in better condition, a beautiful fresco over the second altar of the Madonna on her heavenly throne, with Saint John the Baptist and Saint Bartholomew. This theme was repeated over the third altar, where this time the Virgin was portrayed in her glory with an array of saints. The gold-leaf of the frescos shimmered in the candle-light, giving the illusion that the church was larger than it really was, as a lake glimmering through trees will seem like a sea.

Pasquale had contrived to sit as close as he could to the best work in the church. It was in a niche between the third and second altars, a little roundel of the Annunciation painted by Lippi in the Golden

24

Age before the rise of the artificers. For most of the mass, which was a full ceremony paid by subscription from every master, debtor and creditor alike (Rosso had grumbled mightily over this imposition), Pasquale had gazed at this little window into another world, a world of clear colours and clean lines. The grave acceptance of the Madonna at her window, her face and demeanour expressing the fourth of the fifth of the Laudable Conditions of the Blessed Virgin, namely *Humiliatio*; the golden line from the dove of the Holy Spirit to her womb; and the angel Gabriel kneeling in the garden amongst spring flowers. Most of all the angel. Pasquale was collecting angels. Except for his wings (which despite the gold tracery were clearly modelled on the wings of a pigeon; Pasquale had seen another of Fra Lippi's Annunciations where the angel had the Argus-eyed wings of a peacock), this one could have been any youth from some great house in the time of Lorenzo the Unlucky. He was fourteen or fifteen, pale-skinned, with a long, wondering face and blue long-lashed eyes, and was dressed in the sumptuous costume of those courtly days. Stripped of his superficial exoticism he could have been a deacon or a page-boy. What held Pasquale's attention, what he had twice tried to fix on a scrap of paper, was the angel's expression. It was raptly attentive, filled with sorrowing knowledge at the burden which the Holy Child must bear, but also with joy at this compact between Heaven and Earth at last made flesh.

Or that at least was how you were supposed to read it, Pasquale thought. But how could you capture the true feelings of a creature both greater than man (for he stood closer to God than any but the most blessed of the saints) and lesser (for despite his command of legions of lesser angels, Gabriel was in the end no more than a messenger, a go-between who carried the Word from God to man but was not the Word, only its vessel: angels did not choose to serve, for not to serve was to fall)? It was something he had been trying to work out ever since the conception for his masterwork had fallen on him. Piero di Cosimo, who Pasquale liked to think was his secret master, had in a rare moment of lucidity told him to paint truly if he was to paint at all, but how could you paint the truth of something beyond ordinary human comprehension? How could you paint the face of an angel?

Fra Lippi's solution to this question had been to portray his angel as a beautiful courtier; it was the solution of most painters of the Golden Age. And most painters in Florence, at one time or another, had painted at least one Annunciation, a popular theme because the feast-days of both the Annunciation and the New Year fell on the same day, the twenty-fifth of March. But the Golden Age was gone, as fragmented by the devices of the artificers as reality itself. The New Age had arrived, and demanded genius or nothing. In his youth, Raphael had painted angels as idealizations of idealizations, not the best or most beautiful courtier but the ideal courtier of Castiglione's imaginary conversations. It was said that when Raphael painted he caught not just the hues of his model's face, but the very thoughts and personality. But he had not painted an angel since his apprenticeship, except in his depiction of the flight of Saint Peter from prison, and that in shadow. If the greatest painter in the world shied from the task, how could Pasquale meet his self-imposed challenge?

For while Pasquale had his vision and the ruinously expensive little panel he had prepared with great care, he had not made a brush-stroke towards realizing it. He had glimpsed or thought he had glimpsed more than mere beauty or even the ideal of beauty, but did not know how to begin to express what he had been vouchsafed. He only knew that to fail in this was to fail himself, and believed that if he could only talk with Raphael, the great painter would understand.

Poor drug-crazed Piero di Cosimo, with his talk of creatures from worlds that interleaved this, understood more than most, but for all his adventures in the far shores of the New World, his way of seeing was that of the Old World; he had not entirely escaped his training. And as for Rosso, Pasquale had barely mentioned the subject of his painting to his master, let alone his vision. Rosso was a master of the technical problem, of perspective and plastic space, of the swift decisions needed to paint tempera panels and the bold revisions that the new Dutch and Prussian formulae for oil paints made possible, but while he was a good man and a generous master, he was also increasingly bitter with his lot, and more conservative than he liked to admit. Artists were artisans first and last, was his constant motto.

Bells rang for the elevation of the host; following the masters of the Confraternity (Rosso, who had forgotten to go to confession, had to stay behind), Pasquale and the other pupils lined up at the rail to take the sip of blood-red wine, the thin coin of the wafer of transubstantiated flesh. As Pasquale rose, with the wafer dissolving on his tongue, sweetening the ferruginous taste of the wine, he saw that Raphael was kneeling humbly at the end of the line, democratic amongst his school, as if he were only an ordinary man.

The communion over, the prayers for the celebrants said and the dismissal intoned, people began to drift towards the back of the church, mixing with the layabouts and with the ordinary citizens who were waiting for the regular midday mass, which would begin as soon as this one was finished. The pupils were gathering up the banners. When he had wound up his own, Pasquale asked one of Master Andrea's pupils to carry it back for him. He had seen Raphael walking down the aisle, conversing with a few of the masters.

The pupil, a cheerful fellow by the name of Andrea Squazella, said, 'God sees the sparrow fall, so Raphael might look on you, I suppose. But he'll only see a sparrow.'

'I would be more than that, I hope.'

'I know of your ambition, but as for your talent . . .' As Raphael passed by, Andrea grabbed Pasquale and said with mock alarm, 'Steady, don't faint. He's only a man.'

Raphael was of ordinary height, with a mild white face and curly black shoulder-length hair. His black tunic, doublet and hose were of the finest Dutch cloth, cut expensively on the cross. He was gesturing to underline some point. His fingers were as slim as a woman's, and so long that it seemed that they had an extra joint.

Pasquale breathed out when the little group had passed. 'Only a man,' he said.

'There goes someone with a different opinion,' Andrea said. 'Master Michelangelo thinks your Raphael is definitely something lower than a man. A louse perhaps.'

Michelangelo was making his way up the far side the church, craggy head held high, followed by two of his assistants. He looked like a warship beating out of port ahead of a storm, escorted by a couple of sloops.

'My master says that Raphael stole his ideas,' Andrea said to Pasquale. 'Raphael was secretly shown the Sistine Chapel after Michelangelo quit his work there, and as a result he immediately repainted the prophet Isaiah that he had been working on so that it seemed to be a collaboration, although not one Michelangelo knew about. Your Raphael is something of an improver rather than an improviser.'

'If you mean that his inspiration begins where that of others ends, then mine begins with his,' Pasquale said, and Andrea laughed and said he was shameless.

'I'm desperate. How can I talk with him?'

'Tell him you like his work,' Andrea said sensibly. 'Or better still, let my master introduce you. Go on, Pasquale! If you don't stand near him you'll have to shout, and one simply doesn't do that. Even in a Florentine church.'

Andrea was from Urbino, and considered all Florentines boorish, most especially in the way they chattered openly during mass, even on high days.

By now, the party with Raphael in its centre was almost at the door. Someone stepped inside just as Pasquale hurried up, and it was as if a breeze had blown aside a screen of leaves, for the people around Raphael parted and moved back, leaving him to confront the newcomer.

He was a portly, middle-aged man, dressed in a fashion more suitable to someone twenty years younger: a short grey cape spotted with sooty raindrops, and a white loosely laced shirt; an exaggerated doublet, fantastically puffed and slashed, of the kind favoured by Prussian students; particoloured hose. His hectic face still held more than a trace of the beautiful youth he had once been, in his profile and the sulky downturn of his full mouth. His curly hair was still thick; extravagantly arranged, it fell to his shoulders.

Pasquale knew him at once: Giacomo Caprotti, nicknamed Salai, the Milanese catamite of the Great Engineer. He also saw that the man was drunk. He stepped back, but still Salai shouldered into him.

'Don't you know to mind your step,' Salai said, 'when your betters pass by?'

Pasquale retorted, 'I'm sorry, signor, but I fail to recognize the high opinion you have of yourself.'

He would have said more, but one of Raphael's assistants, Giulio Romano, a burly middle-aged man, caught Salai's arm. He turned him aside and said in a whisper, 'Not here. This is not the place.'

Salai shrugged him off and straightened his sleeves. 'Only too true, but I missed you at the tower and would pay my respects, if I am allowed.'

Romano threw up his hands.

Salai turned back to the others and said with a slurred eloquence, 'A million apologies for having missed your little party. I went to the wrong place, which is to say where you used to hold your feast-day mass, when you meant something in Florence. How I searched to find this small church – charming in its way, I'm sure, but obscure. Actually, I'm not sorry at all, I'm only here to represent my master. He paid his money long ago, before he took up his real calling and left off daubs.' Salai faced up to Raphael. He couldn't quite keep his eyes focused. He said, 'So, painter. For once the dog goes before its master, eh? I compliment you on your choice of dress, Signor Raphael, and those of your hangers-on. Somehow, in these circumstances, mourning appears appropriate. You funny little artists have had your day, even you, Signor Raphael. We'll soon outshine you all in capturing the real light of the world.'

Another of the assistants said, 'If you bring a message from *your* master, speak it now. Master Raphael is too busy to trifle with the likes of you.'

'Some love-affair no doubt. An affair of the heart, such as we read of in the broadsheets. Well, I'm not one to stand in the way of love.'

Raphael laughed. He said, 'You weren't sent at all, were you?'

Salai grinned broadly, as if enormously enjoying the fact that his bluff had been called. 'Well, if it comes to it, no.'

The second assistant said, 'Lorenzo de' Medici was murdered in a church, I recall.'

'Be quiet,' Giulio Romano said.

Salai touched the pommel of the French rapier slung from his silver brocade belt. 'Signor, I can step outside if it makes you feel easier. I'll even wait while you arm yourself.'

There was a moment of tense silence, for Salai was well known for his swordswork. The assistant turned red and looked away.

'Go now,' Romano said. 'Go away, Salai. Not here. Not now.'

Raphael said, with a benign smile, 'You have your audience, Signor Salai. Speak your piece.'

Salai bowed. 'I hope I need not speak, Signor – no, *Master* Raphael.

That's the point. We are soon to be blessed by the first of the Medicis to step within the walls of Florence since the Republic was founded. A pity if that dainty footfall were to be lost in the outcry of scandal.'

'I'm not afraid, Salai. Certainly not of any small mischief you can manage to whip up.'

Salai winked and laid a finger alongside his nose in a coarse parody of intimacy. 'And the honour of a certain lady . . . ?'

'That's old gossip,' Raphael said, even as the second assistant pushed forward, hand on the dagger thrust in his belt.

Salai danced back, suddenly not drunk at all, coarse cunning and a kind of eagerness printed on his face. 'That olive-sticker won't do you much good, friend. I suggest you use it to clean your fingernails – they really shouldn't match the rest of your costume.'

Romano laid a hand on his fellow's shoulder. The others of Raphael's party, emboldened by this move, started to jeer and stamp. A few of the Confraternity, Master Andrea amongst them, were shouting out too, crying shame, shame on the honour of Florence, that one of her citizens should insult one of her guests. Salai looked at them, then bowed, mockingly low, before turning and marching out through the door.

Several of the older masters started to apologize to Raphael; off to the side, Rosso was talking animatedly with Giulio Romano. Pasquale tried to push forward, but Raphael's followers had closed around their master, and they moved as one body through the high doors of the church into the gloomy, rainy afternoon. When Pasquale dared follow, Master Andrea turned and said, not unkindly, 'He's here until the Pope leaves, Pasquale. You'll have a chance to talk, I'm sure, but not now, eh?'

Pasquale caught his sleeve. 'What did Salai mean, when he raised up the matter of the honour of a lady?'

'You know the kind of mischief the Great Engineer's catamite likes to stir up,' Master Andrea said vaguely. 'Women are the root of all evil, some say. Or would say, if they were allowed . . .' He set his four-cornered cap squarely on his grizzled head, shook out the wide sleeves of his tunic, and hurried after the receding party. A couple of pigeons detonated into flight from his path: angel-wings.

Pasquale watched the pigeons a while, getting soaked in the gentle, polluted rain, until Rosso came out of the church. Pasquale saw his

30

master's white, anxious face, and said, 'Shouldn't you go with them, master? The dinner in honour of Raphael—'

'Let the old men go and make pictures with their food,' Rosso said. 'I think we both need a drink.'

3

The bar which Pasquale and Rosso favoured was a low dive fre-
quented by a sometimes explosive mixture of artist's pupils, journalists and Swiss mercenaries. The landlord, a fat bullet-headed Prussian
Swiss, had the habit of taking swigs from the drinks he served,
and kept a hound the size of a small horse which, when it wasn't
flopped in front of the fireplace, wandered amongst the crowd trying
to cadge titbits. The Swiss scrutinized each person as they came
in, and if the new arrival was a passer-by he didn't like the look
of, or a regular he'd argued with, he set up a tremendous volley
of oaths and insults until the unfortunate man was driven out.
Otherwise he jollied his regulars along, attempted clumsy practical
jokes that usually backfired, and created a little world outside the
world. Surprisingly, there were few fights. If the Swiss couldn't
handle trouble-makers he set his dog on them, and needed no
other weapon.

The scandal of Salai's confrontation with Raphael was already the
talk of the bar. Pasquale regaled two separate audiences with his
account, accepting drinks from his eager listeners. He was hoping to
see Piero di Cosimo, but the old man wasn't here. Increasingly, he
retreated from noise, living more and more inside his own head.
He'd spend hours gazing at patterns rain made on a window, or paint
spattered on his filthy floor.

Pasquale had taken him food a few days before, but Piero had
refused to let him in, speaking only through the crack in the half-
opened door. He was, he told Pasquale, engaged on an important
work. He spoke as if asleep, paying attention to something only he
could see.

Pasquale said, 'One day the stuff you take, the híkuri, will kill
you. You cannot live entirely in dreams.'

'There's more than one world, Pasquale. You've glimpsed it once
or twice, but you don't understand it yet. You must, if you're to be
any kind of painter.'

'I have yet to master this world. Let me in, just for a moment. Look, I have bread and fish.'

Piero ignored this. He said wistfully, 'If only I'd had you for my pupil. Together – what voyages, eh, Pasquale? Come back in a few days. In a week.'

Pasquale tried not to sound exasperated. 'If you don't eat, you'll die.'

'You sound like Pelashil,' Piero said. 'No. She has the sense not to disturb me. She understands.'

'I would understand, if you would let me. I need to be able to see . . .'

'Your angel. Yes. But you're not a real person, not yet. Don't bother me any more, Pasquale. I need to dream now.'

It occurred to Pasquale now, in the crowded noisy bar, that it was because of that conversation he had drunkenly persisted in asking Pelashil for more of the híkuri, the simple which Piero had brought back from the New World. He looked around for Pelashil, who usually worked in the bar every night, but couldn't see her. He hadn't seen her all evening, and for a moment wondered, because he was young and self-centred, if she had left in disgust at his behaviour, never to return.

A group of loud and foul-mouthed Swiss cavalrymen had colonized Piero's usual corner. The *condottiere* who had hired them was sprawled in the straight-backed chair Piero favoured, elaborating with vivid obscenity why he would never be fucked up the arse or fuck anyone up the arse either, Florence or not, while the rent-boy who sat in his lap pretended to be fascinated. 'I mean, I like my dick sucked as well as any man, and I don't care if it's a woman or a man or a baby who thinks my come is her mother's milk does the sucking. One of the best fucks I ever had was with an old granny that had lost all her teeth. But only Turks and Florentines fuck each other in the shit-hole, am I right or am I right?'

The *condottiere* had a lean pock-marked face, with a moustache waxed to elaborate points. His fist twined a handful of the rent-boy's hair; the boy winced and blew him a kiss, half-mocking, half-placatory. The *condottiere* glared around the room, little eyes glistening under beetling brows, perhaps hoping that someone would contradict him. No one did, for as the broadsheets never tired of pointing out, the citizens of Florence were intimidated by the foreign soldiers they employed. A little shameful silence hung in the room before the man laughed and called for more wine.

It was Pelashil who served him. Pasquale's heart turned when he saw her. After she'd refilled the *condottiere*'s pitcher he called to her, and she sauntered over. Pelashil of the insolent eyes, black as sloe-berries in a face the colour of fall leaves, broad-hipped in a ragged brocade gown, its sleeves ripped away to leave her muscular arms bare. Pasquale had slept with her once, last winter, and ever since had not been able to decide if it had been her choice or his.

'I was in my cups last night,' Pasquale said. 'You're not still angry, I hope.'

Pelashil stepped back when he tried to embrace her. 'Why do men always think only about themselves?'

'You're angry! What did I say? Don't I have the right to know?'

Rosso, who had been drinking steadily, stirred and said, 'You offered to take her away, Pasqualino. Back across the sea to where the sand is white and the sea is blue and the women go naked.'

'That's what you'd like to think,' Pelashil said, 'but it isn't anything like my home. Besides, I suppose you'd rather think of naked boys.' She caught Pasquale's hand. 'The old man is ill again. You must go and see him,' and she went off to fetch more wine, dodging the groping of a drunken soldier.

Pasquale sat back down and drank more wine and thought again of Piero's vague talk, and then of the way that, after he had eaten híkuri, separate moments had folded into a continuous sheaf, and of the blurring of pigeon-wings in rainy light. Angels and time . . . was their time the same time as men endured, moment to moment? Some notion, vast yet as fabulously fragile as a frost-flower, seemed to be creeping across his brain, threatening to fade to nought if he stared at it too hard. He thought that perhaps Piero would know what this revelation meant. Perhaps Piero would feed him another dried leaf of híkuri. He should go and see the old man, yes, but not yet. Not just yet. He needed courage to face the dilapidated claustrophobia of Piero's room.

Giambattista Gellia, a hothead leftist as famous for being a shoe-maker turned tract-writer as for anything he wrote, was pushing through the crowd. The journalist, Niccolò Machiavegli, had just come in, and Gellia was pulling him towards Pasquale's table, saying loudly, 'Niccolò, you must listen to this. Someone who was there, at the root of the scandal.'

'Often you need distance for the truth to emerge,' Niccolò Machiavegli protested with a laugh. 'Besides, I have already written my piece and left it to be set. In fact, I have to go back soon to check it over. Give me the peace of a drink uninterrupted by business, Gellia. Revolution may be your life, but journalism is only my profession.'

'This young man saw it all – or so he says.'

'It's true,' Pasquale said.

'And I see you have profited well from your luck,' the journalist said, and smiled as the others around the table laughed at Pasquale's expense.

'It's true!' Pasquale insisted.

Niccolò Machiavegli smiled gently. 'I don't need words, my friend.'

Rosso said, 'He's right. You don't need words, Pasqualino.'

Pasquale said, 'What about a picture?'

'It is a rich irony that in all of that congregation of artists, no one thought to sketch the confrontation,' Niccolò Machiavegli said, gaining another laugh.

Rosso stood up, gripping the edge of the table. He had drunk more than Pasquale. 'It's a private matter,' he said.

'But it happened in a public place,' Gellia said.

Pasquale dug his elbow into Rosso's hip and said in a fierce whisper, 'We need the money, master.'

'You do what you will, Pasqualino,' Rosso said wearily. One of his black moods had suddenly descended upon him. 'Do it with my blessing. I suppose it will all come out soon enough.'

Gellia stepped out of the way as Rosso plunged into the crowd, moving towards the door. Pasquale said, because they really did need the money, 'I will show you that I was there. You must forgive my master. What happened was a . . . shameful thing.' He drew out the scrap of paper on which he had been scribbling during the first part of the mass, dipped the corner of his tunic in wine and would have wiped away the drawing he'd already made when Niccolò Machiavegli caught his hand.

The journalist said, 'Allow me to look,' and held the paper to his eyes, moving his gaze back and forth across it as if it were a text. He was slight yet straight-backed, with the clever, boyish face of a monastery librarian. His prominent cheek-bones were shadowed with stubble, and his hair, receding around a widow's peak above a high forehead, was clipped short. He said, 'I see Michelangelo Buonarroti brooding on which mortal to dispatch with a well-chosen thunderbolt. You did this?'

'He's the best of us,' Pasquale said.

'If you will, come with me – no, don't drink up, you'll need a steady hand and eye, and certainly not an inflamed memory.'

It had stopped raining, and a yellow vapour was thickening the air. It smelt of wood-smoke and sulphur, and burned in Pasquale's nose, made his eyes itch. Although the six o'clock cannonade that signalled the closing of the city's gates had not yet sounded, the vapour had already brought on the night. People stumbled through it with their faces muffled; two artificers passed arm in arm, faces masked with pig-snouted leather hoods.

'The artificers poison the air, and then must invent themselves a means to breathe it,' Niccolò Machiavegli said. 'A pity only a few can afford their cure.'

It was one of the smogs that plagued Florence when the wind didn't blow and the smokes of the artificers settled like a heavy blanket along the course of the Arno. The journalist coughed heavily, covering his mouth with his fist, and then apologized. He had once been locked up in the dungeons of the Bargello, he said, and had suffered fluxations of the lungs ever since.

'But that was before I had taken up the pen in the cause of truth instead of the cause of the state. As for truth, now you are away from your fellows you can tell me truly whether you saw all.'

'I was as close to Raphael as I am to you,' Pasquale said, which was not accurate enough to satisfy an artificer, but would serve as commonplace truth.

'And you can remember it well enough to draw it?'

'I train my memory, Signor Machiavegli, especially for faces and gestures. If I can't draw it I can at least remember it.'

'Good enough. And please, I am Niccolò. Signor Machiavegli was another person, in another time.'

36

A dozen years ago, Machiavegli had been one of the most powerful men in Florence: as Secretary to the Ten he had been privy to most of the secrets of the Republic, and had been a prime mover in much of its foreign policy. But then the old government had been overthrown after the surprise attack by the Spanish navy on the dockyards at Livorno. Half the Florentine fleet had been burnt at its moorings, and a regiment of the Spanish army had burnt and sacked its way to the walls of Florence before the Florentines had rallied and overwhelmed it. Gonfalonier-for-life Piero Soderini had committed suicide, and Machiavegli had fallen into disgrace. Despite his frequent republican proclamations, and despite the fact that his own family had been killed and his property destroyed by the Spanish raiders, his enemies put it about that he had always been a Medici sympathizer. In the chaos following the attack it was rumoured that he might form the nucleus of a movement to bring the Medicis back into power for the first time since the short but cruel and disastrous reign of Giuliano de' Medici, who thirty years earlier had prosecuted a campaign of terror that had gone far beyond the summary execution of the assassins and their immediate families after the murder of his elder brother and his own lucky escape from a papal-inspired conspiracy. Even while Rome waged war on Florence, and after Rome's defeat by the devices of the Great Engineer, Giuliano had purged every great family as God had purged the Egyptians to secure the escape of the Israelites. It was a brutal time that was still not forgiven.

Thrown out of office, Niccolò Machiavegli had refused to swear an oath of loyalty to the new government, and for his pains – or pride – had suffered for two years in the dungeons of the Palazzo del Bargello. When he had finally been released, with no charges ever brought, he had become one of the new breed of journalists who worked for one or another of the *stationarii* competing to bring out daily broadsheets that proffered a mixture of sensationalism and scandal. After the fall of the old government, the artificers' faction packed the councils of the Eight and the Ten and the Thirteen. Taking advantage of their creed that nothing truthful should be hidden – although taking care never to write anything that would contradict the government's particular version of the truth – Niccolò Machiavegli had blazed a career as a political commentator.

He worked for a *stationarius* who used as offices the shop where once Vespasiano da Bisticci had worked, an irony since this most distinguished of publishers had retired to his country estate rather than introduce the new-fangled printing-presses which had driven copyists out of business. Some said that this coincidence was an indication that Machiavegli was bankrolled by the Medicis, for Cosimo de' Medici had once been Bisticci's best customer, ordering a library of two hundred volumes which forty-five scribes had completed within a record two years. Florentines liked nothing better than to gossip, and much gossip was founded on association or coincidence with events long past, for Florentines were also acutely aware of, and acutely proud of, their city's colourful and turbulent history. Men might struggle against fate, but they could not defeat the past.

Even at this late hour, lights burned along the length of the broadsheet's offices. Half a dozen men were lounging inside, sharing a meal of pasta and black bread and wine at one of the writing-tables. A blue haze of cigarette smoke drifted in the air above their heads. A couple of printer's devils slept in a kind of nest of rags under the gleaming frame of the spring-driven press. Bales of paper were stacked in the back, and printed sheets hung from lines like drying washing. Candles backed with reflector mirrors burned here and there, and one of the new acetylene lamps depended on a chain from the ceiling. It threw out a bright yellow light and permeated the stale used air of the room with a garlicky stink.

Machiavegli was greeted with cheerful cynicism by his fellows. The publisher of the broadsheet, Pietro Aretino, was an ambitious man half Machiavegli's age, stocky and running to fat, with a full beard and black hair greased straight back from his forehead. 'An eyewitness, eh?' he said, when Machiavegli introduced Pasquale. He was puffing on a green cigar that gave off dense white smoke as poisonous as the smog outside. He peered at Pasquale with kind yet shrewd eyes. 'Well, my friend, we only print the truth here, isn't that right, boys?'

The men around him laughed. The oldest, his bald pate fringed with fine silver hair, said, 'Do the public care so much for a squabble amongst artists?'

'There's a deal more to it than that,' Niccolò Machiavegli said. He had poured a measure of a yellow-green liquor in a tumbler of water;

38

now he drained this cloudy mixture with a shudder that was half eagerness, half disgust.

'Steady, Niccolò,' Aretino said.

'It's good for my nerves,' Niccolò said, as he commenced to mix another drink. 'Now, as to this squabble, it is the visible symptom of something that underlies the whole state. The Spanish pox begins with an innocent-looking sore, not even painful, as I understand. I hope you realize that I'm not speaking from experience,' he added, to laughter. 'But the unfortunate who finds the shepherd's golden coin on the end of his cock ignores it at his peril. I often think we're like doctors, advising the best way of living, drawing off excess humours. This little incident seems a trifle, I know, but it's diagnostic.'

Aretino blew out a long riffle of smoke. 'The public only cares about what we want them to care about. As long as we print it, it is news. If we print it big enough, it's big news. Remember the war in Egypt? Well, there wasn't a war until we reported it, and then the Signoria had to send in a squadron.'

'There would have been a war anyway,' Niccolò said mildly. Somehow, he had finished his second drink, and half-finished a third.

'But not the same war!' Aretino said. 'You are too humble, Niccolò. You should enjoy your power.'

'I know well enough where use of power can lead,' Niccolò Machiavegli said.

'Without risks there can be no gain.'

Aretino rolled his cigar from one side of his mouth to the other with epicurean relish. Candle-light was blankly reflected in his eyes. He looked like the devil, Pasquale thought. On a night like this it was easy to imagine that these few cynical men really could manipulate the world with their words, as they so clearly believed.

The elder journalist said, 'But what makes this petty squabble significant, Niccolò? What's the disease?'

'Please read my report, Girolamo. It's so late that I fear if I told you it over, I might contradict myself.'

Aretino said, 'It's the old against the new, the artificers against the artists, the Medici Pope against our dear Republic. Our question should be, which side are we on? Who are the angels here?'

'Whoever God favours,' one of the others said.

'That's fine,' Aretino retorted, 'but we can't wait on Heaven's judgement, which is often slow and passing strange.'

'This is hardly news,' the elder journalist said. 'Anyone with eyes knows the Pope is coming in two days' time. Anyone with ears knows that this embassy could bury the ashes of the long war between Florence and Rome. Rome once tried to destroy the Medicis by assassination and war, and now a Medici is Pope, and comes to treat with the same artificers whose devices saved the government of Giuliano de' Medici. A silly little squabble is a slender peg on which to hang something so weighty as a conspiracy to hide the truth from the citizens.'

Niccolò said, 'It's well known that Raphael is an outrider for the Pope. All artists have eyes, eh, young man? And Raphael has the best of them all, to spy out the mood of the city. There's also the matter of the wife of a certain important citizen, a woman with a personal interest in the arts –' here all the men smiled, and even Machiavegli looked amused '– but we'd best not mention her name here, well known though it is.'

Pasquale, wondering just who this woman was, said boldly, 'The catamite Salai threatened to reveal her name, if Master Raphael would not keep his peace.'

'An idle threat,' Aretino said, 'since your Master Raphael's amorous exploits are amongst the most widely publicized in Christendom. Many husbands are eager to be cuckolded by that young genius, it seems, although I fear they mistake Raphael's cock for his paintbrush, and believe that their wives are made more valuable by his amorous strokes just as pigment turns to gold when he wields his brush.'

'Perhaps he should sign his women as well as his works,' one of the younger journalists suggested.

'There is a feeling,' Niccolò Machiavegli told Pasquale, 'that the Great Engineer has already made arrangements with the Pope, and that Raphael is the conduit for this commerce. Naturally, this would not be in the interests of Florence, for our empire is founded on the fruits of the Great Engineer's genius. There is also the matter of the Spanish navy, at present on manoeuvre off Corsica under the command of Cortés himself.'

'Cortés the killer,' one of the journalists said.

'Cortés of the burnt arse,' Aretino said. 'Greek fire saw to his fleet when he tried to invade the New World, and will again.'

'The Spanish have ironclads now,' the eldest journalist said, 'and they have not lost their lust for gold and converts. Having rid their own land of the Moorish caliphate, they would take their Holy War to every corner of the New World. Imagine what would have happened if it had been Cortés, instead of Amerigo Vespucci, who first made treaty with Motecuhzoma!'

Pasquale said, 'And what of Salai in all this?'

'Salai feels himself threatened by Raphael, no doubt,' Niccolò said, 'and hence the blustering attack that you witnessed. The Great Engineer has a penchant for pretty boys, and Salai has long lost his bloom.'

'The bloom of the grape has replaced the bloom of his manhood,' one of the other journalists said.

'Raphael is a man whose taste runs only to women,' Aretino said. 'And the Great Engineer is an old man who eats leaves like a peasant, and he probably hasn't managed to get it up since he erected his tower. But Salai lives by his cock, and so he'll die by it too, one of these days. If he doesn't have the Spanish pox, then no one deserves it.'

'They say the Great Engineer has it,' the elder journalist said. 'They say he's crazy. I've heard that he keeps birds in his apartments. They fly free there.'

Aretino said, 'That's less fantastic than the story that he has reanimated a corpse. Or rather, a patchwork man sewn from the pieces of a number of cadavers. Even I do not believe that story, boys! As for birds, well, every man must have a hobby, eh? There's no harm in birds.'

'Unless you think you are one, and not a man,' the elder journalist said. 'They say he crouches on his bed-rail and caws like a rook, and flaps his elbows all the while.'

One of the younger journalists sniggered and said, 'I have it from a whore that one of the leading members of the Ten of Liberty and Peace likes to have in half a dozen wenches at a time and strut around naked with a feather up his arse, crowing like a rooster.'

Machiavegli said with a smile, 'If we believed all we heard, then, to give but one example, every man and woman in Florence would have died of the Spanish pox a dozen times over. Sex isn't the issue here, despite its universal popularity. The issue is alliances. Salai's the wild card who may force all to reveal their hands too soon. I do not believe that Raphael is here to seduce the Great Engineer – it would be too public a seduction. But if Raphael has come to bring the Pope's terms to the Signoria, so that they may have their reply ready when the Pope arrives, then such a secret embassy would be embarrassing to the government if it were revealed. After all, their motto is that democracy lives only by discussion and honest debate. That's why this incident is so important, and why we must run it as hard as we can, especially as not one of our rivals has thought to cover it at all.'

'It's the exclusivity that interests me,' Aretino said. 'Here's something that combines sex and honour and high matters of state, and we have it and no one else does. That means money, boys.'

'And that means you'll run it,' the elder journalist said, stiffly rising from his tall three-legged stool. 'I'll see what we can cut.'

Aretino stubbed out his cigar, suddenly all business. 'Everything else, if we have to. Gerino, kick those two young devils awake and have them break apart the type. We'll need a two-column space fifty lines deep, and I'd like it as near to the top as possible. Leon, write up a hundred-word piece on Signor Salai, nothing gratuitous, but with enough exaggeration to flatter him and serve our purpose. He's the villain of the piece, but a dupe too. As for you, young master painter, what do you know about copperplate engraving?'

Pasquale took a deep breath. His head was still packed with the fumes of all the wine he had drunk and the marijuana cigarette he had smoked: everything seemed slightly blurred and inflated. He said, as steadily as he could, 'I've practised it.'

'Good. There's a desk over there. Jacopino – drag it under the lamp, and turn up the gas, too. This young man will need good light to work by. Fetch – what will you want?'

Pasquale drew another breath. 'Paper of course, with as fine a surface as possible, and tracing-paper and stylus to prick a transfer for the outline. A good pen. Signor Aretino, I have practice of woodcuts, would that not be cheaper? Holly-wood is almost as good as copper.'

'But I have no holly-wood, and I have a liking for copper plates because they can make very many reproductions. There will be

42

hundreds of this edition produced. Let the last be as sharp as the first. How quickly can you do this?'

'Well, perhaps three or four hours to get it right.'

'You've an hour,' Aretino said, and clapped Pasquale on the back and left him standing there.

The youngest of the journalists helped Pasquale drag the desk under the hissing circlet of gas, showed him how to turn the key that regulated the drip of water on to the white rocks in the fuel-pan; as more water trickled in there was a palpable hiss and the yellow flames blossomed, starkly lighting the white sheet of paper, and throwing shadows across the room.

Pasquale lit a cigarette and shaped the scene in his mind, used his hands to block out the spaces on the paper. Space, Rosso had taught him, was the primary consideration in composition. The relationships of figures in the volume of space which contained them must draw the eye in the correct sequence, or else all was chaos. Salai at the left, then, foregrounded by Raphael who, in three-quarters profile, slightly turned from view, was the centre of the picture. Raphael's followers ranged around him in a half-circle, and the masters behind them, made half-size because they were not important. Detail only for Raphael and Salai, generic postures and expressions of shame and horror for the others. To depict shame, draw a figure with its fingers covering its eyes; for horror, bent fists and shaking arms.

When Pasquale had sketched in the outlines of the two main figures he worked in the background frieze of watchers, most prominent amongst them Giulio Romano, holding Salai in check, and the assistant who had feebly threatened Salai now transfigured into a loyal and fierce servant ready to defend his master to the death, hand on dagger, face defiant. Then Salai himself, his eyes narrowed, his grin crooked, and his posture crooked too, twisted left to right. Raphael the proud upright centre, the column supporting the weight of the little picture, steadfast while others shrank from Salai's bitter attack.

Pasquale worked his cramped fingers, then laid the drawing on the block of soft copper and bent to prick first the outlines of the figures, then the necessary details. Once this was done he commenced to incise the main lines, working with the rapid decisiveness and delicacy that Rosso had taught him so well. Then work in the detail, dot and dash and cross-hatch, shade and highlight.

He worked in a fever, hardly aware of what was happening around him except when he paused to work his cramping fingers, straighten his stiffening back, and light another cigarette. The printer's devils were firing up the little stove that drove the rocking springs of the printing-press. Bands of interleaved alloys creaked and groaned, stretching away from the heat to work the screw mechanism that wound the big barrel-spring, contracting back down to be heated again. The elder journalist was stooped over a tray of type, measuring lines with a marked stick. Aretino was quietly talking with Niccolò Machiavegli, puffing at a cigar which he also used to punctuate his sentences.

Their talk fell through Pasquale's fever. Niccolò was expounding a theory of power, suggesting that every society, to be stable, must in its construction emulate the Egyptian pyramid, broad at base and crowned at apex. Italy's troubles, Niccolò explained, were caused by diffusion of power, so that the ruthless could exploit the masses. States ruled by absolute decree could always conquer those ruled by democracy, for decision by one strong man was always more rapid and more flexible than decision by committee, where what emerges is not the best action but compromise. Aretino laughed and said this was all very well, but Italians would always destroy their rulers in the end, for the needs of the family always outweighed the needs of the state. Somehow Pasquale became lost in this talk, and didn't realize for a few minutes that he had sat back from his work not to rest but because it was finished.

Aretino wanted a test print at once, and insisted that the block was fitted into the press. One of the boys set the ratchet levers with a practised hand and released the brake on the barrel-spring. With a rattle of leaf-springs and caged ball-bearings, the carrier shot back to grab a leaf of paper as the ink-roller ran over the surface of the plate, ran back to scrape off excess ink as the paper was deposited. The loom of the press fell with a rattle of counterweights, sprang back up.

The boy nimbly caught up the paper, and there, beneath the broadsheet's device, between close columns of ornate small type, was the picture Pasquale had made, shiny with wet black ink.

As Aretino took the broadsheet and held it to the light, the door of the printing-shop was flung open. Everyone turned; the man who had burst in caught the door frame, panting as if at the end of a bitter race. Wisps of smog curled around him.

'Speak up, man,' Aretino said.

The man caught his breath. 'Murder! Murder at the Palazzo Taddei!'

Someone else said, 'Fuck. That's where Raphael is staying.'

Aretino set down the broadsheet and took his cigar from his mouth. 'Boys,' he said soberly, 'I do believe we have us a story.'

4

The Palazzo Taddei was a four-square building with an imposing frontage of blocks of untrimmed golden sandstone. Windowless, it loomed out of the smoggy darkness of the Via de Ginori like a fortress wall. It was eight o'clock, but even at this late hour, when most honest citizens should have been abed, a small crowd was gathered at the Palazzo's great round gate. Niccolò and Pasquale had to use their elbows and knees to push through to the front.

Niccolò had a word with the sergeant in command of the unit of city militia which kept a space before the gate, handing over a cigar with a smile. The sergeant shook Niccolò's hand and spoke into the brass trumpet of a speaking-tube beside the gate. With a sudden arthritic creaking the dozen wooden leaves of the gate began to draw back into their sockets. A ragged opening widened into a circle. One of the upper leaves stuck, like the last tooth in an old man's jaw, and although a servant appeared and gave a hearty shove to try and force it, Niccolò and Pasquale had to duck under it as the sergeant waved them through.

Pasquale turned to watch as the gate closed up with a rattle of chained weights that in falling recompressed the spring mechanism, regaining all the energy used to open the gate except that lost through heat or noise. Successful merchants like Taddei were in love with such devices, which signified status in the way that sponsoring an altarpiece or a fresco had once done. There were tall mirrors of beaten silver on either side of the door, and Pasquale looked himself up and down before hurrying to catch up with Niccolò Machiavegli, crossing the marble floor of the sumptuous entrance hall and following the journalist through an open door into the loggia that ran around the four sides of the central garden.

The Palazzo was built in the new fashion of architecture inspired by the excavations of the Roman city of Herculaneum. Acetylene lamps on slim iron columns cast a yellow pallor that made the grass and clipped bushes of the formal garden look like their own black shadows. A scaly stone fish gushed water into the central pool, and a mechanical songbird twittered in a gilded cage, turning its head back and forth, back and forth. Its eyes were pinpoint rubies, its feathers fretted gold-leaf. A signal-tower rose above the garden; it was built into a corner of the loggia, the curve of its smooth stone wall gleaming white against the night sky. Niccolò looked up at the signal-tower for a long minute. Pasquale looked too, but saw nothing except a lighted window round as a ship's porthole, and the green and red lamps burning at the end of the long T-shaped signal-vane.

Niccolò hailed another civil guard, this one with an officer's short red cape. 'The captain of the precinct station,' he told Pasquale after he had had a brief word with the man. 'You would expect no less than that in a case like this. He tells me it happened up in the signal-tower. He will let us through, as long as Signor Taddei is agreeable.'

Pasquale said, feeling a kind of sick eagerness, 'Was it Raphael that was killed?'

Niccolò took a pull from a leather flask, screwing the cap back on with deliberation. He was quite drunk, Pasquale realized: he had been drinking steadily ever since they had entered the office of the broadsheet. As a man plodding through a blizzard will choose his steps with care, so Niccolò said, 'Oh no, of course it wasn't Raphael. No, it was one of his followers. A fellow by the name of Giulio Romano.'

Pasquale remembered the man who had challenged Salai. He said, 'He defended Raphael against the Great Engineer's catamite, as I showed in my picture. If someone wanted to strike terror and despair into the heart of Raphael, then killing his best assistant could not do it better. And if Salai did this, then he would choose the man who stood against him.'

'We do not know that it was Salai who did this,' Niccolò said, smiling.

'Call over the captain,' Pasquale said, 'I'll tell him what I think, at least.'

Niccolò took Pasquale's elbow and said quietly, 'You are here to record the scene, if we can but see it. In a case like this . . . it would be better if you kept your own counsel.'

'I don't want to accuse anyone,' Pasquale said with a sudden indignation that surprised himself, 'but I want the truth of what I saw to be known.'

Niccolò said, 'Signor Aretino has given me leave to rewrite my account: all of the front page is mine. Ours, I should say. Do you realize what that means, young Pasquale? Well no, I don't suppose you do. But believe me that it *is* important, and it is important that enough of what I write is new, not retold common knowledge. I have had enough of that. If you tell me your story first, and to the guard the next day, where's the harm? The man is dead, and if Salai killed him it is not very likely that he will flee, for that would confirm his guilt. And if he does flee the city militia will capture him in short order. Listen, Pasquale. You are in deep water here, and do not know it. I admire your desire for justice, but think: would you die if it would save a thousand men?'

'That depends.'

'If they were your fellow citizens?'

'Well, perhaps.'

'Ah. And if your death would save only five hundred? Or seventy? Or ten? And if you would still lay down your life for ten men, what good would it do you when you were cold and dead and they were in the tavern drinking to you, and eating *arista*? What good is laying down your life for the common good when you can't enjoy the taste of pork and rosemary – or anything?'

'Perhaps my children will enjoy it.'

'A good answer, but I don't think you have any children.'

'Well, none that I know about.'

Niccolò laughed. 'And if you die now, you never will, and so you will be killing them. Listen: if you want to lay down your life for others, then confront your enemy in mortal combat and let him kill you, for then at least you will have saved one life: his.'

'I have no enemies.'

'You think not? Perhaps you don't. Then why lay down your life?'

Pasquale said, although he knew how weak it sounded, 'I only want to tell the truth.'

Niccolò laughed. 'If you are to indulge in the vice of honesty, I hope you can afford its price.'

'What's wrong with the truth?' Pasquale thought that Niccolò's love of argument would make him steal another's soul simply for the joy of it.

'Your truth is very different from that which the killer of Giulio Romano believes. You see it as murder; he as survival, perhaps, or a task which will put bread in the mouths of his children.' Niccolò uncapped his flask and took another drink, shuddering with exaggerated satisfaction. 'Ah. I'm an old man, and the night air settles easily in my bones.'

'It seems so matter-of-fact. Like accounts. Bloodless.'

Niccolò made a vague gesture, and dropped the cap of his flask. As he stooped awkwardly, he said, 'Morality is not a guessing-game. There are laws, checks and balances. Where is that cap?'

Pasquale picked it up for Niccolò, who took a while screwing it back on. 'I'm tired,' Niccolò said, as if the matter were over. 'Now I must talk with Signor Taddei.'

Pasquale followed the journalist through the formal garden. A stout man in a heavy embroidered robe, a Turkish cap set squarely on his tousled thinning hair, had appeared at the edge of the loggia. This was the master of the Palazzo, the merchant Taddei, who explained calmly that the household had been preparing for bed when a terrible scream had been heard. His servants had rushed about in a panic until someone had noticed a light burning in the signal-tower, and that was where the corpse had been found, although they had to break down the door to reach it: the murderer had locked the door after him.

Niccolò listened to the merchant without interruption, and now he paused as if in thought before asking if the house had been locked up at that time.

'Of course,' Taddei said, 'although it saddens me to say so. These are the times of enlightenment, yet even within the city walls we must protect ourselves from vagabonds and thieves. The Swiss mercenaries who are here to protect us cause more deaths of innocent citizens than the Spanish pox, it sometimes seems.'

'And of course you had your guests to protect.'

'Master Raphael is attempting to calm his followers. If not for him, they would all have rushed incontinently into the night, in pursuit of the murderer.'

'Master Raphael is a sensible man,' Niccolò said. 'Has any of the

49

guard looked along the walls of your house? No one could have left by the doors, if they were locked, so perhaps our murderer left by a window. And if so, then there will be marks where he landed, for he would have to jump from one of the upper storeys, there being no windows at ground level.'

Taddei said, 'I will ask the captain to order it done, if it has not been done already. But the murderer must have had a key to the signal-tower, for that is always locked at night if I have no messages to send, and expect to receive none. If he had a key to the tower, then he could also have a key to one of the doors to the outside.'

'A good point,' Niccolò said. 'Thank you for your time, signor. Is it possible that we might see the infamous scene now?'

'Of course, if the captain will allow it.'

'With your permission. One more thing. Did you send any signals tonight, or receive any?'

'No, none. As I said, the tower was locked. When the murder was discovered, one of my servants went for the militia straight away. Their quarters are at the end of this street.'

Niccolò considered this for a moment. 'There may be a simple solution to the puzzle,' he said at last, 'but I must see the tower before I can reach any firm conclusion. Come on, Pasquale.'

They walked across the garden to the other side of the loggia, where two or three of the militia, in white waistcoats and red and white particoloured hose, clustered at a door. Niccolò said, 'What do you think, Pasquale?'

'It could be a servant who did it – he may have a key to the tower, and would certainly know where one is kept. If no keys are missing, well, he could have replaced it in the confusion before someone thought to see if it were missing. And a servant would not need to escape. Or it could be one of Raphael's other assistants, or one of his pupils. But that would not explain why the murder was done where it was, in a high place in a strange house.'

'Bravo, Pasquale! Your thoughts mirror mine.'

'Why didn't you say any of this to Signor Taddei?'

'It would insult him to imply that one of his servants would kill a guest. When asking questions of a man, you must never slight his honour, even though that means you must come upon the truth by a crooked path. Slight a man's honour, and he will tell you nothing more. Flatter him, and by and by he will reveal more than he ever intended.'

One of the militia, a slim boy hardly older than Pasquale, let them through to the wooden stairway that wound widdershins inside the signal-tower. It was so narrow that Pasquale had to follow on Niccolò's heels. Niccolò stopped half-way up and banged the flimsy rail back and forth, then went on at a quick pace. Near the top he turned to Pasquale and said, 'Have you ever seen a dead man?'

'Certainly.'

'One killed violently?'

'This past winter I attended the dissection classes at the New University, to learn how a man is put together for my painting. I've no fear of tripes.'

'Bravely said. But remember that dead men do not bleed. I fear there will be a lot of blood. And then there is the matter of the bowels, which loosen at the moment of death. You didn't press your study in summer because of the smell, eh? Do not worry if you grow faint, or even are ill, Pasquale. It is no disgrace.'

With two militia guards as well as the red-caped captain in the tower's little wooden cabin, it would have been crowded even if they had not had to keep to the sides, because Giulio Romano's body was laid on the raised round platform in the centre. Someone had already tracked through the sticky pool of blood around poor Romano's head, adding footprints to the spatters and streaks that spangled the polished ash planks of the floor. The air was thick with a slaughter-house reek; it coated Pasquale's mouth. There was paper everywhere, torn into scraps the largest of which were no bigger than a man's hand, and broken black glass in a heap by the little round window.

Despite Niccolò's warning, Pasquale did not feel faint; rather he was filled with an eager curiosity. He wanted to see what the journalist would do and ask, and besides, he had never before been in a signal-tower. The corpse bore little resemblance to the lively fellow who had stayed Salai's hand in the church only that morning. Rather, it resembled a badly modelled mannequin dressed in expensive black and curled around itself, remote from the affairs of men. Nothing done to me, it seemed to imply, can be worse than that which was done to me before my death. Furrows had been ripped from the flesh of its face down to the bone of the jaw, and there was a deep ragged wound in its throat, packed with a kind of clotted black jelly.

The wooden cabin was no bigger than the private cabin of a ship, brightly lit by a hissing acetylene lamp that hung from the apex of the domed roof. The corpse lay on a round platform lifted waist-high above the walkway that ran around it. This little platform was where the signaller would stand, using his spyglass to watch, through the windows let into the domed roof at each compass point, one or another of the local repeater arms, or the big multiple-route complex on top of the Great Tower. Directly opposite the door was the counterbalanced arm which operated the tower's small signal-vane. There was a brass speaking-tube beside it, and a slate washed milky white, and a ball of chalk on a string. One of the small round windows hung open, and through it Pasquale glimpsed lights burning red and green at the top and bottom of the signal-vane.

Niccolò greeted the captain again, took out a little notepad and a sharp sliver of black lead, and asked if the corpse lay just as it had been found. Pasquale remembered what he was here for, and took paper and chalk from his scrip, although he was not yet ready to start sketching.

The captain said, in answer to Niccolò's question, 'Not at all. It was jammed up against the door; you can see where blood pooled. We had the devil of a job getting in even after the door was unlocked, and then laid him out there so the surgeon could look at him.'

Niccolò bent to inspect the door. He peered at the lock, then stooped further and ran a finger along the lower edge before standing. 'He was dead when he was found. That's what the servant said.'

The captain was a tall man with a cap of black hair and a neatly trimmed beard around the line of his square jaw; he looked like a Roman centurion. Pasquale had his likeness in a dozen nerveless lines. The captain said, 'Quite dead. His throat was torn out; there must have been a race between suffocation and blood loss to finish him off, the poor devil.'

Niccolò paced around the edge of the walkway, circling the cabin once, twice. While the captain and the guards watched the journalist, Pasquale started to sketch the corpse, its huddled arms and legs, the torn throat tipped back, the face set in a remote expression Pasquale had never seen on any living face. His head felt very clear as he worked. He was beginning to understand that death was not simply a loss of vitality, but a profound change. It was something he would never forget, and it made him fear death less. You did not suffer after death. There was nothing left to suffer.

Niccolò reached through the open window, drew in his hand and showed the captain the blood smeared on his fingertips. The captain said, 'There's blood all over. As if the poor devil staggered around in a mad frenzy before dying, perhaps even while his murderer tore the place apart – you see, of course, the paper everywhere. The signaller keeps a log of all messages sent or received, apparently – that's where most of the paper came from. Whoever killed Romano will be covered in blood, like as not. That's why I don't think it was anyone in the palace. We had them all lined up as soon as we could, and that was not twenty minutes after the alarm was raised. No trace of blood on any of them, and no one could have washed so quickly and so thoroughly. And no mark of a struggle on any of them either, no scratches or bruises. Whoever did this was a madman, and poor Romano there fought back bravely – perhaps even tried to follow his killer out the tower.'

'You're very thorough,' Niccolò said. 'And I agree, the murderer came from outside the house. But he came through this window, and left the same way. There is blood on the sill of the window, but no blood on the stair-rail. Look through Romano's clothes: you'll find a key. He locked himself in here for some purpose, and then the murderer surprised him. There was a violent struggle, and Romano tried to unlock the door to escape – there are new scratches on the wood around the lock where he tried and failed to thrust in the key before he was overcome by his murderer. And when he was done, the murderer left the same way he'd come, through the window here that Giulio Romano opened to light the signal-lanterns. They are still burning, as they were when I came into the garden and looked up at the tower, yet Signor Taddei told me no signals were sent this evening. He was wrong, but could not have known that one of his guests was making use of his signal-tower without his permission. I would also guess that there was still life in Romano's body when his murderer left, for he tried again to open the door, but could only scratch at the bottom edge before he died. And so he was found. The murderer could hardly have wedged the body up against the door, and then closed it from the outside.'

The captain said, 'But no key is missing. The murderer must have locked the door when he left.'

'No, it was Romano who locked the door. Search his body and you will find the key.'

The captain gave the order with a smile, as if Niccolò were providing a rare entertainment he was only too happy to co-operate in, just to see where it was going. That was what Pasquale felt, at any rate, as if he were in the centre of an unfolding play, and only Niccolò Machiavegli knew how the threads of plot wove together.

The guard who was searching the body held up a key, and the captain took it and tried it in the lock of the door. The tongue snapped back and forth, and the captain smiled. 'One to you, Niccolò. But if no key is missing, where did this one come from?'

'Signor Taddei will have a key, for he is master of the house. And the major-domo will have another, for he must have the means to ensure that his master's orders are carried out. But there will be a third, too. No doubt that person assured you that his key was not missing – perhaps he even showed you a key. But it was not *the* key.'

The captain swore. 'Of course! You there, Acciaioli! Fetch up the signaller!'

The other guard, the one who had found the key, said, 'Here's something else.'

He held up a little construction of white stiff paper and wood splinters, a kind of boat with a double helical screw instead of a sail. It was small enough to fit into his open palm.

The captain took it and said, 'What do you make of this, Niccolò? Ah, here, there's a band of that new rubber stuff, and a spindle for winding it. A toy do you think?'

Using his thumbnail, with surprising delicacy, the captain turned a needle-sized ratchet. The little boat started to flutter and shake. The captain let it go. The paper screws whirred around and the thing wound itself into the air, rising with such force that it struck the glass bull's-eye of one of the observation ports. Then the energy of the rubber band was spent, and with its helical screws revolving slowly the other way, the boat sank back down.

Pasquale, who had the quickest eye, caught it before it reached the floor. It was as light as a feather: in fact, the sparring which gave it rigidity was made of the shafts of a bird's primary feathers. A pigeon. Angels, pigeon-wings too small to sustain them. Artificers. 'Artificers,' Pasquale said. 'Artificers and angels.'

The captain said to Niccolò, 'There's talk amongst the artificers of machines that can row the air as lightly as a peasant's coracle crosses the Arno's flood. You don't think—'

Niccolò said, 'With your permission, Pasquale,' and lifted up the little flying toy, peered at it with his dark eyes – pigeon's eyes, Pasquale thought, pink-rimmed and rheumy with years of drink, but still sharp.

Niccolò handed the little flying boat back to Pasquale and said, 'We need invoke no fantastical explanation until all mundane possibilities are exhausted. Only then do we begin to search for the footprints of angels. This is only a toy, popular in Rome. I have seen others like it.' He cocked his head as footsteps were heard mounting the wooden stairway. 'Here is our missing key, in more ways than one.'

The signaller was a boy at least five years younger than Pasquale, with a tonsured cap of blond hair and a fringe of fine blond hairs along his acne-speckled jaw. He was dressed in the four-pocketed ankle-length brown tunic of his order, cinched with a broad leather belt from which depended a leather pouch and a small rosewood cross. The Order of Signallers was a congregation of the Dominicans which, although secular rather than monastic, was nevertheless under strict religious rule.

The captain asked the boy pleasantly enough if he would use his key on the lock of the cabin's door, and from the way the boy looked from one man to the other Pasquale knew that his nerve was already gone. The boy signaller straightened his back and said, his voice reedy but steady, 'Sir, Signor Romano bribed me to use this tower. I ask that you put me in the hands of the masters of my order.'

'Not just yet,' the captain said. 'There's a man dead here. He's the one who bought the key from you?'

The boy gave a small tight nod. Sweat stood out on his forehead.

The captain said sharply, 'Did he explain his purpose? Speak, boy! He's dead, and won't complain.'

'Just, just that he wanted to make a private rendezvous.'

'Not to send a message?'

'I would not have allowed him to use the apparatus, sir.'

Niccolò said, 'All messages sent from here would be passed through the Great Tower.'

The signaller, eager to please, said, 'We call it the mains trunk. It handles all traffic routed across the city, and is the relay for the land-lines south and north.'

Niccolò told the captain, 'The Order of Signallers are very thorough record-keepers. If Romano managed to send a signal, then you will find a record of it. No doubt it will be some simple, apparently honest and trivial message, but it will be code for something else. Signor Romano would have sent it himself because this lad refused. He would have sent it in plain talk, which is easy enough to master – even I have knowledge of it. Anyone who practises a simple signal beforehand could send it with sufficient skill to deceive those receiving it into believing it had been sent by the proper person, which is to say our signaller lad here. Not so, boy?'

'He didn't say he wanted to use the apparatus, sir. As I said, I wouldn't have allowed that.'

'But letting him borrow your key gave you a clear conscience, eh?' the captain said. 'And now there's a man dead. Think on that, signaller. You'll spend the night in our lock-up before we hand you over to the tender mercies of your order.'

When the signaller had been marched away, Pasquale asked what would happen to him.

'The Order of Signallers deal with their own more rigorously than we would,' the captain said. 'They must, to enforce and protect their scrupulous code. If the signallers were believed corrupt, who would trust a message to them?'

Niccolò said, 'I can add little more to my tale, Captain. I hope you find it satisfactory.'

'Your reputation is upheld, Niccolò,' the captain said. 'If you could tell me the content of the message, and who received it, then we would have the whole of it, I think.'

'There are still many questions to answer, the least of which is the content of the message. I am more concerned with the motivation of the man who sent it. Was he a spy? And if so, did his master, Raphael, know of it or even order it?'

'Unfortunately, Raphael and his crew have diplomatic status, and so cannot be questioned, let alone arrested,' the captain said. 'Certainly, they will be kept under strict observation from now on, but that is not my duty. I am only a poor precinct captain who must try and catch a murderer. As to who that was, and why he murdered Romano, I am afraid your tale, satisfactory though it may be from a narrative point of view, is lacking in an ending.'

'I can't tell you much about your man,' Niccolò said. 'Except that he is unskilled in killing, and perhaps not even armed. There is no sign of use of a blade, for there are no clean rents in Signor Romano's clothing or on his face or neck, and neither are there cuts on the palms of his hands of the kind which you would expect to find in an unarmed man trying to defend himself, or an armed man defending himself at the last from a superior opponent. A man will grasp at the blade in a last vain attempt to save his life even though it cuts him to the bone. There are no such cuts, but instead wounds made by nails and possibly teeth, and bruises in the pattern of a strong grip. Romano was bludgeoned to death in a hot fury, I would guess, by someone far stronger than he, even in his last desperate throes; even a woman may call up unguessed reserves of strength when pressed to the point of dying, and we must imagine Romano possessed of such strength, yet still he was overcome. Our murderer is a strong man then, perhaps of uncertain temper. And this man was not an accomplice to whatever Romano was up to, for if he entered with Romano, who locked the door behind him to ensure he would not be disturbed, he would have known of a key and taken it. So we must assume that he climbed in through the window and fled the same way – and I have shown you the marks of his escape, the blood that he left on the sill of the window. So while Romano's murderer is a strong man, he is also small or slender enough to enter through that small window.'

'In my experience,' the captain remarked, 'a thief may enter through any aperture large enough to accommodate his head. Certain thieves employ young children, who can wriggle through a chink you would swear would bar entrance even to a snake. And I must say that with all my experience in housebreaking I have never known any who could scale a tower such as this without equipment. Signor Taddei is a wealthy man, and employed builders who fit blocks of stone almost as closely as those in the ancient villas of Herculaneum.'

'You have visited that unfortunate city? You're a lucky man.'

'My wife's family has a farm close by; they grow grapes on the slopes of Vesuvius.'

'If I must bow to your knowledge of housebreakers and of Roman ruins, and indeed of architecture, I do know something of mountaineering, and would judge that it is not impossible for a skilled mountain-climber to scale what we Tuscans, who find hill-walking troubling, would assay impossible. I also note that Romano has coarse hairs caught in his fingernails; not the hairs of a man, but perhaps of the coat or collar of a coat that his murderer was wearing. In winter, and on unseasonably cold nights such as this, the Prussians and Swiss take to wearing overcoats with fur-trimmed collars. Perhaps you might start your inquiries amongst the ranks of Florence's mercenary army. A slim strong ruffian, from one of the rural cantons rather than Zurich or Geneva, and with recent deep scratches on his face or hands; there are shreds of skin along with the hairs under the victim's fingernails.'

The captain said, 'The Pope employs Swiss soldiers, as well as Florence. These are deep waters, Niccolò. You write this up, and I don't know what kind of trouble it might lead to. You will, I think, need the permission of the Signoria itself, and meanwhile, I must take your notebook, and the sketches of your young assistant there.'

Niccolò sighed. 'Of course I'll co-operate. We always do, Captain. Facts, not sensationalism.'

The captain said, 'That's why you were allowed here. I trust you to keep to the facts, Niccolò.'

'I hoped to flatter myself that it was for my forensic skills that I was allowed to witness this terrible scene.'

'I am always grateful for your opinions, Niccolò. You know that. And I will report your opinions, but the matter will soon be out of my hands, I am afraid. Now, your notes and sketches, if you please, and I will see that you are safely escorted from the palace.'

The street outside the gate of the Palazzo was empty. The foul smog and unseasonable cold had defeated the crowd's thirst for sensationalism. Niccolò walked quickly to the corner, where he fumbled out his flask. He drank everything he had, and wiped his mouth with the back of his hand.

Pasquale lit a cigarette and said, 'You might have left me some.'

'My thirst admits no generosity,' Niccolò said. He was shivering, hunched in on himself with his hands thrust between his thighs.

Pasquale took the journalist's arm, and they started down the street towards the publisher's office. He said, 'What will you do now the militia have stopped your story?'

Niccolò laughed. His voice was congested. 'It would take more than confiscation of my notes to stop me writing up what I've seen.'

'But the captain—'

'He followed the form of the law to protect himself. He has my notes, and your sketches, and can tell his superiors that he tried his best to stop me. But he knows I will write the story anyway, and I know that you can draw the scene from memory. You have already shown how well your memory serves your art. And you have the little flying device.'

'I put it in my scrip. Do you think the toy is important?'

'It isn't a toy. That's just a story I told the captain, so he would not wish to keep it. Instead, you must guard it, Pasquale. Will you do that for me?'

'Of course. But why—'

'Ah, but I'm weary, young Pasquale! Turn down here. There's a drinking-den that stays open all hours, if you don't mind vagabonds and whores.'

It was a low dive in a cellar lit only by a small brazier in the centre of the straw-strewn earth floor. A dozen people sat on crude smoke-blackened benches around this rude hearth, drinking new rough red wine they dipped from a common dish. Rats rustled in the dark corners. The slattern who kept the den threw stones at any which ventured near the warmth of the brazier.

Niccolò thawed after a couple of draughts of wine. 'I haven't sustained such a passage of thought since my interrogation,' he said. 'I had forgotten how brain-work tires you.'

'Is it all true, what you said?'

'Some of it, certainly. Although I'm not entirely sure about the motives which the captain ascribes to the murderer.'

Pasquale said, 'Perhaps the murder has nothing to do with Romano. Perhaps he merely surprised a thief or spy rifling through the messages.'

'Then we must believe that Romano chose to use the tower illicitly at the same time this thief broke into it. I do not say that it is impossible, but it is highly unlikely. We can only consider the unlikely when the probable has been ruled out, and the impossible when nothing else is left.'

'But there must be a conspiracy. There must! Surely it is no coincidence that an assistant of Raphael was murdered on the eve of the Pope's visit!'

Niccolò smiled indulgently at this outburst. Pasquale drained his cup and dipped more wine from the common dish – if he was to pay for this, he would get his rightful share. When he sat down again, Niccolò told him, 'We are only at the beginning, Pasquale. I can assure you that I crave the thrill of the hunt – there is no finer way to keep away boredom than to solve a puzzle like this – but I must make sure I am following the right quarry.'

'What of the little flying device? I've never seen anything like it.'

'It may be everything, or nothing. I do not yet know. A man will carry all sorts of odds and ends with him, especially artists. What do you have in your scrip, Pasquale? Apart from the coin you'll need to pay for this vigorous wine? I will guess that there will be charcoal and goose-quills, and a little knife for sharpening the quills, scraps of paper for sketching, some English lead, a bit of bread for rubbing out lines. A block of lampblack, and a dished stone for mixing the ink. Those set you apart as an artist. But I'll wager you also have bits and pieces which set you apart as an individual, and have nothing at all to do with your profession. So perhaps with Giulio Romano. We find a little toy, and if we are not careful it takes on a significance out of proportion to its worth, and we are astray, gone from the path direct, chasing imagined shadows. Yes, it may be important, but it may also mean nothing.'

Pasquale said, 'In a painting, everything can be riddled for meaning. Things resonate because they have been used before, and because there is a story or a tradition behind each gesture, each flower. I saw that little toy flutter up and I thought of angels . . .'

Pasquale wanted, but did not dare, to speak of his vision, the painting that glowed in his mind, still obscure yet slowly growing clearer, as an object hidden in mist grows clearer as the viewer advances towards it. No, it was not at all like the way Niccolò had worked, piecing together a brief history of violence from its scattered aftermath. He was suddenly gripped with an ache to begin painting at once, but knew that if he did it would be a botched beginning that would set him back days, weeks, months. Whole sight, or none at all.

The cellar was dank, but the brazier's fire warmed Pasquale through, and its smoke was better than the sharp chemical stench of the artificers' smog that still clung to his tunic. On the other side of the brazier, a skinny weasel-faced fellow in rags was slowly inserting his arm in a fat whore's massive pendulous bosom, as if he hoped eventually to climb all the way into this maternal cleft. The other customers mostly nodded, befuddled by rough wine, transfixed by the glowing brands in the brazier and their own unguessable thoughts.

After a while, the old white-haired man sitting beside Pasquale spoke up. A livid sheet of scar tissue stretched across the left side of his face, drawing down his eye and the corner of his mouth. He laid a finger alongside this scar and said in a thick Milanese accent, 'You're wondering where I got this, young fellow. Let me tell you I got it when I was building the waterway to the sea. The artificers used Chinese powder to blow through the solid rock at Seraville, and one of the explosions threw burning fragments amongst the tents where we workers was living. A lot didn't get away from the fire, because it touched off a store of powder, but I was fortunate, you might say. More men were killed that night than in the Egyptian War, but I escaped with only a scar. All those factories there now, using the power of the water we channelled to make their goods . . . but what did I get out of it but a pension and a face to curdle milk? They say the artificers have freed men to be themselves, but their machines make men like me less than beasts, working to their pace until we can work no more, and when we have outgrown our use we are thrown aside.'

The old man shifted a cud of tobacco from one cheek to the other, and spat a long liquid stream towards the brazier. Leaning forward to look past Pasquale, he said, 'I know you, Signor Machiavegli. I seen you here before, and heard you talk, too. I know you'd agree with me.'

Niccolò was cheerful and alert once more, Pasquale saw. The wine had done its work, its fire driving away his dolour as a torch will drive away mist.

'We've always been free to be ourselves, in our heads, signor,' Niccolò said. 'But only a few can ever free themselves from the physical lot of the many. It can be proven mathematically that the work expended to produce material wealth can never enrich but a fraction of the population that must labour. Indeed, it is best for the Republic if it remains rich yet its citizens remain poor, for individual wealth engenders sloth. Think of Rome, which for four hundred years after it was built harboured the greatest poverty, yet those years were also the last happy times of the republic. Think of Aemilius Paulus, who with his triumph over Perseus brought much wealth to Rome, yet remained poor himself. Like conquest, work should not make a man rich, but keep him in active, not idle, poverty.'

'Now, forgive me, Signor Machiavegli, but you sound like one of those Savonarolistas,' the old man said. 'I can't say that I hold with them.'

'I've had good cause to favour the followers of that grim prophet,' Niccolò said, 'but I thank God I've enough sense never to have done so.'

Pasquale said, 'All this talk. What good is talk.' He was dismayed to realize that he was drunker than he had believed.

A figure sitting in the shadows beyond the play of the firelight stirred. It was an immensely fat, completely bald man, wrapped in a much-darned woollen cape. 'The last days are here, journalist. A beast sits on the throne of Saint Peter, and will soon die. The false towers erected by the pride and vanity of the artificers will be overthrown. Put that in your paper.'

'It is well known that words and not bombs are my weapons.' Niccolò drank off his wine and turned his cup over, shaking the last drops over the straw between his boots. 'Pay the host, Pasquale, and we will be off. We must put our story to bed before we can think of bed ourselves.'

62

5

Pasquale returned to the studio at cock-crow. He was tired yet a long way from sleep. As he worked through the night on an engraving of the murder scene in the signal-tower of the Palazzo Taddei, Signor Aretino had treated him to several cups of thick bitter coffee, the new and expensive drink imported from the Egyptian Protectorate. Aretino had said that it cured all ills, and most particularly sleep. He was right in the last; although Pasquale was bone-tired, he felt a frail peculiar lucidity, as if he had just woken from a strange and wonderful dream.

The artificers' smog was lifting. In the veiled airy distance, beyond the swayback red-tiled roofs of the modest old houses along the narrow street, the traceries of lamps that limned the bulk of the Great Tower were fading into a watery dawn. Green and red signal-lights winked and glittered. Little arms swung to and fro on one pinnacle at the tower's top. Flocks of messages on the wing, as invisible as angels.

The city was waking with the light. Housewives were rattling open cane shutters of first- and second-floor windows and throwing slops towards the street's central gutter – the artificers' new drainage scheme had not yet reached this part of the city – and talking to one another across the width of the street like swallows chattering in the eaves of a barn. The bells for the first mass were tolling, here and there, far and near, a communion of bells across the roofs of the city. The high chimneys of the sleepless manufactories on the other side of the Arno were sending plumes of smoke high into the dawn air, each kinked at the same height by the westerly wind which had blown away the smog. The rumble of their engines and looms was faint and regular, the monotonous heartbeat of the city's trade.

Pasquale stopped a baker's boy in mid-cry and bought a length of hot bread, its crust crunchily charcoaled. Two silver florins, payment for his night's labours, nestled in his scrip, along with the flying toy, which Niccolò Machiavegli had charged him to keep safe, and a crisp folded copy of that day's edition of the broadsheet, his two engravings anchored amongst the columns of Niccolò Machiavegli's rhythmic, urgent prose. He felt at one with the city, as if he were a part of a great intricate mechanism poised an instant from happiness. He even welcomed the company of a scrawny yellow cur that joined him on his way home and trotted at his heels until it suddenly remembered some business of its own and loped off down an alley.

The door of the studio was open at the top of the stairs; a light burned inside. Rosso was already at work. He was grinding blue pigment, seated astride the smoothing-block, his loose, colour-stained apron girdled at his waist, sleeves rolled back from his freckled forearms as he worked grainy vinegared copper back and forth across the surface of the block, reducing granules to fine powder with brisk strokes, pushing the powder into a pannier already half-full with skyey colour.

Pasquale felt a surge of guilt and affection at the sight of his master at this humble task. He hurried in, apologizing, but Rosso brushed aside his excuses.

'You do as you must,' he said. There were smudges of blue on his forehead and cheeks; his fingers were dyed blue to the knuckles. It seemed that he had been working all night; at the work-table by the window, sections of his painting had been blocked in with washes shading to a deep, almost black umber, limning the volume which framed the figures.

Pasquale showed his master the two florins, and then the broadsheet, which Rosso took to the window and looked at for a long time. 'Poor Giulio,' he said, at last. 'No one knows who killed him?'

Pasquale started to tell his master about Niccolò Machiavegli's investigations, while Rosso stared out of the window in a distracted way. A blade of light fell between the shutters, illuminating precisely one half of his face. When Pasquale had finished, Rosso said, 'I have it in me, Pasquale, to be a great painter. That fool of a hospital director – he knew nothing, nothing! They knew about painting here in Florence, once upon a time, but no more. It is all artificers and their devices, and trade, and talk of an empire to rival that of ancient Rome. But without art it is hollow, Pasquale. It is nothing.'

So it was back to the business of the misunderstanding over the cartoon – the devilish-looking saints Rosso had sketched as a misfired joke, the director's outrage at seeming sacrilege. Rosso turned from the window and added, 'That fool of a monk shouted up to me a few minutes before you came in. He was asking if we had rats.'

'He must take a census of his grapes every day.'

'You will look to Ferdinand,' Rosso said sharply. 'He's caused enough trouble, and I need no more distractions while I'm working. I tied him to your bed, Pasquale, so don't go untying him.'

He had Pasquale write up the two florins in the workshop's leather-bound account book, weighed the coins in his hand and then handed one to Pasquale. They were equals, he said, they had been so for some time. He could teach Pasquale no more, and soon enough Pasquale should make his own way in the world.

'Master, I'll never stop learning from you.'

'That's kind,' Rosso said, with a vague sadness, although he smiled. 'In better times, if things were different . . . More and more, it is not what we can do, but we have done, Pasquale. We are fading into history.'

'You know that isn't true, master,' Pasquale said, and suddenly yawned.

'Get some sleep. A few hours. We have work to do today for that crazy artificer.'

Pasquale fell asleep as soon as he lay down on his bed, hardly noticing that the Barbary ape was tied by a length of rope to the frame. He awoke to the sound of the ape screaming, and sat up and saw that it was gone. It had slipped the loop of rope around its leg. Men were shouting, too, Rosso in the next room, and the monk in the garden below. Pasquale sprang to the window and saw the ape cowering in a corner and chattering and screaming as the monk tried to dislodge it with a pole, and all the while Rosso hurled curses on them both.

Pasquale cut the rope from the bed-frame with his knife and flung an end towards the ape. It saw its chance and swarmed up the grape trellis using hands and feet. As the trellis started to collapse under its weight the ape managed to grab the rope – and almost pulled Pasquale out of the window. The monk flung aside his pole and dodged backwards as vines and trellis collapsed around him.

The ape climbed to safety, leaping across the sill and landing on the floor. Suddenly, Rosso was in the room, belabouring the ape about head and shoulders with a broom. Pasquale got between them, shouting that Rosso should stop, please, it was over. Rosso's face cleared, and he flung aside the broom and buried his face in his hands. The ape jumped on to the bed and threw the blankets around its head.

Pasquale didn't know whether to comfort master or ape. The monk was shouting up from the garden, using words no man of God should know, let alone voice, shouting that he would call on the Officers of Night and Monasteries.

'Pray for us, brother,' Pasquale shouted back. 'Show some Christian charity.' He banged the shutters closed and turned to Rosso, who had calmed himself.

When Pasquale started to apologize, for after all he had taught the ape to clamber up and down the rope, and to steal grapes, Rosso said simply and flatly that it wasn't his fault at all. 'It is the nature of the beast, Pasquale. I got it as a joke, you know, and here it is still, a burden around my neck like the old man of the sea, or a demon.'

'Do you think he'll call on the magistrates?'

Rosso pressed the heels of his palms against his eyes. 'Oh, no doubt he will. He has a narrow selfish soul. Remember that Dante reserved a circle of Hell for those pillar-saints who retreated from the world to enrich their own spirituality, as a miser hoards his coins. Monks are just the same, in my opinion.'

The ape, hearing their voices, took the blanket down from its face, and they both had to laugh to see it looking at them like an old woman peering around a fold of her shawl.

Rosso sighed. 'There is still much to prepare for today's work.'

Pasquale helped Rosso grind the rest of the pigments they would need for their commission. The blue salt made by placing copper over vinegar, the new white lead pigment, red from crushed beetles, bright yellow sulphide of mercury. Each was suspended in egg-yolks thinned with water and vinegar (which turned the blue green), or in size (which kept the blue blue), mixed in the big wooden buckets reserved for fresco work.

The commission was simple enough. They were to paint a fresco of primary colours in sinuous shapes on the wall of a bank in the Piazza della Signoria. The Pope, entering the piazza in the shadow of the Great Tower, would be confronted with this fresco, somehow changed by artificer's trickery into a marvel. Or so the artificer promised: so far he had told the painters nothing about how the trick would be done, being a man who delighted in secrecy. Still, a commission was a commission, and the artificer paid well, and in advance.

The façade of the bank had been given its first layer of plaster and the outline of the design had been drawn on it in charcoal under Rosso's supervision two days before. Newfangled scaffolding had been erected, based on modular units jointed like the legs of an insect, with a regularity quite unlike the forest of props which underpinned the irregular wooden planking of traditional scaffolding. The artificer was waiting for Pasquale and Rosso when they arrived shortly after noon, with the little gang of labourers who carried their pigments and brushes and buckets and sponges and the rest.

The artificer was a plump young man with a round, shining, olive-skinned face, watery blue eyes and a neatly trimmed beard. He was dressed in the usual artificer's uniform of a many-pocketed leather tunic, loose black Turkish trousers and shiny black leather boots with iron toe-caps and buckles at the knees. His name was Benozzo Berni; he was a distant relative of the great satirist.

Berni had been commissioned by the bank to create this spectacle, and was consumed with a high nervousness that he might, through some fault of omission, fail and be destroyed. He had already raised a great fuss because of the delay caused by the celebration of the Feast of Saint Luke, and now made a great deal of the fact that his apparatus was already in place. This was a device a little like a cata-pult, except that instead of a ballista cradle it held an array of acety-lene lanterns, and a series of lenses and mirrors through which the light would be projected. It sat in front of the scaffolding like a skeletal goggle-eyed frog. Just how this device would combine with the big amorphous shapes of the fresco was, Berni said, still a secret.

'You will see on the day. That is, if we are finished.'

Berni did not treat Rosso as a skilled craftsman hired to carry out a task as best he might, but rather as a labourer, and insisted that he and his assistants, two beardless boys younger than Pasquale by at least five years, check every line of Rosso's translation of the outline pattern on to the wall, using little brass sighting instruments hinged on a semicircular scale. The pattern was not complicated, and it only took an hour more to go over the charcoal lines with brushes loaded with red ochre, and then to brush away the charcoal to leave only the red ochre outline, the *sinopia*.

Rosso and Berni then fell into an argument over the best way to proceed. Rosso insisted that he should work as he had always worked, from one area to the next, from top to bottom, but the artificer wanted each colour done in order because there must be no tonal variation, something he deemed impossible if different patches of the same colour were painted at different times. Rosso, slighted by this implication, pointed out over and over, his voice rising each time, that his skill would ensure that different patches of plaster could be painted to exactly the same hue, and at last Berni threw up his hands and stalked off, quivering, to light a cigar.

'We'll start at the top, as we always work,' Rosso told Pasquale. If he was still upset by the behaviour of his ape, this small victory had done something to restore his self-esteem. 'The fool needed convincing that otherwise drips would fall on finished work. We use the blue first, on the dry plaster. I've had them overplaster the *arriccio* for the blue yesterday, to save time. Let's hope they've done it properly. It's getting dark, and Berni promises light from his machinery, but I don't know, Pasquale, I have never worked with artificial light.'

Pasquale and Rosso worked with tacit agreement, quickly finishing the areas of blue, then supervising the labourers who mixed and applied the plaster to the remaining areas of the *sinopia*. The trick was to make sure that the plaster was thin enough to dry quickly to the right consistency, yet had enough tooth to take the pigment. They worked area by area, painting on pigments diluted in lime-water with quick sweeps of the largest hog's-hair brushes once the plaster was at the right stage of drying. Half-way through the work, with daylight fast fading, the artificer had the big acetylene lamps of his apparatus lit, and its mirrors and lenses adjusted to cast diffused yellowish light across the face of the building, so that now Pasquale and Rosso had to work with the angular shadows of the scaffold-framing and their own shadows thrown across the face of the fresco.

'This isn't painting, but a race,' Rosso grumbled.

Pasquale said, 'So now we're house-painters, master.' In fact, he was happy enough because of the sheer physical pleasure of slopping on pigment.

'We will work as best we can, as we have always worked,' Rosso said. 'We are still craftsmen, first and last, no matter what the work.'

Pasquale had worked on enough frescos to know about the problems. Rough walls had to be made smooth by applying a thick coat of rough plaster, *arriccio*, either directly to the brick or stone, or to thin mats of reed laid over it to protect the work from moisture, the greatest enemy of fresco. That was an art in itself: the *arriccio* had to be smooth, but not so smooth that it lacked the roughness necessary for the adhesion of the final layer of plaster, and its consistency had to be carefully controlled. The point of dryness at which you applied the paint affected not only the resulting colour, but also the life of the fresco: too damp, and the paint would sink too deeply and thinly into the plaster; too dry, it would not take properly, and flake. Blue pigments, mixed in size, could only be applied to dry plaster, and had to be patched and replaced every thirty years or so. For that reason, the fresco was divided into small areas by the *sinopia*, a quick sketch or a finished detailed drawing covered in turn with one more layer of plaster, the *intonaco*, put on in patches: small patches where detailed work was needed, as in a face or a hand; larger areas where little detail was required, such as the background drapery or landscape.

If this had been a proper fresco, they would have worked one patch at a time, one day to one patch. Here, with two dozen patches of similar size but irregular shape, each washed with just one primary colour, they could work at speed, laying relatively dry plaster on three patches one after the other, so that by the time they had plastered the third the first would be ready for painting.

Even with the help of the labourers, who mixed plaster and paint to specified dilutions and carried the trowels and buckets to and fro, Rosso and Pasquale were hard-pressed. There was no time to think. Pasquale was absorbed in the task at hand: the sweep of the smoothing trowel over a freshly applied patch of plaster; the slap of the big coarse-haired brush over the grainy, absorbent wall. The sky bruised beyond the glare of the artificer's lanterns. Moths kept blundering into Pasquale's face, attracted to the light as to a candle-flame; his bare arms, scaled with spots of dry paint, were itchy with mosquito-bites. Pasquale hardly noticed, and was so caught up with his work that he had to be told to stop by Rosso when at last they were finished.

6

Pasquale was watching the labourers dismantle the oddly jointed scaffolding when Niccolò Machiavegli found him. He was sitting on an overturned crate, eating black bread and salt cod with one hand, making quick notes about the workers' postures with the other; a flask of coarse red wine was at his feet. The taste of coppery pigments and dry plaster-dust mixed with the salt tang of his food. His arms quivered with exhaustion. One of the workmen, a yellow-haired Prussian, had a perfect unmarred physique, and Pasquale resolved to try and get the fellow's name: perhaps he'd pose for a few pence.

Rosso was talking with the artificer beside the light-throwing device. The ape, Ferdinand, leaned against its master's leg, pleased to be freed from the chain which had tethered it to the foot of the scaffolding during the work. The artificer's assistants were wrestling with the lenses of the device, thick greenish glasses in copper rings on jointed armatures which they moved this way and that in response to their master's fussy orders. Circles of light moved on the painted wall; shadows thrown by the scaffolding rearticulated themselves, drew up in new configurations. The lamps made a steady roaring.

Niccolò Machiavegli walked through the glare of the lamps, and Pasquale jumped up when he recognized him, happy to see the journalist. Perhaps he had solved the mystery already.

'I'll take some of that wine,' Niccolò said mildly, and while he drank Pasquale asked about his investigations.

'Do you remember that I believed that poor Giulio Romano had sent a message before he was murdered?'

Pasquale lit a cigarette and blew out smoke with a luxurious voluptuousness. 'You found out what it was? The captain of the militia was going to make inquiries.'

'There was no message. The captain had the relevant logs searched. Nothing.'

'Then Romano must have used the tower for some other purpose.'

'And yet he had lit the signal-lamps, Pasquale. Why would he do that if not to send a message?'

'Perhaps that was the signal.' Pasquale thought of the little toy tucked away in his scrip.

Niccolò smiled. 'That is just what I think. Perhaps Romano was not sending a signal to the relay-tower, but to someone close by the Palazzo. Perhaps a signal that it was safe to enter by a prepared way. Perhaps Romano was not a spy, but a turncoat within Raphael's circle. Or perhaps he had business of his own. Or perhaps he was tricked by the murderer, which means that someone wanted him dead – or wanted to hurt Raphael by killing his best assistant.'

'Well, we can't know that Romano was a traitor. The man is dead. God must judge him.'

'The captain has charged me with a task, Pasquale. I'd have you help me, if you would. I would interview Raphael himself, for the captain cannot. Raphael has the Pope's embassy, after all. Will you come? You needn't say a word, but use your sharp eyes, your artist's sensibility.'

'I'll do it gladly.' Pasquale would do anything to meet Raphael. How jealous the other pupils would be!

'We have one call to make before we visit Raphael,' Niccolò said. 'I have made a list of the enemies of Raphael, and this is the second name on the list. Michelangelo Buonarroti.'

'Surely not!' Pasquale said, with a mixture of scandalized affront and prurient interest.

'It's well known that they are bitter rivals. Michelangelo claims that Raphael has stolen his ideas.'

'They say that's what caused Michelangelo to quarrel with the Pope. But I do not think Michelangelo would kill one of Raphael's assistants because of it.'

Niccolò said, 'Certainly, to do so in Florence would be very foolish, but anger can make a fool of anyone.'

'He really will talk with you?'

'On this hour.'

'And if Michelangelo is only the second fiercest enemy of Raphael, who is the first?'

'Why, the husband Raphael has cuckolded, of course. Unfortunately, as he is one of the optimates who currently rule this city, and who was among those who had me imprisoned on trumped-up charges, I can hardly put him to the question, much as I would like.'

Pasquale said, 'Am I allowed to know who he is?'

'If it is necessary . . . but it is not yet necessary. There's one more thing,' Niccolò Machiavegli said, his mild face bent to look straight into Pasquale's. 'I have received what I may suppose is a death threat, a broken knife in a package. Of course, it may mean nothing. We journalists are often threatened, and this arrived long after the broadsheet was distributed. I would take it more to heart if it had arrived before the broadsheet went on the streets.' He raised the flask to his lips and tipped back his head. 'Ah. This is terrible stuff, Pasquale. Surely Signor Aretino paid you properly?'

'More than enough. Signor Machiavegli—'

'Niccolò. I'm no landowner. Not any more. The Spanish took that away.'

'Niccolò . . . Do you really think Raphael is involved in a plot against our city?'

'There's no evidence for that. I'm not going to put him to the question, Pasquale. I'm just going to ask him about his poor assistant, who was so brutally murdered. This is no official investigation, you see. There can be none, for Raphael is under embassy from the Pope. He cannot be prosecuted, or arraigned, or even accused. To do so would be to yield the moral high ground to our enemy. That this is not official, in fact, is just why we are allowed to proceed. There is to be no scandal, no rumour. You understand?'

'Completely.'

'Then if you are finished here, say farewell to your master. We have only a little time.'

Despite Niccolò's haste, Pasquale persuaded him to make a detour to the studio, where Pasquale changed from his work-clothes to his best black serge jerkin, a doublet with deep slashes lined with expensive red silk offcuts, and red hose. He washed his face and hands, carefully brushed his curls and pinned a soft velvet cap to the back of his head, Niccolò by now pacing up and down with impatience, then splashed his palms with fresh rose-water and rubbed dried lavender flowers between them, patted the fragrance under his jaw, on the sides of his neck.

'How do I look?'

'You'll make some lucky man a fine bride,' Niccolò said.

'I'm visiting the two greatest artists of the age – of course I must look my best. Just one more thing.' Pasquale found the lily he had made from scraps of gold-foil, and pinned it to his breast. 'There,' he said, 'now Raphael will know my allegiance,' and wondered why Niccolò laughed. He added, 'Should I take my sword, do you think?' It was a short, sweetly tempered Flemish blade with a pommel he had reworked with gold-leaf and red leather.

Niccolò's smile was both amused and sardonic. 'We are petitioners. As such, we persuade with a keen edge to our intelligence, not our swords. Put down your sword, Pasquale, and follow me.'

Michelangelo owned a large property on the Via Ghibellina, three houses side by side. He had his workshop in the middle one, which had a large stable he had converted to a studio by raising its roof to the height of three storeys. One half of this big room was screened off; behind the screen, as Pasquale well knew, was the half-finished heroic statue commemorating the victory of the Florentine navy at the Battle of Potonchán, when the Great Engineer's underwater vessels had sunk half the Spanish fleet bent on invading the empire of the Mexica, and his Greek fire had destroyed most of the rest. Michelangelo had been working on this monument, fitfully, for the last ten years. He would allow no one to see it, not even members of the Signoria, which had sponsored it, and his enemies said that he would never finish it.

Two apprentices, in long smocks and paper hats, were working on a small block of pure white stone under a flaring crown of acetylene lights. The ringing taps of metal on stone echoed in the high space as they made the preliminary passes to free the shape trapped in the stone. The smell of fresh stone-dust sharpened the air. A trestle-table was littered with their tools: pointed punches, flat chisels and toothed and clawed chisels, battered mallets of different sizes, files, a bow drill. Tubs of abrasives – emery, pumice and straw – stood beneath the table. Above all this, like the skeleton of one of the fabulous antediluvian dragons, towered the steam-winch which manoeuvred large blocks of stone in and out of the studio.

Michelangelo took Niccolò and Pasquale into his office, a small shed tacked to the side of the studio, its walls scaled with perspective drawings. He had them sit on low stools, handed them glasses of bitter artichoke liqueur, and smiled when Niccolò, who immediately drained his glass, said that it was good of him to agree to this interview.

'I've nothing to hide. I was working here last night, at first with my assistants, and later on my own, but that was very late. Several friends were here – I can give you their names if you require it.'

'That's very kind, but I'm sure it won't be necessary.'

Michelangelo said, 'I'm sorry for Giulio Romano's death – he could have been a first-rate artist if he had not chosen to live in his master's shadow. But I never had a quarrel with him. Do have more of this liqueur, Signor Machiavegli. It is the only thing about Rome that I miss. Do you know, by the way, of the Fraternity of Saint John the Beheaded?'

'That, like your excellent liqueur, is also of Rome. I believe its brothers comfort condemned prisoners.'

'Exactly. I was a member of it, you understand. We believed that some good could be found even in the worst of humanity, just as I found my David in stone that had been hacked and botched by Simone da Fiesole (perhaps you have heard of him, Pasquale), a crime, in my opinion, as bad as murder. Through my involvement in the Fraternity, I know all about justice, signor, and the rewards of murder. I have a good business, as you see. I would not give it up for anything, and certainly not for Raphael.'

'Perhaps,' Niccolò said, 'you know of someone who may have quarrelled with Signor Romano.'

'I don't keep up with the gossip in Rome,' Michelangelo said dismissively. He was a lean, sinewy man with excessively broad shoulders, and a keen gaze beneath a craggy brow furrowed by seven deep lines. He leaned forward, his head alertly cocked, gripping the edge of his stool with his powerful hands. His fingers were nicked and scarred, and one nail was blackened by a fresh bruise. They drummed the edge of the stool to the rhythm of his assistants' work on the stone.

'Old grudges are often the most deadly,' Niccolò said.

Michelangelo laughed. 'That's true enough. Everyone thinks I have a quarrel with Raphael, but anyone who fights with a good-for-nothing gains nothing. My opinion of Raphael is well known, I won't deny it, but I have better things to do with my time than campaign against his reputation. The light in the public square will reveal that for what it is, by and by.'

Niccolò said, 'I believe you once said that no one who follows others can ever get in front of them.'

'Oh, exactly. Those who can't do good work on their own account can hardly make good use of what others have done. My quarrel is not with Raphael, but with those who don't see him for what he is. As for Giulio Romano, no one had reason to dislike him, unless there was some quarrel between assistants. The way Raphael runs his business, it wouldn't surprise me. He is so careless he must appoint a man to manage his affairs. So long as he wants to be rich, he'll remain poor.'

'I'm certain that whoever killed Romano was known to him, but that it was not someone of Raphael's immediate circle.'

'I'd question his assistants closely, Signor Machiavegli – you are going to interview them?'

'Tonight, as you probably know.'

'And you, Pasquale? Are you going to give Signor Machiavegli the benefit of your advice?'

'I'll help him if I can,' Pasquale said, pleased and embarrassed by Michelangelo's attention.

'Then I hope you're a strong swimmer,' Michelangelo said. 'Your master, Rosso, helped gild my David when he was the assistant of Andrea del Sarto. I trust you're as diligent a pupil as was he.'

Michelangelo excused himself and had a brief but earnest conversation with his assistants, then returned and poured another round of artichoke liqueur, and affably exchanged political gossip with Niccolò for a few minutes, before gently making it clear that he had much work to do before the next day, when he was leaving for the quarries at Serevezza.

Niccolò Machiavegli did not seem disappointed by this interview, although Pasquale felt that it had been a waste of time – they had learned nothing that they did not already know.

'On the contrary. We know that Michelangelo still fiercely resents Raphael, and we also know that he will leave the city for the next few days.'

'A polite withdrawal, so that he will not need to meet the Pope,' Pasquale said. 'That's been known about for weeks.'

'Without doubt. But if anything happens while Michelangelo is away, then we will know he is innocent.'

'He could hire ruffians to do his work.'

'Perhaps,' Niccolò said cheerfully. 'But did you not observe how he treated his assistants? He could scarcely bear to let them work unobserved, and dashed out to check their work as soon as he was able. A man like that, a master of his trade, would not trust others to complete his work for him. I've made a long study of the behaviour of men, Pasquale, and Michelangelo is one who will never delegate important work. Now let us hope our interview with Raphael goes as well.'

There was no crowd of onlookers outside the Palazzo Taddei, and only a single militia guard remained. The man waved Niccolò and Pasquale past with a smile. The gate irised open, and as before one segment stuck; Niccolò gave it a rap, as if for luck, as he and Pasquale ducked beneath it. The major-domo of the Palazzo, splendid in a crimson uniform trimmed with gold, his air grave and faintly dis-approving, led them to the half-dozen rooms of the top floor which had been allotted to Raphael and his followers.

The chambers, lit by candles as scattered as stars, casting more shadows than light, had a rich disordered look, like an encampment of gypsies endowed not only with fabulous wealth but also a ravishing artistic sensibility. The stone walls were swagged with drapery or covered with Flemish tapestries. Canopied beds were in disarray, clothes scattered across them, trays of half-finished meals set on their rumpled sheets. In one room, a naked young man slept face-down on a couch, his buttocks pale crescents in the half-light; in the next, black hunting-dogs sprawled on rushes before a cavernous, empty fireplace; in a third, two men at a chessboard hardly looked up as Niccolò and Pasquale were led past by the major-domo.

Raphael lay on an immense bed in the last of the rooms, propped up on a heap of bolsters. He wore a white chemise loosely tied across his smooth-skinned chest, black hose with an obscenely large codpiece, red felt boots. A young woman slept beside him, her hair unbound and her shoulders bare, the coverlet carelessly cast over her.

A grey-haired man sat on a stool by the bed; three more of Raphael's followers sat at the fireplace, close to a roaring blaze. One of them, a fat man with sweat standing on his jowly face, loudly and jovially told the major-domo that they would have to start chopping at the furniture if more wood wasn't brought. The major-domo bowed and said without demur that he would see what could be done, then announced Pasquale and Niccolò and bowed and withdrew, more like a polite host than a servant doing his duty.

Raphael sat up straighter, stroking the hair of the woman beside him when she stirred in her sleep. He welcomed Niccolò as an old friend, looked askance at Pasquale. Pasquale stared back at him boldly, although he was beginning to sweat in the close heat of the room.

'My assistant,' Niccolò said.

The grey-haired man whispered something in Raphael's ear; the artist nodded. 'He's the pupil of Giovanni Rosso,' Raphael said, staring directly at Pasquale. His eyes were heavy-lidded and half-closed; his eyebrows made a straight black line across the bridge of his proud nose. Threads of gold were wound in the mop of his long black curly hair. In a few more years, Pasquale thought, he would be fat: you could see it in the way his neck made a fleshy bulge to meet his chin as he lounged amongst the bolsters like a sultan; in the thickening of his wrists. The thought did not lessen Pasquale's awe – here was the richest painter in the world, painter to princes and popes. He looked around, hoping to see sketches, cartoons, perhaps a half-finished canvas propped on a chair. There was nothing of the kind.

Niccolò said, 'Pasquale has been good enough to help me. He was here last night. Perhaps you saw the drawings in the broadsheet that illustrated my article.'

Pasquale said with dismay, 'They are nothing.'

Raphael flicked his fingers, as if at a fly. He wore rings on every finger, heavy gold rings studded with rubies and emeralds. 'I don't read the broadsheets. I do see that Florentine painters still dress with their customary flair. Is that paint in your hair, or a new tint?'

Pasquale blushed and said, 'For your honour, sir, I would have preferred to have had enough leisure to remove all traces of my day's work, but the matter is urgent, although Master Niccolò is too polite to tell you.'

The grey-haired man whispered in Raphael's ear again. Raphael said, 'Painting a backdrop for an artificer's light-show isn't really working, but I suppose you must take what you get.'

The fat man by the fire said with jovial malice, 'There's the motto that made Florence the centre of the artistic world. How often I heard it, so that I never wished to hear it again.'

A second man said, 'We have enemies here, Signor Machiavegli. Michelangelo Buonarroti in particular. He is consumed in a fury of jealousy since he lost the Pope's patronage. We have been subject to his false accusations, his crazy assertions that he invented every technique in the history of painting. He is a dangerous man.'

Raphael said, 'We do not fear Michelangelo. But he can be trouble-some, and he has many friends.'

'Many friends amongst the so-called artists,' the second man said.

Niccolò said, smoothing things over, 'I have suffered enough false accusation to understand your caution, but let me assure you that we are here as servants of no one, except truth. You all know me. You all know I cleave to no faction, take no side.'

This seemed to satisfy Raphael. He clapped his hands and loudly called for wine, then winked at Niccolò. 'I assume one of Signor Taddei's vintages will be acceptable.'

'You're very kind.'

'Taddei is a good friend to me, Niccolò. What's happened is dis-tressing enough. That it should happen in the house of my friend makes it worse. I'll help you if I can, if in turn you'll be frank with me. Is there a chance that his murderer will be found by the city militia?'

'I don't think so.'

Raphael said to the grey-haired man, 'I told you! They care nothing for us. We are amongst enemies here, and there is danger on every side.'

The grey-haired man said, 'We mustn't speak of that.'

'No,' Raphael said, 'no, I suppose not. All in good time, eh?'

A sleepy-eyed boy half Pasquale's age brought in a gold tray bear-ing a flask of wine and half a dozen gold beakers. He poured wine, handed round the beakers, smiling when Pasquale gasped at the solid weight of his beaker, its buttery smoothness. It was pure gold, worth a year's profit. The wine gave off a rich, heady aroma.

Raphael drank his wine down in a gulp, held out his beaker to be refilled. He said languidly, 'What do you think, Niccolò? Be truthful. You know I respect your opinions. Who murdered my friend?'

'In truth, I have yet to form an opinion, except that I am certain that the murderer does not live in this house.'

The fat man by the fire said, 'Which leaves only two hundred thousand of my fellow Florentines, every one of them with a knife in his purse and murder in his heart.'

'Be quiet!' Raphael thumped the bed. Wine slopped from his beaker and stained the coverlet. The woman beside him stirred, but did not wake. 'Be quiet,' Raphael said again, softly. 'Giovanni, you're a fine painter, most especially of animals, but right now you don't see the nose in the middle of your face. I loved Giulio best of all of you, and he is dead. I want to find who killed him, but more important than that, I want all of us to get home safely. We are the focus of some terrible conspiracy, our enemies are everywhere . . . but it is nothing that we cannot overcome, eh? A day, two days, and Papa Leone will be here. Meanwhile we must be vigilant. You all know how much my fame has cost me. For every admirer there are two who say I am only derivative, that I am only a reflection of Perugino, or that I stole from Michelangelo. I, whose ideas have been stolen more often than any other, whose works are copied and printed in every country without my permission . . . !' He took a breath, clearly struggling to master his emotions. 'Niccolò, what would you know?'

Niccolò waited until he had everyone's attention. 'In my experience,' he said quietly, 'the best way to understand how a man came to be killed is to work backwards from the moment of his death. That is, to know what he said and what he did, and what was said to him, and by whom. To know who hated him, and who loved him, to know his enemies and his friends. I'd talk with you and your disciples, if I may, about all that befell Giulio Romano after his arrival in Florence. That, to start with.'

'You ask a lot,' Raphael said.

'Forgive me, but I ask only because I know what your friend meant to you.'

'Only that? You don't know how much you must work, to earn one-tenth part of what Giulio meant to me.' Raphael inclined his head to listen to the grey-haired man's discreet whisper. 'All I ask,' Raphael said, 'is that your assistant waits outside while you put us to the question, Niccolò.'

Pasquale's anger flared. He said, 'Romans are very fond of secrets, it seems. If I speak plainly, forgive me, but I can't help it, being a mere Florentine.'

The grey-haired man said mildly, 'Myself, I am from Venice. As to secrets, I have heard that Florentines love secrets above all else, particularly those of other people.'

'Excuse me, signor,' Pasquale said, 'but we haven't been introduced. If you are from Venice, why then you must love secrets more than any Roman, and certainly more than anyone in Florence. Your city is a city of secrets.'

'Lorenzo is my agent,' Raphael said. 'I trust his opinion. Please, young man, as a favour, wait outside. Baverio,' he said, to the boy who had brought in the wine, 'look after the friend of my friend.'

'It's all right,' Niccolò told Pasquale, adding in a whisper, 'I'll tell all after.'

'And have them send up more wood,' the fat man said, as the boy servant led Pasquale away. 'Florentine air is bad enough; but I'd forgotten that Florentine cold is worse.'

'They don't mean any harm,' the boy, Baverio, told Pasquale as they left the room. 'My master is convinced that his mission here has put him in mortal danger, and his assistants are all convinced that they will be cut down one by one. We are painters, not soldiers or ambassadors.'

'Then you do have a mission,' Pasquale said. 'We thought as much.'

Baverio looked unhappy – a pout, a toss of his shoulder. 'Please, I'm not skilled in these games. Here, sit, I'll fetch wine, we'll talk. I want to help.' They were in the room where the black hunting-dogs dozed in the cold fireplace. Pasquale sat on a carved stool, let the dogs smell his hands and rumpled their folded ears. His father had owned two such dogs; their soft mouths could bring back shot songbirds without hurting a feather. His anger was gone. He was simply tired.

Baverio brought a flask of wine and a round of hard cheese; Pasquale sliced off a hunk of cheese and chewed and sipped alternately. Baverio watched him. He wore a velvet tunic striped in dark green and black, elaborately buckled breeches of the same material, and black stockings. A gold circlet rested on the mop of his springy brown hair.

Pasquale remembered the circlet Rosso had placed on his own head – but Baverio's was real gold. He told the boy that he looked more like a princeling than a servant, and asked if he too was a painter.

'I draw a little, but not well enough.'

'Anyone who is properly taught can draw well enough. Surely, with a master such as yours—'

'Then perhaps I lack ambition. It is enough to serve my master as best I can.'

'You said you wanted to help. Perhaps you can tell me . . . do you know why Giulio Romano was in the tower?'

Baverio shook his head. 'I was helping my master at his bedside toilet when we heard the screams. We rushed out, all of us, and that was when we realized Giulio was not amongst us. But as to how he came to be in the tower, and what message he was sending . . .'

Pasquale took a risk, calculating that one disclosure might be worth another. 'Giulio Romano sent no message, but perhaps he sent a signal, simply by lighting the lamps on the signal-vanes. A signal to someone outside the Palazzo, someone waiting to come in, or wanting to know that it was safe to come in.'

Baverio said with some agitation, 'You must not think that Giulio would betray my master! He was my master's best friend, a master in his own right who for love pure and simple used his talent to help my master complete his commissions. Listen, Pasquale, if Giulio was killed by someone outside the Palazzo, as Signor Machiavegli implied, then why was Giulio signalling that it was safe to enter? And if that person had entered on Giulio's signal, why did he make his way to the tower and kill Giulio and then escape?'

'I think that's why Niccolò wants to ask his questions. It's like the cartoon for a painting. We have the lines, as it were, but none of the details. I don't think Giulio meant to harm your master or any of his friends, Baverio, but perhaps he was mistaken in his choice of allies on whatever business he was about.'

'That is my master's burden,' Baverio said. 'Take more wine, against the cold if not for your stomach's sake.'

'It's very good.'

'Then you must thank Signor Taddei.' Baverio grew serious, leaning forward and fixing his eyes on Pasquale's face, and enveloping Pasquale in a cloud of musky perfume from the silk pomander hung at his breast. 'I said that I want to help, and it was not an idle boast. While the others were trying to break down the door of the tower, and then trying to find a key, I went to look for Giulio. I do not know what I was thinking of, except that it seemed to me that he might have returned to his bed. It seemed that if I could find him there, then all would be well, all would be as it had been.'

'I understand.'

'He wasn't there, of course. He slept in the room adjacent to my master's, in the same bed as me. I knew his satchel was still there, hidden under the bolster, and I looked in it. I don't know why. I am ashamed of having done it, and haven't told anyone, not even my master. Especially not Raphael.'

'I won't tell anyone, Baverio, not even Niccolò.'

'It was the wrong thing to do,' Baverio said, 'but it may have been the right thing to do, too. I found something there, and have it still. I heard the guards coming, you see, and thrust it into my scrip. Here.'

Baverio drew out a square of shiny glass. Pasquale thought at first it was a small blackened hand-mirror, but the black coating was too friable, and he could scrape off a curl of the stuff with his thumb-nail. He sniffed: a piercing chemical reek.

Baverio said, 'It was wrapped in black silk, and when I drew it out it changed from grey to black, I swear this. There was also a box of stiff black-painted leather. On one side of the box was a kind of sliding cap, covering a little hole. But the guards took that away, with the rest of Giulio's luggage.'

'An artificer's toy of some kind,' Pasquale said. 'There was glass like this, broken in a heap, in the signal-tower. And there was this, too.' He drew out the little flying toy from his own scrip. 'Here,

83

look. Your friend's dead hand was clutching this. These are common in Rome?'

Baverio took it between his fingertips, turned it around and handed it back. 'I've never seen one before.'

'I thought perhaps some artificer in Rome might have made them.'

'Your own Great Engineer is the greatest artificer of them all. Perhaps he would know.'

'I'm pleased to hear that there is someone of the embassy from Rome who sees some good in Florence.'

Baverio said, 'I saw your Great Engineer only yesterday. We had an audience with him, and he spoke alone with my master for an hour. He will attend the feast in honour of the Pope, my master says.'

'Then it will be the first time in twenty years that he has left his Great Tower. He awaits the new Flood, that will sweep away the wickedness of the world and leave only the pure in heart behind. He has written pamphlets on this – some say that is why he invented the movable-type printing-press. But I'm not the Pope, Baverio. I can't ask him about these things.'

'Then ask some other artificer.' Baverio cocked his head. 'My master calls.' He handed the flying toy and the blackened glass to Pasquale. 'These things were important to Giulio, Pasquale. You keep them. Find out what they mean.'

7

As they were led out by the impassive major-domo, Pasquale asked
Niccolò what he had learnt, but Niccolò Machiavegli shook his head
and whispered, 'Not here.'

Outside, as the sections of the round door ratcheted shut behind
them, Niccolò told Pasquale that they would wait and watch from
the other side of the street. They sheltered in a doorway, watching
the Palazzo's gate through traffic rattling past. This was a main
thoroughfare, busy with carts and carriages, velocipedes and *vaporetti* in the last hour before the city gates closed. The city was filling
with people from nearby towns and villages who had come to see
the Pope. Acetylene lamps shed a weary simulacrum of daylight.

Pasquale asked, 'Who do you expect to arrive?'

'We are waiting for someone to leave. I believe that not only Giulio
Romano is involved. We will wait and see who leaves, and then we
will know who it is. And we will follow him, for he will lead us to
those who plot with him.'

'Everyone sees plots everywhere.'

Niccolò took a little nip from his leather flask. 'When I was
Secretary . . .'

'Is this the time for drinking?'

'There were plots everywhere, back then. There are always plots.'

Pasquale felt a pang of sympathy. 'Those memories must be painful, Niccolò.'

'All memory is painful. We remember what was, and in remembering inevitably think what could have been. It is the nature of men
never to be content with their lot, no matter that they are rich or
poor. The beggar may curse the optimate in his carriage as it goes
by, thinking that there goes a man without worry, but that same
optimate may look out and see a free man in rags, without the res-
ponsibilities of power. By Christ's balls, it is cold out here.' Niccolò
blew on his hands. Stray light from a distant lamp made his stubble-
shadowed cheeks look blue, his dark eyes black.

Pasquale lit a cigarette, and offered another – his last – to Niccolò.

Niccolò smiled his sadly pensive smile. 'That's one vice I don't have.'

'Unlike drink, it is a simple pleasure that will not kill you.' Pasquale instantly regretted his moralistic tone. 'You talked with Raphael, and now you seem unhappy.'

'In wine I escape from my past, forget what has happened to me and what I fear might happen, and think only of the moment. A problem like this, Pasquale, is nearly as good as wine. One needs problems, to keep back the past, and boredom. There! Look there, Pasquale!'

Pasquale saw a paired spark, red and green, high above the tiled roof of the Palazzo. The sparks moved away from each other, then back again.

'The signaller has been dismissed, yet someone uses the tower,' Niccolò said, with a certain satisfaction. 'Unless of course Signor Taddei is a part of this conspiracy.'

'Can you read the lamps? What was the message?'

'I can read plain-talk, if it is transmitted at a slow enough rate. But that was no message, just a simple swing of the signal-arms. Now we will wait and see what has been summoned.'

'What did Raphael tell you?'

Niccolò said, 'Raphael has much to protect. He is a careful man, friend of princes . . . and of course of popes. In such company you learn circumspection should you wish to survive. You cannot behave like our own Michelangelo.'

'He talked of plots. He dismissed me because he feared I was part of a plot.' Pasquale remembered the little square of black glass in his scrip, nestled next to the flying toy. He knew that he should tell Niccolò about what Baverio had said, but did not know how to begin.

Niccolò said, 'There are always plots, in the circles in which Raphael's ambition has thrust him. Such men can trust nothing and no one. It was not a personal thing, Pasquale. It is just business.'

'I know that, but thank you.'

They smiled.

Niccolò said, 'It is my understanding of human nature that men are evil-ready. Since the Fall they must struggle against their nature to achieve goodness, because their nature tends to evil. Think of the single virtue of goodness, and the army against which she stands: ambition and ingratitude, cruelty and envy, luxury and sloth. In particular, sloth. We are all drunkards at heart, and curse the drunkard not out of hate but jealousy. If we were brave enough, we too would roll in the gutter with him.'

'Niccolò, are you talking about men in general, or men in particular?'

'Oh, I feel it in myself,' Niccolò said, and took a long pull on his flask.

There was a silence. There was less traffic now. Passers-by hardly spared a glance for Pasquale and Niccolò: after all, they were doing no more than lounging and watching the world go by, a popular sport in Florence. They watched the guard walk to and fro in the circle of lamplight by the closed maw of the gate in the Palazzo's forbidding wall. Once, he stopped and bent over a flare of light, then sucked on his lighted pipe and blew out a long riffle of smoke, flicked away the spent match.

Niccolò, watching its arc, remarked, 'Lucifer falls.'

'More and more I find myself thinking of an angel . . .'

'Lucifer Morningstar was the prince of angels, the most beautiful until the instant of his rebellion. I've always wondered which wounded God more, Man's Fall, or that of His chief lieutenant.'

'Well, He sent His son to redeem us.'

'Perhaps our redemption is only the first step towards the redemption of Lucifer. But that is not a thought you must repeat, Pasquale. Even in excommunicated Florence, it may be enough to send you to the stake as a heretic, as they tried to burn Savonarola. You cannot count on a thunderstorm saving you. But what angel are you thinking of, Pasquale?'

'The archangel Michael, who drove Adam and Eve out of paradise.'

'Never a popular theme, I must admit. You know, I have always found it odd that the Fall does not have a feast-day. Perhaps then there would be a tradition for you to follow. Although I suppose you have seen the painting by Masaccio.'

'In the Cappella Brancacci, yes. I admit there is a certain despair conveyed in the attitude of the figures of Adam and Eve, but they are somewhat crudely rendered – poor Adam will never straighten his leg, which is curved inward. I have also seen Mantegna's allegory in which Pallas expels the vices from the garden of virtue. But I am interested in the angel himself. I wish to paint only him, yet in such a way that the viewer at once knows what is happening.'

'They would know that by his burning sword.'

'Then perhaps I would omit the sword, too. I want to make something new . . .' Pasquale was embarrassed. Ordinarily he enjoyed talking over the problem he had set himself, yet this was no tavern brag about a commission, but a personal truth. He confessed, 'I do not yet know how to begin.'

Niccolò said, 'I suppose that, like writing, the beginning is always the hardest part of a painting. Ah, here now. What is this?'

A carriage had pulled up at the gate of the Palazzo. It was one of the new designs. Pulled by a single horse, its black body was taller than it was long, an enlarged upright coffin set between two large wheels. The driver leaned down from his high seat to have a word with the guard, and then the leaves of the circular door grated back, and a man stepped out.

It was the fat assistant, the painter of animals, Giovanni Francesco.

He clambered into the carriage, and at once it started off. As soon as it had driven past their doorway, Niccolò rushed out into the street, waving at a *vaporetto* with an empty load-bed. He shouted to the driver that if he could follow the carriage there was good money in it, and waved Pasquale over.

'Show this good fellow your purse.'

'Niccolò—'

'Hurry! We'll lose him.'

The driver, a gnarled ruffian with a sacking hood cast over his head, seemed convinced by the florin that shone amongst the little slew of clipped pennies, but told them they'd have to ride in the back and started up his machine even as they clambered aboard.

The little *vaporetto* trundled down the Via de Ginori and swung around the symmetric church in the Piazza San Giovanni, which shone a pure white in crossed beams of light thrown from lensed lamps burning at its base. The *vaporetto*'s boiler, fired with soft Prussian coal, sang a dreary unvarying note; its exhaust waved a vast smut-laden plume of steam in the night air like a banner. Pasquale and Niccolò clung to the rail of the load-bed, jounced and buffeted as the unsprung wheels rattled over bricks and Roman paving-flags. They jolted down the Via Romana, tangled in traffic going east and west across the Mercato Vecchio where carriages, carts and *vaporetti* threaded around each other in a clangour of bells and hooting of steam-whistles, and the shouts and curses of the drivers.

Niccolò leaned out and shouted to their driver to go as fast as he could, and the man said sharply, 'That's just what I'm doing, signor. Don't think I don't know my own business.'

'Of course not, my dear fellow.'

'Any more than this and the gears will strip. The new models have gears rimmed with beaten iron, you see, but this is one of the first made, nothing but wood in her drive-train. And besides, the road will do for her axle-trees.'

'A horse, my dear fellow, would go faster. I'm minded to find one.'

'You do that if you want, but I'm your man that will take you where you want to go without delay. I still have sight of your carriage, don't worry. Looks like he's heading for the river.'

'We can't run all that way,' Pasquale said.

Niccolò told the driver, 'Your cursed smoke-stack hides my view. I trust you to follow correctly.'

'I'm your man,' the driver said again. 'There he goes, see, straight down the Via Calimara. Don't you worry, he's going to cross the river at the Ponte Vecchio.'

'If I could see him, I'd be a great deal happier,' Niccolò said.

Pasquale leaned out and, sighting around plumes of steam, glimpsed the high profile of the black carriage only a little way ahead of them. The driver's guess was right. They entered a queue of traffic that was slowly making its way past the little shops that lined both sides of the bridge. Lamps strung high above the roadway cast a cold glare; the doorways of the shops, most of them butchers' or tanners', threw patterns of warmer yellow light. Frescos on their stone façades were faded under soot and grime. People were threading amongst the slow-moving single line of traffic, offering food or drink or machine-made trinkets to the drivers and passengers. Once, the line of traffic stalled entirely, and the driver of the *vaporetto* took the opportunity to stoke his vehicle's boiler. Pasquale leaned out again and saw the top of the black carriage half a dozen vehicles in front and told Niccolò.

'He'll turn left at the end of the bridge,' Niccolò shouted at the driver, who nodded.

There was a gap in the buildings at the middle of the bridge. As the *vaporetto* passed, Pasquale could look down at the central channel of the Arno's tamed braided flow. Far off, a great two-masted ship, lights burning on every spar, was making its way upstream towards the new docks across from Sardinia. It was the *Our Lady of the Flowers*, towed by a wood-burning tug with churning paddles, at the end of its long voyage from the New Florentine Republic of the Friendly Isles. Pedestrians had stopped to watch her approach out of the darkness. Pasquale felt a great stirring in his breast. Then the *vaporetto* edged forward with a hiss of steam and he saw her no more.

At the end of the bridge, the carriage turned left, just as Niccolò had predicted. 'He would hardly be going to the Palazzo Pitti,' the journalist said, 'and there's little enough up-river but the shanty slums of manufactory workers and the manufactories themselves. If our man was going there, he would have stopped at the bridge and walked, so as not to draw attention to himself.'

The carriage turned left again, on to a dark dusty road which, with cypress-trees on either side, climbed the side of the valley towards the southern city wall. Crickets made their chorus; a full moon stood low at the head of the valley, made red by the fumes of the manufactories. The *vaporetto* followed the carriage at a respectful distance, its boiler labouring.

At last the carriage drew up at a gate leading to the extensive walled grounds of a large villa. A crest of a lion rampant was set in the arch over the barred gate. The driver of the *vaporetto* drove on without slowing, and at the last moment Pasquale managed to get Niccolò to crouch down. Fat Giovanni Francesco was leaning at the window of the carriage, talking to a uniformed guard.

'For the sake of Christ, we must keep out of sight,' Pasquale said to Niccolò, who tried to stand up again. 'If they see us, the game is up.'

'I want to see what he is doing.'

'Going to the villa, I should think. Stay down!'

'You must learn never to assume anything,' Niccolò said, but he stayed where he was.

As soon as they were safely out of sight, Pasquale told the driver of the *vaporetto* to stop and turn around. Niccolò jumped down, and told Pasquale to give all his small coins to the driver. 'Wait here for us,' he told the driver, 'and you may exchange that money for the florin we have.'

'I'm your man, signor.'

'See that you are. Come, Pasquale.'

They walked back down the road in cricket-filled moonlight. On one side were the walled gardens of the villa; on the other, a grove of wide-spaced olive-trees where the wooden bells of goats grazing in the moonlight made a random clattering. Pasquale protested mildly that Niccolò was very free with money that wasn't his.

'I was responsible for your commission, if you remember. I know that even if you spend that florin, you'll have one left over.'

'And to think that I started out with two this morning,' Pasquale said, remembering his act of generosity when he had given both florins to Rosso, remembering how glad he had been to receive one back. But he could not have seen how things would have fallen out, and besides, there would be a little money from the fee for painting the fresco for the artificer.

Niccolò said, 'You'll earn more from this. This is just the beginning. A story like this, in episodes, will keep the populace buying the broadsheet for days. They would rather waste their time reading idle gossip and speculation than Plato or Ariosto, and I am in no position to deny their wishes. Well, but do you know whose villa this is?'

'He's a Venetian, by the crest over his gate.' Pasquale was thinking that he'd earn little enough from this: there were no dramatic images to be had from sneaking up on a walled house at night, even by moonlight. Or rather, if there were such images, he would be in no position to draw them.

'That's very good,' Niccolò said with approval. 'In fact it is the villa of Paolo Giustiniani, a writer and mystic, a nobleman of Venice, and a disciple of Marsilio Ficino. You know of that last gentleman?'

'I know that he was a magician.'

'He was a priest and philosopher first, but his studies led him to the black arts, and astrology. And into trouble with Rome. He took his magicks entirely too seriously.'

Pasquale took Niccolò's arm, halting him. 'We can't just walk up to the gates,' he said. 'Giovanni Francesco will know at once that we followed him. I'm not certain that we weren't seen as we went past. You were standing as plain as the Gonfalonier in a procession.'

'They would have thought us honest labourers on their way home from a hard day's toil.'

'Labourers don't ride *vaporetti*, Niccolò. And even if you might pass for one, no labourer has ever dressed like me. If we want to learn what is going on, I think it will be best if we skirt around the wall, and climb it well away from any lights.'

It was not, of course, as easy as that. Wild thorn-bushes grew in the ditch at the base of the high rough-dressed stone wall. Niccolò's cloak kept catching in their canes or amongst tufts of rank grass, and to his vexation Pasquale's best hose was torn in two places. He climbed to the top of the wall easily enough, but then had to haul up Niccolò by main force.

They jumped down, landing amongst dusty laurels. Beyond was a long formal lawn crossed from several directions by gravel paths which met at a big sea-shell fountain standing in its centre. An avenue of cedars bordered one side. The branches of the trees, black in the moonlight, each seemed to float at a different level. This part of the garden was higher than the villa, so that Pasquale could see, beyond its tiled roof, the night-time city spread in the valley below. The largest buildings caught the light of the rising moon – the golden dome of the Duomo, the Great Tower and the smaller tower of the Palazzo della Signoria beside it, the towers of churches, the private *palazzi*. A scattering of small lights limned the main streets, while the green and red lamps of signal-towers made a radial pattern converging on the Great Tower's constellation.

'We must beware,' Niccolò said in a hoarse whisper. 'I hear that Paolo Giustiniani is accomplished in his arts.'

'Surely a rational man has nothing to fear from magicians.'

'Magicians have kept pace with the artificers. They are science's black reflection, and should not be underestimated. Or better, magic is science's shadow, for surely where light is cast there must also be shadow.'

'Not if the light is directly above the object, or if the light comes from all directions equally.'

Niccolò said with asperity, 'I should not suppose that I could argue optics with an artist. It was merely a figure. Come now. We will learn little here but how diligently the gardeners attend to their labours.'

'Not diligently enough outside the wall. My clothes are ruined. If I had foreseen this, I would have left them behind, and brought my sword instead.'

'I'm not unprepared,' Niccolò said. 'Keep close to me, and do as I say.'

They started towards the house, keeping to the shadows beneath the cedars. Pasquale fumbled in his scrip and drew out the square of black glass. He said simply, 'While you were talking to Raphael I was given this.'

Niccolò held the glass up to the moonlight, sniffed it, then scraped its friable coating with a fingernail, which he put in his mouth. 'It may be nothing, or it may be something.'

'It was in Giulio Romano's possession,' Pasquale said, and explained about the box that Raphael's boy servant Baverio had also found.

'Then it may well be something. I think you may have learned more than I, Pasquale. You must keep it safe, together with the flying toy.'

'Venice is in alliance with the Pope, isn't she?'

'Yes, but Paolo Giustiniani is an unlikely representative. He was forced to flee Venice in disgrace after an incident involving a virgin and, I believe, a black cockerel.'

'Perhaps he wishes to return to favour.'

'Perhaps. Or perhaps Giovanni Francesco is also a practitioner of the black arts. Or perhaps they are simply friends, who enjoy each other's company. Speculation can be useful, but it is always better to learn. Quietly now, Pasquale, and carefully. There may be traps, and there will certainly be guards.'

The single-storey villa was built of white-painted stone, with a roof of red, ridged tiles, and a square tower at one corner. Lights blazed from every one of its tall arched windows, and Pasquale and Niccolò slipped from one to the other until they came upon one which looked into a room where fat Giovanni Francesco stood. His back was turned to the window as he faced an older man who sprawled carelessly in a high-backed throne-like gilded chair. Dressed in a black robe, with a square black cap on his long straight grey hair, he rested a fist under his chin as he listened to Francesco expound some argument.

The window was closed to keep out the night's chill – a fire burned in the grate of the room's fireplace – and Pasquale could only hear the murmur of Francesco's words, not their sense. Beside him, Niccolò took out a short hollow wooden rod. It had a kind of trumpet at one end, to which he applied his ear after setting the other end against the glass. 'A trick I learned from a physician,' he whispered. 'One must master all of the arts and sciences, to be a good citizen. Keep watch, Pasquale.'

They squatted there for several minutes, Niccolò listening through his hollow rod, Pasquale dividing his attention between the dark garden and the lighted room. Then the voices of the two men inside rose, and Pasquale heard Giovanni Francesco shout something about pictures. He brandished a small wooden frame that held a picture done on glass.

The grey-haired man, without doubt Paolo Giustiniani, rose from his high-backed chair and snatched at the picture. Francesco stepped back from Giustiniani's advance, then bowed and handed it over.

Black-robed Giustiniani, his face showing a cold contempt, listened to what Francesco had to say, then threw the picture into the flames. Francesco waved his hands and protested in his high, slightly hoarse fat man's voice that as there was another made at the same time, it would be well to keep to the agreement, and Giustiniani said, in a loud clear voice that made the glass in the window shiver, 'I've no more need of our agreement!' He snatched his cap from his head and pressed it to his face, and dashed something to the black and white tiles of the floor.

Brown vapour boiled up, and Francesco stumbled back, choking, as the other man made for a door, slamming it shut behind him. The room was dim with brown fumes. Francesco was on his knees, then on his belly. The fire guttered, sending out black smoke to mix with the deadly vapour.

Niccolò threw off his cloak, wound it around his left arm and smashed in the window with his elbow. Vapour poured out, a vile acrid stink worse than any artificer's smog. Pasquale pulled Niccolò out of the way and said, 'Francesco is surely dead.' He was frightened that the noise of the breaking glass would alert the guards.

'Perhaps,' Niccolò said, 'but the worst has blown out – look, the fire burns again.'

He knocked out the rest of the glass and clambered over the window's low sill. Pasquale took a deep breath and followed.

At once his throat started to burn, and his eyes stung and filled with tears so that he could hardly see. Groping together, he and Niccolò turned Francesco's heavy body over, but it was clear from his bulging eyes and the froth on his blue lips that he was dead. Pasquale remembered the picture and managed to snatch the charred frame from the rekindling fire. The effort was almost fatal. His whole chest was filled with a burning pain; his mouth and nose flooded with watery mucus.

Then Niccolò got his bony shoulder under Pasquale's arm and helped him to the window. They tumbled through it together, and Pasquale promptly vomited as cold fresh air strong as heart of wine hit his face.

He still had the charred picture-frame in his hand.

Niccolò got him to his feet, and together they made a stumbling run for the shadows beneath the avenue of cedar-trees. Pasquale's throat was parched, and a band of iron had tightened around his brow, but with every step he felt his strength return as the magician's poisonous smoke was purged from his lungs.

Just as they reached the trees they heard the clamour of several voices raised in alarm. Pasquale threw himself flat and Niccolò dropped beside him. The grass was wet with cold dew. 'I am too old for this,' Niccolò groaned.

Pasquale pointed to the three men silhouetted in the light from the broken window. He said, 'They'll think that Francesco brought friends with him. There, see!'

The three guards, each carrying a lit torch, set off in different directions. Somewhere else a dog barked.

Two more figures broke out of the shadows at the corner of the villa and sprinted across the lawn towards the high wall. A cloak flapped around the taller of the two as he ran with clean strides; the other ran bent almost double, with a curious loping gait. The guards saw these two and shouted and gave chase, their torches hairy stars streaming sparks.

'Francesco had friends after all,' Pasquale said, astonished.

Niccolò said, 'We will go towards the gate.'

'It is already guarded!'

'Perhaps the guard is one of those giving chase.' Shouts, and then a single pistol-shot. Niccolò said, 'One thing is clear. We cannot stay a moment longer.'

They turned the corner of the villa, ran down the wide gravelled path towards the gate. The path divided around a statue of a griffin sitting on its haunches, one front paw supporting a shield. As Pasquale ran past it, ahead of Niccolò, he felt something tug at his ankles. He stumbled, caught himself on hands and knees.

Above him, the statue of the griffin stirred. It shook at every joint, then reared up on its hind legs. Pasquale crouched beneath it in terror and amazement. The shield fell with a wooden clatter. Steam burst from the griffin's mouth and it made a tremendous grinding roar as its head turned to and fro. Its eyes were red lamps. All down the long path to the gate great flares burst into flame, hissing and sizzling and throwing up thick smoke that glowed whitely in the moonlight. Somewhere distant a brazen gong clanged and clanged.

Then Niccolò was pulling at Pasquale, shouting that it was only a mechanical device, a festival trick. Pasquale got to his feet, feeling foolish. The griffin's movements were already subsiding. Niccolò was right; it was a mechanical device of the sort constructed by artists or artificers as centrepieces for those great public spectacles so loved by Florentines. No magic – or not yet.

Niccolò flourished a pistol, an odd weapon with a kind of notched wheel over its stock. 'Have a brave heart,' he said. His face was alive: Pasquale realized that this was what he lived for, desperate moments where courage and luck determined whether you lived or died.

They ran on, and as they neared the gate its guard took a wild shot at them. Niccolò fired back as he ran, fired and fired again without reloading, the wheel of the pistol ratcheting around with each shot. The guard fled through the open gate, and a moment later Pasquale and Niccolò gained the dusty country road and saw the *vaporetto* jolting towards them at top speed, fast as a galloping horse, and wreathed in vast plumes of steam.

They waved at it, and had to jump aside as it slewed to a halt, wheels spinning in the road's soft rutted dirt. The driver shouted that they must climb in and released the brake at the same moment, so that Pasquale had to jump on to the load-bed and haul Niccolò after him, his arms almost starting from his sockets with the effort.

There were pistol-shots as the *vaporetto* banged down the steep road. Something burst overhead, a bright glare that grew and grew until it outshone the full moon. By this floating magical light Pasquale saw that a carriage, perhaps the same one that had delivered poor Francesco to the magician's lair, was chasing them at full tilt. Niccolò saw it too, and calmly told the driver to go faster. When the man started to argue, Pasquale took the florin from his scrip and held it over the driver's shoulder. Without looking, the driver reached up and plucked the coin like a grape. The *vaporetto* leapt forward, throwing Pasquale and Niccolò backwards on to the load-bed's rough planking.

Niccolò rolled over on his belly, making a kind of choked laughter. 'Did you see how that guard ran? I would have killed him if I could. I shot to kill. My blood was up.'

'From your talk it still is,' Pasquale said, feeling his bruises. He tried to sit up and a great jolt as the *vaporetto* shot over a hummock in the ill-made road knocked him back down again. He swore and said, 'We still aren't free yet.'

'I have my pistol. The self-loading wheel does little for its accuracy, but rapid fire is certainly discouraging to those who face it. Did you see the guard? He ran like a Spaniard.'

'This isn't a war.'

'Any kind of combat makes beasts of men. They revert to their base nature.'

'You may have another chance to enjoy your base nature very soon,' Pasquale said, squinting past the tattered clouds of the *vaporetto*'s exhaust into the night behind them. The black carriage had fallen far behind, for its horse could not keep up with the *vaporetto*'s breakneck downhill speed, but he was certain that it would not give up the chase.

The slope of the road flattened out, houses crowding now on either side, and the *vaporetto* began to slow. The driver shouted that water in the boiler was low, that he would have to stop soon and refill it.

'Go on as best you can,' Niccolò told him.

'If the tubes boil empty over the burners, they'll blow,' the driver said. 'There's an end to it.'

Pasquale said, 'I think you will need your pistol, Niccolò. They are gaining on us.'

As he spoke, crossbow-quarrels flew out of the darkness with shocking suddenness. Most missed the *vaporetto*, but two thumped into the load-bed and promptly began to give off acrid white smoke. Pasquale wrestled one from the plank in which it had embedded itself. Its shaft was almost too hot to hold, and its point was hollow and fretted with slots from which the smoke poured. Pasquale threw the quarrel over the side, but burnt his hand when he tried to pull out the second. Then more quarrels whistled past and he ducked down. One thumped into the splintered planks a hand's breadth from his face, burying itself up to its flight feathers; an ordinary quarrel, but still deadly. The new crossbows fired quarrels with such force that even a glancing blow could kill a man.

Niccolò clutched one of the posts of the load-bed, waving his pistol. The shaft of the smoking quarrel that was still embedded in the load-bed suddenly started to burn. In a moment, bright blue flames spread across the tarred planks. Niccolò steadied his pistol with both hands and fired back at the carriage, laughing wildly all the while, so that Pasquale feared he had lost his reason.

The *vaporetto* made a sharp right turn on to the Borgo San Jacopo and was suddenly amongst a crowd of workers. Workmen flung themselves to either side as the *vaporetto* ploughed into their midst. They were the *ciompi*, the shift-workers of the sleepless manufactories. They were dressed in shabby patched tunics girdled with rope, shod in wooden clogs, and wore shapeless felt hats on their heads to keep off the night's cold. Many were shaven-headed, a result of a scheme of the artificers to eliminate lice. They shouted and jeered as the *vaporetto* sped past. The carriage was very close now; Pasquale could see the driver standing on his bench, his arm rising and falling as he whipped the horse on.

The driver of the *vaporetto* looked over his shoulder, his face white and his eyes reflecting the flames leaping up from the load-bed. He uttered a wordless cry and threw himself from his bench into the crowd. The *vaporetto*, rudderless, slewed and slowed, and ran into the wall of one of the houses that fronted the river. Its boiler-tubes split open and vented live steam; the burner-pan broke loose and spilled burning coals that set fire to the undercarriage.

Pasquale jumped down at once, but Niccolò stayed defiantly atop the burning vehicle. He emptied his pistol at the carriage, which had pulled to a halt, its terrified horse rearing in its traces. Here was a picture for the broadsheet, Niccolò raving and firing his pistol through flames, the crowd backing away, the black carriage and its plunging black horse. It burned itself in Pasquale's brain.

Then Niccolò threw away his pistol and jumped down. Pasquale grabbed him and they ran. *Ciompi* parted before them like the Red Sea before the Israelites. More shots from the carriage. Pasquale saw a man in a hemp jerkin struck in the teeth by a pistol-ball; he collapsed spouting blood from his ruined mouth.

Niccolò was out of breath, and Pasquale had to haul him along by main force. He was after all an old man of fifty, and for all his wiry frame not fit to run this race. Suddenly, he staggered and swore and clutched at his thigh. Blood welled over his hand. 'I'm hit!' he shouted, and seemed strangely exhilarated.

Pasquale hauled him on, daring to look back and seeing the carriage stranded amongst the angry mob. The Ponte Vecchio was ahead. Its angle-tower loomed over the heads of the crowd. Pasquale and Niccolò limped on, dodging through streams of *ciompi* shuffling wearily towards their shanty-town hovels at shift's end, or marching in resignation towards that night's work. From a viewpoint high above Florence, from the top of the Great Tower perhaps, there were no individuals visible in the gaslit crowd. Two men escaping with their lives were less disturbance than a pebble thrown in the river. Along the Borgo San Jacopo, there was a commotion around a burning *vaporetto*, and a carriage was surrounded by an angry mob, which suddenly drew back as the carriage was enveloped in a spurt of flame and coloured smokes, which blew away to reveal it empty. But this was only a temporary disturbance. All disturbances in the calm unfolding of the city's routines were temporary, no more than an incalculably minute faltering, as of a speck of grit caught and crushed in a gear-train, in its remorseless mechanisms.

PART TWO

As Above, So Below

1

The caravan of carriages which carried His Holiness Pope Leo X, lately Giovanni di Bicci de' Medici, his advisers and attendants, his page-boys and cooks, his dwarfs and jesters, including his favourite, Father Marioano, his physicians and his Muslim rackmaster and bodyguard, and cardinals Sanseverino Farnese, Luigi de' Rossi, Lorenzo Pucci, Lorenzo Cibò and Giulio de' Medici, and their own lesser entourages of servants, moved in a great cloud of dust visible for many miles as it toiled past the little villages of Pozzalatico and Galluzzo. A squadron of the Swiss men-at-arms marched at the rear, their burnished chestplates, helmets, pike-heads and halberds glittering like a river in the clear fall sunlight; a pipe and drum band of fully fifty men in scarlet and white uniforms marched ahead.

Rumours of the procession's approach flew ahead of it as birds fly ahead of a forest fire. The chain of signal-towers along the Siena road passed messages back and forth in a continual flutter of semaphore arms. As the procession reached the brow of the last hill before the valley of the Arno, it began to pick up a tail of private citizens who had ridden out on horseback or private carriage or *vaporetto*, adding to the official escort of city militia that flanked the papal procession as it rattled down the long dust-white road, banners flying and drummers beating a frenzied marching-beat even though their hands were blistered and bleeding.

It was noon when the procession at last reached the great open space before the Roman Gate in the city walls. Here it stopped, and with a flurry of attendants the Pope climbed down from his carriage. He wore a dazzling white silk rochet embroidered with heavy gold thread, white gloves of fine kid, embroidered with pearls, and white silk slippers. He was a heavy man, with a coarse face and bulging short-sighted eyes, rolls of fat at his neck and a generous paunch. A jewelled tiara was pinned to his vigorous black hair. He looked bothered by the fussing of his attendants, although he bore it with stoicism, and did not neglect to wave to the crowd gathered at the gate.

A mounting-block was brought, and the Pope was helped on to it. He drew out a little brass spyglass and stood for a few minutes looking at the city in the valley, spread either side of the channelled river beneath its own umber haze. He turned this way and that, taking in the bristling defences of the rebuilt walls: the organ cannon, rocket-launching tubes, ballista, broad cannon, and from each tower the diamond shapes of tethered man-kites flying high in the brisk wind. He focused on the Great Tower rising out of a tumble of red-tiled roofs and dominating the square crenellated tower of the Palazzo della Signoria, the great gilded dome of the Duomo beyond, topped by its shining gold ball and cross. The smokes rising from the manufactories along the river, the angular maze of docks packed like a pincushion with clustered masts of ships, the complex geometry of the sluices and channels and gates that tamed the flow of the Arno: the Pope looked at them all.

Perhaps he was thinking of the cruel assassination of his father in the Duomo, at the hands of the Pazzi conspirators, or of the uprising against the tyranny of his uncle which until now had banished every one of his family from the Republic. At any rate, tears rolled down his florid cheeks as he put away the spyglass and submitted to the indignity of being hauled on to the side-saddle of a fine white Arab stallion. Although he was a passionate huntsman he was a poor rider, and suffered from anal fistulas that made sitting in a hard narrow hunting-saddle agony after only a few minutes.

Still, he was smiling as the procession ponderously got under way again, and became a pageant that slowly rolled through the great gate and along the Via Maggio.

Crowds lined the wide street, ten deep. The Pope ceaselessly signed his benediction with plump hands cased in pearl-trimmed white leather gloves. Half watched in silence, remembering the heavy yoke of Giuliano de' Medici's rule when, bent on revenge for his assassination of his brother, Lorenzo, he had purged half the city's merchant families and robbed the rest to repay his debts, or remembering the words of Savonarola's famous sermon which had started the brief but bloody civil war in which the Medicis had been overthrown. Savonarolistas in the pay of the King of Spain had been busy defacing walls with slogans culled from their exiled leader's published works, and workmen were still busy washing them away as the procession moved past. The other half of the crowd, drunk with faith or wine, or both, cheered and waved pennants and shouted out their approval.

Palle! Palle! Papa Leone! Palle! Palle!

The Pope rode slowly, with two pages leading his white stallion by its gold-encrusted bridle. Eight Florentine citizens of noble birth held over his head hoops of moire silk cunningly locked together to form a canopy in the shape of a butterfly's wings. Despite this shade, the heat of the day soon turned the Pope's heavy face an alarming tinge of purple. Now and again he would halt to admire the banners and decorations that hung from every building, or watch the staging of brief tableaux. In one, a child dressed as an angel announced the birth of Christ to a young woman dressed as the Virgin, and burning halos swung above both their heads while a mechanical dove fluttered down and emitted a ray of dazzling light that struck a mirror stitched into the woman's dress above her womb. In another, an actor in the burnished silver armour of Saint Michael fought a copper-scaled mechanical serpent, piercing it through its mouth so that it gushed realistic blood from every orifice. There was a brief pageant in which Cristoforo Colombo stepped from his boat through waves represented by twisting blue cloths, to be greeted by actors naked but for loincloths and with feather head-dresses and skins stained red with tobacco juice, the noble Savages of the Friendly Isles of the New World. Further on, Amerigo Vespucci was received by King Motecuhzoma II of the Mexican Empire, who was seated on a small white, stepped pyramid amidst a cornucopia of maize, hog plums, guavas, pitahayas, avocados, sweet potatoes and manioc set on gold and silver plates.

The Pope only glanced at this last tableau before jogging his horse forward. Rome supported the contention of Spain that the Savages of the New World, from the innocent Indians of the Friendly Isles to the proud bloodthirsty Mexican and Mayan empires, must be conquered in the name of Christ, and that Florentines were endangering their souls by consorting with Savages and accepting them as equals.

At each halt the Pope's huge escort stopped too; by now it was stretched so far down the street that by the time the tail had halted the head was setting off again. At each halt the drummers drummed and the pipers blew shrill trills; chamberlains threw coins into the crowd from bulging moneybags; the men-at-arms marched smartly on the spot, their faces luminous with sweat; and cardinals leaned out of their coaches and craned forward to see what now had caught His Holiness's attention, for later they would have to remark on every feature of the procession. Firecrackers and coloured smokes made the soldiers uneasy. On the rooftops, sharpshooters armed with the latest long-barrelled rifles stood against the sky, watching for any trouble.

So the Pope gradually made his way down the Via Maggio and across the bridge of Santa Trinità, riding slowly beneath a triumphal arch of canvas and wood painted by the workshop of Raphael and erected only that day by over two hundred men. Fully five hours after he had mounted his horse at the great gate, Pope Leo X finally entered the Piazza della Signoria to a tremendous clangour of bells and thunder of cannon that set every bird in Florence on the wing.

The welcoming shouts were louder and more numerous there, for the more favoured citizens had been drinking sweet white wine from gilded barrels, and there were trestle-tables groaning with food under awnings pitched along the sides of the square. Spectators leaned out of every window of every building, and the confraternities raised up their standards and banners so that a flock of strange hieratic images of saints seemed to bend their attention towards the Pope as his horse was led slowly across the square. Patterns of coloured light revolved across the plastered front of the First Republic Bank, swarming in the gathering dusk.

The councillors of the Signoria and other officials sat on a canopied stage, with the miraculous statue of the Madonna, brought from Impruneta and arrayed in cloth of gold, raised on a platform behind them. The pair of pages led the Pope's horse to them and men rushed forward and assembled a kind of platform around the horse so that the Pope could step from the side-saddle directly on to the stage. The Gonfalonier, bareheaded, in black silk robes slashed with scarlet, stepped forward and knelt at the feet of the Pope and kissed the tasselled tips of His Holiness's white slippers while priests shook bells and swung censers which poured forth sweet sandalwood smoke and aspersed everyone in range with holy water.

The Pope raised up the Gonfalonier and kissed him ceremonially, his hands either side of the Gonfalonier's face as if he were his most beloved son. The crowd cheered wildly.

And in the middle of the square, with a rattle of gears barely disguised by a fanfare, the two halves of the huge cosmic egg swung open in front of a great white curtain. Along the edge of the bottom half of the egg were windows engraved with the signs of the zodiac and illuminated by lamps. There was a sudden flare of light as the lensed lamps of the sun in the centre of the engine were ignited and, to strange stately music played by a host of mechanical devices, actors, costumed according to poetic descriptions of the planets and standing on gold discs, rotated slowly and smoothly in their orbits.

The Pope took in this spectacle with a bemused short-sighted gaze. The crowd cheered the cunning of the workshops of the Great Engineer.

There was more. Lights blazed down from the Great Tower itself. Brighter than the setting sun, the shafts of light seemed solid as they slanted above the heads of the crowd. Images rose and melted on the white screen behind the cosmic egg, suddenly coalescing into an angel that suddenly moved in jerky steps. Half the crowd screamed, the rest gasped. The Pope, suddenly unnoticed in the midst of this miracle, touched his pectoral cross.

The angel smiled and bowed and briefly closed its great white wings. When they opened again, a vision of a detailed landscape was revealed, an artificer's Utopia in which every river was regulated and channelled, every city was symmetrical, and great machines rowed the air.

And then the vision faded. A great murmur went up from the crowd, and fireworks shot up from all around the circumference of the cosmic egg, cascading tails of sparks like comets and bursting high above in showers of gold and silver. A thousand white doves were released to whirr high into the air above the heads of the cheering crowds, and from within the cosmic egg stellar divinities arrayed in silver, their faces and hands painted gold, rose up on pillars and stepped down on to the stage to greet the Pope.

2

Pasquale saw the fireworks from the tall double window of Niccolò Machiavegli's room. He was sitting at the writing-table, sketching poses and attitudes of angels, particularly concentrating on the relationship between wings and arms and body. The window overlooked a narrow dark courtyard, and Pasquale could hardly see what he was doing. The sky, bruise-coloured above the clutter of terracotta roofs, seemed to soak up the last light, but he was reluctant to light the thick candle on the desk.

He bent close over the sheet of heavy paper, the back of some official document from the last century, quickly and minutely hatching the folds of the sleeve of the gown of an angel that hung in mid-air with feet together, arms flung wide. Shadows and light in the folds of the gown blending without lines. Soft cloth contrasting with the long primary feathers of wings taller than the figure they framed. He saw the form of the angel clearly. A furious light was burning behind it, and behind the light was a great wild parkland threaded with white paths and populated by animals of every kind, including the great dragons which had not survived the Flood, all of them fleeing the light, the fire of God's wrath.

All this: but he still couldn't see the angel's face.

Papers littered the writing-table, loosely stacked or bound with ribbons, along with a bundle of goose-feather pens, ink-pots, a tray of sand, a tilting writing-stand. Beside the desk was a rack of a hundred or more books, some calf-bound octavo volumes, the rest the cheap paper-covered editions from the new printing-houses. Works ancient and modern. Ariosto's *Orlando Furioso* in three volumes, Terence's *Andria*, Cicero's *The Republic*, Dante, Livy, Plato, Plutarch, Tacitus. And Koppernigk's *De Revolutionibus Orbium Celestium*, Guicciardini's *On the Paths of Light* and *Microcosmonium*, Leonardo's *Treatise on the Replication of Motion*. And two by two, Niccolò's own plays, *Belfagor*, *The Ass*, *Mandragola*, *The Temptation of Saint Anthony*, a thick sheaf of polemical brochures and pamphlets. More unchained books than Pasquale had ever seen in any one place.

As for the rest of the room, there was a black patent stove with a pair of spoon-shaped chairs flanking it, pictures in gilt frames crowding the walls, prominent amongst them blotchy oil-portraits of Niccolò's dead wife and children, a *cassone* with a cracked front panel, and a truckle bed on which Niccolò Machiavegli slept amongst dusty cushions, breathing through his open mouth. The bandage tied above the knee of his left leg was spotted with dried blood. An empty bottle of wine lay on its side on the carpet. Niccolò had deadened the pain of his wounded leg with wine and cloudy absinthe, drinking with an increasing desperation, until finally he had slept.

Pasquale too had slept through most of the day, curled on one of the old Moorish carpets that lapped the splintered wooden floor. He had had no sleep for almost two days, and was exhausted by the night's escapades. By the time he had cleaned and bandaged Niccolò's wound, a deep bloody groove in the flesh above the back of the knee, and examined the glass in its charred frame that he had saved from the fire, the sky had started to lighten and the automatic cannon had fired to announce the opening of the city gates, and the bells of the churches were ringing for the first mass.

Pasquale draped his best black serge jerkin, stained with sweat and smoke as it was, over a chair and slept, and was woken after a few hours by Niccolò's housekeeper, Signora Ambrogini. This was a small fierce old woman, no more than four feet tall, her back bent by years of labour, still dressed in widow's weeds, layer on layer of black, for a husband who had been dead ten years. She looked after all the rooms in the rambling building where Niccolò had his lodgings, off a court backing on to the Via del Corso, midway between the Piazza della Signoria and the Duomo. She was feared and loved by the bachelor scholars and itinerant writers and musicians and artificers who lodged there, chastened by her scorn at their lackaidaisical absent-mindedness and cosseted by her fierce stern loyalty.

She burst into Niccolò's room in the early afternoon, gave a faint scream when she saw Pasquale sleeping curled up on the carpet by the writing-table, and then a louder scream on seeing Niccolò's wounded leg, propped up on cushions on the truckle bed.

Alarm gave way to a kind of angry mothering. Signora Ambrogini banged to and fro, ordered Pasquale to boil up some water on the stove, told Niccolò, who was still dazed with drink, to pull down his leggings. She bathed the wound and neatly bandaged it, looking sideways at Pasquale as if to blame him for the suffering of her tenant.

Niccolò bore this stoically and with good humour; he was used to her ways. 'We had a little adventure,' he said, and smiled when she scolded him.

Signora Ambrogini threw up her hands. 'A man of your age! You shouldn't take up with young ruffians like this,' she added, darting a fierce black look at Pasquale. Her eyes were bright and black in a face folded with deep wrinkles. White hairs coarse as wire sprouted from her chin.

'I know I've learnt my lesson,' Niccolò said. He was eyeing a half-finished bottle of wine that stood on the writing-table, but did not dare ask for it. Signora Ambrogini disapproved of his drinking. He added, 'But I think it was profitable, all the same.'

'Gallivanting shamelessly!' Signora Ambrogini cried, and rolled her eyes with dramatic pathos. 'And now you will miss the arrival of the Pope, and so will I, by the time I have finished with you. Oh! What a time of it you give me, Signor Machiavegli.'

'Now you know you would never go and see the procession,' Niccolò told her with fond patience, 'because of the crowds. And as for me, there will be plenty of journalists there. All of the journalists in Florence, I shouldn't wonder. My contribution won't be missed.'

The old woman bent to tie the bandage around Niccolò's leg. 'And I suppose this young blade is another of your journalist friends. You, young man, you should be about your work, not lurking here bothering my tenants.'

Pasquale protested that he was an artist, but the old woman refused to believe him. She tied the bandage tightly and neatly, and Niccolò leaned back when she had finished and sighed and told her she was a miracle-worker, and he would truly believe it if she could fetch them some broth.

'That young fellow is strong enough to fetch his own broth,' Signora Ambrogini said sharply.

'He is helping me,' Niccolò said. 'Helping me on a truly important project. And he really is an artist, a good one too, an apprentice of Giovanni Rosso.'

'Can't say I know the name,' the old woman said with a sniff, but went off to fetch some broth all the same.

'She means well,' Niccolò said, leaning back on his pillows. 'For the sake of God, Pasquale, pass me the bottle, there on the table.'

'How is your leg?'

Niccolò drank straight from the bottle, and used his sleeve to mop spilled wine from his chin. 'I'll try it later, but now I feel like resting. Pasquale, you still have that glass?'

'Of course.'

'Let me see it again.'

Mounted in a wooden frame that was flaking with black char, the glass had been cracked by the heat of the fire, and the picture printed or drawn upon it was so browned by heat that only a segment was visible. In fact, the picture seemed altogether darker than it had when Pasquale had rescued it, as if the medium on which it had been made was undergoing a transformation. Still, it was possible to make out figures, muffled in robes and hoods, stiffly modelled yet depicted with exquisite meticulous care, that stood behind a kind of altar on which a naked woman lay, drawn in such a way that it was impossible to tell if she was supposed to be dead or alive. Giustiniani, his hood thrown back from his hawkish face, stood with a sword, its blade softly blurred, raised above his head.

'A black mass,' Pasquale said.

'Blackmail,' Niccolò said.

'What did you hear, at the window?'

'I heard the name of Salai, and I heard Francesco threatening Giustiniani in a feeble but quite desperate manner. It occurs to me that Francesco has evidence that Giustiniani is performing rites such as that shown here, and is blackmailing him to provide a service.'

'What service would that be?'

Niccolò became animated. 'What indeed, Pasquale! And why blackmail? Magicians like Giustiniani are always in need of money, and someone like Francesco would have money enough, I should think.'

'Unless it is some task so terrible even someone like Giustiniani would hesitate to perform it.'

'That's the obvious explanation, although – forgive me, Pasquale – it smacks of the plot of some cheap melodrama. Perhaps Giustiniani has already performed the task, and Francesco was trying to threaten him to keep quiet. There may be a connection with Salai, and with Romano's murder. I must think hard about this,' Niccolò said, and drained the rest of the wine. 'Fetch my little flask, and pour a tumbler of water from the pitcher there.'

'That stuff will send you crazy, and then kill you, Niccolò. I know what it is. It has wormwood in it.'

'Seven parts to a hundred parts water is the correct measure. Please, Pasquale, I do not need to be lectured about this! I need to think!'

'You shouldn't excite yourself. You're wounded.'

Niccolò shook his head. 'There's still much to discover. This is deeper and trickier than I first thought. Perhaps the scandal of the age lies around us!'

'I'll do it just the once,' Pasquale said reluctantly.

'Seven parts to a hundred,' Niccolò said, watching closely as Pasquale poured the yellow-green liquid dropwise. He took the glass from Pasquale and drank the cloudy stuff straight down, then lay back, his eyes closed, his thumb and forefinger pinching the bridge of his nose.

Pasquale sat and watched Niccolò. Presently he heard footsteps on the stair outside the door, and set the picture of the black mass face-down on the writing-table just as Signora Ambrogini returned. She carried a tray bearing two bowls of soup and a hunk of dry bread. Niccolò said to the housekeeper, without opening his eyes, 'Why, what would I do without you, Signora Ambrogini?'

'Drink yourself into the gutter, I shouldn't wonder,' Signora Ambrogini said, departing after another fierce look at Pasquale.

Niccolò said that reminded him, and burrowed under his bed, coming up with a bottle of wine. He drew the cork with his teeth, drank off a good draught. He met Pasquale's look, and said, 'For medicinal purposes only. Besides, it's the last.'

Pasquale drank a glass with the soup, but it was thin and bitter stuff, and he was happy enough to let Niccolò drink the rest. Niccolò hardly touched his soup and later slept again, and Pasquale sat at the table in the fading light and studied first the darkened picture, and then the little flying device. Try as he might, he could make no connection between the two, and set them aside and sketched first the sleeping journalist and then Signora Ambrogini, calling up her likeness by remembering her characteristic glare at him, half turned away, quick and cross. That was how he had taught himself to remember faces, not by individual details, but by an attitude or expression which called up the whole memory. He sketched the scene moments after the *vaporetto* had crashed, mostly from imagination, and finally turned to drawing angels, losing himself in the work until fireworks burst in the darkening sky and Niccolò woke.

The journalist's wounded leg had stiffened. He hobbled around the room, cursing under his breath, then collapsed on the bed. Pasquale said that he should rest, but Niccolò was determined to get out. There were questions to be asked, he said. There had been two murders, and it would not stop there.

'You don't have to come with me, Pasquale. You have done enough, risked enough. These are deep dangerous waters in which we have dipped, and I must needs go deeper. Now, I have some idea of what might lurk there, for I have charted these waters before, but you're an artist. Your world is light, the surface of things. Go home.'

'I'll go with you,' Pasquale said, with passion. 'I'm no innocent.'

He had surprised Niccolò at least as much as he had surprised himself. The journalist rasped the black stubble on his chin with his thumb. Eventually he said, 'I'm tired, it is true. I would not object to help, if such help was offered for a good reason.'

'Well, if it is reason that you need, you still owe me the money I flung at the driver last night.'

Niccolò laughed. 'And in the end that fare was hardly enough for the man's trouble, eh?'

'I want to know what this is about. I've never before been involved in plots. It's more exciting than etching portraits of the Pope, which is what we'll be doing next week to earn our bread.' He was thinking of the bare cold rooms he shared with Rosso, the grind of poverty. If he could regain the florins paid to him he could at least afford most of the materials for his painting. And when that was done he would not need to search for money. He scolded himself for believing this so fervently and foolishly, for hope is foolish, given the hard ways of the world, yet he could not help his hope.

'I forget how young you are,' Niccolò said, looking shrewdly at Pasquale. 'Help me around the room a few times to loosen this stiffness in my leg. There will be a good deal of walking to be done before this is finished.'

But before Pasquale could help Niccolò to his feet, there was a knock at the door and Signora Ambrogini burst in, saying that there was a lady who wished to see him.

Niccolò sat up, suddenly alert. 'A woman? Who is it?'

'Not a woman, but a lady,' Signora Ambrogini said firmly. 'She would not give her name.'

'Well, send her up, send her up. If she wishes to speak to me I can hardly refuse.'

'With your room in the state it is! Really, Signor Machiavegli, you can hardly receive a lady here. It isn't proper.'

'If she is desperate enough to wish to see me, she will not be concerned with my circumstances. Please, Signora Ambrogini, do not keep her waiting.'

'I am thinking,' Signora Ambrogini said with great dignity, 'of my reputation.'

'Your reputation will shine forth, signora. Now please, my guest if you will.'

She was indeed a lady. Pasquale recognized her at once, for she was Lisa Giocondo, the wife of the Secretary of the Ten of War. He would have whistled with pleasure, if Niccolò had not shot him a sharp look.

Niccolò settled his guest in the best chair in the room, taking her heavy velvet cloak and handing it to Pasquale. In the last light that fell through the window, her indigo gown, of the finest silk trimmed with Flemish lace, set off her white shoulders and black hair, which was thickened with swatches of black silk. She wore a net veil held by a circlet of gold, which softened the contours of her face. As Pasquale lit candles, he glanced sidelong at this face: Signora Giocondo did not have the beauty of an angel – her nose was perhaps a little too long, and one of her dark eyes was slightly higher than the other, and besides, she was a mature woman with fine lines at the corners of her eyes, while the beauty of angels was the beauty of youth – but she had a solemn radiant grace that seemed to light her oval, pale-skinned face from within. Her perfume, a sweetened musk, filled the room.

She was as direct about her business as her gaze. She folded her

hands and said that she would not be here except for a certain unfortunate event at the Palazzo Taddei, and could not stay long for her
husband would soon expect her at his side at the service which the
Pope would hold in the Duomo. She hoped that Signor Machiavegli
would forgive her candour, but she must speak to clear her husband's
name.

'I hope that you will forgive my candour in turn,' Niccolò said,
clearly enjoying himself, 'but while I have yet to form an opinion of
your husband one way or the other, it is certain that it is in his power
to commission a death should he have need of it.'

'My husband is indeed a very powerful man.'

'I'm not likely to forget that,' Niccolò said.

Lisa Giocondo said with resolve, 'Signor Machiavegli, I know that
we can never be friends, for my husband has the office which you
once enjoyed, but perhaps we can at least not be enemies. I would
help you in your investigations, and hope that in your heart there is
a measure of Christian charity that will respond to my plight.'

'Let me assure you, signora, that I am pursuing not a vendetta,
but the truth. It's truth that interests me.'

'In that we can agree.'

'Then if I may ask a few questions.'

Lisa Giocondo looked up at Pasquale, who at the moment, with
a piercing thrill, understood that she was the lover of Raphael. She
was here to assure Niccolò that her husband had not had Romano
killed for revenge, or as a warning.

Niccolò, who was leaning forward at the edge of his bed with a
hungry look, said, 'He will be as discreet as I, signora.'

Lisa Giocondo said, 'If what you ask me can help uncover the
truth, then I'll answer as truthfully as I'm able.'

'Does your husband know of your friendship with Raphael?'

'He does not approve, but he . . . tolerates it. He is an old man,
signor, caught up in the affairs of state, and I am his third wife. Our
marriage was never one made from love, although you must believe
me that there is love, and since our only child died we have been
apart more than I would have wished.'

'And his honour, signora. Does he worry about that?'

'He would worry about his position, but that is secure. A man
raised up as he is, as you will know, Signor Machiavegli, is subject

to many attacks, including rumours about my . . . conduct. He takes them without hurt.'

'But there is some truth to these rumours, or you would not be here.'

'I am at your mercy, Signor Machiavegli.'

Niccolò pinched the bridge of his nose between finger and thumb. It was his characteristic gesture while he was thinking. After a moment he said, 'Your husband was instrumental in arranging the Pope's embassy. In fact, he has many contacts in Rome.'

'He would not interfere with the affairs of the Republic because of personal matters.'

'Not directly, of course. But was Raphael invited by your husband?'

'Why would he do that?'

'Perhaps to arrange that Raphael be humiliated.'

'An interesting idea, Signor Machiavegli, but I believe that it was the Pope himself who sent Raphael as an ambassador.'

'The Pope himself, and not Giulio de' Medici?'

For the first time, Lisa Giocondo looked perturbed. She said, 'I have it from Raphael that it was the Pope himself. I believe him, Signor Machiavegli.'

'As is your right, signora. I think, for now, that I have asked enough. I see that you glance out of the window, and worry about the passing of time. Of course you must do your duty to your husband. I would not keep you from him.'

Lisa Giocondo rose. She was a tall woman, as tall as Pasquale. She dropped a small bag on the writing-table and said, 'You will no doubt incur expenses in your investigations, Signor Machiavegli. I would not wish to see you out of pocket.'

Niccolò got to his feet with Pasquale's help, apologizing that he had already been hurt in his investigations, a trifling wound but a nuisance even so. 'I had not thought to serve the Republic again, signora. May I ask, if my inquiries should lead to your husband . . . ?'

'I also am interested in the truth. You will, I trust, keep me informed.'

When she had gone, Pasquale could finally whistle. He said, 'I hadn't realized the depth of your hate, Niccolò.'

Niccolò said, 'Francesco del Giocondo is a good silk merchant, a competent secretary, and a bad poet with an inflated opinion of his worth.'

'You imitate Michelangelo's opinion of Raphael.'

'It is a matter of fact, not opinion. What is your judgement of Signora Giocondo?'

'In the tender soul of a woman there dwells prudence and a courageous spirit.'

'Indeed. And a most determined one.'

'And generous,' Pasquale said, spilling half a dozen florins from the small bag, which was heavy with Signora Giocondo's musky scent.

'We are embarked on a voyage over deep and dangerous waters. Those may help speed our passage. Do you know how our lady became Raphael's mistress?'

'Until now I didn't even know she *was* his mistress. I am only a painter, after all.'

Niccolò smiled. 'Raphael painted a portrait of her, but not at her husband's commission. It was her lover at the time, Giulio de' Medici, who set Raphael to the task, while our Florentine secretary and his wife were on embassy to Rome.'

'So you think that perhaps Giulio de' Medici sent Raphael here, into certain danger?'

'Signora Giocondo certainly believes it may be possible, and more, that perhaps her husband was involved in Romano's murder, although she hopes otherwise.'

'Yet what we saw at Giustiniani's villa would suggest that Romano was involved in a plot of his own.'

'Or lured into a plot,' Niccolò said spryly, 'although that would be a very complicated way of performing a simple task.'

'You didn't tell her of Giustiniani.'

'She did not pay for that. Let her wonder and worry. She may be moved to tell us more, although I doubt it. She has a core of iron. Now, hand me the money, young Pasquale. We will have need of it before the night is out. We will make inquiries, and this will ease our questions.'

3

When Pasquale and Niccolò left the apartment building it had just turned night, with three stars pricking the patch of blue-black sky between the roofs above the courtyard. Pasquale tacked his likeness of Signora Ambrogini to her door, saying that now she would know he was an artist, and Niccolò drily remarked that Pasquale shouldn't count on public opinion.

Dusk usually drove most honest citizens indoors, but that night the city was embraced by the carnival begun by the entry of the Pope. Florentines loved carnivals and festivals, and any anniversary or occasion of state was an excuse for celebration and holiday. The streets were lit as much by the lanterns and flaming brands carried by parties of costumed men tramping here and there as by the infrequent acetylene lamps. Groups of youths serenaded favoured girls who sat at their lighted windows. One gang strode along on stilts that doubled their height. Music and singing and cheering sounded from near and far, but Niccolò led Pasquale away from the celebrations, into the maze of narrow passages and courts behind the imposing façades of the buildings that lined the main streets. Always, Florence's private lives turned inward, hiding from public gaze, breeding vendettas and dark plots behind high walls and narrow barred windows.

Niccolò was still limping badly, leaning on a stick of ashwood tipped with iron at either end, and the way was difficult, over slick flagstones or rutted earth, lit only by infrequent shafts of light leaking from high shuttered windows. Pasquale was nervous, and kept his hand on his knife. This was just the kind of place where people imagined that cutthroats and robbers lurked – although because of that, any robbers would have a poor time of it, and were no doubt lurking elsewhere.

After a little while, Pasquale asked, 'Who are we looking for?'

'A certain physician of ill repute. A man who goes by the name of Dr Pretorious. It is not his real name, of course, and as far as I know he has never been examined for his doctorate, although he has been thrown out of at least a dozen different universities in five different countries. But none of his kind use their real names, in case demons learn them. He was put in jail in Venice for trafficking in dead bodies, although he had some influence that meant he was not put to the question but instead served his sentence on the galleys. There were rumours that he was trying to construct a woman, a new Venus or Bride of the Sea, from parts of corpses, and planned to animate this patchwork construction by substitution of an arcane liquor for blood.'

'Another black magician, then? Venice seems to breed them.'

'Do you know, Pasquale, I'm not quite sure where Pretorious was born, but it was certainly never Venice. As for black magic, *he* does not call it that. He calls himself a physician, and it is true he has done some good amongst the *ciompi* shanties, where he holds a clinic and takes whatever people will pay in return for treatment. His clients are in love with him. There were rumours some years ago that he was associated with the disappearance of children, but to his credit the *ciompi* did not believe them.'

'And you think he is an associate of this other magician, this Giustiniani.'

'Ah, because both have fled the city by the sea, for the same reason! All I can say now is that it is likely that Pretorious may be able to shed some light on the business of Paolo Giustiniani, for they move, if not in the same circles, in circles which intersect. Moreover, Dr Pretorious is a collector of facts. He hoards them until such time as the right buyer comes along. Meanwhile, Pasquale, we must be vigorous in our examination of the facts *we* have collected, and in the conclusion we draw from them.'

'As rigorous as the artificers?'

'Well put,' Niccolò said with a smile. 'Down here.'

The tavern they were seeking was in a dark courtyard bounded on three sides by tall houses, on the fourth by a reeking stream that gurgled throatily in the darkness. Pasquale had to half pull, half lift Niccolò up the steep arch of the bridge which crossed this Stygian waterway.

Just as they reached the far side of the bridge, fireworks burst overhead, and the courtyard began to throb to the solemn tolling of the cathedral bells. The mass in honour of the Pope was over, and he was departing for the feast at the Palazzo della Signoria. By the brief light of star-shells, Pasquale caught a clear glimpse across the courtyard, and saw a bundle of twigs crooked over a doorway masked with sacking, and scattered tables where figures hunched over bowls or flagons. Little lamps, wicks floating in saucer of oil, cast faint reddish lights. Someone was playing the bagpipes, and doing it badly.

Pasquale said, remembering the dive where he had taken wine with Niccolò after witnessing the murder scene, 'You know many interesting places.'

'Not all business is transacted on high, and besides, news always falls from high to low, just as water seeks the lowest place.'

'This Dr Pretorious must have fallen far.'

'He doesn't believe so,' Niccolò said. 'Listen carefully, Pasquale. Pretorious is as subtle and poisonous as a serpent. Be careful. In particular, be very careful what you say to him. He'll use any unguarded remark as a way into your soul.'

'You make him sound like the devil.'

'He is,' Niccolò said, and pushed aside the sacking at the door.

Dr Pretorious sat at a corner table, playing single-handed tarot whist. A tall white-haired old man, he was thin to the point of emaciation, fastidiously dressed in a russet tunic with puffed sleeves and a white shirt trimmed with Flemish lace, and seemed quite oblivious to the dirty straw on the floor, the mice that scuttled to and fro. Exuding a brittle charm, he stood and bowed to Niccolò and Pasquale, and called to the landlord for his very best wine. His servant, a hulking Savage with a square scarred face and a helmet of coarse glossy black hair, sat beside him, a knife as big as an ordinary man's sword laid across his thighs.

The wine served was as bad as anything Pasquale had ever tasted, although Niccolò sipped it without complaint, and Dr Pretorious seemed to relish it. He said, 'I have not seen you for a long time, Niccolò. I had hoped it would be longer.'

'You have been quiet, or if not quiet at least careful.'

'I've been working,' Dr Pretorious said. His eyes looked black in the flickering light of the rush-lamps, like deep caves under the overhang of his craggy brow. 'And with great success, too.'

'I'm not here to talk about your work, or anything else you've done. In fact, I'd rather not hear about it.'

'Oh, don't worry! It is, you might say, the antithesis of my previous research. Instead of subverting death, I attempt to subvert life itself, to short-circuit the Great Chain of Being. I have made mannequins, small as mice, and infused them with a spark of life. How my children dance and sing!' There was a measured silence. The gloating way he said *children* chilled Pasquale's blood. Dr Pretorious added, 'Well, you'll know all about it soon enough. Everyone will.'

Niccolò said, 'I've come about the business at Paolo Giustiniani's villa.'

Dr Pretorious started to gather together his tarot cards. He had long white fingers, and yellow nails trimmed close and square. He licked his bloodless lips with a tongue as pointed as a lizard's. 'Ah, so you were involved. I had heard as much.'

'From Giustiniani's men?'

'Perhaps,' Dr Pretorious said carelessly, and folded the cards together and wrapped them in a square of black silk.

'I don't think so. If Giustiniani knew I was involved, then he would have come straight away to my room.'

Dr Pretorious shrugged. 'Well, perhaps I heard it somewhere else. At a time like this, there are many stories. You know that my sources are as various as those of the Nile.'

'You did not welcome the Pope.'

'I have no cause to celebrate. After all, he *is* only the Pope, you know. Not the one we hoped for.' Dr Pretorious looked directly at Pasquale for the first time. 'You've brought an artist along, I see.'

Pasquale felt a queer compulsion to say something. Light lived deep in Dr Pretorious's dark eyes, floating and faint. He said, 'Who were you hoping for?'

Dr Pretorious said, 'We live in the time before the end times. The Great Year has come and gone, and soon the black pope, the antipope, will rise. Then the Millennium will begin, but it will not be what most fools believe it to be, young man. Tell me, did you see the entry of the Pope into this foul city? Did you see him enter the square in the shadow of that ridiculously high tower of the so-called Great Engineer?'

'I was . . . otherwise engaged.'

'Then perhaps I have something you would like to know. I wonder now, what it would be worth.'

Niccolò said sharply, 'Remember that we have serious business here, Pasquale.'

Dr Pretorious smiled, cruel as a knife. 'Ah, this would not of course be a social call. It never is. I suppose that is why you did not introduce your catamite here. From the country, by his accent, although he has taken pains to disguise it. Fiesole I would say, a town well known for its quaint rural ways – they favour goats over women there, I believe.'

'Sit!' Niccolò pressed down on Pasquale's shoulder as he started to rise.

Pasquale subsided, anger a thick taste in his mouth. The Savage smiled broadly at him: his front teeth were gone, and his incisors had been sharpened to points and capped with gold. Pasquale returned the big man's yellow gaze, but he had to lock his hands between his thighs to keep himself from shaking.

Niccolò said, 'He is here to help me, should I need help.'

'Times must be bad for you,' Dr Pretorious said, with a bright smile. 'And of course, they'll shortly be worse still for all artists, if the Great Engineer's new invention proves as popular as it deserves. I sympathize.'

'I need your help,' Niccolò said. 'Times are bad enough for that, at least.'

'Ah. Well, I wondered when that debt would be called in. What shall we say . . . three questions? I'll need paying, too, of course. My debt to you isn't that great.'

Niccolò drank down his wine, and Dr Pretorious quickly poured him some more. Niccolò drank that too, and said, 'You always liked playing games. This will be payment enough.' He set the little bag of florins on the table.

Dr Pretorious breathed deeply through his nose and said, 'From a woman – a rich one, too. Well. There are rules you are not even aware of, my friend. Perhaps to you what I do seems a game. It is not. Ask away. You have my attention.'

'What interest does Paolo Giustiniani have in the painter Raphael?'

'So you *are* involved in that sordid little business. Fascinating.'

'I asked the question.'

'Oh, he has no interest, at present.'

'If I may say so, that is not a very full answer.'

'It is the truth. Aren't you satisfied with that?'

'Perhaps that depends upon the answer to the next question.'

'Press on, my friend,' Dr Pretorious said, with a knife-edged smile.

'On what Great Work is Giustiniani engaged?'

'I can tell you what little I know, so it cannot be a full answer.'

'You are an honourable man.'

'I take this more seriously than you because I know about the consequences of error, dear Niccolò.'

'Then tell me what you know. As full an answer as you are able.'

'I believe he is either engaged in enlisting into his service a great prince and his army of lesser demons, or invoking one of those who serve the celestial throne.'

'These are hardly small matters,' Niccolò said. He was sweating, Pasquale saw, a dew gathered just below his receding hairline.

'It depends on how you go about it,' Dr Pretorious said carelessly. 'Giustiniani is using the worst kind of necromancy, the kind of thing that hedge-wizards long ago abandoned. I hardly think he'll succeed. He is an amateur, you know. He even uses his real name. Most likely, he'll succeed in consigning himself to Hell. That kind always do.'

'And you hope to evade it?'

'Oh, of course,' Dr Pretorious said. His sudden smile was bright and generous – it was then that Pasquale realized that the man was quite insane. There was a chill in the air, as if somewhere near by a door had opened on to the hyperborean regions, radiating anti-heat.

'There are always ways of avoiding the attention of Hell, for those who know,' Dr Pretorious said. 'Of course, my friend, I know that you don't think Hell such a bad place. I've read your play on the matter, where a demon discovers that matrimony is in truth a living hell, and Hell itself is a corner of Heaven ruled not by the Fallen One, but by rich Pluto. Who is rich, of course, because in the end death claims all, and rules not over eternal torment but over a garden where those whose deeds or intellect exclude them from Heaven, the heroes and philosophers, converse. A place that you, foolish Niccolò, perhaps yearn for. Perhaps you should examine your own soul, my friend. Lapses like that are hooks for the claws of demons.'

Pasquale was almost hypnotized by Dr Pretorious's mellifluous voice. The noise of the other patrons of the low tavern had receded, as if Dr Pretorious had created a world within a world, where each was intimately connected to each by words. Then Niccolò laughed, and the spell was broken.

'You read too much into my fantasies,' he said. 'Although I am flattered, you shouldn't misunderstand my interest in Hell. If one is to find the way to Paradise, one should first learn the road to Hell, so that it can be avoided. Without temptation, there can be no Fall, and so no redemption.'

Dr Pretorious said sweetly, 'We are both seekers after power. That is why we are so alike, you and I.'

'Not at all,' Niccolò countered. 'It is true that we both seek power, but by different roads, and for different ends. You wish only to serve yourself, and none other, and so avoid falling into Hell for beside such as you, the damned would seem pure.'

'Spare me the analysis. You have asked two questions. Ask me the third and be done with it.'

'No. No, I don't believe I will. I have learned enough for now.' Niccolò rose, and for a moment Dr Pretorious looked up at him with astonishment. 'Come, Pasquale,' Niccolò said. 'We have much work to do, this night.'

Dr Pretorious said, 'No! Wait! You have one more question to ask me.'

'Perhaps some other time.'

Dr Pretorious swept the table clear of beakers and sprang to his feet. Behind him, the Savage also stood, his head brushing the ceiling. 'No!' Dr Pretorious shouted. 'You will not keep any hold over me after this, I swear it! It is done!'

'I have no more questions for now,' Niccolò said mildly, and took up his stick. 'Come, Pasquale.'

Pasquale dared look back only after they had crossed the bridge over the little stream. No one seemed to be following.

Niccolò said, 'Don't worry. In his own way, Dr Pretorious is a man of his word, and while he still owes me the favour of an answer he will not harm us.'

'What favour could you possibly do a man like that?'

'I once showed that he could not have done what he was accused of having done. I thought that I was acting on the side of justice, for if the wrong man had been hanged then the real criminal would have remained free to continue his dreadful work. Those were terrible times, and I had to act without foresight. If I had known that the real killer would have evaded justice after all, then perhaps I would not have helped Pretorious. There are many things he has done for which he deserves death. But in hindsight it is easy to judge your actions, less so in the heat of the moment. You still look troubled, Pasquale.'

'I was wondering what new artificer's device he was alluding to, that he said would greatly impoverish all artists.'

'You must remember that Dr Pretorious seeks to gain power over everyone he meets, Pasquale. It was probably no more than a snare set to catch your attention. Dismiss it from your thoughts.'

Niccolò seemed troubled and exhausted, and they walked on a way, through dark narrow courts and passages, with Niccolò's stick tapping in the darkness, before Pasquale asked him what he had learned.

'That this is not as great a matter as it might be. If Raphael is not involved, then in all likelihood Giulio Romano and Giovanni Francesco were not acting for him, or acting to protect him, but were acting for themselves. The little flying device you keep safe, and the picture you rescued from the fireplace, undoubtedly have something to do with the matter, but I do not think they are ends in themselves.'

Pasquale remembered, with a guilty shock, that he had left both the picture and the device on Niccolò's writing-table, but thought it best to keep quiet about this lapse. 'Is Giustiniani really a magician? Dr Pretorious seems to believe no one is, save himself.'

'It is true that men of that kind delude themselves into thinking only they have true powers, but that is precisely the point. Dr Pretorious is well placed to see through any trickery, none better, for he believes himself to be a true magus – the only true magus. In the end, men like him deceive no one but themselves.'

'Artificers think they know everything, too.'

'No, Pasquale. While they do believe that they have the means to unriddle locked mysteries of the universe, they share their knowledge because it is discovered by a common system. Men of Dr Pretorious's kind hoard it, and each one believes that only he understands the operations crucial for the conjuration of power. There's the difference.'

Pasquale couldn't help letting his disappointment show. Signora Giocondo's florins lost so quickly. His best clothes ruined. He said, 'Then this may not be important after all.'

'We are starting from a lower rather than a higher place. We may yet climb far. Don't worry, Pasquale. You'll get your money.'

So Niccolò saw through Pasquale, too. He saw through everyone it seemed, even (unlike Dr Pretorious) himself.

They reached the main thoroughfare, and as they passed under the light of the first of the acetylene lamps Pasquale at last took his hand from his knife. Moments later, between the first lamp and the next, they were attacked.

4

Four men ran out of a passageway on the other side of the road, ran right at Pasquale and Niccolò before they realized that these were not revellers. In an instant, Pasquale was wrestled away from Niccolò. His assailant, breathing heavily and stinking of bad beer, locked an arm around his neck and Pasquale shoved backwards, unbalancing the man, and slamming him against a wall. Breath knocked out of him, the man loosened his grip for an instant, and Pasquale stamped on his instep and pulled free.

Then it was knife against knife. The man, a burly bully-boy, grinned when Pasquale drew his knife. He tossed his own from one hand to the other with a streetfighter's ease and taunted Pasquale in a slurred voice, telling him to come on, come and get it, come and get fucked good. They warily circled each other before the man suddenly leapt forward. Pasquale dodged a slashing blow which might otherwise have unseamed his guts, and caught the man's knife-arm with a lucky swipe. The man squealed like a stuck pig and dropped his weapon. Pasquale kicked it away and the drunken fool grinned and ran at him, and Pasquale sank his knife to the hilt in the other's guts. The man gasped and sagged, clutching Pasquale's shoulder with one hand and pawing at his wound with the other. The haft of the knife twisted from Pasquale's grasp and the man fell to his knees, swearing that Pasquale had killed him.

Niccolò had already disabled one ruffian with a blow of his stick; the man curled in the road, sobbing and holding his smashed knee. Niccolò threw the stick at the second and gained enough time to draw his pistol, but the third stepped up behind him and sapped his arm. The second man grabbed the pistol and turned towards Pasquale.

For a moment it seemed that all was lost, but then someone growled and ran out of the darkness, brushing Pasquale aside. It was the giant Savage, Dr Pretorious's servant. He smashed into the ruffian who brandished Niccolò's pistol, swung him into the air by neck and hip, and threw him against his companion.

For a moment everyone froze, like actors at the end of a tableau. Then the two fallen men picked themselves up and ran down the street, shouting. The man with the smashed knee looked whitely at Dr Pretorious's servant and picked himself up and hobbled after his companions, gasping with pain.

'My thanks,' Niccolò said. He was out of breath. So was Pasquale, whose heart was banging against his ribs.

The Savage fixed Niccolò with a stare and said in a low voice, 'My master says that the debt must be discharged.' And then he ran into the shadows and was gone, moving with incredible lightness for so big a man.

Pasquale said admiringly, 'He showed no fear at all.'

'He believes himself dead,' Niccolò said. 'Dr Pretorious once told me that the magi of his godforsaken island, when they wish to enslave a man, make from the liver of a certain fish a potion which renders a man so insensible that he is taken for dead by his family, and is duly buried. The magus then digs up the supposed corpse and revives him, and so gains an obedient servant who is without fear. A potion sewn into a pouch is slung at the servant's neck, to mark him as the property of the magus. Such a one is Pretorious's servant, although how he came by him, Pretorious did not say.'

The brute wounded by Pasquale's knife started to whimper. He was curled up on the ground, both hands pressed to his belly. Niccolò grasped the man's hair and wrenched his head up and asked him who had paid him, but the man only sobbed that he was killed.

'What shall we do with this fool?' Pasquale asked. He had wounded someone before, but that had only been a trifling scratch in a sudden quick drunken fight over something both he and his opponent had forgotten about in the instant of blood-letting. He knew now that he could, if he willed it, fight to the death. He had it in him. It was both exciting and disturbing. It made his blood sing.

Niccolò said, 'We'll find the militia.'

'We should leave him to die.'

'That's hardly Christian charity. Besides,' Niccolò said with a smile, 'he may then wish to tell us about himself. Such as who sent him—'

Pasquale stooped and grasped the brute's ears, shook his head from side to side. The man groaned.

'Who sent you! Was it Giustiniani?'

The brute said in a slurred voice, 'You've killed me, you motherfucking bastard.'

Pasquale tried the question again, but the man would only groan and cry. Niccolò said, 'He will talk, if not now, then later.' Then he lifted his head and said, 'Hush. Someone comes.'

They came from the direction in which the other assailants had fled, half a dozen men in carnival motley, masked as griffins and dragons and unicorns. They were led by a giant – no, it was a man on stilts, stamping along with quick adroitness. He wore a white mask which covered his entire face, with triangular eyeholes rimmed in black. He pointed at Pasquale and Niccolò, and began to whirl a slingshot around his head. His troops surged forward with a yell. Pasquale and Niccolò fled just as the first slingshot load whistled past their heads.

It was a glass globe which shattered on the paving-stones, spraying liquid. A fog whirled up, thick and yellow. Pasquale and Niccolò plunged through the vapour, choking on a vile thick scent like burning geraniums. The ruffians gave chase, yelling loudly. One blew a tinny toy trumpet. Niccolò was labouring, leaning heavily on his stick, and Pasquale dragged him along by main force.

Then they reached the Piazza del Duomo and were suddenly amongst crowds. The congregation of the mass celebrated by the Pope, and supporters of the Medici, and revellers who had joined the party for the fun of it. Pasquale pulled Niccolò through the noisy people, glancing back and seeing the stilt-man looming above the crowd's swirling heads, his white masked face looking this way and that. For the moment they were safe, but Pasquale felt suddenly more exposed than he had when being chased, and imagined a masked assassin whirling towards them out of the festive crowd at every turn.

The cathedral reared above the heads of the crowd, its great gold-skinned cupola shining in focused lamplight, its white marble walls shrouded by cloths on which, by artificer sleight of hand, transparent scenes trembled and shook. The white tower of the campanile was lit too, and its Apostolica bell solemnly tolled the hour of ten.

Pasquale supported Niccolò, and they made slow progress through the noisy crowd. 'Who are they?' Pasquale said, and realized that he was almost as breathless as Niccolò.

'I would guess that they are Giustiniani's. If Dr Pretorious knew of our involvement, then so surely must Giustiniani. The devil is after us for what we know, or what he thinks we know.'

'We have that picture.'

'Which he thinks he destroyed. More likely he knows us as witnesses to the murder of Giovanni Francesco.'

'Or as his accomplices.'

'Very good, Pasquale!'

'Well, they will know us for certain now, because I left my knife behind, and it has my name on its blade. At least I have lost sight of the stilt-man.'

'We have a long way to go this night,' Niccolò said. 'Confound this crowd. The fools should all be abed.'

'A poor thing to say for those who have unwittingly hid us. I would have all the citizens of Florence awake all night, until we are saved.'

'It will take more than one night,' Niccolò said grimly.

'Then I'll stay with you. I'm marked now anyway. Though I would like to know where we are going.'

'Whatever the reason, I am glad of your support, Pasquale. The devil take this crowd! Where we are going, if it is at all possible, is to the Palazzo della Signoria, because that is where Raphael will be dining this night, with the Pope and the first citizens of Florence. We must warn him of what has happened.'

The Piazza della Signoria was scarcely less crowded. The people had taken the long platform in front of the Palazzo on which the Pope had been received, and were carousing like Moorish pirates celebrating the capture of a fat merchant vessel. Bands of university students roamed to and fro, roaring the songs of their nations. There was a clash between the Prussian and French nations around the Great Engineer's cosmic engine. The latter seemed to want to tear at the engine which commemorated the great truth discovered by Canon Koppernigk, while the Prussians were defending the honour of their national hero. 'Still it moves,' they shouted, taunting the French. Beyond this, dancers danced in a circle around Michelangelo's great statue of David. The statue's gilded hair flickered with reflections of the torches they juggled.

Artificers were celebrating, too. Great figures of light rotated over the wall that Pasquale and Rosso had so carefully prepared – was it only yesterday? The artificer, Benozzo Berni, was tending his light-cannon, and greeted Pasquale cheerfully. The big acetylene lamps of his device hissed and roared, their light concentrated through slits on to revolving wheels of painted horn, and big lenses of thick bubbled glass threw the changing patterns vastly magnified on to the painted wall. Light splinteringly refracted from the edges of the lenses threw Berni's shadow a long way across the paving-stones as he came over to Pasquale and Niccolò. The artificer had taken off his many-pocketed tunic and was sweating into his hemp undershirt from the heat of his great lamps. Grinning like a madman, he clapped Pasquale on the back and whirled him around to face the show of lights with a grand expansive gesture.

'Now you see!' he shouted exultantly. 'Moving light making its own picture. What do you think of that, painter?'

'Perhaps I am not sophisticated enough, signor, but I see no pictures, only the kinds of patterns a candle-flame may make against a wall.'

'That's the point! The light patterns act on the eye itself, and deceive it into making pictures. This is a new way of thinking, you see! The marvel of it is that the machine operates upon you.'

'It is certainly a marvel, but perhaps machine thoughts are too difficult for me to understand.' Perhaps Piero di Cosimo might appreciate this light-show, Pasquale thought, but it seemed a costly way of reproducing the random patterns found everywhere in nature.

Berni laughed. 'Have it your own way for now, but you'll come around. We stand at the threshold of a new age. The curtain is hardly raised, and we glimpse only the first flickers of what is beyond, and these are so bright that we can scarcely believe our eyes. But soon we will have to deal with these visions. Machines force new ways of making things, of doing things, and now seeing things. The progression is inevitable.'

'It seems there is no room for the artist,' Pasquale said. To his tired mind, Berni seemed a kind of devil, full of restless energy, celebrating change for change's sake.

Berni dashed sweat from his brow with a scorched red rag. 'The age of representative art is past. There will be new kinds of artists, painting directly with light, producing fleeting images that linger in the screen of the eye. My kinetoscope draws patterns which the eye seeks to interpret, and then there is the marvel of the Great Engineer's moving pictures as produced by his ipseorama! And tonight he will capture the true likeness of the Pope in light itself. Surely you must agree that the age of interpretation and laborious symbolism is past!'

'As a matter of fact,' Pasquale began, 'I know nothing of these moving pictures—'

Niccolò had sat on an upturned crate to rest. Now he struggled to his feet and said, 'I don't know you, signor, but I hope you will not mind if I ask a question.'

'But I know Niccolò Machiavegli!' Berni sketched a bow. 'Perhaps your broadsheet might wish to report the new miracles first demonstrated here.'

'Perhaps. That isn't for me to say. What I would ask, Signor . . .'

'Benozzo Berni, at your service!'

'Signor Berni, I would ask you if any soldiers have lately entered the Palazzo.'

'Why, no. None, since the great procession made its way from the Duomo to the Palazzo for the feast. That's still going on, and I will run my engine until it is over – which means until well past midnight, for I hear more than twenty courses are to be served.'

'Then we may not be too late, Pasquale.' Niccolò smiled vaguely at Berni. 'I'm sorry, signor. Perhaps we will discuss your marvel another time.'

'You are witnessing the dawn of a new age, Signor Machiavegli! Just remember that!'

As they crossed the square, taking a long route to avoid the rowdy students, Pasquale said, 'What are you expecting to happen?'

'I'm not sure, only that something will. Wait, look! Perhaps we are too late!'

Niccolò pointed up at the Palazzo. It loomed at the eastern corner of the square like a ship. Every window in its bulk was ablaze, even in its square high tower, and flags bearing the Medici emblem of twelve gold balls flew amongst Republican banners showing the Florentine lily. Someone had flung wide a window under the overhang of the castellated top floor and was shouting to a group of soldiers below.

More figures appeared at the window. Two men struggling with a third, who suddenly tipped over the sill. People shouted in the square below. The man plummeted, jerked, swung, kicking and kicking at the end of a cord.

Soldiers were jogging smartly around the corner of the Palazzo towards the main entrance. A bell rang out with a quick urgent jangle. Pasquale and Niccolò chased after the soldiers as best they could. City militia in red and white hose, polished breastplates over white tunics, steel caps on their heads, were trying to block the high narrow door of the Palazzo with their pikes, but with little success; Pasquale and Niccolò were not the only ones who wanted to know what was happening. They pushed in with dozens of others, into the cold echoing cortile.

More soldiers, the Pope's Swiss Guards, were pushing a wedge through the crowd. Men were flung out of the way; an officer barked an order and the soldiers cocked their pikes with a rattle of ratchets and held them forward, fingers on the catch-releases. People scrambled backwards, falling over each other; fired at close range, a pike-head could go clean through a man.

Pasquale pulled Niccolò around a pillar just as the Pope appeared. He was bareheaded, in a white cope that fell in generous folds around his bulky body. Servants liveried in black velvet supported him on either side. A flock of red-hatted, scarlet-robed cardinals trailed behind, amongst a rabble of servants. Screams and shouts, a tremendous tramping of boots, soldiers clashing their pikes as they came to attention. The Pope swept past, so close that Pasquale could see the beads of sweat on his blue jowls, and then he was gone, through the narrow door into the night.

Niccolò snagged a councillor at the end of the procession; the man struggled in a moment of panic before he recognized Niccolò and relaxed. 'I can't talk to you here!' he said loudly.

Niccolò spoke directly into the man's face with a quiet firm intensity. 'You can tell me what happened at least, my friend.'

The councillor blurted, 'Murder! Murder, Niccolò!'

'Hardly the first time the Palazzo has seen blood shed.'

'Blood? No, no, it was poison. Right before the Pope himself. It is a miracle I am here to speak to you; my own glass was almost at my lips when he fell—'

'Who was it?'

'We could all have been murdered! All of us! Any hope of alliance is done for. As for what will happen now—'

Niccolò grasped the lapels of the councillor's heavy fur-trimmed robes. The man goggled at him. His hat was askew; his face was white above his full black beard.

Niccolò said softly and urgently, 'Who was it?'

The councillor gathered himself together, shook off Niccolò's grip and straightened his robes and his hat with a kind of distracted dignity. 'Niccolò, old friend, please, for the sake of Christ keep clear of this. It is dark dark business, dark and terrible.'

'I want only to know who it is that was murdered.'

'The painter. The Pope's painter, Raphael. He made a toast to the Pope and drank, and we were about to follow him when he clutched his throat and fell. Horrible, horrible! There, I've already said too much and will say no more. Take care, my friend. Don't even dip a finger in these waters. My advice is to get off the streets at once. Go home. There'll be a terrible reckoning this night – if we're lucky, that will end it. If not—' The councillor had been looking around as he talked. Suddenly he shouted to an officer of the militia, shook off Niccolò's hand and hurried away, two soldiers falling in behind him.

'We must go up there,' Niccolò said.

'Then Raphael was involved after all!'

'Perhaps, perhaps.' Niccolò looked drawn, suddenly looked every one of his fifty years. 'Stay close to me, Pasquale. Help me as you can. I've always tried to see things as they are, not as they ought to be. Christ knows that I will need all of that ability now. If I'm right, this little conspiracy into which we have fallen has spread further than it should. Those in wise council see only a small part of it, and may mistake it for something worse than it is.'

Soldiers barred the way to the grand staircase, grim-faced behind their closed visors. Niccolò hailed a clerkly man, who shook his hand and began to repeat the story of poison. 'I need to see,' Niccolò said. 'I believe it less worse than it is.'

The clerk said, 'They have precipitately hanged the assassin,

Niccolò. There's no way to put his corpse to the question, and besides, you're not the man to do it. Go home.'

'You're the second person to tell me that. It makes me more determined.'

'No one can go up there, Niccolò. I certainly can't, so please, don't ask me.'

The soldiers parted to let two or three people up the staircase. Pasquale recognized one and called to him. The boy, Baverio, turned and stared. He was dressed in the same dark green tunic and breeches as before. His face was quite white, as if powdered with chalk, and his eyes were red-rimmed and wet.

Pasquale quickly explained what Niccolò wanted. Baverio shook his head and said, 'The man who killed my master is dead, and nothing can hurt my master now.'

'Raphael's name must still be defended. Please, Baverio. For the sake of your master's name. You helped me before, and I remember and am grateful. This one more time.'

The boy bit his lip. 'Yet you have not found out why poor Giulio was killed. And now my master is dead, and Giovanni Francesco has disappeared.'

Pasquale could not tell the boy that Francesco too was dead. 'It is all a piece, Baverio. We see only a few parts of the picture. We must see the rest to understand it.'

'If it will help, then follow me.'

The boy, after speaking with his companions, led Pasquale and Niccolò past the soldiers and up the stairs. He explained that Raphael had been struck as if with apoplexy after making a toast at the serving of the fifth course of the feast. The Pope's own physician had rushed to his aid but in vain, except to say that it was poisoned wine.

Baverio said steadily, 'Two of my friends rushed from the room and caught the wine steward, looped a cord around his neck and threw him out of the window. A soldier who ran in at the cry of murder helped them. I was not there, Pasquale, and I should have been. If I had tasted the wine first my master would not be dead.' Tears stood in his eyes, and he tipped his head back so that they wouldn't run and spoil his powdered cheeks.

'There's no end to what might have been,' Pasquale told the boy. 'What's important here is the truth of what has happened.'

The feast had been held in the Hall of Victory of the Republic, the big high-ceilinged room at the heart of the Palazzo della Signoria. Two long tables ran down the room, and a third was set across the head of these, beneath the fan of stairs that led up to the balcony. The tables were strewn with dishes and bowls of food, fine fluted glasses, silver spoons and knives. Burning forests of candles filled the room with heat and steady light. Pasquale gaped at the frenzied glory of Michelangelo's gigantic friezes of the war against Rome and her allies, the Battle of Cascina on one wall, the Florentine victory at Anghiari at the other, where the Great Engineer's armoured turtles had marched through the enemy lines, and multi-barrelled cannon had decimated what was left of their ranks. Then he remembered himself and hurried after Niccolò and Baverio, towards the knot of people gathered at the end table, where the canopied papal throne stood.

Raphael's body lay under a heavy tapestry someone had torn from the wall. Niccolò bent and gently uncovered the face. There was foam on the blue lips; the eyes were closed by silver florins. Niccolò looked up at the men around him and asked who was the physician. When a handsome grey-haired man stepped forward and bowed and said he had that honour, Niccolò said, 'How quick was this?'

'It was very quick, thank Christ, or there would be many more dead. It struck at his lungs – you see here the foam and the cyanosis of the lips – and it paralysed his breathing. He was clawing at his throat, then suffered an apoplectic fit. He would have known only a little pain before dying.'

'A strong poison, then.'

'Obviously, signor.'

'Administered in the wine?'

'His glass is here. Raphael knocked it over when he fell, so the wine is spilled, but I have tested the spill and found poison. A miracle, as I say, that Raphael drank before anyone else.'

'He made a toast,' Baverio said. 'He was a loyal friend to His Holiness, and it has killed him.'

The captain of the Palazzo Guard said, 'The wine steward was responsible for testing for poison. Instead, he must have stirred poison into the wine himself.'

'It was not friendship that killed him,' Niccolò said, 'nor was it the wine, I think.' He peered at the black stain left by the test on the heavy linen table-cloth, then took the fallen glass by its foot, sniffed it, and said, 'It is subtle. You have not tested the glass.'

'What need? The wine—'

'If you would, signor. The rim of the glass, but carefully. Perhaps someone else will fetch the wine that was served.'

The captain of the Guard said, 'The wine steward is already executed.'

'Yes,' Niccolò said with asperity, 'but they did not fling out his wine with his body. Bring me what was served here at the high table.'

The physician exclaimed, and held up the glass. The poison-specific stain had left its black deposit around the gold band at the rim of the glass.

'Well,' Niccolò said, looking pleased. 'Here we have it. It is a long time since I have had the honour of attending one of these feasts, but I do seem to recall that new glasses are set out with the serving of each wine. I fear that the wrong man has been accused and tried and executed. It was not the wine that was poisoned, but the glass.'

The physician said, 'Surely the glass shows a positive trace because it was in contact with the poisoned wine.'

'Ah, but not a trace like that, signor. If the glass was contaminated by the wine it held, then the trace would be evenly spread over the inside surface. Here, though, we see the trace is in a distinct ring, a very narrow ring, around the inside. This poison – is it a contact poison, or must it be ingested?'

'It would not pass through the skin unless there was a cut or a wound, if that's what you mean.'

'That's precisely what I mean,' Niccolò said, his eyes gleaming with excitement. He was possessed by the spirit of inquiry. 'Here is how it fell out. The assassin would have known that there would be checks for poison in the kitchen, and by the head stewards, before food or wine was served. So he smeared poison on his finger and wiped his finger around the edge of the glass before setting it before poor Raphael. You can see the break in the ring where Raphael sipped, and took the poison on to his lips. We will haul up the body of the wine steward, and test his fingers for poison. I am sure that it will test negative. Ah, now here is the wine. Have we a clean glass?'

Niccolò poured a generous measure, then downed it in one. People around him gasped. He smiled. 'You see. I am unharmed. The wine was not poisoned – indeed, it would be a mortal sin to pollute this fine vintage. No, it was Raphael's glass that was poisoned, quite deliberately. This is not a general plot against the Pope and the good councillors of the Signoria, but a specific one, to murder poor Raphael.'

The captain of the Guard called up four of his men. To jeers from the crowd gathered in the square below, they hauled up the dead weight of the wine steward's body and laid it on the floor beneath the window from which it had been flung. The physician applied his stain to the dead man's fingers while Niccolò hummed tunelessly.

'There's no trace,' the physician said at last, creaking up from his knees.

Someone said, 'That only proves he did not contaminate himself.'

Niccolò said sharply, 'You would have him wear gloves? Where are they? Who would have set out the glasses, Captain?'

The man considered this gravely. 'No one specific, I would suppose. Any of the servants of the first table.'

'Then we will round them up and put them to the test! Pasquale, you can best help by comforting poor Baverio here.' Niccolò grasped Pasquale's shoulder and added in a whisper, 'Go with him, see what else you can find out. Perhaps Raphael was killed because he knew something.' He raised his voice. 'Captain, we will not find the assassin by tarrying here.'

When they had gone, and when the soldiers had removed the body of the unfortunate wine steward, Pasquale took Baverio in hand and had him sit at the end of one of the tables. Pasquale was hungry, but he couldn't bring himself to touch the fruit and bread piled in baskets of woven gold in the centre of the tables, not with Raphael's body still lying there on the floor at the far end of the huge candle-lit hall.

As if reading Pasquale's thoughts, Baverio suddenly said, 'We came for my master's body.'

'The soldiers will be back. Or I can go and look for them now, if you'd like.'

Baverio shook his head. 'Signor Machiavegli will find who killed him?'

'We'll help you, if you'll let us.'

'Is this to do with the glass I gave you?'

'Yes, yes I think so.' Pasquale could not put off the moment any longer. 'Baverio, we saw Giovanni Francesco murdered. He too was poisoned, by a choking vapour.'

Baverio's face was chalk-white, but his voice was steady. 'I knew that he was dead. When he did not come back this morning, I knew it, and so did my master. That was why he was determined to speak out.'

'If there is something that your master knew, can you tell me what it was?'

'He would only say that it was to do with a secret of your Great Engineer. He believed that Giulio Romano was being blackmailed in some way, which was why poor Giulio took the little devices, the flying toy and the box and its glass, although that last secret is no longer a secret, of course, not after tonight. But he did not know that Giovanni Francesco was also involved.' Baverio looked down the length of the candlelit room, to where Raphael's body lay under its tapestry shroud, looked back at Pasquale, his eyes brimming with tears. 'My poor master, Pasquale! He cared so much for his assistants!'

'Do you know why Romano was being blackmailed? Was it the usual?'

'The usual?'

'Well,' Pasquale said, thinking of Signora Giocondo, 'I mean an involvement with a married woman.'

'Oh, no! Nothing like that. My master . . . but I won't speak of that.'

There was a silence. Pasquale prompted the boy, 'And Romano?'

'My master thought that he had been involved in a commission to produce . . . a certain kind of art. You know the kind.'

'Stiffeners, you mean. Hardly a matter of honour, I would have thought.' Pasquale thought at once of the picture he had rescued from Giustiniani's grate – he supposed that it was a kind of stiffener, if your tastes ran to blasphemy.

'I didn't ever see what it was,' Baverio said, 'but I know that it was something different, something more real than the usual woodcuts or engravings. My master saw something of it, and said it was a perversion of art in every sense. I think that the glass I gave you was something to do with it.'

139

'How so?'

'It is the great secret that the Great Engineer revealed this night. A way of registering light and shadows. His assistants brought into this room bright lights and a larger version of the box I found amongst Giulio's possessions. All present at the first table, the Pope and my master and members of the Signoria, had to pose stiffly before it. *Taking a picture*, the Great Engineer called it.'

Pasquale thought of the glass plate blackened by some chemical process, and then of the picture he'd rescued from the fire, the strange shadowy picture. Shadow art, art of shadows . . . Dr Pretorious had said that the artificers would put the artists out of business, although this business of simply capturing a likeness of a scene could hardly be the full answer. Even if it could be done, it would be no more than simple reality. There would be no narrative, no grace, none of the dense allusive symbolism by which paintings gave contentment and pleasure and glory to God.

He started to ask Baverio about this, but even as he began to speak a strange dull tremor shook the floor. Knives and glasses jingled along the tables; candle-flames bobbed. As Pasquale and Baverio looked at each other with wild surmise a tremendous clamour was raised somewhere outside the hall. A moment later the captain of the Guard ran in with his soldiers at his heels, and shouted that they must leave.

Baverio started to say something about his master's body, that he was here to take it away. His voice rose in panic, and the captain slapped his face and said with a hysteria hardly more controlled than the boy's, 'No time for that, you fool. We are under attack. Your master's safe enough lying there – he won't be going anywhere.'

Pasquale was hauled to his feet by two soldiers; Baverio by two more. As they were marched towards the door which opened on to the great staircase there was a thunderclap in the balcony that ran above the far end of the room. The windows there blew in with a crash of glass, followed by a tremendous outpouring of smoke.

The captain began to shout about fire, but then the acrid stench of rotting geraniums reached Pasquale. His eyes and nose stung and watered, and he knew at once who was responsible for this.

The soldiers holding Pasquale began to choke. He twisted out of their grip, clapped one hand over nose and mouth, caught Baverio's sleeve with the other, and dragged him through the door.

At the bottom of the staircase, the cortile was filling with the choking orange vapour, and a panicky throng of soldiers and clerks and bystanders were pushing and shoving as they all tried to get out at once. Pasquale kept hold of Baverio's sleeve in the crush as the crowd carried them along – then they were outside, in the cold black torchlit night.

Pasquale, dragging Baverio with him, found shelter in the lee of the ceremonial platform that jutted out from the Palazzo. Half his mind, caught up in the crowd's fear, believed that anything could happen, at any moment; the other half, the rational half, coldly observed, with an epicurean particularity, that it was indeed a kind of magic that could make people suddenly distrust the very skin of things they'd previously thought of as solid and unchangeable. He wondered where Niccolò was.

Overhead, orange smoke was pouring out of windows on the second floor of the Palazzo. The Great Engineer's cosmic engine lay wrecked, its lower half blown apart and on fire from the oil spilled from the smashed lanterns of its central sun. Bodies lay around it, reduced to bloody rags. Some cried out, feebly stirring in pools of their own blood. People ran here and there, soldiers amongst them as panicked as the rest. From the crenellated roof of the Palazzo burning rockets shot down into the square with keening howls and whistles, trailing great tails of sparks, striking paving-stones and bursting with sharp thundercracks or skittering off amongst the legs of the mob. And here and there masked men on stilts strode about, tossing little glass globes that burst into clouds of orange smoke. The very air was alive and inimical, stinging the skin of the face, making eyes and nose water. It was altogether a scene out of one of the paintings of that school of Flemish artists who delighted in depicting the grotesqueries of Hell.

A soldier fired his pike at one of the stilt-men – the pike-head went wide and flew straight across the square and struck Berni's light-cannon, smashing the armature of its lenses. The patterns on the façade of the bank froze around a blurred white web. Another soldier whirled his mace-net around his head and flung it, entangling the legs of one of the stilt-men, who crashed to the paving-stones and erupted in thick jets of vapour that jerked his body this way and that: a cache of gas-bombs, letting go all at once. The mob surged back from this new horror.

Baverio broke from Pasquale's grip and ran across the square in the direction of the Great Engineer's tower, which loomed above the turmoil, its lights as remote as stars. Pasquale screamed after Baverio and ran too, dodging amongst people running in every direction.

A stilt-man stalked forward to intercept him, blowing hard on a toy trumpet. He was unmasked, with a narrow white face and a shock of red hair. Pasquale changed direction, running now not after Baverio but to save himself, running hard towards the narrow passage at the side of the Loggia. The red-headed stilt-man lobbed a gas-bomb that blocked the way. He was laughing wildly, enjoying this sport. Pasquale turned again, and saw, above the heads of the crowd, two more stilt-men swiftly picking their way towards him in one direction, and a coach and pair galloping at full tilt towards him from another. The coach bore the crest of the house of Taddei.

Before Pasquale could make a run towards the coach, the shadows of the pair of stilt-men loomed over him. Pasquale yelled defiantly. The nearest bent towards him – and then arrows sprouted on his chest and he staggered back, blundering into his companion. The coach swung past, its pair of white horses tossing their heads. The carriage door banged open and a man leaned out and caught Pasquale around the waist and drew him in, just as the mortally wounded stilt-man toppled and exploded.

5

The Palazzo Taddei was busy with men coming and going even at the late hour, past midnight, when Pasquale and Baverio arrived. As soon as they climbed down from the carriage, Baverio was taken off in one direction, and a page led Pasquale in another. Pasquale, excited and curious, and certainly in no condition to sleep after his close brush with the stilt-men, followed readily enough. He was taken inside to see Taddei himself, who was holding an audience in the great hall on the first floor of the Palazzo, listening to a report from a sergeant-at-arms of the militia.

Taddei was sitting in a high-backed chair near the cavernous fire-place, his jowly, pugnacious face lit on one side by the crowns of hissing acetylene lamps that hung from the ceiling, on the other by the shuddering light of the fire. He wore a richly brocaded robe, and a turban embroidered with gold thread. His eyes were half closed as he listened to the sergeant's stuttering account of a riot in the workers' quarter across the river. His secretary sat at a table beside him, taking down the sergeant's words. On the other side of the fireplace sat a thin young man clad in black, and a cardinal in scarlet robes and a red skullcap, both listening keenly.

The sleepless manufactories had shut down, it seemed, because the workers, the *ciompi*, had left their labours and were looting and burning their way through the commercial district which served their impoverished quarter. Pasquale realized that the point of the report was the defence by a detachment of the city militia of a warehouse owned by Taddei.

The sergeant concluded, 'Those scum will burn their own houses in their rage, but if we are lucky they won't think or wish to turn to the factories or warehouses, or cross the bridges. They know that if they do, they will have to face mercenary troops as well as us, and I do not think that they have the stomach for a real fight.'

The cardinal leaned forward. He was a spry handsome man of some forty years, with lank black hair cut in a fringe, a long straight ncse, and a heavy-lidded gaze with which he fixed the soldier. A big jewelled cross on a heavy gold chain rested on his chest. 'Be assured that they will try the bridges. The Savonarolistas are behind that riot, of that we can be certain.'

The sergeant said in a nervous rush, 'Begging your pardon, your eminence, but even the Savonarolistas, of which I admit to having seen no sign, would be hard put to lead this many-headed mob. The *ciompi* aren't led at all, not this time. They have no cause, but are rioting for the sake of it, every man for himself, taking what he can and burning the rest. They live like animals, and so they behave.'

The cardinal wore rings on every finger of his hands, and he rolled these back and forth on the carved arm of his chair with contained impatience as the sergeant spoke. Now he said, 'The Savonarolistas will show their hand soon enough. They have been much abroad recently, amongst your manufactory workers.'

'That's true enough,' Taddei said. 'One was discovered in my weaving-sheds only a month ago. He was disguised as a loom operator, and was preaching sedition amongst the other workers. I had him flogged to the city wall and back, and thrown in jail, and sacked all the workers on that shift. But where there is one, there are others, if not in my warehouses or manufactories, then in those of my less careful friends and associates.'

The sergeant said, 'Signor Taddei, I ask for your recommendation.'

'I'll pay for guards on all my manufactories and warehouses. You know the arrangements, and I know they will be acceptable to you. Go now, Sergeant, you have a long night ahead of you.'

'Signor,' the sergeant said steadfastly, 'if the Savonarolistas are involved, I may be ordered to help guard the bridges.'

The young man in black said sarcastically, 'If you have to defend the bridges, they won't be attacking the manufactories, will they?' This fellow was hardly older than Pasquale, with a mop of tousled blond hair and a face as keen as a knife-blade, his hollow cheeks hectic with acne. His left hand was tucked beneath the bend of his knee, thumb and forefinger working on the ligament there.

'You'll do your best to make sure that those orders never reach you,' Taddei told the sergeant. 'I'm sure a man used to being rewarded so well can manage a small task like that.'

The sergeant said slowly, 'If the worst comes to the worst, we can always dispose of any messengers, make it look like rebel work . . .'

'I don't want to know about *how* you'll do it,' Taddei said with distaste, and turned to his secretary. 'Marchetto, you won't write that down. I'll have no part in sedition.'

'No visible part,' the young man said, with a humourless smile.

'No part,' Taddei repeated firmly. 'Go to your work, Sergeant. We'll pray for you.'

The sergeant saluted and marched out, and Taddei smiled at Pasquale as if he had seen him for the first time. 'Come here, boy! Come along. Perhaps you can tell us more of these matters, and enlighten my friend here. This is the boy I told you about,' he added, turning to the cardinal.

The cardinal lifted a pair of spectacles, shaped like the handles of scissors, to his eyes. He peered at Pasquale for a long moment. 'Ah, the apprentice of Giovanni Rosso. I have a small painting by Rosso's master, Andrea del Sarto. An old-fashioned piece, but it gives me pleasure.'

Pasquale said eagerly, 'I have learnt many things from my master, and from Piero di Cosimo, too. Perhaps you saw the drawings of the scene of Giulio Romano's murder – those were my own engravings. I am also skilled in all kinds of drawing, especially silverpoint, and in all aspects of the painting of frescos, and of any kind of picture your eminence might require. At this moment I am engaged in the painting of an angel the like of which has never been seen before—'

The cardinal said, 'How I wish I was here to discuss painting.'

'If it please your eminence, perhaps he would at least accept this token of my skill.' Pasquale unfastened the emblem of the Florentine lily which he had pinned to his black serge jerkin – its gold-foil loops were a little crushed by his adventures, but it still shone with a fine buttery lustre – and held it out. He wondered if he should kiss the cardinal's ring. He had never met a cardinal before, after all, and knew vaguely that you should kiss the Pope's foot – there had been a small scandal some time ago, when it was discovered that Leo X, when he went hunting, wore thigh-length soft leather boots which made kissing his foot impossible. Certain broadsheets had commented that the Medicis were corrupting the Holy See for their own convenience, just as they had once corrupted the government of Florence.

The cardinal took the little brooch and twirled it between his long white fingers. 'If only I could wear this openly,' he said, 'I would be the happiest man in the world.'

Taddei made a gesture, and the page-boy brought a stool. Pasquale sat, and found that he had to look up at the others.

Taddei explained, 'This young man has been involved with the inquiries of Niccolò Machiavegli into the murder of Giulio Romano. He was rescued from the Palazzo della Signoria this night, and brought straight here.' He said to Pasquale, 'I must suppose that you were with Signor Machiavegli, investigating Raphael's murder.'

'Well, that's true,' Pasquale said. He was not sure just how much he should admit, but that seemed safe enough.

The cardinal said, 'I had believed Machiavegli reduced to a petty journalist, a poor enough occupation for a man of his talent. This news heartens us. Do the members of the Signoria relish the thought of having him involved in matters of state once more?'

'I do not believe they are much aware of it,' Taddei said. 'I engaged Machiavegli myself, for the private matter of investigating the death of poor Giulio Romano. His murder—'

'Yes, yes. I heard all of that sorry tale from Raphael, not an hour before he himself was murdered. I had not believed that Florence was so dangerous. But I did not know that Machiavegli was investigating these matters. A provocative choice,' the cardinal said, 'and one that pleases us greatly. We have always considered Machiavegli to be supportive of our family.'

With a soft sinking shock Pasquale realized who the cardinal was: Giulio de' Medici, the Pope's cousin. He wondered what he had fallen into. Of course, Signor Taddei was a good friend of Raphael's, and so would know the Pope, but Pasquale was beginning to understand that nothing was simple in these circles. As in a painting, where every object is not only itself but also its allegorical meaning, so here each action had a sinister shadow.

Taddei said to Pasquale, 'I see that you recognize my illustrious guest. Be assured that he is a friend of Florence.'

'I do not doubt that any friend of yours is a friend of Florence, signor,' Pasquale said.

Taddei said, 'I must also introduce Girolamo Cardano, a mathema-

146

tician, and more germane to the matter at hand, a scientist of natural magic and my personal astrologer.'

The young man in black, Cardano, shifted on his seat with a grimace. He said, 'In my opinion, Machiavegli is a summer soldier, a competent playwright, a no more than ordinary poet, and a failed servant of the state. He's not to be trusted. Even his friends say that, for love of this city, he has pissed in many a snow. But then you never take my opinions into account when you act.'

'On the contrary, my dear Girolamo,' Taddei said, 'there's always a good deal of truth in what you say. But the thing of it is that Machiavegli has a fascination with problems and riddles. A problem can possess him and consume his entire attention if it is sufficiently complex, and I believe that this problem has indeed possessed him. He needs no commission from me, now. It has become his life.' Taddei's forthright gaze bore down on Pasquale. 'Tell us about his investigation, my boy. More to the point, tell us where he is now. My men could not find him, or he would be here with you.'

'In truth, signor, I would wish that he was here with us too, for I do not know where he is, and I greatly fear for him. I saw him last at the Palazzo della Signoria. He left with the captain of the Guard to question the servants who had been in attendance when Raphael was assassinated, after he discovered that it was not the wine steward who poisoned Raphael.'

Pasquale told of what had fallen out at the Palazzo della Signoria, speaking mostly to Taddei, but with sidelong glances at the cardinal. When he was done, he realized that the page had appeared at his side, holding out a gold tray on which stood a jewelled beaker of wine. He drank gratefully, and at once the rich wine's fumes invaded his head, as if driven by the heat of the fire.

Girolamo Cardano shifted in his chair, with a sudden wince as if he'd been struck. Pasquale saw that his thumb and forefinger had closed, pincer-like, on the soft muscle under his knee, and that this self-chastisement had brought tears to his eyes. The young magician caught him looking and said with a sneer, 'Like Machiavegli, I need to be reminded of the failing of my body.'

Taddei said, amused, 'Niccolò Machiavegli drinks; Girolamo inflicts pain upon himself. He says that otherwise he is overcome by a certain mental anguish. He does not believe in himself, you see, unless he is subject to some small hurt.'

Cardano ignored this and said to Pasquale, 'You do not tell us why the stilt-men were pursuing you.'

'In truth, signor, I do not know why. It seemed to me that the stilt-men were attacking any of the crowd that took their attention.'

'He dissembles,' Cardano declared. With a languorous flick of his wrist, he pulled a white mask as if from thin air, held it up so that its angles flashed in the light of the fire. He tossed it to Pasquale, who caught it by reflex. It had triangular black-rimmed cut-outs for eyes, and black ribbons to tie it around the wearer's head. The ribbons were stiff with dry blood.

'A Venetian carnival mask, taken from one of the men on stilts,' the astrologer said. 'What would you have us know of Venetians, painter?'

'Nothing more than what you already seem to know.'

Cardano made another languid gesture, and held up a little box. It was covered in black leather, and the astrologer flicked a hinged slide that covered a pinhole opening at one end. Pasquale knew at once what it was: Baverio had described it well.

Signor Taddei said, not unkindly, 'We found this amongst poor Giulio Romano's possessions.'

'There's something missing,' Cardano said. 'You have it, I believe.'

Pasquale discovered that he was sweating hard, although he felt as if he was bathed in ice. 'It was only a piece of glass, covered in some black stuff.'

He could see it quite clearly. It lay on a pile of papers on Niccolò's writing-table, with the flying device resting beside it.

'Ah,' Cardano said, 'exposed, then. If we are to believe you that is.'

'You can ask Raphael's page. It was he who entrusted it to me, out of the best of motives. He believed it would help me find Romano's murderer.'

'Hardly,' Cardano said. 'Where is it?'

Pasquale said, 'I do not have it.' Signor Taddei's uplifted eyebrow compelled him to confess, 'I gave it to Niccolò, to Signor Machiavegli. If you please, I would know what it signified.'

'Something or nothing,' Cardano said. 'It depends what image it captured.'

Pasquale said, 'Then it was a kind of mirror magic.'

'More powerful and exact than that,' the astrologer said. 'This box throws an image on a coated glass plate, which captures it and is blackened to various degrees by various degrees of light. That plate you had may or may not have held an image, but it had not been treated to make it insensitive to light. That's why it turned black when it was exposed. Don't tell me that you are ignorant of the process, painter. You shouldn't be: it will be the end of your profession.'

'I have heard of such things,' Pasquale said.

Taddei said, 'The Great Engineer decided to reveal his invention once he realized that a spy had discovered it. With a masterly stroke, he did so by making a likeness of the Pope and his immediate entourage.'

'It is a very slow process,' the cardinal said. 'How Leo complained! We had to sit still for a full two minutes, and Leo had to rest his head in a brace devised by the Great Engineer, for any movement would blur the image.'

Pasquale suddenly understood the true nature of the charred picture in his scrip. It was no drawing, but a true image, a residue of something that had really happened. Giustiniani had posed for it, out of monstrous pride or arrogance, and Francesco had tried to bribe him with a copy. But if this was an invention of the Great Engineer's, how had Raphael's assistants come by it? Had Salai given it to them? And if so, for what purpose?

In answer to these questions, which tumbled one upon the other in Pasquale's brain, Taddei said, 'One of these devices was taken from the Great Engineer's workshops. It seems that Romano was a spy.'

The cardinal said, 'Not for Rome, despite his name. It seems that Giulio Romano had been promised advancement and employment in return for the smallest of favours. He was not a disloyal man, but was beginning to believe that he had laboured too long in Raphael's shadow. The court of Spain offered him a position there, if he performed certain tasks. But poor Romano was an innocent, killed once he had learnt what his masters needed to know, or so we believe.'

For a moment, Pasquale thought that he was falling into the sudden silence of the long firelit room. He said to Taddei, 'And you set us to the task of finding the murderer, knowing this?'

Taddei protested. 'I knew nothing until tonight. I learnt it from a message from which arrived only moments before you did. It would seem that whoever has taken Raphael's body wishes to exchange it for you, young man.'

'Was this message sent by Giustiniani?'

'It was sent anonymously. It told of Romano's betrayal, and asked that you be delivered to the south side of the Ponte Vecchio at a certain time. Why do you suspect Giustiniani?'

'I saw a man killed at his villa,' Pasquale said.

Cardano leaned forward. 'That would be the missing man, Giovanni Francesco. It would explain all. It seems that Francesco was an accomplice of Romano, and it may be that he killed Romano to win all the glory for himself. In any event, he was killed in turn because he failed in his task.'

Pasquale decided not to tell them about the picture of the black mass, or of the flying device, or of Francesco's attempt at blackmail. It could well be that Francesco was Romano's killer – Romano would certainly have opened the door of the signal-tower to him – but it was unlikely that Francesco could have cleaned himself of Romano's blood in the short time between Romano's dying cry and the search which it immediately started. And even if Francesco was Romano's murderer, why would he have gone to treat with Giustiniani? Surely he would have first tried to win back the box – it was in Taddei's possession, and so within reach – and he would also have taken the flying device from Romano. For the moment, exhausted and more than a little drunk from the heady wine, Pasquale couldn't unriddle it. He wished that he could benefit from Niccolò's sharp, clear insight . . . and with a pang realized that he might never see him again. Giustiniani's men could have killed him in the confusion at the Palazzo della Signoria.

Taddei said, 'You had better explain to us, Pasquale, just what happened at Giustiniani's villa.'

When Pasquale had finished, omitting any mention of blackmail, there was a silence. Finally the cardinal said, 'It pains us to hear how badly things have fallen out here. My cousin was thinking of presenting Raphael with a commission to complete the chapel which Michelangelo has left unfinished for so long.'

'There's no doubt that Giustiniani was the broker in Romano's compact with Spain,' Taddei said, 'and would be still if he could. That is why his men tried to capture this boy. But Raphael's assassination is the kind of devilry the Savonarolistas might use in their clandestine war. Suddenly it appears that we are playing a three-handed game here.'

The cardinal said, 'Raphael's body must be returned. For all that my family love Florence, my cousin cannot avoid war if he returns to Rome without it.'

'Raphael was a guest of this city,' Taddei told Pasquale. 'That he was murdered is bad enough, although it can be excused as a Savonarolista plot. But that his body was taken and Florence cannot return it . . . There will in truth be war between Rome and Florence if it is not returned. And with the alliance broken, Spain will win all. It is well known that she will not be content with the south of Italy, but would rule all, and our colonies in the New World as well. The Spanish fleet has been standing off the coast this past week, and no doubt will land as soon as the alliance fragments into war. They have been funding the Savonarolistas for so long, and at last the unrest they have sought is coming about.'

Pasquale said, 'Surely no one will attack Florence. We are defended by the genius of the Great Engineer, whose inventions defeated the armies of Rome and Venice after the assassination of Lorenzo.'

The cardinal said, 'How ironic that Lorenzo's son may have to make war on Florence because of this sorry affair.'

Taddei told Pasquale, 'All states are now armed with similar weapons, copied from the originals that Florence has first used, and in many cases improving upon them. All governments have their rocket cannon, their mobile armoured shields, their Greek fire and the rest. If the Great Engineer has invented new weapons, then he has kept them secret even from the Signoria.'

Cardano said, 'He is an old man. It is said that he is crazy, and obsessed with escaping a deluge that will end the world. What Spain hoped to learn I do not know, but in the end two men are dead for an invention which is of no use in war, and which in any case has now been revealed to all the world.'

'You know that I saw your Great Engineer today,' the cardinal said. 'I will say that he seemed to have withdrawn from everything around him. He spoke not at all, and did not once look at the marvel of his cosmic engine, while his assistants worked to capture my cousin's likeness with no word or order from him.'

'He has not invented anything for a long time,' Cardano said. 'As his university has grown, so his own powers of invention have dwindled.'

Taddei said, 'Nevertheless, this misadventure threatens the very existence of the Republic, and its renewed alliance with Rome.'

The cardinal nodded, suddenly grave. Cardano was staring at Pasquale with a dark intensity, his lower lip caught between his teeth.

Taddei said to Pasquale, 'Understand that we do this out of dire need.'

'It's nothing personal,' Cardano added.

There was a crash of armour; a dozen soldiers passed through the arch of the door at the far end of the room, marching in quickstep. Cardano drew a slim short sword and Pasquale sprang to his feet and lifted the stool to parry the blow. A second swing knocked the sword from the astrologer's hand. The weapon flew the length of the Persian carpet and Pasquale ran and snatched it up and turned to face the soldiers, flicking it from point to point to keep them at bay.

For a moment, only the soft sounds of the fire.

Then a corporal made a sweeping movement and his pincer mace shot forward. Its toothed maw gripped the top of Pasquale's head and his left shoulder. Pain lived between these points, pure as light.

The corporal twisted his weapon. Stone smashed into Pasquale's hip, his back. The sword fell from his hand, ringing on the flagstones. His body was numb. He was looking up at the white vaults of the ceiling. At each of the bosses of the ceiling's vaults a gilded putto, with round cheeks and a rosebud mouth, smiled down. A shadow fell across Pasquale. Cardano bent and gently pressed a reeking cloth to his nose and mouth.

6

The vaporous liquid which soaked the cloth did not put Pasquale entirely to sleep. It was as if he were hovering at the border of dreaming and waking, might again be in his truckle bed in the narrow little room of the studio he shared with Rosso and the Barbary ape, nursing the dull pain of a hangover and easing into day. He felt motion, and dreamed, or thought he dreamed, that he was being carried swiftly on the back of a demon eagle, like the magician Gerbert, who had ridden a demon to save himself from the Inquisition and had lived to become Pope Sylvester II. The eagle turned its terrible horned face to him and with a flick of its wings tumbled him from its back. He tried to scream, but no words would come. A great mouth rushed at him, grinding its teeth as it opened and spat him out into night.

When Pasquale woke, it was to the jolting of a carriage. His head seemed cramped by a band of iron; his mouth was thoroughly coated with a foul sweet taste. He was lying on his belly on the carriage floor, slung lengthwise between benches where two soldiers sat. His hands were bound by a thin strong cord, and although his feet were free he did not yet have the energy or will to try and sit up, let alone stand.

The soldiers, as massive from his prone perspective as statues of Roman emperors, wore iron breastplates and helmets with an elongated beak and an upswept crest that broke into horns, the sort of fantastication loved by the Albanian mercenaries who were employed by private merchants to protect their wagon-trains. Taddei was making good his promise, then. Pasquale was being delivered as ransom for Raphael's corpse.

The coach rattled to a stop, and one of the mercenaries leaned out of the window – Pasquale heard the bang as he slid the shutter back, then felt a draught of cold air – and shouted something to the driver. With the cold air, which helped revive Pasquale's strength, came a diffuse sound like the roar of the sea, and a smell of burning.

The coach set off again, and the roar grew louder: men shouting; a random peppering of shots; screams. The carriage stopped again. One of the mercenaries was talking to someone, saying look, look, here was the pass, here was the seal of the Ten. The carriage door swung open, doubling the roar of the mob. A ray of lantern-light shot into the interior. Rough hands dragged Pasquale to a sitting position; just in time, he remembered to close his eyes. Let them think him unconscious.

The first mercenary said, 'This is the piece of shit we have to deliver across the river.'

'And by tonight,' the second mercenary said.

A third, Florentine-accented voice said, 'You'll have to do the best you can, but you won't get across this bridge, or any other.'

The first mercenary said, 'It must be this bridge, Captain. We have important business at the other end. Here, it says we can ask for your help.'

The captain said, 'I'm giving you my advice. It is all I have.'

'Then keep it,' the second mercenary said, 'and give us a few men instead.'

'You'll need a fucking army to get through that mob,' the captain said, 'and I can't spare even one man.'

'It says—'

'I can read it,' the captain said sharply, 'which is more than you can. Bring me the man who wrote it and I might listen to you. Instead, I'll tell you what you can do, and that's turn this carriage around and try and get a ferry-boat across the river down by Sardinia. The seal on that piece of paper might possibly impress some poor oarsman.'

The second mercenary said, 'We report you, when we return. I remember your face.'

'You do that. Meanwhile, turn around and get off the bridge. Anyone trying to force a way through that mob will only inflame them further. Try a ferry. If you have no luck with your bit of paper you can always steal the boat. That's what you mercenaries are good at, isn't it?'

Both mercenaries swore at the captain, fluently and inventively, and the man laughed. Then there was a rattle of steel in the distance, a great shout and the captain shouted, 'Now you see why you must turn back! Turn back right now!' A cannon boomed out close by and the carriage rolled forward a pace as its horses started.

The carriage door slammed so hard the vehicle rocked. Pasquale allowed himself to be laid back on the floor and risked opening an eye as the two mercenaries argued in their own guttural language. Firelight flickering on the roof of the carriage, a glimpse of heads moving past outside the window. Then the horned helmet of one of the mercenaries blocked the view as the man leaned out of the window and shouted to the driver to get on. The driver must have argued, because the mercenary swore and shouted that they must reach the far end of the bridge, to go, go now, go now at a gallop!

The carriage lurched forward so abruptly Pasquale rolled against the boots of the mercenaries, who kicked him back as one might roll a log, bruising his hips and shoulders. Blows thundered on the sides of the carriage; a window was punched in with a sharp clatter. The carriage rocked as the blows doubled and redoubled; then the carriage gained speed.

Shots, thunderous in the small space. The mercenaries were crouched at either window and firing pistols through them at a rapid rate. Pasquale started to sit up, feeling an airy panic, and one of the soldiers cried out and fell backwards, sprawling across him.

Pasquale felt the man's hot blood soaking his tunic. He writhed beneath the dead weight and groped for the man's belt with his bound hands, but could find no knife. Then the weight shifted and the first mercenary lifted him by the hair so that he howled as he was dragged from the carriage into noisy firelit night.

They were on the Ponte Vecchio. It looked like the gateway to Hell. Shops burned in unison on either side, their roofs fallen in, flames leaping high and sparks whirling higher. Broken acetylene lanterns spat hissing geysers of yellow flame. The far end of the bridge was crowded with men, their faces red-lit by fire, their eyes pinprick glints. Some capered on the parapet, or on the roofs of those shops not yet burned. A great ragged chanting came from them, and a rain of small missiles, visible only as they arced down through the firelight. Most passed over the carriage, but some struck the pavement around it, stones smacking with sharp thumps, bottles shattering. A corpse lay a few *braccia* away, and others were scattered up and down the roadway, indistinct bundles in the leaping firelight.

Shots plucked the air overhead – soldiers holding the barricade through which the carriage had driven were returning fire. Pasquale saw a man spin and topple from the parapet into the river below, any sound he might have made in his last fall lost in the howl of the mob.

On either side of the burning bridge, along the bank on either side, buildings burned too, squatting over their inverted reflections.

The mercenary wound his fingers in Pasquale's hair and jerked his head back. The mercenary said, 'Your bastard militia shot the driver and Luigi. You try and run and I shoot you. I shoot you dead.'

Pasquale's mouth was dry. He rubbed his tongue over his palate until saliva flowed and said, 'I think your master wants me alive.'

'I was told to deliver you to the other side of this bridge, that's all. Dead or alive makes no difference to me. But I think the soldiers back there want you alive, or they'd use their cannon on us, like they used on the mob to keep them back.'

'What would you have me do?'

The mercenary wrenched Pasquale's head again, and started to march him backwards. 'We're walking back there, and you tell them to guarantee safe passage across the river. Maybe they listen to a fine gentleman like you.'

Pasquale couldn't believe the fool, and laughed right in his face. The mercenary lost his temper and knocked Pasquale down. Pasquale saw his chance. He rolled under the carriage, scrambled to his feet on the other side, started to run towards the barricade, the only thing he could think to do, waving his bound hands above his head and shouting that he was kidnapped. Behind him, the howl of the mob doubled: it was surging forward. Little lights blinked and flickered amongst the militia behind the barricade; then the first bullets struck the paving-stones around Pasquale. One grazed the parapet and went whooping away into the darkness over the river.

Pasquale threw himself down and tried to make himself as small as possible. Incendiary quarrels rained down too, and where they struck the coach they started to burn. The mercenary suddenly sat down, clutching his pierced breastplate. Burning quarrels littered the paving-stones; horribly, one had set fire to a corpse, which in a hideous parody of life slowly writhed in the middle of a ball of orange flame and greasy smoke as the heat shrivelled its muscles.

A cannon boomed. Its round whistled overhead, skimmed the top of a burning shop and vanished into the darkness beyond. The mob retreated, men trampling their fallen fellows in panic. The two horses harnessed to the carriage stamped forward, eyes rolling, foam running from their mouths as they pulled against the brake.

Pasquale ran towards the carriage, for it was the only shelter on the bridge. With his hands crossed and bound, he couldn't use the grab-rail, but he got a foot in a bracket and kicked up. The driver slumped on the bench; Pasquale got blood on his hands when he untangled the reins from the dead man's grip. He kicked back the brake and flicked the reins across the horses' sweating backs and they promptly charged towards the mob. For an exhilarating moment, it seemed that Pasquale might succeed, but then the carriage smashed into an overturned velocipede which tangled in the spokes of the front wheels. The carriage slewed, its iron-bound wheels dragging rooster-tails of sparks from the paving-stones.

The horses stumbled, mad with panic because they were caught in a narrow corridor between burning buildings. Pasquale tried to haul on the reins, but had no strength left. The carriage slewed towards a burning butcher's shop and Pasquale jumped, rolling over and over.

As he staggered to his feet, two men ran at him from the mob. No, one was an ape. It was the Barbary ape, Ferdinand. It squatted a little way from Pasquale, gazing at him with brown, intelligent eyes. The man who caught hold of the ape's iron collar and grinned down at Pasquale was Giovanni Rosso.

7

As the mob surged forward, striking up their jeering chants again, Rosso squatted and cut the cord which bound Pasquale's wrists. Pain surged into Pasquale's fingers. Skin had been torn from every knuckle, and more pain came when he flexed his hands, fearful that he had broken bones.

He hadn't.

Rosso helped him through the dense-packed swirling mob. Pasquale had once spent a day watching the madmen stagger to and fro amongst the rocks and skinned carcasses of horses and mules at Sardinia, noting and sketching. Those same expressions surged around him now, from incoherent rage to slack-mouthed idiocy. Heat beat on either side from the burning butchers' shops. The smell of roasting meat was sickening. The light shaking above the writhing bodies of the mob was vermilion and cinnabar and gold. Sweat, the stink of smoke reaching back into the throat, the crisp noise of the fires. When the cannon boomed out almost everyone dropped to his knees, then slowly picked himself up and moved forward again.

'They could kill us all with one shot!' Pasquale shouted to his master.

'And smash the bridge, most likely,' Rosso shouted back. 'No, they're firing to let us know they can, angling shot over into the flood-channel where it's deepest. The time for killing hasn't come, not yet. They need orders for that.'

Pasquale's head was swimming, and it didn't seem in the least odd that his master should be here to help him. He asked, 'Where are we going?'

'Away from here. Before they do get orders to aim the cannon into the crowd and clear the bridge with chain-shot. Ever seen that? Pairs of small iron shot linked by a chain maybe a span apart. One will cut a man in two. They call them the Great Engineer's balls, because they will never engender a child.'

After Pasquale and Rosso reached the far end of the bridge, shouldering past opportunistic hawkers and their customers, they took the steep steps down to the New Walk that had been cantilevered out above the river not five years ago. It was a promenade much in favour with the artificers, who could look on the system of channels by which they had tamed the Arno, on the Great Tower in which the chief of their number lived, and the manufactories which had made them wealthy and powerful.

Rosso stopped, and made one of his grand gestures at the burning bridge a little way down-river. 'Don't you love this, Pasqualino? I'll paint such a picture as has never been painted before! Fire and black water and men baying for the blood of men! They have talked about my handling of highlights and shadow – I'll show them the true worth! If I find the right client it'll fetch four hundred florins at least!'

Pasquale had to smile. 'Master, only you would think of a commission in the midst of this. Are we to go much further?'

'What's wrong? Hurt your leg? Quite a tumble you took, although you handled it like an acrobat. Ah, Pasqualino, I never understood why you thought it was so wrong to try and better yourself. A man must be on the lookout for any opportunity. The trouble with us Tuscans is that we're too given over to frivolities of this sort, which is why we're afflicted with wretchedness and poverty.'

Pasquale began to laugh. It welled up from deep inside and would not stop. He laughed until he had to clutch the railing of the walkway to stay on his feet. The iron rail was hot under his hands.

Rosso said, 'Yes, I know how business amuses you. But a little more business and a little less dreaming, Pasqualino, and you would be a rich man. Look up-river! That will be the cloth manufactory of the merchant Taddei burning. See the colours that the dyes lend the flames!'

Pasquale said, 'I was with Signor Taddei not an hour ago.'

'Of course.'

'You know? Master, how do you know?'

Rosso said casually, 'I saw the insignia on the side of the carriage, of course.'

He called to the ape, Ferdinand, which was swinging idly on the rail. The creature swung down and ambled over, with a sailor's careless rolling gait. It put a hand on its master's thigh and looked up at him with beseeching eyes, and Rosso dropped a grape which it caught between its strong yellow teeth.

'Damn you,' Rosso told it affectionately, knuckling its bony brow, 'I should feed you something other than grapes. Grapes are your Eve's apples, and how you grin to show that you know it. Wicked wicked *wicked* fallen creature. You should not have taught him to steal, Pasquale. It was his undoing.'

Pasquale said, 'You are a part of it, master. Tell me it's true or I will go mad!'

Rosso was amused all over again. 'Tell me what you think is true, Pasqualino.'

'You knew Raphael's assistants. I remember now that you told me so much about them at the feast-day mass, but until now I didn't think about where you had learnt that gossip.'

'But surely you know how much I love gossip? Ah, Pasqualino, you have spent so much time with the famous journalist Niccolò Machiavegli that you see conspiracies everywhere, and no doubt Spain at the bottom of all of them.'

Pasquale shivered. He said, 'Would you have a cigarette, master?'

Rosso handed one over, stuck another in his own mouth, and lit both from his slow-match. Pasquale greedily drew cool smoke deep into his lungs. His hands were shaking so much he had trouble keeping the cigarette pinched between thumb and fingers. The cold night air stung his skinned knuckles. He said, 'It was in Niccolò Machiavegli's company that I saw you, although I did not recognize you at the time. It was in the gardens of the villa of the Venetian magician, Giustiniani. I think that you went there with your name-sake, Giovanni Francesco. Something had gone wrong with your plans after the murder of Giulio Romano. Perhaps he was the leader? Or something was stolen from him, that you were going to trade with the Venetian for the promise of new positions.'

'Something was stolen, perhaps. Or let us say taken by mistake.'

It was an admission that set Pasquale's heart racing. He said, 'If you mean the box which captures and fixes light, I no longer have it.'

'Ah, no. That was always ours. An experimental device, but one soon to become common knowledge. Raphael had been given one to try out – although he tired of it soon enough, and Giulio was able to put it to better use. More rewarding use, let us say for now. He wasn't murdered, Pasqualino, except if you count a ridiculous accident murder. Let us say for now he didn't die at another man's hands.'

Rosso's face, lit from one side by the burning bridge, looked amused and cruel and remote. He blew out a riffle of smoke between pursed lips. So Lucifer might look, at a foolish sinner's boasting, for Lucifer's crime was so great that it was beyond the measure of human sin, no matter how black the heart of the sinner – unless the artificers could mount a challenge on Heaven.

Pasquale said, 'I suppose that you know how Giulio Romano died, then, but you will not tell me.'

'I'm sure you'll work it out if you need to. But really it isn't important. Not poor Giulio's death, I mean, but the way he died.' Rosso pushed away from the rail and put an arm around Pasquale, pushed him forward. 'We have a little way still to go,' he said. 'Amuse me as we walk.'

'Well then,' Pasquale said doggedly. 'After Giulio's death you had to try a new tack, perhaps by threatening the Venetian magician. Instead, he murdered Francesco, and you fled with Ferdinand. I saw you both cross the lawn in moonlight. I thought that Ferdinand was a dwarf.'

'You're moving in strange circles, Pasqualino.'

'Stranger than you think, perhaps.'

'Taddei and his tame magician are hardly strange,' Rosso said. 'Staid, I would have said, but not strange. Even the Pope employs an astrologer: presumably the powers of the Holy See do not extend to prognostication. Talk on, Pasqualino, you haven't the half of it yet, although I'm impressed that you know even that much.'

Pasquale confessed that he knew only a little more, and that by guesswork. 'I would suppose that the Venetian had Raphael murdered because he believed that Raphael was a part of your plot, although I must suppose that he was nothing of the kind. And now someone has the corpse of Raphael, and wants me, too. That's why I had to escape, master. Taddei planned to ransom me for Raphael's body.'

'That's beside the point. At one time Giustiniani was acting as broker for us, and after the stupid accident which killed Romano he began to pressure us for delivery of what we had promised. Francesco thought that he could return the pressure, and went to parley with Giustiniani. That was against my advice, I should say. I knew that snake Giustiniani would simply laugh at any attempt to blackmail him. He revels in degradation – after all, it is an advertisement of his power. So I earnestly treated with Francesco, and when the poor fool refused to listen I followed him. As did you, and so you know what fell out there, and that I could not save poor Francesco but had to flee for my own life. But now I need not treat with any agent, for I can deal directly with those who can give me what I want, and I them.'

They turned off the promenade, and climbed the clanging iron stair, and started across the wide street. Pasquale said, 'Where are we going, master?'

'To see some friends of mine. You may be able to help them. And they in turn . . . we will see, eh Pasqualino?'

Rosso led Pasquale along a narrow street that wound up the steep hillside, leaving behind the tall fine houses that looked out across the Arno. The shanty town of the *ciompi* spread across the hillside, a densely packed wave of dark shapes against the dark land. Few lights showed. The paving-stones of the street gave way to mud. There was a sharp smell of burning in the cold night air, cutting through the ripe stench of the open sewer that ran gurgling down the middle of the street.

Pasquale stopped and said, 'Would your friends be Spanish, master? If so, I'd rather not go any further.'

'Here's fine gratitude, after all my help.'

'A million thanks for your help, master, but I don't want to be involved in this.'

Rosso laughed. 'But you are involved, Pasqualino. Besides, I know things you need to know. For instance, I know where your friend Niccolò Machiavegli is. Don't you want to see him again?'

When Pasquale tried to run, Rosso caught his arm and managed to throw him to the muddy path. Pasquale sprawled in shock. He was stronger than his master, but the fight was gone from him. The ape chattered, plucking anxiously at Pasquale's chest, his torn jerkin, touching his face with hard horny fingers. Pasquale calmed the animal and slowly got to his feet. 'That wasn't necessary,' he said.

'I know what you're going to say, Pasqualino. That I am a traitor, consorting with enemies of the State. But it really isn't so. Ever since we left the bridge we have been watched, by the way. I have saved your life, because if you had run away they surely would have killed you.'

'If you're caught, you'll hang as a traitor. Master, you can't think of this!'

'These are hard days for artists, Pasqualino. We must find sponsors where we can. It doesn't matter who the sponsors are – it is the art that we can make because of their support that matters. And I am tired, Pasqualino, tired of scraping a living painting pots and carnival masks, and dirty pictures for lecherous merchants and their vapid wives. I know that I have it in me to paint great pictures, and I need a comfortable position to do it. Many of our fraternity have fled to France for support, and even there the artificers are winning, driving out good art with bad reproductions. Spain, though, is still a friend to us. There are so many in its royal family, so many dukes and princes who wish to show themselves a better patron and connoisseur than their neighbour, who wish to glorify themselves through commissioning great paintings. Ah, but I forget that you think that you can work without any kind of sponsorship, and live on air, I suppose.'

'Please, master, I'll take no more of your mockery.'

Rosso gave no sign of having heard Pasquale. He said mildly, 'Look now, look down there on their work. What wonderful catastrophic light! I shall paint such a picture . . .'

They were high above the Arno now. The huddled roofs of the rude dwellings of the *ciompi* spilled downhill towards the river. The Ponte Vecchio still burned, a small and intense line of fire. The river either side of it was a ribbon of molten copper, molten bronze, burning light alive on its sluggish surface. Beyond was the prickly city, the lighted dome of the Duomo, and the towers and spires of the *palazzi* and churches, and the tower of the Great Engineer with its scattering of lighted windows and crown of red and green signal-lamps. Sounds were small and faint, a distant roar punctuated by the sound of cannons.

Pasquale said, 'People are dying down there.' But it *was* beautiful, in a powerful strange exhilarating way. He saw swarms of sparks flying up from the burning buildings on the bridge, dimming as they rose, like an inversion of the long fall of the rebellious host.

Rosso recognized his pupil's ambivalence and said, 'Ah, but we are elevated above that. Catastrophe always compels from a distance, eh Pasqualino? Battles are the finest subjects of painting, when all conflict is resolved into one desperate hour. All life, and all death, in a tightly focused struggle.'

'I'll always remember the many fine discussions we had about the theory of art, master. How much further do we have to climb?'

'Why, we're here. That's why we stopped,' Rosso said. He stepped up to the plank door of a hovel, said, 'I'm sorry, Pasqualino,' and flung open the door and pushed Pasquale across the threshold.

8

A man sprang upon Pasquale as soon as he stumbled into the hovel. He was knocked bodily to the ground, and a sack stinking of mouldy earth was thrown over his head. He tried to struggle to his feet, but the man knelt on the small of his back and tied his hands together behind his back before lifting him up. Then the sack was jerked from his head, and he saw Niccolò Machiavegli.

The journalist was twisting in the air, his feet a handspan above the dirt floor, hanging by his arms from a rope which passed over the main roof-beam. It was a crude version of the torture employed by the secret police: the *strappado*, the rope. A brutish man hauled on the other end of the rope and lifted Niccolò a little higher.

Niccolò gasped, and Pasquale cried out too. Then a hand was clamped around his mouth and he was shoved down the length of the room.

The one room was all there was to the hovel, under a ceiling slung with bunches of gorse to catch any drips of rain that might seep through the loose slates of the roof. Two men sat on benches drawn up to a poor fire of dry turf and wood-chips that sent up a trickle of sweetish smoke. One wore the dark homespun robe, girdled with a rope, of a Dominican friar. He was young and plump and shaven-headed, with small features centred on a mild moon-shaped face. The other smiled at Pasquale, and Pasquale's heart turned over with fear, for he knew the man. It was the Great Engineer's one-time catamite, Salai.

Turning on the rope, Niccolò called out, 'Be careful, Pasquale!'

Rosso ducked through the door of the hovel, dragging the ape with him. Pasquale twisted from the grip of the ruffian who had bound his hands, and called on his master to put an end to this at once. Rosso twisted the chain of the ape once more around his hand, fed the creature a grape and said without looking up, 'I can do nothing for you, Pasquale.'

Salai made soft ironic applause.

Niccolò cried out again as he was jerked another hand's breadth above the filthy floor. The brute who hauled him up was bigger than any man Pasquale had ever seen before, with a bristling beard and an eye-patch, and a knife with a curved, notched blade thrust through his belt.

The friar said, 'Oh, but you must not cry out yet, Signor Machiavegli. We have not begun.'

Salai said, 'The roof's not high enough for proper *strappado*, so count yourself lucky, journalist.' He winked at Pasquale. 'You know how it's done?'

Pasquale did know how it was done. He had once made sketches of the questioning of a Savonarolista, for the newsletter that peddled the Signoria's line. He remembered too the game he had so often played as a child, hanging from a branch of a tree in his father's olive-grove, waiting and waiting as sharp needles dug into his arms and shoulders, and his wrists ached and his fingers burned, until the burden of his body could be borne no more, and then the airy rush of release when he let go, the wonderful feeling of rolling over and over, free, in the fragrant summer-dried grass. And he thought of how it would be with no release, and turned from the sight of Niccolò's torture, ashamed and angry.

Salai said, 'I'll tell you how it was once done to me. They haul you up and then the rope is abruptly released. You fall but you do not fall all the way, and the halt almost tears your arms from your sockets. Then they haul you up again. They do it four times before they put you to the question, and by then you're ready to say anything.'

Rosso dared take two steps into the room, hauling the ape with him. He said, 'You talked, of course.'

Niccolò lifted his head and said, 'Of course he talked.' There was a sheen of sweat over his white face.

Salai laughed. He was quite at ease in the hovel, with its damp smoky air and its dirt floor strewn with filthy rushes, in which black beetles as big as mice rustled. He was as elegantly dressed as always, in a cloak of black Dutch cloth fastened with scarlet cord over a red silk tunic that must have been worth the annual wage of any ten *ciompi*, and which almost but not quite concealed his paunch, and red breeches with a padded codpiece in the Flemish manner, and black hose on his fleshy legs.

He said, 'Of course I talked. I squealed like a happy pig. Why not? I told them something like the truth, and even if the names were wrong, they arrested the right number of men. Who because they were innocent protested their innocence even under question, which made their guilt all the more convincing.' A silver box was open beside him, from which he took a square of Moorish jelly, dusted with fine sugar. He popped the confection in his mouth and smacked his rosebud lips together. 'It is time this farce was put to rest, Perlata,' he said to the friar. 'The sooner I am out of this flea-ridden pit the better.'

Niccolò said, 'I agree. For the love of God, let me down. Why do you do this?'

The young friar, Fra Perlata, said, 'For the love of God, of course. These matters can't be rushed.'

Rosso laughed. 'For the love of God!'

Fra Perlata said quietly, 'Look in your pupil's purse. See if he has it.'

'I've done all you asked me to,' Rosso protested. 'That and more.'

'And you will do this,' Fra Perlata said.

Rosso said, 'I'm sorry for this, Pasquale,' and unbuckled the flap of Pasquale's scrip and poked through its contents. He said, 'It isn't here.'

'Of course not,' Salai said. 'You think he'd carry it with him as a keepsake?'

Pasquale told Rosso, 'Master, I hardly believe you can watch this. Your need for patronage is truly great. It astounds me.' He knew now why Rosso had been so frivolous all the way up the hill; it was how Rosso, who was fundamentally honest, always hid a lie, a misdeed, a betrayal.

Rosso said, 'You got mixed up in this of your own free will, Pasqualino. Tell them what they want, and they'll let you and Machiavegli go. I swear it.'

'Be careful what you say,' Niccolò called, and groaned as the brute jerked him up by another notch.

Salai made an impatient farting noise with his lips. 'Enough sentiment. Let's find out what these fools have done with it and we can get on with our business. I'll heat my knife in the fire here and test him myself rather than watch him twist like a spider. It's making me dizzy!'

Fra Perlata said, 'Please, Signor Caprotti, have patience. When we have the proof you will have your reward.'

He was the centre of power in the room, this plump young friar, his fanaticism scarcely disguised by a superficial mildness, like a sword sheathed in kid leather. It was quite clear what he was, for Savonarola himself was a Dominican, dying even now by slow degrees, it was reported, in a Dominican monastery in Seville. It was said that a cancer had taken away Savonarola's voice, that instrument which had once shivered all of Florence to its collective soul, yet even on his deathbed he wrote an endless stream of tracts and letters and sermons and pamphlets about the great time to come, when the pure in heart would be bodily raised up to Heaven, and the sinners would be left to face the war of the Antichrist. Fra Perlata was one of the foot-soldiers in this holy cause.

As for the brute who held Niccolò suspended, and the ruffian who had taken charge of Pasquale, it didn't matter what they were, loyal Savonarolistas or hired muscle. More likely the latter: both had a Prussian rather than Spanish look. They were landsknechts perhaps – there were plenty of those looking for work after Luther had been caught and tried and hanged by the forces of Rome – but whatever they were really didn't matter, because they were there simply to hurt Pasquale and Niccolò until they talked. It was their job.

'All we have to do is tickle these two,' Salai said. 'Why make such a fuss about it?'

'What is important is the liberation of the Holy City,' Fra Perlata said. 'The hour is at hand. We must observe the proper form.'

'A few *ciompi* are not God's Holy Army,' Salai said with scorn.

'We're not to say how God's will is manifested,' the friar said.

'He seems to be moving in mysterious ways,' Salai said, popping another sugar-dusted square into his mouth and masticating loudly. 'Certainly if he is using this oaf of a painter as his vehicle for returning what's rightly ours, and an ape as the agent of our misfortune. Rosso, what do you say? Should I kill that flea-ridden brute of yours? I mean the ape, of course, not your pupil.'

Rosso, who had regained something of his swagger, said, 'Forgive it, Lord. It does not know what it has done.'

The ape sat on its bottom beside him, arms folded over the top of its head, peeking from beneath the angle of its elbows at Pasquale like a child. Pasquale smiled back at it, remembering how he had taught it to steal the grapes from the choice vines of the garden of the friars of Sante Croce. Ferdinand was an intelligent animal, and would not have forgotten. But he could not make the signs to it because his hands were tied behind his back.

Salai said, 'In Prussia they burn dogs whose barking has been judged to cause thunderstorms.'

Rosso said, 'God save us that we are not in Prussia.'

Fra Perlata said to Pasquale, 'You know what we want. Where is it?'

'Signor Taddei has it.'

'Bad news for you if he has,' Salai said.

Fra Perlata said, 'Please be quiet. I'll attend to this.' He stood up, dusting the skirt of his robe, and told the brute to raise Niccolò higher.

Niccolò made a terrible sound as he was raised: he didn't sound like a man at all. Pasquale cried out too, then flinched when Fra Perlata put a hand on his shoulder.

The friar said, 'Your friend has hung there long enough, don't you think? Much longer and he'll be a cripple for life. He won't ever be able to write again. Help him. Tell us the truth, and be sure you do. We have a man in Signor Taddei's household, and all the worse for your friend if you lie.'

Pasquale said, 'If you mean the signaller, then he was arrested.'

'I know of the signaller, but he was never privy to our cause. How would we have known where you were being taken for ransom, Pasquale, if we had not been told? Now think carefully, and speak the truth.'

Pasquale said quickly, 'Signor Taddei took the box. He has it. I'm sorry Niccolò, I had to tell them. Forgive me.'

Niccolò shook his head from side to side. 'No more,' he said.

Salai giggled. 'Box? You think we'd worry about a trifle like that? It was good for making dirty pictures, but not for waging war.'

Fra Perlata said, 'Hold, signor! We'll put him to the drop before we question him.'

Salai said, 'I tell you the drop is not great enough. Peasants do not make their holes well enough to lend them to torture – in fact, I'm surprised that the roof-beam hasn't split in two by now. If you really want to hurt them, then hang on to their legs. It is the weight that does it, you see. We grow heavier in the moment that we stop falling, something the old man once explained to me. Better still, I'll carve a few slices from them, eh? Maybe trim the boy's fingers joint by joint. A painter loves his hands as much as a musician.'

Fra Perlata said, 'You will put away your knife. We are on God's business here.'

Salai said, 'This little blade? Why, it isn't really what you'd call a weapon.'

Pasquale said, 'You'd best kill me, because if it is not the box that you want, I have nothing.'

'Oh, but you have,' Salai said. 'The flying device. You took it from Romano's corpse, in the signal-tower.'

Niccolò laughed.

'Be still!' Fra Perlata said, his voice ringing under the low ceiling. The ape Ferdinand looked at him with momentary interest, then yawned, showing a ribbed liver-coloured throat behind strong yellow teeth.

Salai said lazily, 'Don't threaten me, monk. We're on the same side, and I want to help you. Believe me, I've had experience in these matters, and the *strappado* will not work here. Besides, even if it made them talk, they might not speak the truth. I did not, after all.'

Pasquale said, 'It's the toy you want? I can take you straight to where I left it!' He could see it, for a moment, on Niccolò Machiavegli's cluttered writing-table, sitting on a pile of manuscript leaves, faintly luminous in the shadowy room.

Niccolò said, 'No more, Pasquale. They'll kill us anyway.'

Salai smiled and said, 'Well done, painter. But no one will believe you until you're put to the test. We must have our fun, after all.'

'Leave off this,' Rosso said. 'Leave it off! I'd know if he's lying, and I tell you now that he speaks the truth.'

Salai turned on him with a snarl. 'You know nothing of the kind. Your ape lost us the fucking thing in the first place.'

Suddenly, Pasquale knew what had killed Giulio Romano, knew how his body could have been found in a locked room atop a tower climbable by no man. He and Niccolò had been straining after the answer and now it had been placed into his hands and it was worthless, so that he must laugh.

Salai said, 'You see how he mocks us! A little blood will let out the truth. Are you afraid of blood, monk?'

'You know that I am trained in medicine. But I will do this the proper way.'

'Perhaps you mean the scientific way? Even torture has its artificers. Better the pain of the knife. It is slow, exquisite. Unlike the *strappado*, it does not stop. It works cut by cut, mounting by degrees. He's a pretty enough boy, so perhaps I should cut away one of his ears, piece by piece, eh?'

Niccolò said, 'Hold your tongue, Salai.' He had to draw his lips back from his teeth to speak, and took little breaths that broke his sentences. 'I think you're no more, no more than an idle boaster. Not even a good one. If you want to hurt me, try flaying.'

'Let him down,' Salai said coldly, 'and we'll see. No, monk. We'll try my way first.'

Niccolò said, 'You don't dare, Salai,' but stiffened when Salai laid the blade of his knife flat against his bandaged thigh, where he had been wounded by a pistol-ball.

Rosso said with a trembling edge to his voice, 'Tell them what they want, Pasquale. It can't hurt you, and will save your friend.'

Pasquale, for a moment the centre of attention, felt an odd sense of control. He looked directly at Salai and said, 'I've already told you I have the toy, in a safe place. Cut him, and I'll tell you no more.'

'But I think you will,' Salai said, and jabbed the tip of the knife into the tensed muscle of Niccolò's thigh. 'Tell me the truth, painter.'

Rosso cried out, 'For the love of God, Salai! Let Pasquale speak.'

Pasquale bit the inside of his lips to stop himself from crying out too, and the taste of his own warm salt blood filled his mouth. He spat on the straw, and the ruffian cuffed his head.

Niccolò grinned down at Salai: a death's-head grin. 'That's the best you can do?'

171

'Worse, far worse,' Salai said, and thrust again, laughing.

'Leave him be!'

'Stay your hand!'

First Rosso, then Fra Perlata, had spoken. Rosso had drawn his knife. The ape dragged against its master's grip, intently watching Pasquale.

Salai laughed again, stepping back so that everyone in the room could see him. He raised the bloody knife and licked its blade, grinning around it.

Niccolò groaned, and said, 'Kill me for the truth. You know the boy doesn't lie.'

Salai shrugged and raised his knife. Rosso shrieked and the ape wrenched free from his grip and with an odd sideways bound threw itself on the ruffian who held Pasquale. Man and ape went sprawling, and then Niccolò fell as the brute hireling let go of the rope, plucked the ape from his compatriot by an arm and a leg and threw it across the room before it could fasten its teeth on him. The ape jumped up, chattering with rage and flailing straw with its hands and its hand-like feet. Fra Perlata told Rosso to keep it quiet and bent over Niccolò and quickly examined his wounds.

Salai screamed insults at Rosso. His curly hair shook around his mottled jowly face. When he ran out of breath, Fra Perlata said, 'You've done enough harm. This isn't one of your games.'

Rosso said, 'None of this is necessary. None of it.'

Salai laughed and said, 'I'll kill you, Rosso. I swear it.'

Fra Perlata turned and said quietly, 'This is God's business. You must all understand what we're about. These are the End Times, bringing distress as bitter as a dish of borage, and change as relentless as a mill grinding out the flour of wisdom. Florence is at the centre of Italy through God's plan, as will shortly be revealed. It must be ruled by the Holy Word, or a sword will fall upon it. It must repent while there is still time. It must clothe itself in the white garments of purification, but must not wait, for soon there will be no time for repentance. Do you all understand?'

'You still need me,' Salai said. 'Don't forget it.'

'I forget nothing,' the friar said. He told the brute hireling to attend to Niccolò and crossed the room and bent his round face close to Pasquale's. His breath stank of onions. 'I forget nothing, and by

172

God's grace I see what I need to see. Look at me straight, boy, and tell me, or we will continue what we have started.'

Pasquale saw Niccolò's blood pooling under his wounded leg and gathering around the fingers of his bound hands, which were twisted behind his back. Fra Perlata pinched his cheeks between sharp-nailed fingers, so that Pasquale had to meet his eyes.

Pasquale said, 'I have what you need. I can lead you straight to it.'

The brute hireling washed Niccolò's wounds with salt water and bound them with cloth torn from his shirt. Fra Perlata inspected this work and told Niccolò that it was God's will if he lived or died now, and then ordered Rosso to quiet the ape. Salai said he knew a quick way, and was told to be quiet in turn. The Savonarolista friar was making the best of it that he could, Pasquale saw, masking his anger with decision and action. Niccolò was bound by the rope from which he had hung, turned four times around his body and tied tight, and then the bonds at his ankles were cut and he and Pasquale were walked outside and down a foul alley to where a horse-drawn carriage waited.

The ride was not long, but every jounce of the carriage hurt Niccolò's leg and drew a stifled cry from him. He lay across one of the carriage's benches: Pasquale sat on the other between Fra Perlata and Salai, who was cleaning his immaculate nails with the tip of his knife, careless of the jolting ride. The two hirelings and Rosso and the ape rode up with the driver. The curtains were drawn across the carriage's windows, so Pasquale could not tell which direction they were taking, but at one point the noise of a mob rose ahead and passed by and subsided behind, and he knew they would not cross the Arno by any bridge.

All too soon he was proved right. The carriage halted and he and Niccolò were bundled out by the hirelings. They were at the edge of the new docks. The brute slung Niccolò across his shoulders like a sack of meal, and Fra Perlata gripped Pasquale's elbow and marched him down a stone slipway to the ferry which rocked on the dark water of the river.

The Savonarolistas had taken it. There was a dead man on the decking, lying in a pool of his own blood, and the crew was muffled in scarves.

The ferry got under way at once. Steam billowed from the vents of its burner-pipes and with a laborious flexing of the wooden beams the paddle-wheel churned water into a creamy froth. It moved at an angle against the current, driving towards the far end of the complex series of weirs and steps that controlled the flow of the channelled river.

It was bitterly cold. Downstream, beyond the new docks, where the ocean-crossing *maona* loomed above lesser vessels, the waterway ribboned away across the dark flood-plain under a sky crowded with crisp bright stars. Upstream, Florence lay under a mantle of smoke: not the fumes of the manufactories, but the smoke of many burnings. Fire still illuminated the arch of the Ponte Vecchio, and fires burned along the bank which the ferry had just quit. Otherwise the city was dark and still, save for the winking of signal-lights. Pasquale heard the bells of the public clock in the tower of the church of Santa Trinità toll the hour of four.

He sat with Niccolò Machiavegli, massaging the journalist's arms. 'I had never thought to have to bear the rope again,' Niccolò said wryly, 'yet I am pleased that I could bear it straightforwardly. A million thanks, Pasquale, I do feel something in my hands again, where you move the blood into them. Blood is the conduit for pain it seems, for it always hurts us to spill it, and now it hurts when it returns to its natural place.'

'I wish I could mend the wound that Salai gave you.'

'It hurts no worse for his attentions than it did when the ball of the pistol first struck it.'

'How did you come there, Niccolò? Did the Savonarolistas kidnap you at the Palazzo?'

'Not at all. It was the work of Giustiniani's men. I knew them by their white masks, and the vapours they used. They put me in a carriage, but it was stopped at a bridge and they were overpowered. I thought I was saved, but I was placed in another carriage and delivered to the attentions of Perlata and Salai.'

'Then Giustiniani and the Savonarolistas are at each other's throats, although they work for the same master.'

'Giustiniani does not work for Spain, Pasquale, but for what money he can gain by selling the device. The Savonarolistas do it to overthrow the government of Florence and save us all for the love of God. And you, Pasquale?'

'It was in precisely the opposite way. I was betrayed by Signor Taddei, who received an anonymous note asking that I be delivered in exchange for Raphael's body.'

'Raphael's body was taken? I wonder for what end?'

'If the body is not returned, then there will be war between Florence and Rome.'

'Ah, I see. And Spain will be the victor.'

'That's what Signor Taddei said.'

'He is a patriot.'

Pasquale said bitterly, 'He is foremost a business man.'

'The two go hand in hand. And what was taken – I won't speak of it here – is wanted by both Giustiniani and the Savonarolistas. One would sell it to Spain, and one would give it.'

Pasquale explained what Rosso had told him about Giustiniani's role as agent for the dissident artists, and Niccolò laughed and said that now he understood why what was sought was sought so eagerly by all.

'But there are also the pictures made by the Great Engineer's device, which Giulio Romano used to copy the Great Engineer's notes about his flying toy. It is a device that captures light, Niccolò, and fixes it precisely. The blackened glass I had from Baverio was one such, and the picture I rescued from Giustiniani's fireplace another.'

'Do you not remember the signal-tower, Pasquale? Think. What did you see beside the body?'

'The open window.'

'Yes. And?'

'Glass, below it.'

'Yes. Yet the window was unbroken, and besides, the glass was black.'

Pasquale remembered the glass plate that Baverio had given him, blackened from its exposure to light, and understood. The glass had been the remains of pictures of the Great Engineer's notes. Only the model remained. He said, 'What will happen to us, Niccolò?'

'The Savonarolistas aren't known for killing without reason. If they are given what they want they may let us go. They believe, after all, that they are working God's will. If they win, then once again it will be as it was during the brief reign of Savonarola. Blessed bands of children will roam the streets of Florence, singing hymns and seeking out every vanity from rouge-pots to paintings, from chess-boards to every kind of artificer's device, and throwing stones at those not yet virtuous. There will be fasting and religious pageants and great bonfires of vanities. The Savonarolistas dream of a pure and simple world, Pasquale, in which all men turn entirely to Christ whether they like it or not. Yet their plans are founded on the certainty that God speaks directly to Savonarola, and I am not persuaded of that, for all that many in Florence once believed it.'

'Yes, but I do not trust Salai. I would kill him if I could.'

'Many have tried, yet he lives. Don't underestimate him, Pasquale.'

Fra Perlata was talking to one of the Savonarolistas who had captured the ferry. Pasquale caught a few of their words, brought to him on the bitter wind that blew past the labouring ferry. Something about fire, and the last times, and justice. No doubt that was what the Savonarolistas promised the *ciompi*, Heaven's justice here and now on Earth, but it seemed to Pasquale that even justice in Heaven was a remote possibility, and he said as much to Niccolò.

'It's true that we are enveloped in the laces of sin, but we must always hope, Pasquale. Without hope there is only despair, and with despair, evil. If we are to have God as a friend, we must hope for redemption. The Savonarolistas promise it, but it is not theirs to give. Ah, we are making for the shore now.'

The note of the boiling tubes of the ferry's Hero's engine rose in pitch, a keening whistle at the edge of hearing. The paddle-wheel thumped faster, spraying the deck with cold droplets of water. The ferry was coming about, heading into the quieter water along the edge of the river as it made for a landing at the foot of the city wall by the river gate. The head of the dead crewman was rocked back and forth by the vibration. Its eyes glimmered in the moonlight, blind and foolish-looking. Death makes fools of us all, Pasquale thought.

Most of the crew of Savonarolistas had lined up on the landward side of the ferry, muskets and rifles bristling out at the stony barren shore. Pasquale called to the brute hireling, asking if trouble was expected, and the man grinned and drew his thumb-nail across his throat.

Rosso pushed away from the rail, where all this time he had leant and watched Florence burn. He said, 'We're enemies to our own city now.' Beside him, the ape shifted and rattled its chain. It hated water, and was uneasy and subdued on the little ferry.

'You knew what road you were setting on,' Pasquale said. 'I hope to see your paintings, master, when you have your commissions.'

'I do not know if I can paint again,' Rosso said. 'This is a bitter business, Pasqualino. You should hate me, and I would not blame you. I've been a fool.'

Niccolò said, 'There is always redemption.'

'No talking,' one of the masked Savonarolistas said. 'You do what we want, now. All of you.'

The shore was suddenly visible, and the city wall looming beyond. Signal-lights winked green and red atop the nearest tower. The ferry was aiming into a small cut that ran back into the shore along the line of the wall, labouring against the current. As it neared the mouth of the cut, lights rose up: rockets.

At first Pasquale thought that they were signals from Savonarolistas waiting on the shore. But more and more rose, scrabbling quickly into the night and bursting in showers of white sparks at the tops of their toppling arcs. Pasquale remembered Giustiniani's men sending rockets bursting through the panicky crowd in the Piazza della Signoria. Smoke blew out across the black river, softening the harsh glare released by the exploding rockets. The Savonarolistas started firing into the smoke, and red muzzle-flashes snapped back at them.

The ape, Ferdinand, was sent into a frenzy by the noise, dashing to and fro in the narrow arc permitted by its chain. Rosso made a gesture, throwing up his hand, and at the same time the ape shrugged free of its chain; or no, Rosso had released it. It bounded away towards the foredeck, after the grapes that Rosso had thrown there. The brute hireling and Salai, his sword drawn, closed on it from different directions; the ape dodged both men by scampering up one of the rope stays of the ferry's steam-vent.

Rosso put a hand on either of Pasquale's shoulders, and pushed him overboard.

The shock of the cold water drove away Pasquale's surprise. For a moment he thought he would drown in darkness; he made frantic frog-kicks, straining to free his hands, which were still bound behind his back. Then Rosso appeared beside him and got one arm under his chin. They were drifting away from the ferry, which had reversed

177

its paddle-wheel as it tried to turn from the shore. Stray shots splashed and pattered around Rosso and Pasquale; one hit the water close to Pasquale's face, tugging at the sodden folds of his jerkin as it sank. The ferry's paddle-wheel stopped and the craft began to drift sideways in the current. It was silhouetted against the smoke and light from the shore; then something rushed out across the water, spitting sparks, and smashed into the stern.

Rosso kicked and kicked, dragging Pasquale with him, and in a minute they were staggering up the shingle bank of a little backwater, where a handful of fresh corpses lay face-down in the water, men killed by the fighting on the bridges, washed here by the river's currents.

PART THREE

The Interrupted Measure

1

By the time Pasquale and Rosso had clambered across the jumble of flood-cast boulders and rotten tree-stumps on the river-bank, the exchange of shots between the Savonarolistas and the forces on the shore had ended. The ferry had run aground and was ablaze from end to end, and those Savonarolistas who had not jumped ship and chanced the dubious mercy of their enemies must surely have perished.

Pasquale would have run to try and find Niccolò if Rosso hadn't held him back. 'We must save ourselves!' Rosso said desperately.

Filled with loathing and despair, Pasquale wrenched free and said, 'He is my friend!' Then he ran at Rosso and knocked him to the gravelly mud, and might have tried to kill him if voices had not sounded close by.

It was a contingent of the city militia, searching for survivors of the ferry wreck. Pasquale and Rosso hid in a pit amongst freshly flayed bodies of horses and mules. By now both were racked by deep shivers, for their soaked clothes were icy cold and not likely to dry in the cold night air. Teeth chattering, they hugged each other for warmth, but both knew that their friendship had died amongst the stink of blood and the yellow grins of the dead animals.

The militia's search was in any case half-hearted. Moonlight turned the tumbled shore into a shadowy maze where a hundred men could have hidden from the searches of a thousand, and it was a cold night and the militia knew better than most that Sardinia was haunted by the shades of those who were disappeared for the convenience of the Signoria and the safety of the city. Besides, they had to pay for their ammunition out of their meagre stipends, and there was no point wasting it on any survivors of those who had (they supposed) stolen the ferry. They marched back to their warm guardroom without bothering to search the area properly, and they didn't even report the incident: there was already enough madness that night.

Rosso and Pasquale arose from their grave and made their way along a track winding between white boulders, over a little hill studded with rotted tree-stumps and the broken skeletons of horses and mules. Rib-cages gleamed like ivory staves in the smoky moonlight. Half-way along, a shadow bounded up towards them, making a faint jingling. It was the ape, Ferdinand, its fur soaking wet and raised in little points.

Rosso groaned, and cried out softly that he was cursed to bear this burden until he died. The ape made plaintive little hootings as Pasquale scratched behind its ears, and it seemed almost glad when Rosso took up its chain again. He roughly wrapped its length around his arm and hauled hard upon it, although the ape trotted along docilely enough between the two men, as if they were simply walking to their favourite tavern after a day's work.

But that time was over.

They quickly reached a little gate at the base of a square ballistics tower, beside a channelled stream which ran out beneath the wall. A mill-house stood on the other side of the fast-running stream; chinks of yellow light showed between the big wooden shutters over its first-floor windows. But the gate was shut, of course, and Pasquale and Rosso didn't dare bang on it and demand entry. It was quite clear that the militia were edgy that night, and would need little excuse to shoot a couple of shivering stragglers, so they had no choice but to pick their way around the wall to the nearest road, to await the opening of the Prato Gate at cock-crow. Walking at least kept the blood flowing.

Rosso told Pasquale that he knew that this rescue would never make amends, but it was all he could do. He jerked the ape's chain said, 'Perhaps you can sell the toy, if the Savonarolistas don't find it.'

'Perhaps,' Pasquale said. He wasn't convinced that Rosso's help was motivated purely by a desire for redemption – anyone able to offer the flying toy to those who wanted it could name his price, although whether he survived the transaction was another matter entirely. As for his former master, Pasquale felt nothing but an empty pity, and that more for himself than for Rosso. He was suddenly cast adrift, rudderless, without a compass.

'It's not just that I can't stomach torture,' Rosso said. He was hugging himself as he walked, slapping his chest with crossed arms like a bird with clipped wings trying to take flight.

'Niccolò found it hard enough,' Pasquale said, finding in himself an unforgiving streak.

'Of course, of course. I suppose that at the end I cannot betray my friends, or my city. It's all very well thinking of these things in the abstract, but the actuality is quite different. It may seem I have no principles, but they are there all the same, buried deep.'

'Then I suppose that you didn't intend to murder Giulio Romano.'

'No, no! That was a foolish accident. And besides, I wasn't even in the tower.'

'I thought you might have put the ape up to it in some way,' Pasquale remarked, and even in the fading moonlight saw that his shot had gone home, for Rosso stumbled and cursed and walked on a little way before speaking again.

'Well, you guessed the main part of it, anyway. But no one put him up to murder. The ape climbed the signal-tower, it's true, and I did set him to it, but not with the intention of killing poor Giulio. No, that was furthest from my mind, and I had thought the ape ready, for I had already trained it to retrieve grapes from a higher and higher place until it would climb anywhere I asked it. How do you think it so easily learned to steal those grapes from that silly monk?

'We had arranged that Giulio would light the lamps of the signal-tower of Signor Taddei's Palazzo at a certain time. I would signal in turn by briefly revealing a lantern, and then send the ape to collect the prize. We had to resort to such devices because all of Raphael's disciples were being watched closely, as you might imagine. In fact, that was why I was there that night, because Giulio feared losing that which he had taken, and would entrust it to me instead, although I had no means of getting it to where it was supposed to be.'

'Then it was Romano who stole the device, and not Salai after all.'

'So you don't know everything, Pasqualino. No, Salai told Giulio how to find the device, that is all, for we knew that suspicion would immediately fall upon him, as indeed it did, once the device was found to be missing. Giulio took the device with ease, when he and his master, Raphael, visited the Great Engineer. He also made pictures of the Great Engineer's notes, for they were too convoluted for easy transcription, even if the Great Engineer did not write in mirror image. How Giulio sweated over each long exposure! The ape wore a harness, with a padded pocket for the glass plates.'

'I see now how things fell out. That same day, Salai met with Romano at the service for our confraternity. But why would Romano pass the device and the picture plates to you?'

'Quite simple. Our plan was beginning to unravel. He became nervous when the secret police made discreet inquiries of Raphael. He was worried that the apartments would be searched. After all, the device was discovered to be missing after Raphael's party had visited the tower. We had already thought of this, of course, and thought too of a way of transferring the device and picture plates from one hand to the other without even meeting.'

'So that was why you were waiting with your ape outside the Signor Taddei's Palazzo.'

Rosso sighed. He seemed weary of the convolutions of his tale, yet set on again, like an ox plodding its round at a water-lift. 'So indeed. After you left the tavern I collected the ape and went straight-away to Taddei's Palazzo, and there I waited, watching the signal-tower through a glass, with Ferdinand by my side watching as keenly as me. The devil was in him that night, I swear. When he saw the arms of the signal-tower move, he straight away climbed the Palazzo's boundary wall and swarmed up the tower, without waiting for my order. You can imagine my feelings as I watched him climb, for all of our plans resided on the actions of that one animal. He climbed quickly and strongly, swarming up the side of the tower and dis-appearing into the open window. As to what fell out then, I can only guess, although I heard Giulio's dreadful cry and must guess that the ape believed that Giulio was attacking it when he tried to take off the harness. Or perhaps Giulio merely made a gesture which the ape in its excitement believed to be a threat. However it fell out, they fought, and so Giulio was killed, and the ape came back down empty-handed. By then Taddei's household had been roused by Giulio's cry, and I had to make my escape. And so it was that you found the little device on Giulio's body, and took it believing it a toy. And here we are, in the cold and the dark.'

'Not for long,' Pasquale said.

They turned the corner of the city wall, and quit the stony ground of Sardinia for a rough heath that saddled away in the moonlight. There was a little wood and beside it a scattering of camp-fires, like a constellation fallen to Earth from the cold starry sky, with the dark shapes of wagons drawn around them.

It was a night camp of travellers who had arrived too late to enter the city the previous day. There were mendicants and refugees from the farms hoping to find work in the city's manufactories, and a train of wagons, a knight and his entourage, and a merchant's party. Hawkers and whores from the city moved amongst them, selling food and wine, or plying the warm commerce. No one slept except the smallest children, for the camp was alive with rumours of what was happening in the city. Pasquale and Romano kept their own counsel, for there were bound to be spies and informers amongst the hundred or more people camped there, and simply said that they had been assaulted by footpads and thrown into the river. They had no coin to buy food, and charity was not immediately forthcoming, but at Pasquale's goading the ape turned a few summersets and walked up and down on its hands, flipping stones with its feet.

This performance brought not money but bowls of soup and dry black bread, and cigarettes and a flagon of smooth red wine from the merchant, an elegant man in a brocaded caped tunic, with rings on every finger of his white hands. He was not much older than Pasquale, and took a liking to him, all the more so when he discovered that Pasquale was a painter, and where he was from. For an hour they talked about Fiesole, which the merchant knew well, and the broken axle-tree which had delayed the merchant's journey, and the paintings which the merchant had inherited from his father, and the murder of Raphael, which the merchant had heard from a signaller who had passed on the news.

The sky grew milky as dawn approached. Pasquale fell asleep and woke to find himself covered in a blanket stiff with rime. He had slept only an hour, but now it was light enough to see the city wall stretching away, prickly with weaponry, and the roofs and towers beyond it, and many threads of smoke already rising amongst them.

The camp was stirring about him. People were hitching horses to wagons, dousing camp-fires, picking up bundles of possessions and loading them on carts and travois, heading along the muddy road towards the Prato Gate. The hawkers and prostitutes were already clustered before its arch, yawning and discussing the night's work.

Pasquale wandered through the disintegrating camp, looking for Rosso, and at last spotted the ape lurking in the shadows of the little wood. It scampered up to him as he approached. It had lost its chain, and was clearly agitated, for it kept dashing ahead of Pasquale and then running back to clutch his leg.

In that way the ape led Pasquale through the little wood. Pasquale was amused, and then annoyed, and at last frightened. In the midst of the wood was a grandfather oak which sent its long limbs twisting out in every direction above the humped, mossy ground. The ape sat down on its bottom and wrapped its arms over its head and rocked back and forth.

Pasquale left it and slowly walked around the oak to where Rosso hung. He had wrapped one end of the chain around one of the heavy lower branches, and the other around his neck. The toes of his leather slippers brushed frost-shrivelled grass-stalks as his corpse turned back and forth in the bitter wind which had sprung up with the rising sun. Crows had already found him and pecked out his eyes, and blood redder than his hair streaked his cheeks like the tears of the damned.

2

As Pasquale ran out of the wood, heartsick and horrified, the ape scampering at his heels, there was a distant flourish of trumpets. The city gates were opening.

But by the time Pasquale gained the road he saw that something was wrong. Those who had been waiting to pass through the customs post were being beaten back by squads of city militia. Hawkers dropped their trays and fled; prostitutes picked up their skirts and ran, screaming imprecations. Those too slow to run, or those brave or foolish enough to stand their ground, were knocked aside. The soldiers' staves rose and fell and rose and fell, and there was a glitter of swords.

A squad of cavalry burst out of the deep shadow beneath the arch of the gate, riding at full gallop, scattering militia and onlookers alike. Pasquale saw the merchant's wagon founder as it was driven off the road, its horses screaming horribly as they tumbled into the ditch.

More riders burst forth from the gateway, riding on either side of a string of coaches whose drivers flogged their teams with long whips. Sharpshooters in cork-lined breastplates and smooth helmets fitting close to their skulls lay on the roofs of the coaches, and more cavalry brought up the rear. This party passed in a thunder of wheels and hooves, and men bawling like beasts, and a great cloud of dust.

Pasquale saw that the middle coach was drawn by a team of white horses, and that it flew the cobalt-blue banner of the Vatican. He had a glimpse of a man's face peering through the thick glass window, a heavy coarse-featured face with unshaven jowls and small, short-sighted eyes. The man looked angry yet resolute, and his fierce stare burned in Pasquale's vision even after the coach had thundered past.

All around Pasquale, people had stopped what they were doing and swept off their hats; some even dropped to their knees, careless of the wheels of the coaches that rattled past less than an arm's length away. Pasquale understood then. The Pope was leaving, fleeing the riots that threatened to tear Florence apart.

Then the carriages and soldiers were gone, leaving only dust blowing in their wake, and a fading rumble. People slowly returned to what they had been doing, moving as if waking from a dream. As they began to pass through the customs post beyond the gate, Pasquale saw that each was stopped and questioned by armed militia.

Rather than risk immediate questioning, Pasquale lent a hand to the merchant and his half-dozen men. They cut the horses free, unloaded the wagon, and dragged it from the ditch by main force. The horses had been thoroughly shaken but were otherwise unhurt, and the merchant's men were efficient. In less than an hour they had mended the traces and hitched up the horses and reloaded the wagon.

Early-morning traffic was moving up and down the road, making a detour around the wagon. The merchant thanked Pasquale, and asked after his friend.

'He had to leave. A matter of honour.'

'Yet I see you have his ape.'

Pasquale turned and saw Ferdinand sitting a little way off, and groaned. He had forgotten about the ape, yet here it was, and when it saw him looking at him it ambled over and flung its arms around his thighs in a clumsy hug.

'I have nothing for you,' Pasquale told it, his heart turning over at the thought of the death of his master.

The merchant looked at Pasquale shrewdly. 'I won't ask the how and the why of it, but I see you are in some trouble.'

'I won't inconvenience you further, signor, except to ask a small favour.'

The merchant, who was a shrewd, kindly man, laughed and said that Pasquale didn't seem to be a dangerous criminal, if criminal he was, and if he wanted only to get past the militia then there was no problem. So it was that Pasquale rode through the gate on the wagon bench beside the merchant and his driver. The little square beyond, usually crowded with wagons, *vaporetti* and horses, and lined with stalls, was almost deserted. As the wagon rolled across the square, Pasquale saw that a frame-gibbet had been hammered together in the middle of the three-way junction on the far side. Half a dozen men, naked but for sacking hoods, hung from it, and each had a sign hung around his neck: *I looted. Look on me and take heed.*

Pasquale started to shake, seeing at once and all too clearly Rosso staring sightlessly, twisting in the wind. The merchant, misunderstanding, said that this was only night business, then shouted out as Pasquale jumped down from the wagon and ran, the ape pelting after him.

Pasquale was soon deep in the maze of alleys and yards somewhere between Santa Maria Novella and the Duomo. He recognized a fading mural of the Madonna on the wall of a shuttered shop, and walked on in the direction of the lodging-house where Niccolò Machiavegli had his rooms. The ape ambled behind him in such a way that Pasquale had the morbid fancy that somehow the essence of poor dead Rosso had become embedded in his pet, as dogs are supposed to grow to resemble their owners. So the ape, with its swaggering bow-legged walk and way of looking sharply around, imitated Rosso's assertive yet nervous manner.

Signora Ambrogini was not pleased to see Pasquale; even less so to see Ferdinand. 'I don't suppose that Signor Machiavegli is with you,' she said, peering through the finger-width gap she had opened after many minutes of knocking.

'I wish that he was. Please, signora, I left something in his rooms that I must have.'

'He was out all last night,' the old woman said. 'He may not be as old as me, but neither is he a strapping young brute like you.'

'You can come with me,' Pasquale said. 'It will only take a minute.'

'There was someone else here asking after his rooms. I sent him away and told him the militia would be after him.'

'When was this?'

'Not long ago. A foreign fellow. I have to set off for mass, young man. I suppose the churches will still be open.'

'I'm sure they are.' Pasquale fell to his knees in a dramatic gesture. 'Please, signora, I implore you. I'll return the key in a moment.'

'Signor Machiavegli keeps strange friends,' the old woman said, 'but that was a good likeness of me, young man, even if you did make me look years younger than I am.'

'That was a mere sketch. My thanks for this favour will be a portrait in oils!'

'Paintings should be of beautiful subjects. I'm old enough that I don't need flattery.'

'None was intended, signora.'

'You can push the key under my door when you've finished,' Signora Ambrogini said. 'I haven't missed second mass since twenty years ago, and that was on the day that my husband died. And don't you let that animal in the room.'

Pasquale took the long iron key, gabbled his thanks, and ran up the winding stairs, slapping every turn with his palm. The room was as he and Niccolò left it, and the little flying device sat like a little boat on the sea of papers on the writing-desk at the high window.

Just as Pasquale had finished folding a sheet of stiff paper into a box for the little device, and was stowing it away in his scrip, a face appeared at the top of the window. It was upside-down, its shock of red hair swinging back and forth. It was the stilt-man who had led the others in the Piazza della Signoria. The man grinned at Pasquale and then his hand swung sharply down. A pane of glass shattered, and orange smoke blew in.

Pasquale ran, and heard the rest of the window smash to shards behind him. He tumbled down a whole turn of stairs and picked himself up and ran again, Ferdinand at his heels, not stopping to return the key (which he had anyway left in the lock), not stopping until he was streets and streets away, and then stopping only to regain his breath before running again, to the one place left in the whole city where he could be sure of safety.

3

Pasquale had to bang on the door of Piero di Cosimo's house for a full five minutes before it swung open a crack. Pelashil peered sleepily at him. 'I must see him,' Pasquale said. 'Please, you must let me in.'

The woman pushed the door wider, leaning back against the wall so that Pasquale had to brush past her as he entered. Her glossy black hair was down over her face, and when she raised a hand to push it back Pasquale glimpsed her small, spiky breasts inside her loose shirt. Ferdinand bounded through the door and scampered down the passageway. Pelashil shut the door and said, 'The old man sleeps. You be quiet, Pasquale, and the ape.'

'You know Piero likes Ferdinand. Please, I need to speak to him. Well, of course, and to you.'

Pelashil smiled slowly. She was not conventionally pretty, but a woman who, when she smiled, was utterly changed, so that a man would do all he could to see that smile again. Despite himself, Pasquale responded to her smile with one of his own. She embraced him quickly, then stepped back, wrinkling her snub nose. Chocolate freckles dusted its bridge. 'You stink of the river! And there is mud in your hair. I will wash you. When did you last wash? You are shy of water, and yet you have so much of it. In the desert, we wash with sand.'

'I've been in the river, and that's enough water for anyone. I'll tell you about my adventures, but first I must speak with Piero. It's very important.'

'You're too young to know anything important. Go to him, if you must.'

Piero di Cosimo owned the whole house, but lived and worked in the big draughty room that took up most of the ground floor. Lit only by a series of rigged mirrors that reflected sunlight to every corner, at this early hour everything in the room was in shades of sepia, that pigment drawn from pulpy body of the common cuttle-fish. Big canvases leaned against one wall, their painted surfaces

191

turned away from the light; one set on a trestle was roughly covered with a paint-spattered sheet. When he had returned from the New World, Piero had made his money by painting small wooden decorative panels, *spallieri*, to private commissions. His scenes of the life of the Savages of the high deserts had been especially popular in a time when anything to do with the New World was fashionable. But now he painted for no one but himself, and kept everything.

As well as paintings, the studio was cluttered with bits of old furniture, tables with one or more legs broken and lashed together, a broken-backed couch in which Pasquale knew that mice nested, rickety stools, an old *cassone* with a cracked front panel and its top entirely missing. Bits and pieces of machinery too, for Piero was fascinated by the inventions of the artificers, and he scavenged broken machines and tried to repair them or make them into something new. There was an automatic music-player, all the strings in its scallop-shaped iron frame frayed or snapped, and the hammers bent or missing. A tantalus cup. A colonial long rifle with an octagonal barrel fully two *braccia* long. A kind of plush puppet moved by clockwork sat slumped on a bench, legs splayed in front of it, head drooping. A clockwork prognostication engine, its springs broken and its jammed registers permanently showing *Patience Becoming Virtue*. A machine that at a turn of a handle was supposed to mix and grind pigments, but which in Pasquale's experience only spattered clouds of fine tinted dust over the user; an automatic double-entry abacus; an automatic loom broken into pieces and put back together with the idea that pictures could be generated using its punch-cards; a clock driven by complex gearing to equalize the progressively diminishing power of its barrel-spring. The tick of the clock's ratchet escapement was for a moment the loudest thing in the room, and then Piero's pet raven saw the ape and shifted on its perch with a scaly scratching and croaked, 'Danger.'

Piero was sleeping on a truckle bed in one corner of the room, behind a screen painted with scenes of the happy isles of the New World. Pelashil went to him and shook him by the shoulder until he woke and feebly tried to push her away. She shrugged and cast a smouldering look at Pasquale before departing.

Piero drew the filthy blanket around himself. His vigorous white hair stood up in all directions around his nut-brown wrinkled face, and he scratched and rummaged in this cockade for a full minute before getting up and scuttling to a far corner of the room and making water into a basin on a stand. Moving so as to keep his back half-turned to Pasquale, Piero opened the window and threw the basin's contents out into the wild garden, where vines scrambled unchecked over untrimmed trees, and hedges had grown monstrously shaggy.

Pasquale said, 'Master, have I offended you?'

'You've been a bad boy,' Piero said, still managing to keep his back half-turned as he scuttled back to his corner and carefully lowered himself on to the bed. He stretched out slowly and clutched the top of the blanket to his neck with his knobbly arthritic hands. He finally looked full at Pasquale and said, 'I'm asleep. You're a dream.' And with that his head fell on to the greasy clout he used as a pillow and he commenced to breathe deeply and raggedly through his open mouth.

'You've been taking that stuff again,' Pasquale said, but there was no reply. He added, 'You should eat. Dreams aren't everything.'

There was a pan of hard-boiled eggs on the stove-top – Piero economically boiled them up in big batches when he boiled his size or glue – but when Pasquale cracked one it gave off a nauseous sulphur reek, and he saw that its white was tinged copper-green.

'Pelashil should cook for you,' Pasquale said, because this usually roused Piero into an argument about oppression, with Pasquale telling him that he shouldn't have brought her back from the New World if he didn't want her oppressed, and Piero replying that this was precisely the point, elaborating one or another fantastical argument along the lines that slavery is freedom, and freedom slavery. But this time Piero defiantly stayed asleep, or at least maintained the pretence. Pasquale sat down on a broken stool and watched the old man for a while. Perhaps he dozed, for Pelashil was shaking him by the shoulder, and now Piero really was asleep, snoring with his mouth open to show rotten black teeth in pulpy gums.

Pelashil put her finger to her lips and led Pasquale out into the scullery, where a pot-bellied stove radiated heat, and blankets woven with bright geometric shapes covered the flaking calcined walls, so that it was like being in a tent in some far Moorish land, where the sun blazes so hot at midday that the sands of the desert fuse into glass.

Half-dazed with exhaustion, forgetting why he had come here, Pasquale allowed Pelashil to undress him. His clothes were stiff with mud. She washed his body with a damp cloth, and then thrust a bowl of soup into his hands. Burnt crusty bread had been broken into it, so that he could eat it without a spoon. He wanted to know where the ape was, and she shrugged and pointed to the garden; she had let it out. When he tried to get up to see what had become of it, she pressed him back, and with a strange inward smile bowed her head, brushed his chest with her wiry black hair, then moved lower, so that his manhood stirred to the tickling touch and he groaned and drew her to him.

When Pasquale woke, the sliver of sky that showed through the window had darkened, like a scrap of violet cloth caught amongst the tangled branches of the untrimmed trees of Piero's garden. Pelashil was dressing with careless languor, pulling a tarnished white gown over her tawny skin. Pasquale watched her, swoony with tiredness and affection, and asked her where she was going.

'Work,' Pelashil said. 'He earns nothing, I must.'

'Have him sell one of his paintings,' Pasquale said. He stood up and punched at the air with his fists. It was so warm that it felt like a solid substance. 'If he sold no more than one, he could live as he does for the rest of his life.'

Pelashil shook her head. 'No! He needs them. He lives there.'

'In the paintings?'

'In a place he finds by making the paintings,' she said. 'He is the first mara'akame of your people, but perhaps not the last. You can learn much from him, Pasquale. I followed him because he is a great mara'akame. He has travelled far along the branches of the Tree of Life.'

Pasquale said, 'I thought that Piero had enslaved you, to make you follow him, to make you share his bed.'

Pelashil made a sound that was half exasperation, half laughter. She started to fasten her dress across her breasts. 'When I first knew him he was younger and more virile, but not as advanced in knowledge as he is now. Power takes power.'

'You left your people because you wanted to? I always thought . . .'

'That I am his servant? No more than you are the servant of Rosso. Ah, why do you start at the mention of your master's name? What is wrong?'

'I have much to tell you, Pelashil, but I'm not sure if this is the right time.'

Pelashil finished fastening her dress, and calmly wrapped a shawl around her shoulders, casting a corner of it over her head. 'If I tell you one thing, Pasquale, you must promise not to tell anyone else.'

'Of course.'

'You're a handsome boy, full of life. You shouldn't stay here in this city. When you took Piero as your secret master, I knew that in your heart you were a traveller like him.'

'Pelashil, I may have to leave soon. Will you go with me?'

'I became the servant of a foreign magus because it is the only way a woman of my people can gain real power. Our own mara'akame speak only to other men, although in the past there have been female mara'akame. But although they would not speak to me, they spoke to Piero, and set him on the road to wisdom. He has been walking that road ever since, and I have followed.'

'The plant he eats . . . you eat it too?'

'Was it not me who gave it to you? All of my people eat it. Only we know where to find the true peyote, híkuri, and how to gather it, on the pilgrimages to the sacred land.'

'I thought it would help my painting, Pelashil. That's why I took it.'

'You are still like the rest of your people, Pasquale. You are not in balance. You are ruled by the makers of things, of machines, but they see only half the world. Híkuri reveals the truth behind what we think we see.'

Pasquale thought of Piero's experiments with devices discarded by the artificers. He said, 'Then Piero wants to understand both.'

'He stands in the middle. He is the first mara'akame to do so. Those who follow him will find it easier, and go further. Now listen to me. You must not stay here. You bring trouble.'

'I don't know what you mean.'

'Men came here. Soldiers of the city. Look for you. He was scared by that. You must leave, to keep him safe. And think about what I told you. I will watch over you, because you are about to take the first step.'

And then she was gone, leaving Pasquale to reassemble his clothes from where they had been scattered about the little room. So he was being chased not only by the Savonarolistas, but by the city government too, no doubt put up to it by the merchant Taddei. If they caught him, he would be sent straight away as ransom for Raphael's corpse. And Giustiniani's men would by now have ransacked Niccolò Machiavegli's rooms and be searching for him, for the device he had accidentally acquired. He knew what he must do. It was the only thing he could do. He must return it to its owner.

Piero was standing at a table in the big room, where candles made little islands of unsteady light. His hands spread to take his weight, he leaned over drawings that were scattered like leaves across the table. He had wrapped his blanket around himself in the style of a senator from ancient Rome, leaving one bony shoulder bare, and with his unkempt white beard and elf-locked hair he resembled Saint Jerome in his study, lacking only the traditional attributes of lion and cardinal's hat.

As Pasquale came into the room the raven shifted on its perch and ruffled its wings. Pasquale said, 'Are these new pictures, master?'

Piero didn't look up, but slowly shook his head.

'The woman has left soup for you, master. You should eat.'

'Cooks grow monstrous fat on the odours of cooking alone,' Piero said, 'which is as well, for food grows repugnant to them, just as coal is hateful to a Westphalian miner, and he instead burns wood in his grate.'

It was no use forcing Piero in these matters. Pasquale said, 'If you're not hungry, master, I quite understand.'

Piero shook his head again, and said, 'The shadows are crowding me from my room. No light, boy, no light. How can poor Piero paint without light?'

Pasquale lighted fat tallow candles, and set them before the scattered mirrors and lenses, so that their light glimmered through the big cold room.

'The light doesn't stay still,' Piero complained, when at last Pasquale had finished.

'That's the nature of light, master.' Wistfully, Pasquale thought of

196

his angel – there had not been much time for contemplation of late. He cast his mind back to the glimpse he'd had of its glory, a reflection of the glory of its master, which, like the sun, could not be approached or looked at directly. Yet as sunlight dances upon the face of the waters and multiplies its glory in such a way that its raw beauty is made bearable to the human eye, so with an angel, surely, for it would be driven by the glory of its service, made bemused and breathless by its journey from Heaven to Earth. It moved, it would always move: it would be as restless as light on water. Oh, how to paint that! How to paint its face!

'Bring light here,' Piero said, and Pasquale carried a candle to the table. He saw that the pictures were delicately penned studies of fantastic animals cavorting or coiled amongst strange rock formations, sheet after sheet of drawings, and no beast like any other or like anything Pasquale had ever seen, even in the sketches made by travellers of devils cavorting in the weird Flemish paintings of Heaven and Hell.

'Are these from the New World, master?'

Piero tapped his forehead. In the candle-light Pasquale saw the skull under the skin of his secret master's face, and knew that Piero did not have long to live. He had travelled far from humanity, and the journey had worn him out before his time.

'From the country of the mind,' Piero said. 'Cristoforo Columbo was wrong to voyage out towards the edge of the Earth. There are unexplored regions far wider and wilder and stranger than any glimpsed by a scurvied sailor clinging to the top-gallant of the royal mast of his vessel, scrying for landfall. The country of the mind lives inside us all, yet most know it not. You do not know it boy, and until you do you won't be able to paint your angel. Has the woman talked to you yet?'

'She gave me one of your plants to eat, master.'

'Don't tell me what you saw – it won't have been anything important. Only true masters see the truth. You'll be going away soon. I had hoped that the woman would have had time to initiate you, but perhaps this is better. Anyway, the plants I have are losing their potency after all these years. I envy you, Pasquale. You'll taste fresh híkuri, and I never will again. Have I told you about Pelashil's people, the Wixarika?'

'Several times, master.'

'You'll hear it one more time?'

'Of course, master.'

So Piero told Pasquale how the híkuri was hunted, using the same words as he had when he had first told his tale. He told of how it took place in the dry season before winter, of how, when the maize was still green but the squash had ripened, a party of Wixarika set out on a pilgrimage lasting twenty days. After two days of preparing costumes, of prayer and cleansing confessions, they took the names of gods and, led by a mara'akame who had taken the name of the god of fire, were led across the dry plain beneath the two sacred mountains, searching for deer-tracks, for without deer there could be no peyote, which appeared in the footsteps of the first deer in the morning of the world. The first of the small grey-green plants was always pierced by an arrow and ringed with offerings; the rest were carefully examined and scrupulously packed away. Piero had taken his first peyote on the first night of his first pilgrimage, and had been led by a spotted cat through a series of images set out like booths in a carnival, and had known upon awakening that he would be a mara'akame.

Pasquale had heard this before, told in exactly the same way, but now he understood that everything Piero had told him, and all Pela-shil had done, was to initiate him in this truth: that the world of visions was as real as the world of the artificers. He said, 'Master, please forgive me. I doubted that you were a good man. I was wrong, and now I am in sore need of your advice.'

'I know, I know. They think me stupid, or a fool or a madman, but I'm not. I know why the soldiers came here. Can I see it?'

Pasquale took out the little device. Piero peered at it from every angle, and finally asked, 'And does it fly?'

'Master, as always you astound me. How did you know?'

'Because Giovanni Rosso came looking for it, before the soldiers.'

'I must return it to its maker. Master, you have talked with the Great Engineer. How can I see him? Will you take me?'

'He understands me more than most. But we have talked but twice. I know him not. Not well enough for your purpose.'

'But master, my life is in danger. I am in the middle of a struggle for a prize I would gladly give up, if I could.'

'They say the Pope has left, retreated from the fighting in the streets.'

'That's true enough. I saw him with my own eyes.' Pasquale described the scene at the gate that morning, watching his master's face soften dreamily. Piero was a great supporter of the Medicis: when they had been overthrown he had left Florence too, for the New World. When Pope Leo X had gained Saint Peter's throne, he and Andrea del Sarto had contrived a carnival triumph whose theme was death. At the centre of the procession had been the Chariot of Death itself, drawn by black buffaloes painted with white human bones and crosses, on which stood a huge figure of Death armed with a scythe standing triumphant over tombs which opened and issued forth figures draped in black cloth on which were painted the bones of complete skeletons, so that by torchlight they looked like skeletons dancing in service of their dark lord. As death was exile from life, so the triumph symbolized the long exile from which the Medicis would return to their rightful place, and again rule Florence. But they had not returned. Florence in her triumph was still stronger than Rome. It was the last spectacle that Piero had staged, and afterwards he had retreated from the world.

When Pasquale had finished describing the Pope's retreat, there was a silence. At last Piero sighed heavily and said, 'I will die with a heavy heart. How I danced not two days ago, Pasquale. How I danced. And now Florence stands alone again.'

'This talk of death makes me uncomfortable.'

'I envy you, Pasquale. Suppose you are caught and tried and executed – at least you will go to your death in the best of health, watched by thousands who will mark your passing as only the passing of a favoured few men is marked. You will march to your death to stirring music, on a fête-day, your every need having been catered for beforehand, and the announcement of your death will have been prominently placed in every broadsheet. How much better than most deaths, those small sullen private struggles. I do not fear death, Pasquale, but I fear the indignity of dying.'

Pasquale had to laugh at this fantasy. It was a trick of Piero's, to invert accepted truths and make them seem as exotic as the ceremonies of the Mexica, or any of the lesser nations of Savages.

'You laugh at death,' Piero said. 'That's good, at least. Well, I'll look after the ape for you. I don't mind that, although it will drive Pelashil mad, no doubt, and leave me entirely on my own. Poor Piero, they'll say, with only an ape to mend his clothes and cook his food, and warm his bed.'

Pasquale had forgotten about the ape, and asked where it was.

'Out in the garden, eating the figs from my trees. It is happy there, Pasquale. Leave it be. Sheathe your burning sword, eh? Don't drive it out. It knows no sin.'

Pasquale supposed it was true. The ape had killed, but not out of malice and quite without intent or any knowledge of wrong, and so without guilt. Happy ignorance of the unremembering unfallen – how he envied it, remembering his own burden.

'I may never see you again,' Piero said. 'That has just occurred to me.'

'I'll be back, master. I promise.'

'I don't mind,' Piero said quickly. 'I prefer the sound of rain to that of idle conversation. I wish I could teach you more, but perhaps you know enough already. Let learning be your journey.'

Pasquale cradled the device, turning its helical screw back and forth with a forefinger. So fragile a toy, on which the fate of empires rested. He said, 'I'll be as quiet as a church mouse, master, when I tiptoe back. And I'll wait for a clear day, with no rain. But if you could tell me, please, how to gain an audience with the Great Engineer, I can be gone now, and leave you to your contemplations.'

Piero ruffled the raven's feathers with a finger, so that the bird ducked its head in pleasure, regarding its master sideways with a round black eye shiny as a berry. 'He loves birds,' Piero said. 'That's what we talked about, mostly. I told him of the condor, that soars for hours on outstretched wings.'

'But how do I gain audience, master? When I return the device I must make sure it is into his hands that it falls. I can make my own small talk, if I need to.'

'He's one of the saddest men I know. And one of the loneliest.'

'Can I simply walk into his tower? Is it as simple as that?'

'Of course not,' Piero said sharply, still stroking his pet. 'Don't be a fool. He is more closely guarded than the Pope, for the college of Rome can always elect another pope, but there will only ever be one Great Engineer. But although he is mostly shut up in his tower, his assistants walk here and there about town. There is one who haunts the kind of low taverns that you like, Pasquale. You could try and find him, I suppose. He has a taste for the low life, and for dirty pictures. He is called Nicolas Koppernigk, a poor threadbare sketch of a man, and a notorious miser to boot. You know him?'

Pasquale remembered the cosmic engine, afire in the square. Koppernigk had proved that the Earth went around the sun, which was the centre of the universe. Or perhaps the other way around: it was all the same to him as long as the ground was always under his feet. He said, 'This Koppernigk. How do I find him?'

'Oh,' Piero said vaguely, 'one or other of the taverns of the Prussian student nation, I suppose. But first promise to change your clothes, Pasquale. Have you been swimming in the river at this late season?'

4

Rosso's studio was like a battlefield. Everything had been overturned and smashed. Pasquale's clothes, for which he had risked returning, had all been slashed or systematically slit along the seams: the fine silk shirt for which he had paid ten florins; the white, lace-trimmed shirt of best English cloth and its matching white doublet with gold silk sewn inside deep slashes; the ordinary homespun shirts and hose; the big cape he had bought from an Albanian mercenary and lovingly relined; even his work-apron had been cut to ribbons. The heels of his second-best pair of boots had been broken off. A broad leather belt, which he had tooled with intricate patterns after the Moorish style, had somehow been snapped in two, and its brass buckle bent. His truckle bed was now truly broken-backed, and its mattress cut to ribbons.

Pasquale ripped out the remains of the lining from the cloak and wrapped it around himself. The rest, all the clothes he had carefully collected or mended or sewn together himself, were beyond salvage.

The main room of the studio was in as bad a state as Pasquale's few possessions. The work-bench had been overturned, the grindstone cracked in two, the door of the little kiln broken off. Pigments had been spilt everywhere, making gaudy arcs and splashes across the floor, and every canvas had been slashed, every frame broken. In the half-light of dusk, Pasquale felt in the back of the kiln, and found the small cloth bag in which Rosso habitually kept the studio's takings. It contained more than he'd hoped for but less than it should, considering the fees for the stiffener and for the broadsheet engravings. Rosso, had he still lived, would have been grievously short with the rent.

Pasquale turned to go, and stumbled over the little panel he had so lovingly prepared. A hole had been kicked in it. He held it and felt nothing, for all that he had spent so much skill and time on preparing it. It was made of best seasoned poplar, glued and then braced, and given an ornate frame that Pasquale had gilded himself. He had sanded the wood and filled every small knothole and crack with sawdust and glue, then coated the panel with one thin and three thick coats of liquid size and covered the size with strips of linen. The next layers, of *gesso grosso*, or chalk mixed in size, had taken two weeks to prepare; each had been allowed to dry for several days and then scraped and sanded smooth before the next was applied. Finally, he had applied coats of *gesso sottile*, the first rubbed on by hand, the others each brushed on before the previous one had dried, eight in all. And after that had been dried in the sun, Pasquale had smoothed and scraped it with spatula and *raffietti* until it was as smooth and burnished as ancient ivory.

All for some thug to put his boot through, in a moment.

As he stood there, Pasquale heard someone coming carelessly up the stairs. A moment later there was a brisk hammering at the door. He found a little knife and unbent its blade between two floorboards and crept to the door, which he had left open.

The monk who looked after the gardens of Santa Croce was fixing a magistrate's notice with nails and a hammer. Pasquale caught the monk's hand on the upswing, jabbed him in the neck with the point of the knife, where fat made two rolls at the collar of his habit, and caught the hammer when it dropped.

'I don't have any time,' Pasquale said, 'so please tell me straight. Did you see who did this?'

The monk moved his head cautiously, a thumb's width to either side. His eyes were fixed on the notice he had nailed to the door.

Pasquale added, 'The noise must have been considerable. You didn't come and complain?'

'I was . . . elsewhere.'

'They may have been costumed as militia, or masked. Which was it?'

'I wasn't here!'

The hammer made a very satisfactory noise as it thumped across the floor of the workshop. 'No,' Pasquale said, 'you were at the Offices of Night and Monasteries, to judge by this scrap of paper. What's this about a harness weighted with lead?'

'To stop it climbing. I mean only to look after my garden. It is my duty, and your ape—'

The monk watched, goggle-eyed, as Pasquale slashed the notice to ribbons.

'Pray for me, brother,' Pasquale said. 'I'd speak more of this, but I have an important appointment with a scholar.'

As he hurried down the winding stair, for the last time, he heard the monk shouting that he'd get a new notice restraining master and ape. You can bang on that drum all you like, fellow, Pasquale thought. Two days ago it might have frightened me, but no more.

Doctor Nicolas Koppernigk favoured the taverns used by students of the Prussian nation, where he held informal tutorials and took wine as his fee, being too parsimonious to buy his own. He had a cautious taste for the low life, so long as it cost him nothing, and preferred the company of students to that of his fellow artificers, of whom he was both jealous and suspicious.

A band of strolling musicians was playing dance music in the square outside in the hope that they would please enough of the tavern's patrons to gain a free meal. Small chance of that, Pasquale thought, who had a poor opinion of students in general, and Prussian students in particular. Students were no more than intellectual vagabonds, flitting from university to university until they found one that would sell them a doctorate; they had no discipline and no craft, and inhabited an airy world of ideas. As for Prussians, they lacked even the ideas, and had no ear for the finer aspects of music, liking only drinking-songs and bombastic marches.

The tavern was noisy and smoky, filled with students shouting at each other across the tables, their faces beast-like in the flickering rushlights. One group was beating its table with beakers and singing a dreary tune in bad Latin:

> *The British eat shit because it's all they have,*
> *The Italians eat shit because they're dumb,*
> *The French eat shit because the Italians do,*
> *But we eat shit because we are strong loyal Prussians,*
> *Ha! Ha! Ha!*

Doctor Koppernigk sat in the furthest darkest corner with three swarthy lumpen-faced students who looked at Pasquale with ill grace when he bowed and introduced himself. Koppernigk started up in a kind of befuddled pop-eyed amazement. He was a gaunt man of about fifty, the cheeks of his bony face scraped red, his eyes set close beneath eyebrows that knit together to form a single line that lowered as he regarded Pasquale. He wore a fur-trimmed cap that sat askew his long greasy grey hair, and a long tunic of what might once have been rust-coloured fabric, but was now darkened to a blotchy black.

Pasquale sat opposite Koppernigk and called loudly for more wine, and told the scientist that he would be a new pupil.

Koppernigk's suspicious gaze shifted to Pasquale's face, jumped back nervously away. 'What trick is this?'

Pasquale lit a cigarette and sucked smoke deep into his lungs. 'There is no trick at all, signor. I need your help, and Piero di Cosimo recommended me to you.'

'I need no agent, and no pupils for that matter. I'm a philosopher, signor, no mere teacher.'

'And yet you teach,' Pasquale said mildly, smiling at the three students and getting more scowls in return. He showed a coin, and asked how much a private lesson would cost.

Koppernigk allowed cautiously, eyeing the coin with a kind of hunger, that three times as much might be sufficient.

'It's yours,' Pasquale said, and sat down when Koppernigk had shooed off his lumpen pupils like an old wife scattering chickens.

'Now, signor,' Koppernigk said, 'you can ask me what you want, although I should warn you that I am notoriously short of answers.'

'I must apologize, signor, for driving away your pupils for this night. But in many ways I'm no stranger to you. Ah! Perhaps this wine will help make amends.' Pasquale beamed at the greasy drab who had thumped a flask of wine on the table, and gave her a clipped silver coin with a carelessness he certainly did not feel. 'Please drink with me at least, good Canon, and hear my entreaty.'

Koppernigk poured wine into his beaker with niggardly care. 'I'm a canon at Frauenberg Cathedral, it's true, but I haven't been there since I was installed. My mission is temporal, not spiritual. You call me Doctor, Doctor Copernicus, if you don't mind. My Latin is as good as anyone's, and that's the name that is known in all the countries of the world.'

'It's because of your renown that I came, signor,' Pasquale assured him.

Koppernigk was suddenly suspicious again. 'Who sent you? Why did you come to me? I do not advertise my goods like a merchant, no one does who has any pretensions at greatness in the scientific arts. In any case, too many have made too much from my ideas.'

It was as Piero had said; Doctor Koppernigk, having been forced to loose the truths he had uncovered upon the world, had lost control of them, which was an affront to his soul. His caution was the caution of a miser asked to part with some trifling fraction of his fortune. He would hoard his truths, if he could, for otherwise his rivals might gain from them at his expense. He had divined the disposition of the architecture of the universe, but was not clever enough to profit from his discovery, or indeed to defend it except by evolving complicated epicycles to explain what drove the motions of the planets about the sun. His discovery that the Earth and the other planets revolved around the sun had revolutionized the notion of the place of man in the universe, and yet with his epicycles and equants and epicycles upon epicycles he had sought not to topple the old order, but to reconcile it with his findings through a receding infinity of adjustments. He knew well enough that he could not demonstrate those mechanisms, for in truth they did not exist except in the minds of men, and so, although he had shifted the centre of the universe, he was frightened that his discovery would be taken from him. He trusted no one, not even himself.

Pasquale explained again that he was here only because of the good canon's reputation, and the advice of Piero di Cosimo.

Koppernigk glared at Pasquale and said, 'You say you know me already? I don't think so. Have you been following me?'

'Oh no. Not at all.'

'I won't have people following me about the city.'

'Quite right. I understand exactly.'

'I called the militia on one fellow only last year. He denied it of course, and the militia wouldn't believe me, but it was quite true. Charlatans would dearly love to use my name to further their schemes. Astrologers and the like. I am plagued,' Koppernigk said, and drained his beaker, 'by astrologers and so-called natural scientists, under which disguise so many magicians trade these days. No, if that's what you're after, then you may go now, or I will call the guard.'

'Doctor, I am an artist, not an astrologer. I understand from Piero di Cosimo that you have appreciated some of my depictions of the amorous arts. Please, do take more wine. There's plenty more where that came from.' The wine wasn't too bad, Pasquale thought, or at least, it was by no means as bad as he had expected, and if it left a coppery taste in the mouth, the heat it generated was genuine enough. He freely poured wine for both of them, and drank deep to show goodwill.

Koppernigk drank in rapid sips, his veiny hands wrapped around the beaker as if he were afraid that someone would take it from him. He said, 'If you're an artist I don't suppose you have come to hear about my theory of the aether and the propagation of light. I must ask you again why you are here, signor. Bear in mind my time is limited. You say I have appreciated your work? What was your name again? Firenze? You are named for the city?'

'No, Doctor. My name is Pasquale de Cione Fiesole. The small town, you know, no more than an hour's ride away.'

'I know Fiesole, of course. I have been there several times to make my observations. The city smoke you see, obscures the stars, and then again there are the acetylene lamps . . . Have you more of that wine? This is good wine, for Tuscan wine, although Prussian wine is much better. But I should be careful. It will mount to my head.'

'Not at all, signor. Wine fortifies the blood, and so feeds the seat of intelligence.' Pasquale found that he was grinning at the thought that this crabbed colourless scholar was his only chance of gaining entry to the court of the Great Engineer, and worked his lips to erase his smile. His face felt both hot and numb, as if it had been thrust into a furnace.

'You artists are wrong, of course,' Koppernigk said with grave precision. 'You cannot represent the world by smearing pigments on a flat plane. It only works because the eye is so easily tricked – but it is not real. As for reality, light itself is the key, and the motion of light, of course, as so recently demonstrated by the Great Engineer. You did see his tableau of living light?'

Pasquale lit another cigarette from the twisted stub of the first. 'I regret that I was detained elsewhere. But you have made the very point I wished to raise. There is something I want to learn, Doctor.'

Koppernigk suddenly seemed to take fright, as if he had stepped across a line only he could see, into dangers only he could apprehend. 'I am nothing but a student in those matters. I can repeat only what

208

is said many times, that is. I have no direct experience, no, none at all.'

Pasquale fumbled out the picture he had rescued from the fireplace at Guistiniani's villa. Flakes of silvery stuff were caught in the black cloth he'd wrapped around the glass plate, and the darkening was worse, a lapping rim of shadows encroaching on all but the very centre. He laid it on the table and asked Koppernigk his opinion.

Koppernigk planted his elbows on the table and his sharp chin in his cupped hands, and frowned down at the picture, his eyes wrinkling in the way of the short-sighted. Then he realized what it showed and reared backwards, looking wildly around at the noisy tavern, the students carousing or singing crude national songs. They were drunk; everyone in the tavern was drunk. Koppernigk sputtered that he really knew nothing of that sort of thing, no, not at all.

'I mean the process. I would learn of the process. This picture is crude, yes.'

Koppernigk said with what appeared to be genuine outrage, 'It is the vilest kind of devil-worship!'

Pasquale talked quickly, stumbling over his words, explaining that a composition with artistic merit would be another matter, it was not so much the subject as the presentation. As he talked he took out paper and pen and quickly sketched from memory the outline of a tableau he had once created. His hand was shaking and yet seemed as heavy as lead at the same time; he botched the passage of the woman's hair, and had to peer closely to get her hands right. She was couched on pillows, dressed only in a filmy clinging shift, her face dreamy with delight as she stroked her own self with the bent fingers of one hand, and weighed the globes of her breast with another. The commission had made Pasquale less than a florin, although the *stationarius* had reprinted it over and over.

Koppernigk watched him sidelong, as if he suspected a trick. 'Well, I recognize that, of course. It is of its kind, I suppose you would say, an interesting piece.'

'It was my hand that first drew it, Doctor. But you see how it is, I make a little money, and the printers make much more. This new process, though. This painting with light. If you could tutor me in it, we could together make much money. I'll reward you well for your time – this florin, here, to begin with.'

209

'Anyone can copy out a print,' Koppernigk said, 'especially one as popular as that one.'

'We call them stiffeners in the trade,' Pasquale said. 'I'll take you to meet the model. Then you'll believe me.'

'Perhaps so. Perhaps so. Ah, the wine is finished.'

Pasquale bought another flagon. They drank, to the aether, whatever that was, to Florence, to the Great Engineer. Somehow Pasquale and Koppernigk, without transition, were walking along a road, stumbling arm in arm in darkness towards a distant lamp as dim as a star in the solid darkness. The cold air smote Pasquale's face. Wine, he had drunk too much wine. He smiled foolishly. He was in mortal peril, but at least he could still live a little.

Koppernigk was talking and talking, his hold on his store of words loosened by drink. He was talking about the aether, or the concept of the aether, it being as vaporous as the epicycles which Koppernigk evoked to keep the Earth in motion around the sun. It was, it seemed, no medium at all, but a higher state of matter, of vibration.

'Light is no more than matter, raised to this higher state. It is well known that light travels faster than sound, and my theory shows why. And beyond light, there is God Himself. Dear Christ save me!'

Koppernigk slipped on a wad of filth and had not Pasquale held him up would have gone flying into the open drain that ran not at all sweetly in the centre of the street. Koppernigk hiccuped and whispered, 'I'll say no more because there are enemies all around who would seize on my ideas and misrepresent them. Science is not to be rushed. Those who try will burn themselves out, you mark me. Hush. What do you hear?'

It was the sound of wagon-wheels, muffled in some way, and coming towards them from behind.

Pasquale pushed Koppernigk into a deep arched gateway. The iron gate was locked at this hour, the courtyard beyond dark. Koppernigk made feeble struggles to get free, but Pasquale held him fast, and clapped a hand over his mouth when he started to exclaim indignantly. The muffled noise of the wagon grew closer, closer. Pasquale discovered that he was holding his breath. He knew what the wagon was even before it went past: it was the wagon of the corpsemasters, who roamed the city with a licence to take away any corpses they deemed fit for the use of the dissectors and experimenters in the New

University. Many said that, such was the demand in these enlightened times, the corpsemasters had taken to stealing corpses from their own wakes, and even to murdering stray citizens caught out alone in the late night.

It was a low long black wagon, drawn by a single horse. The driver and his mate were hunched on the bench, both muffled in high-collared black cloaks, and with black leather masks covering their faces. The horse which drew the wagon was shod in leather boots; the wheels were wrapped with rags. There was a distinctive odour, a strong scent of violets overlying the odour of rotting meat.

Then it was past. Koppernigk made another struggle for freedom, banging against the iron gate so that it rattled. Pasquale could have hit him, but that would have been an end to his chance of entering the Great Tower. When Pasquale released him, the artificer said indignantly, 'I know those men.'

Pasquale laughed. 'I suppose you do.'

'I studied anatomy, amongst other sciences, when I was a student. Theirs is an honourable profession, and they are only going about their legal business. Without them, we would not advance in the treatment of illness. There's no need to be afraid, young man. Now where is this accursed place you said you knew? I will see the woman, then I will believe you.'

'I have also studied anatomy, but would not like to meet those gentlemen in these circumstances. You'll help me, Doctor. I must insist.'

Koppernigk said with drunken dignity, and not much truth, 'You needn't threaten me. I am not afraid of threats.'

When they reached the lamp at the corner of the street, Pasquale knew where he was, and remembered where they were going. He had promised to show Koppernigk his model, Maddalena, as proof that he was who he said he was. Wine, there is no end to truth in wine, or the trouble truth can get you into.

Then he and Koppernigk were hammering on the door of Mother Lucia's house. A dog set to barking somewhere, and then the door opened and they tumbled inside, almost falling into the soft fat arms of the whoremistress, Mother Lucia herself. Her face was caked with white lead and rouge, but in the soft candle-light she looked, if not girlish, then more like a doll than the old woman she was. Somehow

Pasquale was sitting, a cup of wine in his hands, blinking at the bright lamplight in the parlour. A trio of girls, bareshouldered in velvet gowns, their breasts pushed up like soft rounded shelves, giggled together on the other side of the room, which seemed to be slowly sinking through the ground.

'My friend, where . . . ?'

'Why with Maddalena, of course,' Mother Lucia said. 'Oh, Pasquale, Pasqualino, you are in your cups.'

Pasquale said stupidly, 'You're a good woman in your way, Mother Lucia. Did I ever tell you that?'

'Business is business, dearie, and you think about doing another nice picture for me and we won't say anything more about it. Brings in business, those pictures. Like now.'

'Can't pay you know. Absolutely broke.' There was the florin, of course, but he had promised it to Doctor Koppernigk.

'Your friend pays. Don't you worry. Where have you been, Pasquale? Your clothes are covered in mud.'

Pasquale, reduced by wine and exhaustion to sentiment, said, 'I'm in a lot of trouble, Mother Lucia. You're a good Christian woman to help me. I'll never go to another place from now on.'

'A fine compliment, I'm sure,' Mother Lucia said, with the air of one who has heard it all before.

'No, no. I mean it! This is a hinge of history, great terrible times. That you should help me, help me now . . .'

'You remember my charity, dearie, next time you take up your pen.' The girls in the corner giggled, and Mother Lucia shot them a severe look. She told Pasquale, 'That's as far as it goes. Meanwhile, don't drink any more wine. I can't bear to see a man cry.'

'If only I could start painting now . . . you're an angel, Lucia. My friend, has he finished?'

'Old men always take a long time,' one of the whores said with a sniff.

'A strange sort of cove,' Mother Lucia observed, taking a cup from another of her whores with a regal gesture. 'Asked me if I did the operation on my girls, you know, the one where a piece of skull is taken out to make them docile. A little hole it is, and a wire is inserted to stir out the devil. I told him this was a straight establishment, and he said it was the other way around, that I was unregulated. Why,

I regulate as I please, you know that, Pasqualino. I know his sort, they'd make us all machines fit only for one thing or another, according to their wants.'

Pasquale must have dozed, for he woke to the echo of a shriek from somewhere in the house. He jumped up and pushed past the whores, who clutched at him and told him to sit down, to leave it be, and found himself running down a candle-lit passage. There was a roaring in his ears. He kept banging into one or the other of the walls. A door burst open and he tumbled inside.

Maddalena was kneeling on a wrecked bed, a sheet pulled up to her chin in bunched fists. Her unbound hair tumbled down to the small of her back. 'He did a runner, right out the window,' she squealed, and the Moorish servant who'd followed Pasquale nodded grimly and ran back out.

'You better go,' Mother Lucia said, out of breath at the doorway. 'We'll sort him out.'

Pasquale flung open the shutters of the window, but there was only an empty alley below. He leaned into the cold dark air, his head spinning with an excess of wine and high excitement. 'Don't hurt him,' he said. 'I have need of his services.'

Mother Lucia said in a splendid rage, 'He gives service and cuts and runs – a fine kind of gentleman he must be!' Her bare upper arms, hung with fatty flesh like dewlaps, quivered. 'He won't do that again at my establishment. Fine kind of friends you have, Pasquale. There'll be a reckoning over this.'

'Two paintings. Three. Big as you like. Where did he go?'

'I heard the corpse-wagon outside,' Maddalena said. 'Maybe it frightened him.'

Pasquale went to the ewer and up-ended it over his head. Gasping and blinking, soaked and more nearly sober, he said, 'I think I'll need to use the back way.'

Then there was a hammering on the front door.

Maddalena gave a squeak of fear and the sheet fell, exposing her breasts. Mother Lucia said, 'You know the back door well enough, I think. Don't be in a hurry to return, Pasquale.'

'Never mind,' Pasquale said, 'they'd follow me that way anyway.'

He swung his legs over the sill of the window and let himself down until he was clinging by his fingertips, then dropped and landed sprawling on the half-frozen muck of the alley floor. He picked himself up, ran to the end of the alley, and squinted around the corner.

The corpse-wagon was parked in the street hard by the door of Mother Lucia's establishment. The two black-cloaked corpsemasters were wrestling with Mother Lucia's big Moorish servant; even as Pasquale watched, one of the men produced a sap and knocked the Moor sprawling. Then the two were inside the house and Pasquale heard Mother Lucia's loud indignant voice.

A man's voice, no doubt that of one of the corpsemasters, rode over it. 'Where is the thief?'

'He ran,' Mother Lucia said. 'One of your artificers had one of my girls and ran off without paying. You should pay, as you also work for the New University. And make recompense for wounding my guard!'

'It was the artificer who told us that the man who brought him here tried to rob him. Where's your pimp? He's the thief we're interested in.'

Pasquale groaned. Clearly, drink and spent lust had inflamed Koppernigk's suspicions.

'I have no need of pimps. I have,' Mother Lucia said with incandescent dignity, 'my reputation. Wait! Where are you going?'

A moment later there was the sound of furniture being overturned, and then a window went out in a cascade of glass, followed by the sound of a whistle blowing, the alarm call for the city militia.

Pasquale could run of course, but he doubted that he would get far. Surely if Koppernigk had alerted these two, then he would alert others. And besides, he must still gain an audience with the Great Engineer. There was only one thing for it, only one way to get into the New University without being seen. He jumped on to the back of the wagon, lifted the heavy oiled canvas sheet, and scrambled beneath.

He barely had time to settle himself before he heard the two corpsemasters coming back, pursued by Mother Lucia's vengeful voice. Pasquale lay still in the darkness, up against a cold heavy body. The rough planks were wet with something that was soaking into his hose. There was a creaking as the two men climbed on to the wagon's bench, then a lurch as they started off. In the heavily perfumed darkness beneath the tarpaulin, a corpse's cold hand fell across Pasquale's face. He didn't dare move it; suppose one of the corpsemasters chanced to be looking down at his load? Another corpse, swollen with gases, made liquid farting noises at every jolt. The smell was not as bad as that in the anatomy theatre in high summer, on the third day of dissection when nothing is left but a shell of spoiling muscle and fat over yellow bones, but Pasquale did not have a pouch of camphor to hold to his nostrils, and although the strong artificial scent of violets burned his throat and eyes, it did not mask the stench but only cut through it. He turned his head and was able to thrust his nose close to the cleated edge of the canvas sheet, and so draw in fresh cold air. He prayed that these corpses had all died violent or natural deaths, and that he would not catch the flux or the French pox from their black air.

The corpsemasters' voices could be heard over the rumble of the wagon's muffled wheels and the creaking of its wooden frame. One, slow and deep-voiced, was grumbling about the arrogance of artificers. 'As if we weren't busy enough, we're bodyguards to the fools to the bargain.'

The other said, 'He's a stubborn blockhead of an old man who thinks everyone is set on robbing him. No doubt some pimp asked too much for the favour of introducing him to a nice warm whore.'

'Well, the pimp ran off too. Or never existed in the first place.'

'It doesn't matter. We'll make sure we get that coin he promised us, even if we didn't find the pimp. Did you see the tits on the girl? I'd have liked to stay there for sloppy seconds.'

The deep-voiced one laughed. 'The way it's going you'll be able to afford her fresh and warm in a day or two.'

'The way it's going we'll be out of business by then. War is good for medicine, bad for the likes of us. Any fool can turn his hand to the trade during war.'

'Don't you worry,' the first said. 'Unless they find some way of preserving corpses in summer we'll always have a job. This lot won't keep the theatres going past the New Year. Look at it like this – at least we don't have to go on the hunt.'

The second said, 'We might have to, even so. Too many hot-blooded young men killing each other, and not enough women.'

'Brains is all they want these days. They're not too particular what kind. Brains are all the same.'

'Brains are the seat of reason, which may be why you don't find them interesting.'

'Now hearts are a different matter. I always have had a soft spot for hearts.'

'Hearts or lights, it's all money in the end.'

'You have no poetry, Agostino. The heart now, with its four chambers and its valves, is a miracle. Think of the way the blood must flow in the heart, because the valves are so cunningly designed that they open inward or outward according to need. You need an education in these matters, as I've always said.'

The second corpsemaster, Agostino, said, 'There's still the medical students to think about. Maybe that young whore you were soft on, the one with the tits. I would look the other way if you wanted to enjoy her before we put her over to the cold side.'

'My father was in this trade, and his father before him. They didn't have to use the knife.'

'I have heard enough about your father, thank you. You turn down here. We'll make this last pick-up and then get back.'

The corpse's hand flopped away from Pasquale's face as the wagon turned, fell back again when it drew to a halt. There was a spell of silence, and then the end of the tarpaulin was thrown back and a corpse slung on to the load-bed. The deep-voiced corpsemaster talked with someone about money. The wagon started up again, rolling ponderously along the silent streets, the corpsemasters talking in subdued voices until at last the wagon stopped again and there was a brazen clash of gates.

The corpsemasters exchanged pleasantries with a guard. The wagon rolled forward a short distance before halting again. Then a lurch, and the sensation of falling amidst the pounding of steam machineries and rattling of iron chains. The wagon was inside the New University.

6

The falling stopped with a thump. Sudden light outlined the edge of the oiled canvas sheet over the load-bed. The wagon rolled forward slowly. Dull echoes, the noise of an engine thumping mindlessly over and over. Pasquale fumbled out his little knife and was about to risk cutting the canvas when the end of the sheet was lifted and flung back.

Pasquale lay still, peeking through the stiff fingers of the dead hand which still lay across his face. Bright lights burned overhead, a ring of acetylene jets depending from a vaulted ceiling painted plain white. It was freezing cold, a cellar deep under the ground. The corpsemasters began to unload the wagon, using an iron hook to pull a corpse to the end of the load-bed, then swinging it away by hair and feet.

Pasquale eased himself up, and saw that beyond the wagon were rows of slabs, most with naked corpses laid on them. The two corpsemasters were busy with the body they had just unloaded. One was taking down details on a scrap of paper while the other made measurements.

Pasquale scrambled up and jumped over the side of the wagon, landing with a clatter on the cold slate floor. The horses snorted and stamped, dragging on the wagon's brake. The two corpsemasters turned and shouted and gave chase. Pasquale dodged amidst bodies laid on slate-topped slabs and ran for the nearest door, slamming it shut on the faces of the corpsemasters.

He was in a small circular closet caged round with a shell of lattice-work iron a hand's breadth away from the rough stone walls. The corpsemasters banged on the door, and the floor shivered and swayed beneath Pasquale's feet. He grabbed at a rope and whooped with surprise as the room rose, carrying him with it.

The room rose a long way, swaying with a small motion, at one point passing a shield of lead that slid around it in a clatter of chains. When the room finally banged to a stop Pasquale did not at first trust himself to let go of the rope, half-convinced that if he did, the room would promptly plunge all the way back down to where it had started. The door, when he pushed it open, let out on to windy night.

The mortuary must have been lodged in the cool deep basements of the Great Tower, for the moving room had delivered him to the tower's very top. He was looking out across the roofs and terraces of the New University towards the river, its channels defined by the lights of the floating water-mills. The dark hills rose beyond, only thinly mantled with lights. Armies gathering out there, an unseen menace heavy in the air, like storm-clouds.

Wind quite blew away the confusion of the wine Pasquale had drunk. He shivered in the tumble of cold air. His hose clung to his legs, clotted with jelly-like corpse blood and worse. He was on a kind of platform that took up half the roof. A confusion of lesser towers bearing signal arms rose behind him. Even as he watched, a set of arms on the tallest structure turned and clapped upwards before commencing their swooping formal dance, sending a message out to the edge of the world. Their lanterns seemed to leave traceries of red and green light in the air.

Winding-gear jutted beyond the edge of the parapet, two sets of triple drums angled either side of a Hero's engine with a tall narrow chimney. The chimney was topped with a kind of cap that spun and clattered in the constant wind. Cables threaded through pulleys rose into the darkness beyond the parapet. Pasquale could just make out the precise geometric shapes that made swooping shadows against the night clouds. Kites, tethered by thin yet strong copper cables, flying in the constant wind above the tower top.

Pasquale laid a hand on a cable, felt its thrumming. Clinging to the cable, he looked down and whooped with exultation. The bulk of the tower diminished darkly, tapering down to its base. Pasquale could see foreshortened lights on the tower that must be windows, and here and there balconies and platforms jutting from its wall like the nests of swifts in the eaves of houses. Lights defined the shape of the Piazza della Signoria, and then the maze of streets that webbed the Palazzo and the floodlit Duomo and a thousand lesser buildings, the whole night-time city stretched between the river and the city walls.

Chains clattered behind Pasquale, unwinding from the drums on top of the shed which housed the moving room. The room was making a fast descent. By the red and green light of the signal-lanterns Pasquale could see the chains swaying down, far down the long long shaft, to the flat disc of the room's ceiling, diminished by perspective to the size of a coin. As Pasquale watched, the disc passed through the ring of the lead counterweight and halted for a few moments before starting to rise again in a roar of chains.

Pasquale looked for something that he could jam into the chains, or into the winding-drums, or the chain-drive which turned the winding-drums, driven by some engine far below, but there were only big drums of cable which he could not shift by even a finger's width. He could hide amongst the signal structures, but not from any prolonged search – and even as he thought of it a hatch banged open on the far side of the tower's roof and a man climbed through and began to shine a lantern this way and that.

Pasquale ducked down, crouching at the base of the winch. The moving room banged to a stop. Its door opened and two men rushed out, one dragging a big leashed hound, the other a lantern whose light shot out across the platform. The man searching amongst the signal-towers turned towards his fellow, and his lantern-beam brushed over Pasquale. The dog barked, pulling its master forward, and Pasquale jumped up and caught a kite-cable and swung out into the rush of the wind.

As soon as Pasquale trusted his weight to the cable, the tethered kite swooped down, and Pasquale was at once plunged below the level of the platform. He kicked out as the smooth stone of the tower rushed past, managed to hook a leg over one of the kite's three cables. He hung upside-down by his hands and the crook of a knee, looking up at cloudy night sky and the tower's looming shadow. He could feel the long drop at his back. Strong cold wind plucked and sang in his ears, lashing his hair around his face and numbing his hands, but he was elated rather than scared, believing that he must have seemed to have run into darkness and disappeared like a wraith.

Then the guards looked over the edge of the parapet, and three lantern-beams shot out, crossing and recrossing.

Pasquale started to climb along the cable, and as he did so the kite rose, unreeling its cables and Pasquale with it. The guards hauled at the cable to which Pasquale clung, but their efforts were nothing compared to the smooth power of the wind, and transmitted only the faintest of jerks. One of them called to Pasquale, something to the effect that he shouldn't be a fool, he wouldn't be hurt if he came down, but most of his words were blown away in the wind. The others were bent at the winch's Hero's engine, trying to spark a light in its boiler-pan with a flint.

Pasquale, knees hooked around the cable, hauled himself hand over hand until he was directly beneath the great kite. Its surface, canvas stretched over a frame of ash, shivered and boomed. By the fugitive light of the guards' lantern-beams, Pasquale saw an open harness or frame of wicker like a short sleeveless tunic lashed to the crossbar of the framing. A steering-bar curved beyond it. He climbed on until he was dangling just beyond the harness, at the point where the cable entered a leather collar and split to fan out in a dozen strands which anchored at the kite's blunt nose.

An urgent vibration started in the cable. Pasquale glanced down and saw that the chimney of the Hero's engine was spitting sparks. In a few minutes it would be warm enough to begin to wind in the triple cables, something that couldn't be managed by main force unless, as Pasquale had seen on carnival days when smaller kites were flown from the city walls, twenty men united their strength.

He steadied his grip on the cable and unhooked his legs and slowly turned himself around. It was no more difficult than his tricks with the ape outside the big windows of Rosso's rooms, even though the drop was a hundred times greater – but he must not think of the drop. His hands were almost numb now, and his fingers seemed to be swollen to twice their usual size. He drew his knees to his chest, then kicked backward. For a moment his feet tangled in the harness and he felt a stab of pure panic, because, stretched out as he was, the twisting of the kite's frame could make him lose his grip. He kicked like a frog, and inched backwards, hand over hand again, until he felt the harness cradle his hips and his chest.

The guards were shouting at him again. Their lantern-beams shook back and forth on the kite's undersurface. Working with one hand, Pasquale pulled the harness-straps tight, something easier than he'd thought it would be; little teeth in the brass snaps let the leather straps slide one way but not the other. His feet found hooked stirrups, and he finally let go of the cable with one hand. The harness creaked and took his weight and held. He grasped the bar in front of his face with both hands and twisted it hard over, as he had seen the carnival kite-riders do so many times that summer, when he had begun to search for the shadow of the reality of his angel.

The kite slid down the air at once, alarmingly fast. Its right edge rattled, letting air spill into the space caused by the wind blowing over the top of its surface. He knew from his conversations with the boys who rode the brief loops of the carnival kites that they flew because air moved more quickly over the top of the cunningly shaped lifting-surface than beneath. Air lifted the kite as it sought to fill the emptiness so created, for God so loves His creation that He abhors any space that is incomplete, no matter how small, and crams the world with detail upon detail.

Now, with air spilling under its right edge, the kite fell sideways. At the same moment someone declutched the cable-drums and the kite immediately gained a good two hundred *braccia* of cable. It swooped down and down before the engine started to wind in the triple cables.

Pasquale had been aiming for a platform that cantilevered out beneath the last tier of the tower, but he misjudged the liveliness of the kite. The balcony rushed by him and then he was below it and falling away from the tower. He tried to tip to the left, and with air spilling under both edges the kite lost lift entirely.

For a horrifying moment it plunged straight down. The lights of the piazza spun dizzyingly. Then the winch made up the slack and the kite jerked backwards with such force that Pasquale's hands were wrenched from the control-bar and his breath was driven from him as the harness crushed his ribs. The cables snagged on the edge of the balcony and the kite swung inward, pivoting on this hinge-point. Pasquale saw a tall stained-glass window rush at him: an angel, a white angel raising a burning sword in triumph over a prostrate serpentine devil. It burst around him in shards of white and red and gold.

7

Fortunately for Pasquale, the guards were quick-witted, and they threw the brakes of the winch as soon as they saw what had happened; otherwise he would have been dragged up with the remains of the kite and smashed into the base of the balcony. Instead, Pasquale found himself caught amongst the burst and twisted lead framework of the window with multicoloured glass falling around him, tinkling to the floor of a big, vaulted room. Its wooden skeleton smashed, the kite's lifting-surface folded around him like broken wings. He looked like a crucified angel.

The cross-braces of the kite and the wicker harness had taken the brunt of the blow, but still his breath had been knocked out of him. Cold air howled, fretting the rags of the kite. By the time he remembered the straps that held him and started to fumble with them, guards had burst through a door and were running towards him between long tables strewn with papers and pieces of machinery. The guards all wore steel armour plated to a mirror finish. Wind blew papers into the air like a flock of startled birds.

An old man, with long white hair and a long white beard falling in waves around his shoulders and over his chest, supported by a guard, blinked up at Pasquale. Another man swaggered in, splendid in red velvets.

It was Salai. Like an actor in a pageant, he threw out an arm, pointing at Pasquale. 'There, master! You see! There is the traitor!'

Despite his dizzy confusion, Pasquale realized at once who the old man must be. He struggled against the bonds of his harness, waking pain in his arms and back. The guards made noise, finding a ladder, moving a table littered with machine parts and glass fragments away from the window where Pasquale hung.

'Don't listen,' Pasquale shouted. 'He is the father of lies. Please . . .'

Salai grinned at Pasquale. He *did* look like a fat little devil in his red tunic and doublet and red and black particoloured hose. He said to the old man, 'I will bring you proof directly, master, and tell you all.'

The old man mumbled something to Salai, laying a hand on the plump man's arm. But Pasquale could not hear what he said, for now the ladder banged into position beside his head and two guards started to climb it while others jumped on to the table and started to pry apart the twisted framework of lead strips in which the kite had become entangled.

Salai made a long speech to the old man, whispering into his ear and now and then glancing sidelong at Pasquale with a mischievous malevolence. When Salai was done, the old man started to speak, but Salai laid his hand on the old man's arm and said something to the guard, who helped the old man away.

A guard cut the straps of Pasquale's harness; then others had his legs, his arms and in a minute they had him down. He tried to struggle as Salai went through his scrip, but the guards were all burly beef-fed Swiss: as easy to wrestle bullocks to the ground. Pasquale could only watch as Salai tossed aside his knife and bits of paper and charcoal with a delicate contempt; then he picked out the little flying device in its paper shell.

Salai unwrapped the device and held it up, turned it this way and that so that shadows and highlights ran amongst its intricate paper spirals and the fretted mechanism. 'You see,' he said to one of the guards. 'Mark this well. The boy had it with him.'

Then he thrust it into his red velvet tunic and told the guards, 'Bring him and follow me.'

They lifted Pasquale up, one man to an arm or a leg, and carried him down a winding stair to a small room shaped like the letter D, or a strung bow, with a curved wall of stone on one side, and a wall of cabinets on the other. When the guards set him down Pasquale picked himself up as quickly as possible and faced Salai, who stood just outside the door, two burly guards at his back.

'Full marks for your entrance,' Salai said, and made soft mocking applause. 'I cannot tell you how convenient this is. I could almost kiss you. My estimation of your abilities has risen, although it seems that I was right all along about your intelligence. I won't ask why you came here, not now. Why, I will not even ask how you gained entrance to the tower, or at least not at once. That pleasure will come later.'

'You know very well why I'm here, Salai.' Pasquale spoke to the guards as much as Salai. 'It was you who stole the device, and when it fell into my hands and I learned just how important it was, I tried to bring it here. I would bring it directly to the Great Engineer. This is the truth!'

'Oh, shout all you want. You see, these are my men, painter.' Salai sniffed the air. 'There's a certain odour about you. Did you shit your breeches when you came through the window? Speak up: it's nothing to be ashamed of.'

'It is nothing but old blood. A smell you should know intimately. How did you escape Giustiniani's ambush, Salai? I know it was Giustiniani – those fireworks had his mark, and one of his men nearly surprised me in Niccolò Machiavegli's room.'

'Who said I escaped?'

'You betrayed my master, and you betrayed the Savonarolistas to Giustiniani. Who else?'

'Ah, such spirit. I shall enjoy putting you to the question, painter. I have not forgotten our last session, of course. We'll start directly where we left off, in far better-equipped circumstances. I'll leave you to think that over until it is light, painter, and then we will have you moved to the Bargello, the better to perform my offices of mercy.'

'Niccolò Machiavegli, Salai! Does he still live? Does Giustiniani have him, and Raphael's corpse?'

'For now,' Salai said, and the door was shut, its wooden lock rattling home.

It did not take Pasquale long to explore the room, using what little light leaked through the grille over the transom. The cabinets proved to be full of skulls, and wax impressions of the brains they had once contained. There were shelf upon shelf of them, all neatly catalogued. The dome of each skull was divided by a grid of fine black lines, and each had a tag wired through the right eye, bearing a label in cramped writing that Pasquale thought at first was code, until he realized that it was mirror writing. *Woman, age 44, palsy. Man, age 22, blind, congenital idiot. Man, age 56, normal. Man, age 35, hanged as thief.* Dust on the shelves suggested that the room had not been used for some time.

There was nothing that could be used as a weapon, and he did not think that he could climb through the narrow window in the centre of the curved wall, which in any case was so high above the floor that he could only touch its sill by standing on tiptoe. Besides, even if he did manage to climb out he would simply be on the outside of the tower, high above the ground, and with no kite to bear him.

He sat opposite the door, in the narrow corner made where the cabinets met the curved wall, legs straight in front of him. The aches and bruises he had suffered throbbed. Whenever he closed his eyes he relived the thrill of his flight and his fall, and the amazing moment when he had burst the window. Perhaps he had become the angel he had destroyed: he imagined Salai as a scaly worm writhing beneath his own burning sword. Or perhaps by passing through the image of the angel he had become its reverse: a black angel fallen from the grace of God and doomed only to torment. In any event, the madness that had gripped him seemed to have passed. It had inhabited him ever since he had dived into the river to escape the Savonarolistas, a rising curve of urgent, increasingly uncontrolled action that had left him stranded here, in this little cell high in the Great Tower. Or perhaps he had been infected long before then, when he had first met Niccolò Machiavegli. Perhaps he had taken the old man's obsessions with plot and counterplot too deeply into his own self, seeing Spanish conspiracies where there was only coincidence. He gripped his ankles and shivered, feeling a lassitude that was not despair but simple acceptance of his fate steal over him.

8

He was woken by the door's cumbersome toothed lock ratcheting backwards. Milky dawn light was leaking through the high window, falling like a blanket around Pasquale, although quite without warmth.

He blinked back sleep as the door opened and a guard stepped through. The man's polished steel armour gleamed in the light of the lantern he carried, reflected fragmented images of the room so brightly that the man's square-jawed clean-shaven face (he was not much older than Pasquale) seemed to float unsupported above a crazy mirror. Behind the guard was the old man Pasquale had seen in the long room. It was the Great Engineer.

Pasquale scrambled to his feet as best he could. His spine seemed to be a column of jagged fused iron, and his every back-muscle ached. The Great Engineer regarded him mildly, stroking his silky white beard with one hand. He wore a pair of blue-lensed spectacles that perched on the end of his nose like a butterfly.

'You had better bring him along,' he said at last, as if to the air, and turned away.

The guard took hold of Pasquale's arm just above the elbow, the thumb and forefinger of his steel-mesh gauntlet nipping the muscles as cruelly and irresistibly as pincers. He half led, half dragged Pasquale up the winding stair, across the great hall where the kite still hung at the burst stained-glass window, its tattered fabric flapping idly, and through a small door on the far side, into a round room noisy with clocks.

Clocks of all kinds were ranged around the walls: clocks powered by falling sand; clocks with water-wheel linkwork escapements; and every kind of mechanical clock, with dials of burnished gold and silver, or carved painted wood, or even of glass, behind which candles glowed through holes pricked to represent the constellations. There were day clocks and calendar clocks which showed the feasts of the saints, and even an antiquated weight-driven astrolabe with a revolving drum that dripped mercury as an escapement. And in the centre of the room, twice as high as a man, was a great astronomical clock, its weight-driven mechanism visible inside a cage of brass, with a seven-sided drum above. Each face of the drum bore a dial showing the movement of one of the seven heavenly bodies, the Primum Mobile, the moon and the planets, and below the drum, within the brass cage, were ring-dials which showed the hour of the day, and the fixed and movable feasts of the Church, and a dial for the nodes. This device made a loud regular knocking, like a magnified heartbeat, measured and stately against the background of the brisk chatter of the smaller mechanisms.

The Great Engineer stood at the far end of the room, looking out of a window, like a section of a bubble, or a lens, that reached from floor to ceiling. The guard walked Pasquale across the room, and when Pasquale started to ask why he had been brought here, told him to speak only when spoken to.

'But the device—'

The guard, a blond fellow with a bumpy close-cropped head, a smooth boyish face, and intense icy-blue eyes, said quietly, 'My master has few words, but each is chosen with care. You will have to get used to his little ways.'

Pasquale was made to sit at a small table inside the lens of the window. Looking out at the waking city stretched far below, he had the dizzy sensation of being housed in the eye of a giant. He was so high, the Great Tower being four times the height of the square tower of the Palazzo della Signoria, that he could see the circle of the city walls on either side of the river. He saw the manufactories strung along the river, with blackened gaps where some had been burnt out, the bridges across the braided river, and, directly below, the seat of government. The Piazza della Signoria, deep in shadow, was still littered with the wrecks of the devices of the artificers. The great statue of David was reduced by Pasquale's elevation to a chip or fleck.

The Great Engineer remarked to the air, 'The guard is Salai's, of course, and will straight away send word to his master, wherever he is.'

'Whatever are you thinking of, master! Of course I won't,' the guard said, and winked at Pasquale. 'Master, don't you want to share breakfast with this young hero?'

'Has he time for breakfast? Shouldn't you take him away?'

'It's the least we can do for him,' the guard said, winking at Pasquale again. 'Salai's men won't check the room until they get orders.' He pulled a red cord set in a channel in the wall, apparently without effect.

The Great Engineer turned and left the window without looking at Pasquale, and started to wind up the weight of the tall astronomical clock, using a toothed key as long as a man's arm. He favoured his left hand.

The guard said, with the air of a stage-manager prompting a recalcitrant actor, 'This is all about the model of the device that went missing, is it not?'

Pasquale said, 'I came to bring it back, but Salai took it from me.'

'Well of course, I saw it myself. Didn't we see that, master?'

The Great Engineer set down the key and said, 'You don't have to humour me, Jacopo. I suppose I must hear how the model fell into this young man's hands.'

'Set on your tale,' the guard told Pasquale.

While the Great Engineer pottered about his clocks, winding them one by one, Pasquale started to explain what had fallen out, how he had come by the device, the murder of Romano that was not after all a murder, the assassination of Raphael and the theft of his corpse, Niccolò Machiavegli's kidnap, Salai's plotting with the Savonarolistas and his double-edged game with Giustiniani.

'I had intended to bring your device straight back to you, master,' Pasquale said, 'but my luck did not run far enough for that.'

The guard said, 'It was a brave try, eh master?'

There was a silence while the Great Engineer finished winding his clocks. At last he said, 'It does not matter, Jacopo. You cannot suppress an idea, as I long ago discovered. Once it is loosed on the world it acquires a life of its own, as in the Greek story of Pandora. Often it is enough for someone sufficiently skilled to know a thing is possible – I once amused myself by telling my pupils that I had done such and such a task in such and such a way, and having them attempt to duplicate my efforts. Most could, and although no one way was exactly the same as any other, there was, as it were, a familial resemblance. The model was not important, but the idea behind it was, and that is abroad.'

The guard, Jacopo, said, 'Well, perhaps we were unsuccessful in keeping the camera secret, but this is a more dangerous matter.'

Pasquale said, 'Salai believes the model important, master, which means he has found a buyer for it. I believe that he's taken it to the Venetian magician, Paolo Giustiniani, who will sell it on to the Spanish. The Spanish will use it against Florence. I helped frustrate his plans the first time, although entirely by accident. He was working through intermediaries last time, but now he has moved openly. I would try and stop him, if I could.'

Jacopo said, 'You mentioned this Giustiniani before. Did Salai tell you why he treated with him and not directly with Spain?'

Pasquale thought back on what Salai had said, and admitted, 'Not in so many words, but the way in which the Savonarolistas were attacked on the river has Giustiniani's mark. Besides, the Savonarolistas are fanatics who would not pay for the device – or not as much as Giustiniani could no doubt promise.'

Jacopo said, 'But you've no evidence, eh? Well, whoever he has gone to, Salai won't be back this time, master. It's treason he's set on. Open treason.'

The Great Engineer put his hands over his ears.

'That'll do no good,' Jacopo said loudly. He was leaning at the join the window made with the wall, idly looking out at the city. He added, 'You know he's really done it this time. You won't be able to buy him out of this kind of trouble. You'll have to rescue him from himself.'

This Jacopo had a sly comfortable air, Pasquale thought, protective but self-serving, too, like the youngest son who humours his father's every whim in hope of a share of the inheritance. There was best Flemish lace at the neck and wrists of his armour, and his sword had a finger-guard of fretted gold, set with little rubies like flecks of blood.

The Great Engineer put down his hands and looked at them. 'How did I get so old, Jacopo? And my beautiful boy?'

'I suppose it was the usual way, master.'

'Salai trusts no one,' the Great Engineer said, 'for after all he knows in his own heart that he is not to be trusted, and so he thinks all men are the same as he. You were right, young man, to call him the prince of lies. I named him in punning reference to the name of the god of the Moorish peoples, for from the first he seemed a very limb of Satan. Such a pretty boy, but such manners and such sulks. And greedy too, of course, taking whatever he wanted. Like a little prince, in a way. So it has come to this. No doubt he will have you killed, by and by.'

'We haven't rescued this young man to let him be killed by Salai's bullies, master,' Jacopo said. 'You know that very well, so stop trying to scare him.'

'It's only the truth.'

'Only if you let it be the truth,' Jacopo said, and winked at Pasquale again.

'Yes, you'd like to see Salai's powers diminished,' the Great Engineer said.

'He has altogether too much power over you, and his faction has too much power over the other artificers. A spot of humiliation will do us all good.'

'And will do you good most especially,' the Great Engineer said. 'Don't think I don't know how you try and poison my mind against Salai.'

'Hush,' Jacopo said. 'Not in front of the servants.'

A page entered, bearing a tray of fruit and soft black bread and a sweating pitcher of water. He set it on the low table in front of the centre of the lensed window and withdrew. Jacopo, still lounging by the window, told Pasquale, 'Eat what you will.'

'What about your master?'

'Oh,' Jacopo said loudly, glancing over his shoulder to make sure the Great Engineer was listening, 'he'll claim he's already eaten. He eats hardly enough for a mouse, and sleeps even less. In anticipation, he says, for the long sleep that is to come.' More softly, Jacopo told Pasquale, 'Eat, and let my master think matters over. He'll warm to the idea, sooner or later. He'll soon see that if Salai succeeds it can only reflect badly on him. And believe it or not, he still has a soft spot for Salai. He won't want him to come to harm.'

Pasquale knocked the tray to the floor; focused by the curved glass of the window, it made a particularly satisfactory crash. The Great Engineer blinked at him, his eyes mistily magnified by the blue lenses of his spectacles. It was the first time he had looked directly at Pasquale.

Jacopo had drawn his sword. 'You fool!' he said.

Pasquale sprang to his feet and said, 'I must ask you to let me go, master. It is not too late to stop Salai. I will do it, if you will not.'

'Sit down,' Jacopo hissed. 'You don't know what he can be like. He still loves Salai.'

'Peace, Jacopo,' the Great Engineer said mildly, 'and put up your sword. Do you think this young man will attack me with a plum, or a handful of figs? As for you, young man, there's no need to get excited. I have said that I will help you, as in fact I already have. If it is in my power, you will leave the tower before Salai returns, or as is more likely, before he learns that you are free and sends the order that you are to be locked up more securely.'

'That's kind of you, master, but I would ask more.' Desperation had made Pasquale bold. Salai had said that Niccolò was still alive, but what would happen if Giustiniani had all he wanted? He said, 'If you let me go free that is one thing. Perhaps I can stop Salai, perhaps not. What I do know is that I must struggle against his plans while also evading the plans of Signor Taddei, who would ransom me in exchange for Raphael's body. I can try my best, master, but I am but a painter, and hardly more than a pupil at that, while you can call upon so much that for you it would be a simple matter to drag Salai from his meeting-place.'

'Keep your counsel,' Jacopo said in a fierce whisper. 'You'll scare him, and then nothing will happen!'

'It is nothing but the truth,' Pasquale insisted.

'You fool – I'm on your side!'

The Great Engineer said, 'Salai has tried to poison me twice, and a few years ago a soldier shot at me. He missed and was killed at once, but I have my suspicions.'

'More than suspicions,' Jacopo said.

Pasquale asked, 'And yet you could not have evicted him?'

'Not now. His influence is too great, and he has intimated that my mind is failing. Well, perhaps it is. Besides, where else would he go? Poor Salai has never known another home.'

'You see how it is,' Jacopo said, flinging up his hands in frustration.

'But I loved him, and forgave him,' the Great Engineer said. 'I still love him, or the wayward child from which he has grown, and which still in some measure lives in him. Besides, the tower is not mine, or at least, this part of it is not. So that I might build it I made a compact with the Signoria, that if they would pay for the construction and allow me to work as I would, the tower would house a university of artificers. They were great days, once! We would work for days on end in pursuit of an idea. I remember when Vannoccio Biringuccio first rediscovered the principle of Hero's engine – he sealed water in a copper sphere, which he heated, and was lucky to survive the explosion. We thought the tower was falling! Who would have believed where that would lead, in fifteen years? Who would have thought that our simple inquiries into Nature would so change the world? What do you see, Jacopo?'

'What, through the window? Why, the city of course. It's still there, if a little singed around the edges.'

'Lately when I look out I see a city in flames. I see flying machines fluttering above defensive walls and dropping pots of fire on those places which will burn best. I see the populace fleeing, harried by the same flying machines. I see men turned into devils. It may yet come to pass. Pick up your breakfast, young man. Eat, drink. Regular habits make a regular mind. We have a little time.'

'It's all right,' Jacopo said quietly. 'He's thinking about it.'

'It may soon be too late,' Pasquale said.

'Hush. He moves at his own pace. You've already caused enough trouble.'

'I hope it is enough,' Pasquale said, and bit into a plum. The rich juice flooded his mouth and awoke his appetite. As he fell to, the Great Engineer finished winding his clocks, and Pasquale observed (taking great satisfaction in the way that Jacopo rolled his eyes) that there was indeed a great deal of time stored here.

'Measured, rather,' the Great Engineer said. 'I find it interesting that it can be measured in so many ways. Sometimes I would rather I had been a clockmaker than an artificer. Or perhaps an artist, as I set out to be. But I have little power in my right hand now, and so cannot steady my left, and besides, it is a trade to which one must devote one's life. I took a different path after Lorenzo was assassinated, and yet sometimes I think I can glimpse what might have been, as when a climber mounts a high peak, and finds he has not conquered the world after all, for beyond it lie others, dwindling into the mists. Time is a tricky thing, as painters well know. We see it as a river, moving always in one direction, but perhaps God sees it differently, and can return to different events and change them as an author might correct a draft. In another life . . . Well, but you smile at these notions.'

'You reminded me of my teacher, Piero di Cosimo.'

'I know him well enough to realize that his fabulations which at first seem only amusing are in fact profound, for they strike at the roots of what we accept only by custom or habit without questioning. In that respect Piero is like a child, to whom all is new. Indeed, it's my contention that all artificers should first see a thing anew if they would understand it.'

'Then I would ask you to see things anew, master. To see that things are not as hopeless as you believe. The device itself does not matter: it is the importance that certain people have placed upon it that matters. It . . . it's like the angel, the angel of the Annunciation! It doesn't matter what message the angel bears, what form of words is used. It is enough that he bears God's radiance. That itself is the message. If we can take the device back, then the advantage will be ours.'

Pasquale would have spoken more on this, and more boldly, but a bell chimed softly and Jacopo said, 'The guards are coming back. No doubt their captain has been informed that you are loose – I never did trust that page. Master, we'll have to go now. Do you understand?'

'Of course I understand. I'm old, but I'm not in my dotage.'

They went through the door which the page had used, down a long corridor with a window as tall as a man at its end, overlooking the city. Jacopo swung this open, and it proved to be a mirror or screen that cleverly reflected a view from a lens, with a stair hidden behind it.

They descended a long way, passing through small rooms that opened out at intervals like beads on a rosary. Jacopo explained that within the tower was a kind of anti-tower, hidden places only a few knew about. Many builders had laboured to construct the tower, but they had worked on one part or another and had not the whole sight of the Great Engineer, just as an ordinary man cannot properly see the city in which he lives unless he is raised far above it so that, like God, he can see all. Pasquale thought that this was taking analogies too far, but the Great Engineer showed him how true it was in the next room they passed through.

It was windowless like all the rest, but larger, and circular, and lit not by acetylene lamps but by sunlight, projected through an aperture in the ceiling, which fell on a small table with a dished white surface. At the Great Engineer's order, Jacopo reached up and moved a lever, and suddenly the dished table was filled with an image of the city, shown as if from the eye of a bird hovering above it. More trickery with lenses, prisms and mirrors, but none the less compelling.

'Show me the house of this Giustiniani,' the Great Engineer said, and after a moment Pasquale was able to find the villa, a white speck on the hillside inside the city wall on the other side of the Arno. For a brief moment, the shadow of his finger erasing the image, he really could believe that this was how God saw the world, that if he could but sharpen his eyesight he would be able to see Salai riding towards the house, or see through the roof of the house and spy upon the magician, or find poor Niccolò in his prison.

'Light is my abiding interest now,' the Great Engineer said. His deep-set sad eyes were pools of shadow, and shadow etched every line of his face. 'Light . . . it is purer than idea.'

Pasquale said, 'Together we can defeat Salai's plot, master. There is still time. The Spanish are a day's ride away. Even if they get the message that Giustiniani has the model, they must collect it. Come with me!'

'Isn't that what I am doing? You have already persuaded me, young man. Jacopo, are you with us? Close your mouth, man. You might swallow a fly.'

'I am amazed as usual, master, by the sudden turns of your mind. I have been trying to persuade you to move against Salai ever since he tried to have you assassinated, and suddenly you will do it.'

The Great Engineer said to Pasquale, 'It was the way you burst through the window, so like an angel. I knew then, but I only now know that I knew. We will rescue Salai from his folly.'

'Your science against Giustiniani's magic, master,' Pasquale said.

'Magic is only science which seeks to hide itself as something else. I suppose that we have only a little time. We must hurry. Where will you take me?'

'But I had thought—'

The Great Engineer groped for a chair, and sat with a weary sigh. 'What, that I could raise an army? There is none, except for the guards, and they are Salai's. All I have is inside my own head. I have no pupils, even. I have not had a pupil for twenty years, only followers.'

'Who glean your least idea like crows,' Jacopo said.

Pasquale said, 'There is only one man who can help us, but I do not know that he will.'

'Never mind. Lead me to him! I have great faith in your powers of persuasion, young man. Together we will make him understand. But first, I must rest. There are times when I wish that I had not built the tower so high.'

Jacopo took Pasquale's arm and steered him deeper into the room. 'He is an old man, and this enterprise will be dangerous for him.'

'It is the only way to stop Salai.'

'I see that we understand each other. Very well, then. Let me show you something – as a painter you are sure to be interested.'

In the furthest reach of the room was a series of stone troughs lit by bloody light diffused through a red-tinted lens. A constant cold wind blew there. Jacopo said that this was where the Great Engineer painted with light. He showed Pasquale a rack of glass plates evenly coated with silver, and the lensed apparatus into which they fitted.

'Although first the silver must be made sensitive, by treatment with iodine vapour. Then, after exposure to light, the plate is held over a trough of hot mercury until the image forms, and is then plunged into hot salt water to fix it. Here is his latest. Be careful! The silver film is fragile, and although he tried a new varnish to preserve it, it is already flaking. Careful I say!'

For Pasquale had grabbed the plate and marched across the room to the table. Jacopo followed. 'Be careful, be careful! You see it is a portrait of the feast for the Pope. There is the Pope himself, with the unfortunate Raphael beside him.'

Pasquale was not looking at the dignitaries, but at the servants who waited behind them, ready to make the second serving of wine. In particular, the servant standing at Raphael's shoulder. He knew that pale face, that shock of hair, and finally understood all.

9

When Pasquale was delivered into Signor Taddei's presence, the merchant was playing chess with his astrologer, Girolamo Cardano, in front of the great stone fireplace. Documents were strewn about their feet; a mechanical tortoise, its ebony shell inlaid with a swirling pattern of tiny diamonds, was making its way across this drift of papers on six stumpy legs. Taddei's secretary was writing at a desk behind his master's high-backed chair, and an assistant was adding figures using an automatic abacus, fixing the settings and turning the handle and recording the result on a long sheet of paper with quick mechanical dexterity.

On the far side of the room, a trio of musicians was playing a sprightly piece, and the servant escorting Pasquale waited until they were done before marching him briskly down the length of the great hall. Cardano eyed him sardonically, while Taddei contemplated the board, a finger stroking his beard. The mechanical tortoise reached his feet: he turned it around and made his move before glancing up. They made an odd pair, the twitchy young black-clad aesthete and the comfortably expansive merchant, but such unlikely couplings were common, for often the master would recognize in a servant or employee an exaggeration of a trait lacking in his own character, and so would raise that man up to become a confidant and sounding-board for his own ideas.

'An unexpected pleasure,' Signor Taddei said, and looked askance at the servant who escorted Pasquale.

Cardano moved a bishop across the board and then set the tortoise marching back towards Taddei.

The servant explained that Pasquale had marched up to the gate and demanded entry. Pasquale said boldly, 'I came with a friend. I believe you should speak with him, rather than play at war.'

'Is that so,' Taddei said, and settled back in his chair and stared frankly at Pasquale. He was dressed in a red robe trimmed at neck

237

and cuffs with dyed black fur, and a square hat was set on his balding pate.

'Beware tricks,' Cardano murmured. His lower lip was swollen, and even as Pasquale watched he bit it so hard that tears stood in his eyes. The astrologer had had a lot to think about, it seemed. He added, 'One man can do the work of many, in the right place.'

Pasquale said, with a lightness he did not feel, 'He is an old man, and no assassin.'

'Appearances often deceive,' Cardano said. 'Be careful, master.'

'In every way,' Taddei said. The tortoise nudged his curl-toed slippers. Hardly glancing at the board, he moved a pawn forward one space and with his foot turned the little device around so that it started to march back towards Cardano.

Pasquale said, 'I have only to glance at you, Signor Cardano, to remind myself of that.'

The servant told Taddei, 'There is an old man, master, and also a man escorting him, in armour.'

'His bodyservant,' Pasquale said. 'He'll give up his sword if you ask him, and has no other weapon.'

'Fetch this old man up,' Taddei told the servant, and said to Pasquale, 'You've caused me a great deal of trouble, boy. Tell me now that you are not in league with the Savonarolistas.'

'You know that I am not,' Pasquale said as steadily as he could. 'It was the Savonarolistas who took me from your men at the Ponte Vecchio.'

'I know nothing of the sort! Two of my men dead, and the third lingering with a bullet in his guts as likely to die as his companions. Perhaps the Savonarolistas took you, but now here you are, unharmed.'

'Although not in the best odour,' Cardano said.

'I had to resort to an unusual mode of transport.'

'Unfortunately,' Taddei said, 'there is still no trace of Raphael's body. Did you see it, when the Savonarolistas held you?'

Pasquale said, 'The Savonarolistas don't have Raphael's body.'

'I always thought that you were poor enough ransom,' Cardano said.

Pasquale said, 'The Savonarolistas did not want me, but something I possessed – and I no longer have it. And in fact it was not they who set up the exchange, but another. They learnt of it because there is someone in your house, signor, who is in contact with them.'

'If you were with the Savonarolistas, that is just what you would say,' Cardano said. The tortoise was trying to clamber over his black boots, and he nudged it away impatiently.

'I'm not accusing you, signor. It will be one of the servants, perhaps the replacement for your signaller. In a way it does not even matter.'

'If it is true,' Taddei said, 'it matters to me.'

Cardano said, 'We can't believe a word this boy says. How is it that he is standing here if he was taken by the Savonarolistas?'

'Hush,' Taddei said. 'It's your move, Girolamo.'

'Oh, that.' Cardano moved his queen so that it stood beside his bishop and leaned back, pinching the inside of his elbow with thumb and forefinger. 'There. Checkmate.'

'It is?' Taddei looked at the board distractedly, then pushed it away.

Pasquale said, 'This is all you can do while armies march on Florence?'

Taddei regarded him with mild amusement. 'I cannot send my goods out by road because the roads are closed by order of the Signoria, and I dare not send my goods by water, as the Spanish navy sits off the coast and like as not would sink any ship that dared try to pass. Meanwhile, citizens are calling for the resignation of the artificers' faction from the Signoria, the city is under martial law but is still threatened by mob rule, and my manufactories are closed because of a strike called by your Savonarolistas – but as for that, I wait only for my spies to identify the ringleaders so that they can be dealt with.' He ground fist and palm together, to show what he meant. 'You will tell me how you escaped from the Savonarolistas.'

'They were taking me across the river, on a ferry they had captured, when they were attacked from the shore by what I believe were forces under the command of Paolo Giustiniani. I dived into the river, and swam to shore.' There was no need to mention Rosso's role in this. The dead are dead, and there's no use speaking ill or good of them. Pasquale added, 'If you need proof that I have nothing to do with the Savonarolistas, here it is.'

He pulled out the plate, which he had carried from the Great

Tower wrapped in a square of linen. He said, 'I know who killed Raphael, now, for I recognize his man. This was taken at the feast after the entry of the Pope. You are there, Signor Taddei, at the end of the table, so you must remember it.'

Taddei took the glass and peered at the smudged black and brown image. 'I remember it being made,' he said. 'We had to sit still for two full minutes, and the glare of the lights was horrible on the eyes. Ah, there is poor Raphael!' The room fell silent as the merchant gazed at the picture. 'Well,' he said at last, 'how does this advance your cause?'

'When was the picture taken?' Pasquale asked.

'Why, between courses. I cannot remember exactly when. No, of course, it was just before Raphael died. What is your meaning, boy?'

'Look in the background, signor. You will see the servants waiting to serve the wine for the new course. Fortunately, they too obeyed the instructions to stay still. You will see one at Raphael's shoulder. I know him. He is a servant of Paolo Giustiniani, the same man who tried to capture me in the Piazza della Signoria, and who later tried to break into Niccolò Machiavegli's room when I was there. Perhaps you remember him, Signor Taddei. He has red hair, and a skin as pale as milk.'

Cardano said, 'Even if you can show that you came by this representation legitimately, we have only your word that this servant is who you say he is.'

Pasquale glanced over his shoulder, and to his relief saw the Great Engineer hobbling along beside Taddei's servant, with Jacopo in his glittering armour behind them. 'As for how I came by this representation, my friend here can vouch for me. I think you know him, signor.'

Signor Taddei followed Pasquale's glance, then jumped up in astonishment, sending the chessboard and the carved ivory pieces crashing to the tiles. With great and apparently genuine effusion, he took the Great Engineer's arm and escorted him to his own chair. Even Cardano seemed overcome by this apparition, and stood aside to watch with eagerness as Taddei settled in the chair opposite the Great Engineer and began to ply him with questions.

The Great Engineer answered with a nervous smile and a shake of his head, and indicated that Jacopo could speak for him. He was after all an old man in bad health, exhausted by the break in his reclusive habits and the short journey on foot from the Great Tower to the Palazzo Taddei. He slumped rather than sat in the chair which Taddei had given over to him, refused wine and, through Jacopo, asked instead for water. His eyes, behind the blue lenses of his spectacles, were half-closed.

Jacopo stood behind his master's chair, visibly amused by this turn of events, and said that his master would help as much as he could in the matter of Paolo Giustiniani. 'He acquired something belonging to my master, a trinket which must be returned.' He bent to listen to the Great Engineer, and added, 'Or destroyed, my master says. In any event, it must not fall into the hands of the Spanish.'

Pasquale explained as quickly as he could that it was this device which Giulio Romano had originally stolen to the order of Paolo Giustiniani, who was acting as agent for the Spanish. That the Savonarolistas, who did not trust Giustiniani, had taken him because they wanted to capture the device and give it straight away to their masters. That this Paolo Giustiniani was not only acting as a go-between in the matter of the stolen device, but that he was also the instigator of the murder of Raphael, that it must be he who had stolen the painter's corpse. 'This surely must have been either on the orders of Spain or simply to make money from its ransom. When Giustiniani learnt that I had the device, he decided that he would kill two birds with a single shot, and offered Raphael's body in exchange for myself and poor Niccolò Machiavegli, knowing that we knew where the device was. Instead, the Savonarolistas took us, although I cannot pretend to be grateful.'

Cardano said, 'Yet is it not interesting that this young fellow escaped when Signor Machiavegli did not? We still have no explanation of that.'

Jacopo said, 'You may believe him. My master considers him to be an honest lad.'

While Pasquale had been speaking, the Great Engineer had picked up a sheet of paper from the litter on the floor and had started to doodle upon its reverse, quickly covering it with small diagrams. Now he held this up, and said, 'With my help it is possible that we can quickly take this so-called magician by surprise. If he does not have the time to do anything beyond respond to the attack, then he will not have the time to destroy the body of Raphael. More importantly, he will not be able to take vengeance on my poor misguided Salai. I will have words for that wicked soul myself.'

'We would wish that no one is hurt in this,' Signor Taddei said, 'but I would ask the cost of this expedition. I am not a poor man, it is true, but I would find it hard to furnish an expedition of this nature, most especially in these suddenly straitened times. Would you say that this device of yours is valuable?'

'It has already cost too much,' the Great Engineer said.

Jacopo said, 'My master means that we could come to some arrangement.'

The Great Engineer grimaced at that, but said nothing.

Taddei said, 'What do you think, Girolamo? Could it be developed?'

'I would have to see it,' Cardano said with a shrug.

Pasquale said, angry and disbelieving, 'You decide matters in the language of double-entry bookkeeping?'

'Peace, young man,' Taddei said. 'I am after all a business man. Perhaps you should look elsewhere if you desire unconsidered action, although I doubt that anyone else would listen to your wild tale. After all, that was why you came to me, was it not?'

'I came to you because you were instrumental in the attempt to regain Raphael's body.'

Taddei gave Pasquale a shrewd look, and Pasquale blushed. After all, Cardinal Giulio de' Medici, the Pope's own cousin, had witnessed Pasquale's dispatch as ransom for the return of Raphael's body, and Pasquale could not even guess at what favours had been promised Taddei for that work, or what favours he had repaid by undertaking it. Nor of course could he ask. One did not speak of things like that directly, for it was too dangerous. Even knowledge has its own worth, and so its own dangers for the owner, as Pasquale now well knew. Unknowingly, he had been the possessor of the very knowledge which had cost the lives of poor Rosso and two of Raphael's disciples, and which now threatened to become the seed from which the destruction of Florence might spring.

Taddei was at base a kindly man, if brusque and practical. He said, 'All of Florence's might and worth are founded on commerce, as I'm sure you realize. As for my own small worth, it springs from that most traditional of our enterprises, that of making textiles. Now, to secure advantage over our foreign competitors, we Florentines have used the banking system to our own great advantage, buying up the production of English flocks two or three years in advance. Thus, even before a lamb takes its first giddy steps on English soil, all the wool that will ever grow upon its back has already been bought. Yet that very advantage may now be our doom, for we must take in that wool and make good our promises of payment even if we cannot now use it to produce cloth. The Savonarolistas well know this, and so they would disrupt the manufactories. You understand then that this *is* a war fought as much on the pages of the double-entry system as it is on the battlefields, and while the war has already been openly declared on the former, the armies have yet even to begin manoeuvring around each other on the latter. So, signor, you see that even the smallest part I can play in this must be carefully scrutinized, for it would be to throw all to the winds should I win one part of the war only to lose the other.'

The Great Engineer said, 'Perhaps Signor Cardano might wish to scrutinize my plans on your behalf, Signor Taddei. I believe that he will find them reasonable. I have no wish to mount a bloody campaign and lose that which I care for, any more than you wish to ruin yourself for the benefit of others. With that in mind, I have devised a way in which the actions of a few will be seen as the actions of many, by use of devices which will cause confusion and panic in the heart and mind of the enemy while exposing those attacking to the smallest of risks. I have spent my life considering the experience of those men who claim to be skilled inventors of machines of war, and long ago I realized that those machines differ in no way from those commonly used in manufactories and elsewhere. So it is with the minimum expense and greatest haste that my devices may be put into effect, and any use that you believe you might find for them afterwards, well then, they are yours.'

It was a long speech, and cost the old man a lot. He slumped in his chair, and it fell to Jacopo to acknowledge Taddei's effusive thanks.

Cardano bent eagerly over the sheet of plans, and almost at once fell to questioning the Great Engineer, who replied only with a smile or a shake of his head. Taddei called for wine, and put an arm around

Pasquale's shoulder in a friendly although unwanted manner, and led him a little way down the room.

'You must tell me why you are in such a hurry, young man. I've always held that if a thing is worth doing at all, it is worth doing well, even though that means patience. You're as impatient as my astrologer there, and as young, the two things often going together.'

'I would save my friend Niccolò Machiavegli. If he still lives, then he is in Giustiniani's hands: he was on the ferry when Giustiniani's men attacked the Savonarolistas, but was wounded and could not escape. The longer we delay, the less likely that he will remain alive. And once the Spanish take the device, then Giustiniani will have no further use for Niccolò or for the body of Raphael.'

'He might still ransom them.'

'More likely he would leave with the Spanish, if there is to be war. Besides, you might pay for the body, signor, but would you pay for the life of a journalist?'

'You're blunt,' Taddei said, not without admiration.

'I find I must be.'

'Then let me be blunt, too. I have it in mind that you will play a leading role in the engagement.'

'Signor, I am a painter, not a soldier. If it was in my power to be otherwise—'

Taddei said implacably, 'You'll go into the villa before the attack. If at all possible you will secure the safety of Raphael's body, and of your friend, and of this Salai. And above all, you will attempt to rescue this device. In that order. I was Raphael's good friend, and it is a matter of honour for me to ensure he has a decent burial. I hope you understand.'

'But how will I do all this if I am to make myself a prisoner of Giustiniani?'

'You're a resourceful young man. If your balls are as big as your mouth, you'll find a way.'

'You don't trust me, do you, signor?'

Taddei dismissed this with a wave of his hand. 'It is not a matter of trust.'

'I could go in and straight away betray your attack.'

'Then I would know not to trust you, eh? I *do* trust you enough to think you will not. But what if you do? We will attack anyway, and if Giustiniani attacks first, then we will fight all the harder. And take no prisoners – you understand me, I hope?'

'Perfectly,' Pasquale said, with ice in his spine. 'There is one favour I would ask. If I survive, I must leave the city. It will be too dangerous for me to stay, knowing what I know.'

'Well, that's true,' Taddei admitted. 'Where would you go?'

Pasquale told him, and Taddei laughed. 'I must admire your ambition. There's a ship leaving this night. If you can reach it in time, there'll be a place for you.'

'Two places,' Pasquale said. He was thinking of Pelashil.

'You ask a high price.'

'The stake is my own life. Tell me, signor, do you think that this assault can work?'

'If it is possible, then let it be so.'

'All things are possible to the Great Engineer.'

'So they say.' Taddei turned back and said, 'Cardano, damn your skin, will it work?'

The black-clad astrologer came over. He pinched one pitted cheek between thumb and forefinger and said in a subdued voice, 'I'm not fully conversant with the uses to which certain principles are put . . .'

'And will it cost me over-much?'

'The Great Engineer's man says that much of the apparatus can be taken from the workshops of the Great Tower . . . no, I don't think so. But the risk if even one part of this does not work . . .'

'Talk with my secretary, give me an exact figure. As to its working, we must trust to our genius.' Taddei turned towards the Great Engineer, but the old man was asleep, his blue-tinted spectacles askew on his face, a half-completed portrait of Salai, young and idealized, fallen from his hand.

10

It rained a little just before sunset, enough to lay the dust and soften
the ground. The night was cold and clear, and Pasquale shivered
as he lay in long damp grass looking across the rutted road at the
gate to Giustiniani's villa. If it kept up like this there would be a
frost, the first of the year. In the vineyards on the hillsides around
Fiesole, peasants would be sitting beside braziers loaded with
tarred brushwood, to keep the frost from the last of the season's
grapes.

Pasquale drew on his cigarette, cupping it in his hands to hide the
coal. It was no more than a few twists of tobacco and marijuana
seeds in coarse paper. The smoke tasted hot in his dry mouth. When
the coal nipped his fingers he pinched it out and let it fall amongst
the grass stems. It could be his last – a thought so morbid he must
smile at it.

The walls around the garden of Giustiniani's villa glimmered in
the light of the waning moon. When Pasquale had first been there
with Niccolò Machiavegli, the moon had been red as it set beyond
the shoulder of the wide valley. Setting now, it was a cold blue-white,
for the manufactories along the Arno were shut down and their
smokes dispersed. A doubly bad omen, then, this clear moon. Signor
Taddei's men, under the instruction of Girolamo Cardano, had had
a hard time of it, making their way through olive-groves that were
a chiaroscuro of moonlight and shadow, every shadow potentially a
servant or soldier of Giustiniani. Two had scouted ahead to make
sure the way was safe before the others advanced, bent with heavy
packs on their backs. Despite the caution of the scouts, Pasquale had
jumped at every quiver of moon-drenched shadow, each scuttling
mouse. He was not a brave man, merely foolish enough not to admit
fear. Pelashil had said that he was a fool, and he believed it now, no
matter how much he had protested then.

He had gone to see her that afternoon, while Cardano, armed with
a warrant that Taddei had arranged through his connections, had gone

246

to the workshops of the New University to requisition apparatus its custodians hardly suspected they possessed. Pasquale had given his word of honour to Taddei that he would return, and Taddei had acknowledged that promise by having him followed discreetly rather than escorted.

Pasquale had come into the bar to jeers and catcalls from his friends: one saying that he thought he saw a ghost; another that no ghost would look so bedraggled; a third that here was a notorious man indeed, with a summons to the magistrates upon his head. A fourth cradled a *viola da gamba* between his thighs, and called forth a plaintive melody from its warm wooden womanshape with dexterous use of a bow. To the percussive beat of his fellows' hands on their thighs – this kind of strong accompanying beat, borrowed from the chants of the New World Savages, was the latest musical fashion, its rude vigour sweeping away the traditional melodies – the viola player half sang the first verse of a popular love song, twisting the words to suit Pasquale's name so that his companions laughed and lost the beat in delighted applause.

Pasquale felt at once that he had returned home, but that while he had changed his home had not. He suddenly felt that he had nothing in common with these dandified youths, with their hair elaborately curled or sleeked to a lacquered shine with gum arabic, their fine clean clothes in carefully matched shades of rose and yellow and cornflower blue, their palms scented with fresh rose- and lavender-water, their languid drawls and knowing smiles, their petty intrigues and feigned passions for fine horses (which they could not afford) and fine women (likewise). The brown hose and doublet and black jerkin Pasquale had been given at Signor Taddei's were no more than serviceable, with a cut ten years out of fashion. He had not had time to wash his hair properly, let alone set it in its usual fringe of falling curls, and instead he'd caught it up in a net, like a soldier. He felt, all of a sudden, grown-up amongst boys. They urged him to sit with them, tell them what he'd been doing, tell them what he knew about Raphael's murder, to have a drink.

He said, 'What's this about a summons?'

'You've been a bad boy,' said the musician, setting aside his instrument and bow. 'Did someone post an accusation in one of the *tamburi* against you?'

'Been banging someone's daughter, Pasqualino?' another said, and a third added, 'More likely someone's son.'

Pasquale remembered the monk and shrugged and asked after Pelashil, and his friends started to laugh again. The mercenary sitting beside the ashes of last night's fire looked over at this noise, scowling. Pasquale met his gaze and looked away nervously.

'Where's Rosso?' someone said. 'Come on, Pasquale, sit with us and tell us all about your wicked ways.'

Pasquale blushed with horrible shame. He could not tell his friends that his master was dead, killed by his own hand. Instead, he blurted that he must see Pelashil, and roused the Swiss landlord, who was dozing in a corner with his giant hound lying across his bare feet. The man cursed sleepily and told him she was out in the back, rinsing the pots.

'You take care,' he added, 'and be ready to duck when you go through the door.'

Pasquale soon found out what the Swiss meant. Pelashil was washing plates in a bucket. Lunchtime herring was cooking on a grill shoved on to the coals of the stove, filling the air with a haze of smoke. When Pasquale started to talk to her, she turned her back on him; when he persisted she started splashing grease-slicked water at him. He jumped back, mortified. He said that he wanted only to say farewell, in the very unlikely event that he didn't come back.

'That's done. So you go. Go now!' She was furious, rubbed at her eyes with raw red wrists, turned her back and tried to shrug him off when he tried to turn her to him.

He tried to make a joke of it. 'Oh well, and I thought you cared for me, and I see you are careless of me instead.'

'You men. So brave. So selfless. So you think, playing your foolish games. Go kill yourself and don't expect me to mourn you. Be a hero and enjoy your grave. Your friends will give you a fine monument, I suppose.'

'This talk of graves is making me nervous. I just came to ask you two favours. To look after the ape, just in case. You know . . .'

'It's no more trouble than the old man, and better company than you.'

'Cleaner? Warmer? Come, I won't have it that you share your bed with such a monster.'

She smiled, just for a moment, a flash of white in her lined brown face. 'You think yourself such a fine gentleman.'

'Well, am I not?'

'I've told you what you could be. You're a fool.'

'Pelashil, I'm not sure if I want to be a magus. All I wanted a few days ago was to learn how to paint an angel in a way no one has painted an angel before.'

'I showed you the way.'

'I'm not sure what I saw, now.' The polychrome bird, that was and yet was not Pelashil. Moments of time like bright beads on a string, vivid and fixed as stars. The creature he'd met in the weave of the cloth hanging.

'You can't learn from the híkuri until you are a mara'akame. Before that time your dreams are only . . . like plays.'

'Entertainments?'

'Yes,' Pelashil said, with a stubborn finality.

'It seems too a long road.'

'Listen. When you first take híkuri, you look in the fire and see the play of colours, the many arrows with feathers full of colour.'

'Yes,' Pasquale said, remembering.

'When a mara'akame looks in the fire, what does he see? He sees the fire-god, Tatewarí. And he sees the sun. He hears prayers venerating the fire where Tatewarí dwells, and the prayers are like music. All this is necessary to understand: it is what you must do so that you can see what Tatewarí lets go from his heart for us. That is what you have taken the first step towards. That is what you are throwing away. There are two worlds, the world of things and the world of the names of things, where their essence lies. The mara'akame stands between them. Except for my master, you are the only one of this great and terrible city to begin to understand this, and you throw this understanding away for a fool's errand.'

'It's hardly a fool's errand. Truly.' Pasquale tried to explain about where he was going, the villa, the Great Engineer's devices. 'If he can save all Florence, then he can certainly save me.'

He was still making the mistake of joking about it.

Pelashil said, 'I'll tell my master that there's going to be war. Perhaps we should travel on, so don't expect me to be here when you come back.'

Pasquale tried to tell her what Signor Taddei had promised, that when it was over he would begin his journey, and she could be there with him, but she wouldn't listen, and turned away when he tried to calm her, then banged the dishes together in the tub of water when he tried to speak again, and wouldn't answer any of his appeals.

So in the end nothing had been settled. He'd gone out through the back alley rather than go in through the tavern again and face his friends. He had felt all of eight years old again.

Now, in the darkness, in the long grass by the road, Pasquale checked the time given by the mechanical timepiece strapped to his wrist. It was as thick as three ducats set one atop the other, with a single wedge which moved around a dial marked with the quarter divisions of the hour. Pasquale's fingers told him that the wedge was more than fifteen minutes from the hour, when according to the plan he would walk up to the gate and surrender to the guard. Cardano wore the twin of this timepiece, and at the end of the next hour he would set the attack in motion whether or not Pasquale had succeeded.

These synchronized timepieces were the least of the wonders culled from the workshops of the Great Engineer. Nor were they his only gift. When Pasquale had returned to the Palazzo Taddei from the tavern, with his tail between his legs, he found the old man awake again, picking at a bowl of heavily oiled fava beans flavoured with rosemary. He had been filling page after page with diagrams, seeking, so Jacopo explained with a shrug, to work out a method whereby a square could be derived from a circle so that each shared the same area.

'In mathematics is truth,' the Great Engineer said mildly. 'Only in mathematics.' Then he added, 'Alas, I waste too much of my time on these problems.'

Pasquale was becoming used to the old man's mood-shifts, whereby he raised something up only to dash it down. He remarked, 'The Greek, Pythagoras, believed numbers embodied pure truth. As if they were the dust from God's robe.'

'Many do believe so still. I receive many letters containing intricate calculations which claim to show how old the universe is, or how big, or how all laws which govern it may be subsumed into a single simple statement. Isn't that right, Jacopo?'

'How would you know, master? You make me read them for you, and very tedious they are, too. Like Pythagoras and his followers, and like hermetic scientists such as this Venetian, Giustiniani, the fools who write to you believe that the universe is a great puzzle, which may be solved by devising the right key. And they further believe that this hypothetical key will grant unlimited power and knowledge to those privy to it. They make offers to you, master, that you will have half the kingdom of Heaven if you help them solve their puzzles.'

'And yet,' the Great Engineer said, 'I am reminded that Pythagoras and his followers, who saw numbers as the true essence of things, were confounded by the simple observation that the diagonal of a regular square one unit to a side is a number which is not a regular fraction, that is, the ratio of two whole numbers. This was so fundamental a flaw that one disciple, Hippasus, was ritually drowned for revealing it. Poor man. I have always sympathized with him. I fear the irrational deluge that can in one day destroy all of man's works.'

Pasquale asked the old man's permission and picked up a sheet of paper to study. 'These abstract designs are almost decorative.'

'Oh, often I have picked out designs for architectural features from these doodlings, most especially for stained glass.'

'I am sorry that I destroyed your window. I would have liked to see it.'

The Great Engineer leaned forward, his eyes suddenly filled with fiery enthusiasm. 'When you burst through it! It was the most marvellous sight I have seen for some time. I have been too long in the tower, away from the world . . . but the world is a confusing place, not well ordered. I need order to think, more and more. The strange thing about these mathematical fancies is not that they generate what we apprehend as beauty, but that one cannot predict which geometry is beautiful. There is no equation of beauty: it arises randomly, as a snatch of song may be apprehended above the buzz of a crowd, before sinking into the general noise again. Euclid proposed that geometry was a solid base for rational exposition of the universe, but even in Euclid's expositions there are puzzles to be found. I have long wrestled with this or that problem . . . perhaps I have wasted my time. Perhaps there are irrational properties in geometry which cannot be derived from Euclid's sand-drawn axioms. But if the absolute certainties of geometry are overthrown, then so too are all our architectures and our artistic endeavours, our navigation and our fixing of the stars.'

Pasquale felt a giddy excitement – if the world was not fixed, then every man was surely free to determine his own fate. Nothing could be measured against one thing, but all was free, true only to its own self. Angels and men. The world of things, and the world of the senses. He said, 'Yet Cristoforo Columbo found the New World.'

Jacopo shrugged. 'While aiming for something else.'

'But others follow his navigation. Piero di Cosimo, for instance.'

The Great Engineer crooked a finger, and Jacopo cleared his throat and said with a certain formality, 'My master reminds me to tell you that Taddei is not to be trusted. Don't count on his sponsorship, Pasquale.'

Pasquale said, 'There is something I would ask you, Jacopo. When I am gone, I'd like you to call on a certain important household. I could never gain entry, but you are the personal servant of the Great Engineer, and I trust that you are well known in such circles.'

Jacopo swelled with self-importance. He asked, 'Who is this person?'

Pasquale told him, and gave him the message, and from Jacopo's look of glee at this intrigue knew that it would be delivered.

The Great Engineer said wistfully, 'If I were younger then I might wish to sail with you.'

'Don't be foolish,' Jacopo said. 'When you were a young man you would never have been allowed to set forth on such a dangerous voyage, for you were too valuable to the city.'

Their talk turned, slowly, to painting. To Pasquale's angel.

The Great Engineer listened as Pasquale explained how he had wrestled with the problem of painting something new, an angel no one had seen before, but then a silence fell. Pasquale believed that the old man had fallen asleep, but suddenly he said, 'He would not look stern or sorrowful, you know. That is what a man might feel, but not a creature of God. An angel would be ecstatic, for he would be doing God's work, and besides, he would also see the future. Your angel would know that the Fall would set man free, for before the Fall man was perfectly attuned to God's will, and since the Fall man must strive to regain the ability to hear the secret and solemn music by which the spheres of the universe are ordered. For having fallen, man has gained the chance to mount higher than angels.'

'How high? Surely you don't mean—'

The Great Engineer smiled, and touched a finger to his lips. They were rose-red inside his silky white beard. Pasquale suspected that they were dyed. The old man's fingernail was long, yet quite clean, and painted with some substance that gave it a pearly sheen.

'Don't say it. It will get you into trouble even thinking it here.'

Jacopo said, 'Signor Taddei is a close friend of the Vatican.'

The Great Engineer added, 'He would say such pride filled Lucifer, and in that instant he rebelled and in the same instant was overthrown. But Lucifer Lightbringer was of Heaven, while we have nowhere to go but to mount higher. Your angel would see this, and so would be filled with joy.'

'A stern kind of joy, it would seem. Perhaps I am not equal to the task.'

'Doubting that you are able to do the work is the first step. When you know what you do not know, you can begin to gain knowledge. Otherwise, in ignorant bliss, you learn nothing. I have always wondered if angels are intelligent, or even rational, for if they are perfect servants of God's will, then they need know nothing, proceeding as they do from that which knows all.'

The guard went past the gate again, the fifth time since Pasquale had settled down in the undergrowth. The lights of the villa could just be glimpsed beyond the walls, glimmering as cold and remote as the moon.

Mastering the science of light, the Great Engineer had told Pasquale that afternoon, would be the achievement of the age. The recording of light and the motion of light would revolutionize the way in which time was perceived. He foresaw a way in which the slow chemical process by which light freed silver from its iodine salt could be hastened, so that an exposure could be made each second, capturing the way in which men and animals moved. Such sequences passed before the eye imitated movement, falling one after the other just as in life. Jacopo added with no little pride that his master had already essayed such a technique before the Pope, but that was simple trickery, as Pasquale would see. Amongst the devices to be used against Giustiniani was one which employed the same kind of trick.

'I hope we do not need to use it,' Pasquale said. 'I must treat with Giustiniani, on Taddei's request.' He thought for a moment, and told the Great Engineer, 'Seeing your drawing, master, has given me an idea of how to set about that task. If you would spare me a few moments, then perhaps there is a way in which I can seriously bargain for the life of my friend, and my own safe return.'

There was the sound of a galloping horse, the creak of harness and the thud of wheels. A carriage swayed up the steep road, pulled by a sweating coal-black horse. The gate clashed open as two guards hurriedly stepped through. From where he lay, Pasquale was no more than a few *braccia* from the nearest, could see his white face under the shadow of his peaked steel helmet – a heavy-set man with a thick moustache that lapped a thick-lipped mouth, eyes blue as the mountains of the moon. A Swiss or Prussian mercenary, like the men Taddei had hired for this expedition. Pasquale had a brief vision of the hireling soldiers of both sides throwing down their arms and greeting each other as brothers: he really had no stomach for the fight.

The carriage was reined in. The guard closest to Pasquale caught at the traces of the sweating horse, which hung its head, blowing heavily through its nostrils, and spoke to the driver in guttural Prussian. The milk-faced driver laughed and swiped off his loose hat, letting curly red hair fall over his forehead. In that moment a sliver of ice seemed to pierce Pasquale's breast. The driver was the servant of Giustiniani, the man who had driven Giovanni Francesco all unknowing to his death, the man who had handed the poisoned goblet to Raphael, who had chased Pasquale in the Piazza della Signoria, whom Pasquale had glimpsed at the window of Niccolò's room.

The guard waved the carriage on. As it slowly rattled beneath the arch of the gate, Pasquale stood up and walked into the road.

The guard levelled his pistol in reflex, then relaxed a little when he saw that Pasquale was alone. His companion said in halting Tuscan, 'No visitors. Go away like a good fellow.'

Pasquale said, 'I have business with Signor Giustiniani.'

He made to pull the papers from inside his jerkin, and the first guard raised his pistol again. The second stepped up, knocked aside Pasquale's hands, and drew out the sheaf of papers.

'For Signor Giustiniani,' Pasquale said.

'We take them. You go.'

Pasquale hadn't foreseen that he would be turned away – but why would the guards recognize him? He said, 'I want payment,' and snatched at the papers.

The second guard pushed him over. Pasquale sprawled in soft rutted mud and for the first time since he had set off for the villa felt anger, fierce and hot. He sprang up and snatched at the papers which the guard waved overhead, out of reach. Both guards laughed at this crude Prussian bully-boy joke. See the spic jump, hear him cry out. How fine it is to be a good strong stupid Prussian!

'You'll be in trouble,' Pasquale said breathlessly, quite beyond fear, 'when Signor Giustiniani hears of this.'

The carriage had halted on the white gravel beyond the gate. Now the driver jumped down and walked back. He recognized Pasquale at once and broke into a broad grin. 'The party is complete. And just in time, too. Tomorrow, we would not be here.'

'Then you have the Spanish envoy with you.'

The red-headed man laid a finger alongside his prominent nose and winked. 'He's in the coach. I admire your balls, signor.'

Pasquale snatched the papers from the guard and held them up like a shield. 'Your master will want to see these. Salai has not told you the whole story.'

The red-headed man shrugged. 'I'm not the person you want to convince. Climb up on the board, and I'll take you straightway to my master.' He turned, and told the guard, 'Close the gate. There'll be no more visitors this night.'

11

As before, light blazed from all the windows of the villa. In every room, glass chandeliers were filled with luminous tapers, like so many burning bushes slung under high plaster ceilings where friezes of putti and cherubs frolicked in buttocky profusion. When Pasquale entered the villa through double doors which stood wide open, following the red-headed servant and the Spanish envoy, he heard a woman laughing somewhere. The echo of her laughter floated across the entrance hall, where white marble statues posed under a pale blue ceiling. The laughter soared, breaking towards hysteria, and then stopped as abruptly as if a door had slammed upon it.

Pasquale realized that he had been holding his breath. He glanced at the red-headed servant, who merely smiled and said, 'This way, if it please you, signors.'

Many of the rooms through which the servant led Pasquale and the Spanish envoy – a straight-backed, taciturn man in ordinary red and black hose and doublet, and a leather tunic cinched by a belt with a big silver buckle – were empty, and the rest held only a scattering of furniture. In one room soldiers played dice before a massive fireplace, so intent on their gambling that they scarcely looked up as the three passed through. A fortune in books, a hundred or more, was stacked along the wall of another.

The door on the far side of this room was shut. There was, incongruously, a kind of door-knocker, in the form of a mask of tragedy, set square on its planks. The red-headed servant touched the lips of this mask lightly and reverently before opening the door and ushering in his two charges.

Pasquale stopped, struck again by fear. It seemed there was no end to fear.

The room was the same room in which Giovanni Francesco had been murdered. There was the same grate in the fireplace, in which logs burned with a fierce spitting sound; there was the same throne-like chair, its dark wood modelled with intricate carvings picked out in gold-leaf. And in the chair, as before, sat the Venetian magician, Paolo Giustiniani.

He wore a square black hat, a black robe embroidered with silk thread and slit to the waist up both sides, his hairy muscular legs bare beneath it. His feet were cased in black slippers with upturned toes. He turned to the two other people in the room so that his spare hawkish face was in profile to Pasquale and said, 'As you see, the sending was successful. Now we are ready.'

One of the men was Salai, who simply shrugged. The other, sitting upright and composed on a stool, his wrists manacled and laid in his lap, was Niccolò Machiavegli. He turned his quiet ironic smile to Pasquale, and Pasquale smiled back, his heart turning over with hope.

'Ill met again,' Niccolò said, 'although I hope you may find this interesting, Pasquale.'

'Do not hope,' the magician told Pasquale. His Tuscan was flavoured with a heavy Venetian accent, with spitting *x*'s instead of *ch*'s. 'There is no hope here, especially not for you.'

The red-headed servant shut the door and leaned against it carelessly, smiling quite without malice at Pasquale.

The Spanish envoy began to protest, in a slow sonorous voice, that he was here on serious business, and business that had been paid for.

'Oh, give him what he wants and let's be done with it,' Salai said. He stuck a cigarette between his meaty lips and bent to light it, then blew out a riffle of smoke with an impatient flourish. He still wore his red velvet tunic, with a slim sword at his side. He added, 'All this bores me.'

'I am not here for your entertainment,' the envoy said, with affronted dignity.

Salai bowed mockingly. 'Forgive me, signor. The way you are dressed I believed that you were here for a masque.'

'Be silent,' Giustiniani said. He cupped his hands together, the left on top of the right. When he parted them, the device stood on the palm of his right hand. 'This is yours, signor,' he told the envoy, and the red-haired servant stepped forward and handed the flying device to the envoy with a flourish.

Giustiniani said, 'Now, let us hear what the painter has to say.' He had a way of holding up a hand when he spoke, to command attention. Pasquale didn't think much of this: if he was any kind of leader, a man should be able to command respect without tricks.

'Surely you know what he will say,' Salai said, 'having drawn him here. Or was the funny business with a mirror and burnt hair a charade?'

'It is all in earnest, as you will see,' the magician said. He pressed his hands together at his chest in a mockery of prayer and told Pasquale, 'Lay on, boy. You have brought me a gift. Show these people what it is.'

Pasquale drew out the crumpled sheet of paper. 'Here, magister. This, for the life of Niccolò Machiavegli. The rest of it when we are released with the body of Raphael.'

'There must indeed be much written there.'

'Salai did not tell you the truth. When he lost the plates he also lost important information. The model is not enough. You will also need these calculations, of which I have brought you the first half. The rest, as I said, on my release, together with my friend, and the corpse.'

The magician took the paper, glanced at it, and handed it to Salai. 'This is your master's writing?'

'It is,' Salai admitted.

The magician took the paper back, and passed it to the envoy.

Salai burst out, 'But there is so much writing. The old man does nothing but scribble scribble scribble. One damn fat book after another. This could be anything, anything at all.'

'Look at the bottom,' Pasquale said steadily. 'You will need a mirror to read it easily.'

The red-headed servant produced one and handed it to the envoy, who used it to examine the cramped backwards writing. There, as Pasquale and Jacopo had conspired to compose, and had patiently dictated to the old man, was written, *This is the record of the true calculations by which a man may fly using a vertical screw to draw himself through the air. I, Leonardo, do so depose this.*

The envoy read this out. Salai spluttered a cloud of smoke and protested, 'A trick. Anyone with any training as an artificer can build the device from the model. There's no need for anything else, no need to pay any other price. No need to trade with that, that *creature*.'

'Be still,' the magician said. His voice rang out in the room, and

258

Pasquale felt his heart pause for a moment, as if obedient to this command.

Niccolò said, with amusement, 'An interesting problem.' His eyes were glittering, and he sat forward in his chair, bright and inquisitive as a bird. The chain which linked the iron cuffs of his shackles was coiled in his lap.

'I delivered all that was requested,' Salai said. 'Nothing was said about any papers. In any case, they may not be the old man's.'

The envoy said, 'You said that the handwriting was his.'

'So I was wrong.'

'You change your mind?' the envoy said. 'It is indeed a conveniently malleable thing.'

The magician said, 'The document was written by a mathematician. Anyone else in Florence would use the Roman system – they use it in accounts,' he told the envoy, 'because it cannot be falsified by adding extra signifiers to the end of a number. That's a measure of how much they trust each other in Florence. But mathematicians use the more sensible Indian system, which is far more flexible. So here.'

The envoy said to Salai, '*You* said nothing about the need for any papers, signor. That is the point here.'

'Oh, exactly,' Niccolò Machiavegli said. 'Right to the heart of the matter. You will trust the Great Engineer, or you must put your faith in the opinion of his catamite.'

Salai made to strike Niccolò, and the red-headed servant stepped forward and caught Salai's wrist. Salai strove against this grip for a moment before wrenching free and turning away.

The envoy said, 'Let them go. What need do we have of these two?'

'Ah,' the magician said, 'but I do need the corpse, as an altar, and it is no coincidence that this number has gathered here.' He was sweating – the air in the room was heavy, as if freighted with a portentous unspoken word.

Pasquale thought of the picture he had rescued from the fire, and felt a chill.

The envoy said, 'The body must not be returned. That was also the agreement.'

'And I will keep it,' the magician said. 'As soon as the ceremony is done, signor, it shall be destroyed. That is, if it is not taken by the one I shall call. And he will come, this time. The time is right. I can feel it.'

Salai started to laugh, but almost immediately fell silent. Everyone in the room was watching the magician, whose face was possessed by a kind of sick eagerness.

Pasquale said, feeling as if he were treading air – as an angel might feel, for an angel could never touch base earth, 'All or nothing. Release us without the body, and the rest of the calculations will not be given to you.'

'I think not,' the magician said. 'After all, why should we release you now, with a great matter at hand?'

Pasquale surreptitiously felt the device at his wrist, and was surprised to find that less than half an hour had passed since he had hailed the guard. He'd done that earlier than planned, and there was still almost an hour before the attack would begin. He tried to make himself relax. He had plenty of time to treat with the magician. Even if he rescued only Niccolò, it would be a victory. Raphael was already dead. Nothing worse could happen to him, because the worst had already happened. Not even being the altar for a black mass was worse than being dead.

The Spanish envoy said to Salai, 'If more information is needed, then you can be sure that we will not pay you, signor. Our agreement was for the whole, or nothing.'

Salai said furiously, 'It will work! I have told you that the model is all you need, no more and no less. This young fool is bluffing, that's all. Oh, perhaps he is brave. I will give him that. Perhaps he is given to fine motives, even. But for whatever reason, he's simply trying to pull the wool over your eyes. Kill him and be done with it. Take the papers he has, if you like. What do I care? They are worthless, you have my word on that. And even if they aren't, why then I will personally guarantee that I will get the rest, even if I have to kill the old man. I swear this.'

'As for assassination, that would be a new commission,' the Spanish envoy said. 'I cannot negotiate with you on that point.'

The magician said, 'If I wanted the Great Engineer dead, I could send an invisible spirit that would blacken the air of the chamber while he slept, and suffocate him.'

The envoy said with obvious distaste, 'I'll not hear of such matters.'

'You'll do a good deal more than *hear*,' Salai said gloatingly.

The envoy said, very much on his dignity, 'All I know, signor, is that you promised much, but it appears you may not have delivered all you promised.'

Niccolò said to the envoy, 'It's like the angel and the devil and the two doors. Do you know the story?'

The magician said, 'We all do. Peace.'

The Spanish envoy said, 'Well, I don't. If it has a bearing on the matter I should like to hear it.'

Salai threw his hands in the air and turned away.

Niccolò smiled and explained, 'Imagine you are in a room, with two doors leading out, one to death, and one to freedom, and nothing to show which is which. In the room with you are an angel and a devil, and you can ask only one of them a single question. The devil, naturally, is given over to telling only lies, while the angel tells only the truth. Oh, and of course both are invisible, so you will not know which has answered. Now, which one question do you ask to make sure that you will escape with your life?'

The magician said, 'No more puzzles. The matter is plain. You,' he said to the envoy, 'shall take Signor Machiavegli with you, as well as the papers this young artist so kindly carried here. If it is true that they are valuable, then I will act, without commission, as courier for the rest, in return for Signor Machiavegli's release. If not, then you may dispose of him as you will. In any event, you shall pay us as you agreed, or none shall leave here except those I choose.'

Pasquale said, 'That changes nothing! You must free my friend, Niccolò Machiavegli, and return the body of Raphael.'

'But things *are* changed,' the magician told him. He was not smiling, but he was amused. He steepled his long fingers together and regarded his nails. 'What has changed is that you are here, and that you may return freely. Bring the rest of the papers and your friend goes free. If not . . .'

The envoy said, 'If you will lend me two men, Signor Giustiniani, then it shall be done as you said. It does not exceed my powers. Although I will say that Admiral Cortés will not be pleased at the delay.'

'I appreciate that you are a far-sighted man, signor.'

The envoy said, 'It is foresight that will win us the world. He who holds the key to the future has the power to hold history to ransom.'

Niccolò said cheerfully, 'I would say that he who holds that key will find himself under siege by those who want it.'

The magician told Niccolò to be silent. 'As for power,' he said to the envoy, 'you will see now how little temporal power matters. I have gathered you all here on this, Saturn's day, to assist me. To begin with, you must be robed.'

The envoy started forward. 'I'll have no part in any devilment!'

The red-headed servant caught him and put an arm around his throat, and held a knife to his eye when he started to struggle. The magician held a candle to the envoy's face and moved it slowly back and forth, all the while speaking in a low monotonous voice. When the servant released the envoy, Pasquale saw that tears were banked in the man's wide unblinking eyes, and that he trembled like a young tree in a gale.

'Does anyone else have an objection?' the magician said. He turned his level gaze to Pasquale, and then to Niccolò.

'Steady, Pasquale,' Niccolò said.

'What does he want of us?'

'I believe he will call up a spirit, if he can. He has boasted that he will gain much power this night, and I understand now that it is not from the Spanish. Are you frightened?'

'No spirit,' the magician said, 'but an angel. One of the seven archangels, in fact.'

Salai giggled, 'This is my beloved son, with whom I am well pleased.'

'Beware,' the magician said quietly. 'This is a serious business. I believe you have an interest in angels, painter. Tell me, would you like to see one?'

Pasquale said, as steadily as he could, 'I do not yet know if my imagination has failed me.'

'Do you believe angels exist?'

For a moment, Pasquale's mouth flooded with the bitter-sour taste of the wrinkled leather button of the híkuri which Pelashil had fed him. He said, 'Oh yes. Yes.'

The magician smiled. 'And if you would paint one, surely you should not turn from the chance to see one? What other painter could boast as much?'

262

Pasquale, remembering his broken panel, said, 'Once I thought of nothing else. But things have changed.'

'They will change again,' the magician said. 'You will obey me, painter, and you, Signor Machiavegli, or I shall be forced to control you too. Do not think I would not do it!'

The red-headed servant released Niccolò from his chain and lifted white linen robes from a chest, and handed out paper hats, of the kind that stonemasons wore to keep dust and chips from their hair. Under his instruction, Pasquale and Niccolò pulled them on. The servant dressed the Spanish envoy, then closed the shackles around Niccolò's wrists again. Pasquale obeyed with a heartsick eagerness. He seemed to be split into two parts. One part wished that he might see an angel; the other knew that this was dark, dark business, and that his very soul was in peril. It was one thing to imagine the face of an angel, quite another to be on the threshold of gazing into that face.

'Courage, Pasquale,' Niccolò said.

Pasquale whispered, 'Can he really call upon an angel?'

'He believes it. But if men such as he have powers such as they claim, why are they not ruling the world?'

'How do we know that they are not?'

'In secret, you mean.' Niccolò considered this for a moment. 'No prince can rule in secret, for even with cabbalistic powers he must at some stage manifest his will so that it may be carried out. No, even I do not believe such a secret conspiracy could exist.'

'It's good to talk with you again, Niccolò.'

'I'm sorry I can bring no comfort. I fear for both of us, Pasquale.'

'No more than I,' Pasquale said, thinking of the devices that Cardano commanded. He did not trust Cardano.

The magician girdled a long broad-bladed sword around his waist and took off his black cap, revealing that he was tonsured like a monk. 'Now we begin,' he said. 'No one is to speak unless I tell him, not even you, Signor Machiavegli, nor will any of you move from his station.'

He led them into the adjoining room. Its marble floor was marked with a huge design. It was drawn in red chalk. A five-pointed star was framed inside a circle, with a second circle drawn outside the first. Lesser circles were drawn inside the five triangles of the star, and in its centre was a square of red cloth a yard on each side, with an ordinary ironwork brazier standing at one corner. In the margin between the circles strange symbols, as if of some hermetic mathematics, were carefully drawn. Pasquale recognized Roman lettering mixed up with Greek and Hebrew characters, but there was not a word or a name he knew, except for the astrological sign for Saturn at the top or north of the five-pointed star. At each point of the star burned a single fat candle of white beeswax half the height of a man. More candles stood at each corner of a kind of altar which stood in a lesser circle to the north-east of the main diagram. On the altar—

Pasquale gasped. He could not help it. Laid on the altar was the naked dead body of Raphael. His skin had been washed and shaved and was covered in red and yellow writing drawn with a kind of grease-paint. His hands were crossed on his hairless chest, and his blue-nailed fingers were wrapped around an inverted cross. A crucible sat in his groin.

The magician looked at Pasquale and with an ironic smile touched a finger to his lips, then held up the little leather pouch that hung around his neck, muttered a few words, and kissed it. It was an evil moment.

The close rich scent of the candles in the shuttered room was dizzying. The red-headed servant showed each man where to stand: Pasquale and Niccolò in the circles in the eastern and western arms of the five-pointed star, Salai and the somnolent Spanish envoy in the two southern arms. The servant handed a flask of brandy to Pasquale, and another of camphor to Niccolò, and told them that when instructed they were to shake as much liquid as a man's cupped palm might hold on to the brazier.

Meanwhile, the magician had folded up the red cloth in the centre of the diagram, revealing a triangle drawn in the same red chalk as the rest, and bordered with ivy. He draped the folded cloth over his left shoulder and plunged his sword into the charcoal heaped in the brazier. It kindled with a muted crackle and immediately sent up a dense pungent white smoke.

The servant took up his position in the circle at the top of the diagram, and the magician used the tip of his sword to score the flagstones and close up the diagram.

'No one is to move,' he repeated, and crossed back to stand by the brazier.

The room was slowly filling with smoke. It was at once sweet and acrid, and as dense as an artificers' smog. Pasquale felt a curious light-headedness. His fingers and toes tingled. At the magician's command, he shook brandy on to the coals of the brazier, and Niccolò added camphor. The servant set down a crucible, and blue flames licked up inside it.

The magician intoned, in Latin, 'Hear me, Uriel! From this valley of misery and the misery of this valley, from this realm of darkness and the darkness of this realm, to the Holy Mount Sion and the heavenly tabernacles, I conjure you by the authority of God the Father Almighty, by the virtue of Heaven and of the stars, by that of the elements, by that of the stones and herbs, and in like manner by the virtue of snowstorms, thunder and winds, that you perform the things requested of you in the perfection of which you move, the whole without trickery or falsehood or deception, by the command of God, Creator of Angels and Emperor of the Ages!

'In the name of Emmanuel, in the name of Tetragrammaton Jehovah, in the name of Adonai, King of Kings, demonstrate to me your terrible power and give to me of your immeasurable largess. To this, I dedicate my altar.'

The magician kissed his sword and plunged its tip into the crucible at the feet of his servant. At once, blue flames licked up its length. Holding it in front of him, the magician crossed the circle and touched the tip of the burning sword to the crucible set upon the groin of Raphael's corpse. Sparks and smoke sputtered up, and continued to fly upward as the magician carefully paced backwards to his triangle.

The smoke was now so thick that Pasquale could hardly see the others, except as featureless shadows looming through a general whiteness. The sparks which flew up from Raphael's corpse seemed to sketch fleeting faces, some near, some far. They were wistful and stern, gay and grave. Pasquale was so drowsy with fear and with the effects of the smoke that the magician had to speak twice before he remembered to cast brandy on the glowing coals of the brazier.

The magician set his naked sword, which no longer burned, across the toes of his slippers. 'I command and adjure thee,' he intoned as solemnly as a priest at mass, 'Uriel, great minister, by the power of the pact I have sealed with thee, and by the power of the armies that thou dost command, to fulfil my work. I call on thee, Pamersiel, Anoyr, Madrisel, Ebrasothean, Abrulges, Itrasbiel, Nadres, Ormenu, Itules, Rablon, Hamorphiel, you who command the twelve angels of the twelve tribes which govern kings and governments, from the fire through the thirty abidings to the ninety-one parts of the Earth, arise, arise, arise!'

For a moment, nothing happened. Then the entire villa shivered under three quick, heavy blows. The air in the room seemed to compress as if great wings were beating it, and the flame of the candle burning in front of Pasquale shivered and then flared up. White smoke writhed before him, as if trying to take shape. For a moment a wild expectation lived in him, as bright as the candle-flame. Then, behind the heavy drapes, glass fell out of the tall windows with a ringing sound. A great wind filled the room and all the candles went out.

12

Pasquale knew at once that no angel had tried to manifest itself. He had been betrayed: Cardano had started the attack earlier than agreed. At any moment Pasquale expected to hear the sound of more missiles. There had been six of them, carried in straw-insulated cradles on the backs of the men, already heated so that the water inside had turned to steam, vigorously pressing for an exit. All that was needed to launch them was to open a valve.

'Stand fast,' the magician shouted, but Salai was already at the curtains, peering around one edge. 'It would seem that someone has set fire to your house,' he said.

The servant came back, carefully closing the door behind him. Pasquale had not even seen him leave. Plaster-dust calcined his bush of red hair. 'Rockets,' he reported, 'although there's no sign of the launch-frames, and no one saw their fires. The men are panicking. I should see to them.'

And he was gone again.

Standing at the centre of his ruined ceremony, the magician brushed lime-dust from his black robe and looked at Pasquale with a grave calm. The big candles flickered around him, throwing his shadow across the far wall; the brazier's smoke poured around his feet, a spreading sea roiled by the air that blew in through the broken windows. The crucible set in the groin of Raphael's body still burned and sent up sparks, making a small but distinct crackling sound. The envoy was blinking hard, staring at his hands as he flexed his fingers.

'You are the Judas goat,' the magician said, and raised his hand. He was suddenly holding a staff made of black ivory.

'I'll kill them now!' Salai sprang to Niccolò's side, drew his sword and held it to Niccolò's throat. Niccolò stood quite still, looking calmly and levelly at the magician as if challenging him, for all that he was chained and a moment from death.

The magician said, 'Leave off, until we know the size of the force ranged against us. We may well need them alive, to bargain.'

Salai shook his head so violently that his ringlets fluttered around his fat choleric face like a bush in a storm. 'No!'

The magician flung out his hand and his staff promptly transformed into a black snake. Continuing the same motion, he threw the snake at Salai. Wild with fear, Salai slashed at the serpent with his sword, missed, and screamed and ran from the room.

The magician stooped and picked up the writhing serpent, and ran his thumb down its back. It went rigid. The magician shot his sleeves and then he was holding a black ivory staff again. There was a noise growing outside, a wild drumming and a mad ear-splitting skirl of pipes, as if made by men with arms of iron and throats of brass. Pasquale remembered the drumming machine, its bellows and weights and clockwork arms.

The envoy said, in the dazed manner of one suddenly awakened from a dream, 'Are we surrounded?'

The magician said, 'My men will fight free, with my help. You will take charge of this prisoner, signor, and follow me.' He bent over Niccolò and brought his hands together. Niccolò's chains fell away from his wrists, leaving his hands bound by a device which locked his thumbs together.

Niccolò said calmly, 'He who moves first in a battle is generally the victor.'

The magician struck him with the back of his hand, so hard that the sound echoed in the smoke- and dust-filled room. 'If you will live, you will follow me,' he said, in a conversational voice.

Niccolò brought his head back and met Giustiniani's stare, a half-smile playing on his thin lips. 'It's never wise to admit to losing the game,' he said.

The magician turned on his heel and grabbed Pasquale by the arm. 'Come,' he said, and marched Pasquale out of the room without looking to see if the envoy and Niccolò followed.

The villa was filled with dust and smoke. The magician marched Pasquale through a series of empty rooms, past mercenaries running to and fro with bound chests or weapons or stacks of books. Clearly, they were preparing to retreat. One half of the entrance hall was afire, a fire that clung to the walls and the frames of the broken windows. The ceiling was down, filling the floor with lath and plaster, and most of the statues had fallen from their plinths. The fire filled the space with a strong dry heat and a great roaring noise and a piercing sweet smell: it was the smell of Greek fire, with which the hollow heads of the missiles had been filled, spilling and catching alight upon impact.

Heat scorched Pasquale's skin as he followed the magician outside. The shouts of the magician's men were mixed with the cacophony of the drumming machine. Vast, vague lights flickered beyond the boundary of the garden, and shadows moved within the lights. Some of the mercenaries were taking pot-shots, their muskets sounding as frail and harmless as twigs snapping in a fire. And indeed they could do no harm, for the shadows at which they fired were no more than that: shadows made to resemble the silhouettes of an army advancing against a background of brilliant lights.

Two men were hard put to hold the stamping horse which was harnessed to the black carriage. They were in silhouette against the fierce light that beat across the lawn, the light of the reflector lamps, each with spinning blades, which Taddei's men had mounted in the olive-grove.

As the magician started to hustle Pasquale down the wide marble steps towards the carriage there were three muffled thumps beyond the wall and the arched gate. Pasquale flinched, but the magician kept him upright by main force, so that he saw the three vapour trails as the steam-powered missiles flung their arcs through the black air. One struck the crown of the gate with a dissonant clang and enveloped it in a ball of orange fire. The other two rose higher, and Pasquale glimpsed their fat shapes turning like fish in the black air as they came down. One burst harmlessly amongst trees, but the other smashed through the roof of the villa. A moment later a ball of fire shot into the air. The horse, maddened by this, reared and plunged. It broke its traces and galloped away around the corner of the villa, dragging its handler behind it.

Down the line of the road to the gate, the griffin stirred on its plinth. Perhaps someone had activated it, or perhaps the shock of the explosion had jarred its mechanism. It rose on stiff legs, eyes glaring red, then started shivering in a kind of mechanical palsy. Steam burst from its joints, from the ruff around its neck. Its beak spasmed, chattering like the teeth of an idiot. Jets of vapour spurted from hidden vents, raising a great cloud that was driven upward by the heat of the burning villa and the burning gate. This mist refracted the lights beyond the wall, so that things took on the aspect of a small grainy dawn suspended in the deep night.

The magician's men were firing in the direction from which the steam-driven missiles had come, running to and fro in the glare of the lights, their shadows thrown in overlapping confusion over the lawn. Some used muskets or crossbows; others whirled slingshots around their heads, hurling glass globes into the glaring lights. But Pasquale had warned of this tactic, and Taddei had equipped his mercenaries with charcoal masks. A stilt-man tottered across the lawn, gaining speed, and plunged into the shrubbery. A moment later there was an eruption of fire and a fountain of bits of burning bush.

Giustiniani drew Pasquale close. He suddenly had a knife in his hand. It had a twisted blade with red characters printed on it. The magician spoke directly in Pasquale's ear, his clove-scented breath feathering Pasquale's cheek. 'How many men, and what disposition? Tell me now.'

'No more than seven, magister.'

The point of the knife pricked the soft skin just beneath Pasquale's left eye. Pasquale could not help but flinch.

The magician wound his hand in Pasquale's hair, and pulled his head back so that he was looking up at the black sky. 'You will tell the truth, painter, or first you will lose this eye, and then the other.'

'A hundred at least! They surround the place, magister!'

'Is this the city militia?'

The knife-point withdrew slightly. 'No, magister. They are the private army of the merchant Taddei.'

'I know the name. A friend of Raphael.'

'He wants the body, magister.'

The magician said grimly, 'He can have yours instead.'

'He calls on demons, as you have seen.'

'My magic will defeat his,' Giustiniani said.

One of the cedar-trees at the edge of the firelit lawn began to shake its lowest tier of branches. The magician turned just as a shadow flung itself from the tree and shot across the lawn. Mercenaries scattered in panic, unable to shoot at the apparition for fear of wounding each other.

270

The magician flung Pasquale away and raised his arms above his head. Gas suddenly whirled up from a scattering of brief detonations in front of him. It was yellow, acrid and choking. Pasquale reeled back as the ape – it was Ferdinand – shot through this cloud. It danced from side to side and beat the ground with its fists. Its eyes redly reflected the fire behind the magician.

The magician stepped back and, with a flourish, produced his black ivory staff. Pasquale shouted a warning just as the magician threw his arm forward. The snake struck the ape in its throat, and it rolled over and over, gripping the thrashing snake by its head and tail. Pasquale ran to the ape just as it flung the broken-backed snake away. It kicked out and quivered, all its muscles in tetany. It could not breathe, and all Pasquale could do was hold its horny-palmed hand as it suffocated.

'Thus I destroy all demons,' the magician screamed, and then he was running. He grabbed a passing mercenary, shouted something at him and pushed him on, ran to grab the next. He was trying to marshal his resources, running to and fro amongst his scattered troops, his white legs flashing through the slits in his black robe.

Pasquale closed Ferdinand's eyes, as if the ape had been a man, and turned away. His eyes filled with tears. Some great grief was threatening to wrench itself free inside him, if he would let it. Then hope returned, for the second time in as many minutes. A figure emerged from the burning villa, one arm flung up to shield his face. The man tottered down the steps and fell to his knees, and Pasquale ran towards him. It was Niccolò, soot-stained and scorched but otherwise unharmed.

Pasquale got him to his feet and they staggered a little way across the lawn. Its grass was withering in the heat. The mechanism that animated the griffin had jammed. It stood in a half-crouch with one paw raised, its mouth clacking emptily on wisps of vapour. Pasquale and Niccolò took shelter by its plinth, and Niccolò explained with a smile that the envoy had wisely decided to look after his own self.

'He has what he wants, after all. The device, and the papers you brought. That was a brave bit of trickery, Pasquale.'

'You saw through it!' Pasquale had to shout to make himself heard over the drumming and the rifle-fire.

'Salai was forced to tell the truth, yet no one believed him. A pleasing irony.'

'And the envoy really let you go free?'

'Let us say I slipped away in the confusion.'

'And your shackles dissolved.'

'Oh no. I took the key from Signor Giustiniani when he hit me. While it seemed that he released the chains by sleight of hand, he of course used a key. By my own sleight of hand, I took it from him, and then used it to open the device which locked my thumbs together.' Niccolò looked about him. 'I believe it is time to leave. What is the plan?'

Pasquale said, 'Taddei would have us die, I think. This attack came far sooner than we agreed. Perhaps we should stay where we are.'

'How many men out there?'

'Seven.'

'No more than that?'

'The Great Engineer supplied certain devices.'

'In that case we have little to fear from those attacking.'

Pasquale saw movement in the flames that engulfed the broken arch of the gate. He said, 'Don't be too sure.'

The device emerged from the burning gate with patches of fire clinging to its burnished hide. It was the utilitarian cousin of Taddei's jewelled tortoise: a thing the size of a hunting-dog, with a dome of steel plates no more than a couple of *braccia* high. It marched forward on a dozen stumpy legs. Rifle-shot rang on its hide as the mercenaries turned their attention to it. Then it stopped. Pairs of spring-driven shafts shot out on either side and began to lift it above the gravel road.

Pasquale pulled at Niccolò's arm and told him to run for it. They had made the corner of the villa when the device exploded and sent discs of sharp-edged metal scything across the lawn. Wounded and dead mercenaries toppled even as another device marched through the burning gate and bumped into the remnants of its fellow and went off prematurely, discharging most of its explosion into the ground, vanishing in a burst of earth and broken metal.

Niccolò said, 'I've always held that man will never rise to grace until his capacity for creation equals that for destruction!' He was dangerously exhilarated, his black eyes gleaming with more than firelight. 'With just a handful of those devices a single man could destroy an army!'

'If we are not careful they may destroy us.'

'There'll be a way out of here, you can depend upon it.'

'How can you be so sure?'

Niccolò grinned. 'Quite simply because Giustiniani would not live in a house with only one entrance and exit from its grounds. Look there! Come on, Pasquale! We have but one chance now!'

The red-headed servant was running in the opposite direction to the surviving mercenaries, who were fanning out across the lawn under the direction of the magician, advancing upon the shadow-play of forces beyond the wall. The magician was making war on demons, finally caught up in his own system of sleight of hand and illusion – for after all, had he not just defeated a demon which had attacked him? He brandished his ebony staff and it ran with blue flames. Pasquale knew then that the snake had been a snake all along, produced by a trick, although this brought no consolation. The real snake had been as deadly as if it had been magical – perhaps more so.

Niccolò gave chase to the red-headed servant and Pasquale picked himself up and followed. They ran past the mechanical griffin. Its head had been blown away by the explosion of the walking cannon, and the ragged stump of its neck erupted a jet of steam. Pasquale told Niccolò to circle to the right, and he himself ran off to the left. They closed on their quarry, who had stopped to kick at the plinth of a statue of a nude woman with the shaggy, horned head of a goat.

The statue abruptly rolled backward. The servant glanced behind him and saw that Pasquale and Niccolò were almost upon him. He drew a pistol but hesitated as to which man to shoot. That was enough for Pasquale to run straight at him and knock him to the ground. Niccolò snatched up the pistol and aimed it at the servant with shaking hands. 'Bravely done, Pasquale,' he said. 'You see, we have our exit.'

The plinth was hollow. The statue had moved back to reveal stone steps that descended down into the ground.

The servant grinned up at Niccolò. Blood ran from one corner of his mouth, but he paid it no mind. 'If you're going to threaten me with that pistol, you'll need to cock it first,' he said.

Niccolò eased the brass lever with his thumb. The pistol was the same pan-loading multiple-action type he had carried on the first expedition to the villa. He told the servant to stand up and move aside.

The man clasped his hands on his bush of red hair but stayed where he was. 'If you were going to shoot me, why, you would have done so. Let me show you the way out. It is as tricky as the way in.'

Niccolò said, a touch wildly, 'I have shot at men before, and have no desire to shoot at you, but I will if pressed.'

Pasquale said to the servant, 'He means that you should lead on, although why we should trust a man who is bent on betraying his master is beyond me.'

'There's no more profit to be had here, that's for sure.' A stray musket-ball cracked past overhead. Niccolò and Pasquale ducked reflexively, but the servant stood straight, hands still on his head. He added, 'In fact, profit is about to become a loss. May I take my hands down? The passage is not particularly easy.'

When the three men reached the bottom of the steps, the statue ground back over the opening. Little beads of blue flame sprang up in scattered niches. The passage was scarcely half Pasquale's height, dry, and lined with bricks. The servant led the way, and Pasquale brought up the rear, with Niccolò breathing hard between.

Half-way along, the passage made a U-shaped loop – to trap any besiegers who discovered it and tried to make use of it, the servant explained cheerfully. They had to wait there while something made giant footfalls overhead, shaking loose thin streams of dirt from the unmortared joints of the bricks.

The servant remarked, 'A fine tomb this place would make.'

'You may yet put that to the test,' Niccolò said.

In the light of the blue pinpoint flames, scarcely brighter than starlight, Pasquale could just see the servant's white face over Niccolò's shoulder. The man was smiling, as cosy as a rat in its burrow. He said, 'What was the answer to that riddle about the devil and the angel? I've been turning it over and can't see an answer to it. Make an end to my torture.'

'Signor,' Niccolò said, suddenly very much on his dignity, 'it is but a pinprick to the humiliations and trials which your master has put me through this past day. Let it rattle your brains. I'll get little

274

enough joy from the thought, but it's more than I expected.'

The servant laughed. 'You have me at pistol-point. I'm sure that's more satisfying. As for your hurts, I was following orders, as you well know.'

It suddenly came to Pasquale in the sideways fashion that answers to puzzles often did. He said, 'You ask what door the other spirit would recommend. It is the only question to which both will answer in the same way.'

The servant laughed again. 'Ah, then the devil will lie, and recommend the door of destruction, knowing the angel would lead you to safety. But the angel, the angel . . .'

'I'm not surprised that you cannot understand the minds of angels,' Niccolò said. 'Despite that your master would call one up, if he could.'

Pasquale said, 'The angel also points to the door to death, knowing that the devil would recommend it, and so both spirits will answer the question in the same way, and you may escape by taking the other door. I'm sorry, Niccolò, I only just now understood.'

Niccolò said, 'Listen.'

'I don't hear anything,' Pasquale said, after a moment.

'Precisely. The war has moved on. So should we.'

After the tight bend, the roof of the passage was a little higher. It ended at another stair, rising up to a small square ceiling.

The servant put his fingers to his lips and winked. 'My master that was would tell you that it's all done by incantations, and the binding of demons. In fact it's simple hydraulics, as I'll demonstrate.'

He shifted half a dozen bricks from the wall. Reaching inside with both hands, he turned something with a deal of effort. There was a rushing noise underfoot, the noise of water evacuating a reservoir. The ceiling that stopped the stairs ground aside, and the servant took the steps three at a time. Pasquale gave chase after him, afraid that the man would escape, or turn at the top and seal them in. But when he clambered out, he discovered the servant sitting on the shelf of rock which had stopped the hole in the heathy ground, the ankle of one leg crossed on the knee of the other. He seemed quite at ease, as if being captured and forced to reveal the bolt-hole were part of his plans all along.

They had emerged about a hundred *braccia* from the verge of the road which ran along one side of the villa's wall. Inside the wall, fire made a welter of orange light and red shadow. The villa was ablaze from end to end, and those trees nearest it had caught fire too, tossing harvest after harvest of sparks into the black air. Near at hand, blue flames of Greek fire clung to the ruins of the gate. The lights of the Great Engineer's devices, on the far side of the burning villa, dimmed by the blaze, crossed and recrossed in the sky, while the noise of the automatic drumming came and went on the hot wind, mixed with the fainter shouts of the beleaguered mercenaries. Suddenly, a great red smoke rose within the walls. As it rose it grew into the shape of a leering demon, but then air rushing to feed the fires took it and tore it apart.

'Just about the last trick,' the servant remarked. 'You gentlemen may run along. I've one loose end to deal with, and for that I'd like my pistol back.'

Niccolò said grimly, 'I would be quite glad to let you go, signor, except that you were a witness to what happened. We shall need you as proof of the schemes of Giustiniani, and of the fate of Raphael's body. On that still hangs a war.'

The red-headed servant stood. 'Why, signor, that's hardly enough to hold me. The corpse is your concern, not mine. As for being a witness, you forget that I was responsible for Raphael's death. I'll not be a witness to my own execution warrant.'

'All the more reason for you to be a witness,' Niccolò said grimly. 'You have been a willing accomplice to this devilry, signor. Hanging is the least of it. We burn witches in this city, and will burn you if you do not co-operate.'

'I've already survived one attempt to burn me,' the servant said, 'so you'll excuse me if I do not tempt fate and put myself forward for a second go-round.'

He stepped forward, and only smiled more widely when Niccolò raised the pistol. Then he reached out, and Niccolò snarled and pulled the trigger. There was only a dry click. The servant moved in a rush, turned Niccolò around and jerked his arm up behind his back so that he had to let go of the weapon.

Pasquale managed to land a blow on the servant's head that sent him staggering, but when he pressed his attack a swipe of the pistol clipped him on the corner of a cheek. Pasquale reeled back, and the servant sprang upon the flat rock. He flipped off the pistol's empty pan, jammed on a new one, and fired once into the air.

Pasquale and Niccolò exchanged a look. Pasquale's own warm blood coursed down the side of his jaw and dripped from his chin. The wound was just beginning to hurt.

Pasquale said, 'The game's not worth our lives, Niccolò. Leave him.'

The servant bowed mockingly, then raised a slim whistle, the kind the municipal swineherds used to summon their charges from roaming the city cloaca. He blew a single piercing note. A man stepped from a clump of trees that stood on a rise off towards the olive-grove through which Pasquale and Taddei's men had approached the villa. He made his way towards them slowly, and before he was half-way there, Pasquale recognized the Spanish envoy.

'That's far enough I think,' the servant called, and raised the pistol.

Pasquale saw the envoy's expression change to astonishment. He reached for something in the pouch at his belt and as he brought his hand up the servant shot him three times in rapid succession. The envoy sat down with a sudden rush. The servant took careful aim and fired again. The envoy's head snapped back and he fell over, and with his last moment of life he set free the thing he'd taken from his pouch.

It was the device. Pasquale saw it quite clearly as it rose into the night, even imagined he could hear the whir of its bands unwinding – but that was impossible, for the drums, the drums, the drums were still beating off in the distance and the fires were roaring, and the magician's mercenaries were shouting and shooting at the shadow-show.

The servant ran out across the heath, leaping and snatching at the device as it fluttered higher, suddenly not borne by its flexing wings but by the wind that fed the fires. It flew sideways, on a rising curve. For a moment it seemed that it would rise above the flames which clung to the ruined gateway, but then the gust of air failed, and the device dipped and instantly kindled. A burning scrap made lighter by its burning, it rose again, a feather on the breath of God whirling high above the destruction. And went out.

The servant had reached the margin of the road, and was staring up at where the device had vanished, as if it might suddenly reappear

277

like the phoenix. As he turned towards Pasquale and Niccolò there was a flat crack and he stumbled and pitched forward.

At first Pasquale supposed he had tripped, but when he did not rise Pasquale knew that he had been shot. He tugged Niccolò's sleeve and made him crouch in the dubious cover of a clump of wiry grasses. A figure was making its way along the road to where the servant had fallen. Suddenly, Pasquale realized who it must be, for no one else would have brought the ape. He stood up and waved and shouted, for all that Niccolò cursed him as a fool, telling him that Taddei would as soon have both of them dead.

But the person on the road had already turned to them. Pasquale ran forward. It was a woman. It was Pelashil.

13

Pasquale, Pelashil and Niccolò Machiavegli made a long way of it back towards the river. They did not trust the road, for Pelashil said that men were waiting there for any who escaped – she had seen them take a fat man in red, which must be Salai, and force him into a carriage. Pasquale asked if one was a priest, or wore robes, and Pelashil said, 'Yes, and a hood, and a big cross, here.' She placed a hand between her small breasts.

'It's as I thought,' Pasquale said. 'Cardano is the Savonarolistas' man.'

Niccolò said, 'Then Fra Perlata escaped. I wasn't sure in the confusion, when the ferry struck the shore and Giustiniani's men swarmed aboard.'

Pasquale dabbed at his bloody cheek with his sleeve. 'Once they find that Salai doesn't have the device, they'll be looking for us. We can't stay here.'

They stumbled across the heath with the burning villa at their backs and the tower of the church of Santo Spirito rising against the scattered lights of the city ahead of them. Pelashil went arm in arm with Pasquale. The long hunting-rifle was slung over her shoulder, its octagonal barrel rising a full *braccio* above her head. She knew he would need help, she said: Piero had seen it in a dream, and so she had brought the ape, intending to break into the grounds and use him as a distraction. But when the ape had seen the lights and the fire, and heard the strange noises, he had broken his chain and jumped the wall.

'He found me anyway,' Pasquale said, and told her how Ferdinand had died.

There was more to the story, Pelashil said. She had seen a broadsheet with Pasquale's likeness upon it, and Piero had told her what it meant. It seemed that Pasquale was wanted for the murder of his master, Giovanni Battista Rosso. 'But that matters not in the least,' Pelashil said cheerfully. 'You are set on the right road at last.'

Pasquale walked on in silence. He was numb. It didn't stop, was all he could think. It was not like the chivalric stories of heroes who slew monsters and brutes or sought the Grail, and after they succeeded there was an end to their labours, and a reward. A woman's hand and rightful ascension to the throne, the Grail found, and Heaven with it.

'Taddei will be behind it,' Niccolò remarked. 'The last of the scandal has been diverted upon your head, Pasquale. Of course, he did not expect you to survive this holocaust, and so you would not be an inconvenient witness at your own trial.'

'So I thought,' Pasquale said at last. He turned to Pelashil. 'Perhaps you will come with me. I was trying to tell you before that there may be a way—'

'I already have a master—'

'After this? You are your own master, or mistress, it would seem. Pelashil, I can take you back to your home. Piero hardly knows you are there. He wants to be alone. That is his fear: fear of the other. Thunder, crowds, anything not inside his head. He is even frightened of me, and I would be his pupil if he would allow it.'

'I have my life here,' Pelashil said. 'Piero took me in, and taught me when my own people would not. I look after him. He teaches me, so that I will be a mara'akame. Is that simple enough for you?'

'I wouldn't steal you from him. I ask only because I don't believe that you are his slave.'

Pelashil let go of his hand and said angrily, 'Why do men understand nothing? I stay with him because I want to. No one owns me. I am not his slave, nor his wife. I look after him because I want to. Yes, he's frightened of me, of many things, but he is a great and skilful mara'akame, and a better painter than you will ever be. There is a reason, if you need one.'

'I'm frightened of you, too,' Pasquale said.

'Good.'

'I didn't even know you could shoot.'

'The old man taught me. In my country, before I came here. Before he came back to this terrible city.'

Pasquale discovered that he did not want to know, as he had often wanted to ask, whether she had ever slept with Piero. He said, 'All

I know has died in the city. What hold has it on me now? Rosso was right after all. If I had agreed to go to Spain with him he would be alive, and so many others too.'

Niccolò had prudently walked a little way ahead of them while they argued, but now he stopped and they caught up with him. He said, 'You may have your wish. Or rather, it may be that Spain will come to you.'

They had reached the crest of the slope. A road ran downhill, gathering houses around it as it descended towards the docks. The city spread on either side, and in every part of the city green and red sparks were making small precise movements.

Pasquale asked Niccolò, 'What are they saying?'

'If you're patient, perhaps I'll be able to tell you in a moment. They are all sending the same message, in plain talk . . . Well,' Niccolò said flatly, 'it is to be war. What a comedy of errors, eh, Pasquale?'

'So we did nothing in the end, except what we thought was right.' It did not seem unexpected. Pasquale found that he felt nothing, not even disappointment.

Niccolò said kindly, 'Perhaps we made a difference, although we should not know it. It would be gross egotism to imagine otherwise. Only princes affect the course of history, Pasquale, and with your pardon, I do not believe any of us are that.'

'Except the Great Engineer.'

'He was once a prince, perhaps. But even princes have their day, and I think he had his long ago, in the war against Rome. His devices won that, but someone else must win this.'

Pasquale saw lights move on the river. The great ocean-going *maona* was preparing to warp out of its dock, a bank of lights looming beyond the prickly masts of the smaller vessels, supplemented by the small, luminous comma of the churning wake of a paddle-wheel tug.

'Come on,' he said. 'I only have this one chance,' and started to run. And as he ran, gathering exhilaration lifted his heart. It didn't matter if his plea had been delivered by Jacopo or not, or even if it had been answered. All that mattered was the hope, the chase. He stopped at the bottom of the hill, breathing like a Hero's engine, and when Niccolò and Pelashil caught up he led them on down to the river, following a muddy path between the tall chandlers' shops and warehouses that looked out over the docks.

People crowded the floating stage of the dock. The ship lay a little way beyond. The tug was laboriously turning it towards the lock that would let it gain the channel of the Grand Canal. As Pasquale fought his way through the crowd, he saw a flash of silver above the packed heads of the crowd. It was the polished armour of the Great Engineer's servant, Jacopo, who was standing on the roof of a carriage and looking this way and that.

When Pasquale, with Pelashil and Niccolò following, won through to the carriage, Jacopo jumped down from its roof and opened its door. 'She would speak with you,' he told Pasquale, smiling.

'And I hope with me,' Niccolò said.

Lisa Giocondo was waiting inside, her face glimmering in the light of a scented taper – the only light in the carriage, for its window-shades were drawn. Pasquale and Niccolò sat opposite her on the plush bench, but Pelashil paused at the door, shook her head and turned away.

Niccolò said, 'No doubt you would hear all that has fallen out since we last spoke.'

Lisa Giocondo folded her long fingers together. Her heavy musk filled the little carriage; as before, she wore a net veil, lifted up from her face. She said, 'No doubt you would enjoy telling me all, Signor Machiavegli, but there is little enough time for that now. All I would know is whether my husband was involved.'

'It was the Venetian magician Paolo Giustiniani who killed Raphael,' Pasquale said. 'Signor Taddei has evidence that it was a servant of Giustiniani who administered the poison, and he will find the body of that servant by the gate of Giustiniani's villa.'

Lisa Giocondo made a breathy sigh. She said, 'Then I am in your debt.'

'As to that,' Niccolò said, smiling his slight, closed smile, 'I would have words with your innocent husband, signora. I have seen the declaration of war made from every signal-tower in the city, and would seek to serve as I once served.'

'I will do what I can, but you must understand that I have only a little influence with my husband. You must convince him of your worth.'

'Readily,' Niccolò said eagerly.

Lisa Giocondo pressed a docket into Pasquale's hands, telling him that two places had been reserved as promised. 'Although it cost me dear. This may be the last ship to leave before war breaks out. Did I see a woman outside – your wife, perhaps?'

'Not yet,' Pasquale said, blushing. 'Perhaps never. She still has a duty here. Niccolò, unless you will come with me, I must make my farewell.'

'You needn't worry about me,' Niccolò said. 'The broadsheets will all be closed, but the Signoria will need an experienced voice to calm the populace. War is a way of life, Pasquale. There has been war, there is war, there will be war again, as long as there are states which strive against each other. War is but another kind of politics, or perhaps its purest expression, for it springs fully armed from the cardinal vice of ambition. All states desire peace, but any state which renounces war will at once find itself besieged by its neighbours. So I do not fear it, just as I do not fear the weather.'

'I'll miss you, Niccolò. You are comforted by the strangest things.'

Niccolò laid a finger alongside his nose. 'Florence is ready for war, and that is the first necessary thing on the road to victory. And unlike Spain, the citizens control the military, which is the second. The Republic will survive, and grow greater.'

Lisa Giocondo smiled at this, and Pasquale told the journalist, 'You're already writing the propaganda, Niccolò. Just say farewell.'

Niccolò grasped Pasquale's shoulders and kissed him like a brother, and said with a quick smile, 'We won't meet again, Pasquale, but I hope that I will hear of your adventures. Go now. You have a ship to catch.'

Pelashil and Jacopo were waiting outside. Pasquale told Jacopo, 'Your master will be pleased that the device is no more.'

'I'll tell him. And Salai?'

'The Savonarolistas have him. Taddei's astrologer, Cardano, is one of their number, and turned the attack on Giustiniani to their advantage. It was only by a stroke of fortune that the flying device was destroyed before it could fall into their hands.'

'The news will break my master's heart, but in my opinion he's well rid of the little shit.' Jacopo looked past Pasquale's shoulder at Pelashil. 'This is the woman you're taking?'

Pasquale blushed again. 'She is staying.'

Jacopo said, 'I suppose I should be surprised that there are limits to your powers of persuasion. My master asks me to give this to you. You'll need to buy wine and provisions for the voyage. You can do that at Livorno, although you'll have to pay through the nose.'

Pasquale weighed the small bag of coins. 'I wish I could thank your master.'

'He is safely in his tower, thinking of ways to deal with Salai. He is a fool for a pretty face, Pasquale. I'm glad you won't be around to abuse his notion that you are some kind of angel. This way now, quickly.'

'But the ship—'

'What would you do, swim to it? Signora Giocondo has arranged a ferry for you, at no little expense. I won't ask what favour she is returning – it must be considerable.'

A small landing-stage floated on the river's flood beyond the berths of the large ships, guarded by two men-at-arms. A small boat was tied up at its end. Its master sat with his back against a mooring-post that slanted above his head. He was an old man, whiskery and wrinkled, one eye white-capped and half-hidden by a drooping eye-brow. He was wrapped in a blanket against the chill of the water, and smoking a cigarette which he pinched between two fingers and stowed behind his ear before clambering aboard his craft.

Before he boarded this leaky shell, Pasquale dared to hug Pelashil, who after a moment unbent to return his embrace.

She said into his ear, 'You know that my people are the Wixarika, that they live in the mountains to the north and west of the empire of the Mexica. It is difficult to reach, Pasquale, for there are many canyons and other deep places, but if you follow your path you will find small villages of round houses, each with a kalihue where the mara'akate dance, and fields of maize all around.'

'Pelashil, I've heard Piero talk about this a hundred times.'

'Yes, and how much do you believe?'

'I'll believe what I see.'

'We say that one day all will be as we see it in Wirikuta, in the place we go to hunt the híkuri. The First People will come back and the sun will grow dimmer and the moon brighter, until there is no difference. All will be one. Until then, we stand between the world of the sun and the dreams of the moon. Remember that, Pasquale.'

Jacopo said, 'The boatman can't row faster than the ship. If you want to board it, you'll have to go now.'

As the boat was pushed out, and the boatman unshipped his oars, Pelashil called out across the widening watery gap, 'Send your first picture back, Pasquale, so that I know you are alive! Piero won't live for ever!'

And then she turned away, Jacopo following, and Pasquale saw them no more. The ship was moving slowly into the lock at the entrance to the Grand Canal, and Pasquale saw that his was not the only boat going out to meet her. She had undocked hours early, it turned out, to make open sea before the Spanish blockaded the canal. Many had no dockets, and Pasquale had to hold his up and call out Lisa Giocondo's name over and over until at last a knotted rope was dropped and he climbed aboard.

It was morning, and the ship was already being towed through the wide channel beyond Livorno, amid a flotilla of small craft bearing merchants who were doing good business selling fresh fruit, clothing, mirrors, beads and other trinkets (for bargaining with the Savages), guns (which must at once be handed in to the armourer) and much else, when Pasquale was finally given a berth. It was no more than a chalked space two *braccia* by four, with a little locker at its head where Pasquale could stow away the necessaries he had bought from the floating merchants and from the quartermaster, a dour fat man who had his office in the black bowels of the ship. The passenger hold was marked out with half a hundred such spaces, but no one was asleep. Along with everyone else, Pasquale leaned at the rail of the ship's promenade, at her waist beneath the raised platform where the captain stood beside the steersman. Pasquale felt a strange thrilling excitement, looking amongst his fellow passengers and wondering which would be his friends, whether any enemies would be made, or lovers found amongst them on the long voyage to the New World.

The merchants' craft fell behind. The paddle-wheeled tug cast off its lines and slowed, so that the ship drew abreast of it, and then it too fell astern. Ahead was a widening line, the hard blue sea under a clear sky.

Pasquale carried under his arm a board with a cover of oiled cloth, and two bands to hold paper down against the wind. He had kept his silverpoint pen through all his adventures, and his little knife, and blocks of chalk. Paper and more chalk was to be had from the quartermaster at a price. But he was not ready. Not yet. He was sure that there was money to be made from sketching portraits of his fellow voyagers, but not yet. He was still filled with tumbling images from his adventures. There was the burning gate and the trees caught afire, the burning bridge and the luminous stained-glass window shivered to pieces around him, the puzzled fading gaze of the dying ape and Lisa Giocondo's smile, the wry wise face of his friend and Pelashil's fierce, scornful independence . . . And gathering form from all this, although he would not yet admit it, were the lineaments of something more than human and less, something that, poised between the world of thought and the world of things, between Word and Act, might possibly be (for how could he ever again be certain of anything?) the fierce luminous wondering face of his angel.